DIRTY MONEY

DIRTY MONEY

CHARLOTTE PHILBY

BASKERVILLE
An imprint of JOHN MURRAY

First published in Great Britain in 2025 by Baskerville
An imprint of John Murray (Publishers)

1

A CIP catalogue record for this title is available from the British Library

Hardback ISBN 9781399812078
Trade Paperback ISBN 9781399812085
ebook ISBN 9781399812108

Typeset in Adobe Garamond Pro by
Palimpsest Book Production Ltd, Falkirk, Stirlingshire

Printed and bound in Great Britain by Clays Ltd, Elcograf S.p.A.

John Murray policy is to use papers that are natural, renewable and
recyclable products and made from wood grown in sustainable forests.
The logging and manufacturing processes are expected to conform
to the environmental regulations of the country of origin.

Carmelite House
50 Victoria Embankment
London EC4Y 0DZ

www.johnmurraypress.co.uk

John Murray Press, part of Hodder & Stoughton Limited
An Hachette UK company

The authorised representative in the EEA is Hachette Ireland, 8 Castlecourt Centre,
Dublin 15, D15 XTP3, Ireland (email: info@hbgi.ie)

For Barney

In memory of David Kirk, 1949–2023

CHAPTER ONE

'Why you saying my name for? I don't even know you, bruv!'

The sound of shouting in the street outside wakes Ramona sometime after eight and she holds the pillow over her head as the voices grow louder and finally subside through the single-glazing of the sash windows.

Fucking crackheads. Every. Single. Day.

If not them, then it's the kamikaze toddlers on scooters tornadoing towards the Steiner nursery on the corner of the street, up towards Dalston. It's not the kids themselves who are the problem so much as the parents with their oat milk flat whites chatting endless self-important drivel, dressed in the ubiquitous beanies they buy for sixty pounds a pop on Stoke Newington High Street.

Give her the crackheads any day of the week.

After the constant rumble of Camden High Street, Ramona had imagined it would be more peaceful living on a residential terraced street in a part of Hackney pretentiously described by the estate agent who showed her around as the Islington Borders. But there is something about the lurching sounds of the city whenever they suddenly spring out from the veneer of silence that is unsettling.

Still, she loves it up here in the neglected Georgian rafters, the silhouette of the treetops just visible through the window.

Monday.

With her eyes still closed, she lies in forced inaction until it's clear she won't get back to sleep. When she sits up, she remains still a while, watching the shadows of the room come into focus through the net curtains that were already here when she moved in.

The room is small and rectangular; a third of a room really, separated from the so-called open-plan kitchen and living area by a single stud wall. Propped precariously against the left side is a narrow, free-standing wardrobe. Opposite, in the right-hand corner, is the armchair she found abandoned on the street a few doors down, along with a note: *Free to a good home!*

Well, it was a home of sorts, she had mused, as she dragged it four floors up with the help of the couple downstairs.

Standing here now, her legs exposed under the thigh-length *Reservoir Dogs* T-shirt she has no memory of buying but can't remember being without, Ramona pulls on a pair of tracksuit bottoms.

Yawning, she fills the kettle and stands with her back against the melamine countertop, looking out at the bare branches that are at eye level with the window as she waits for the water to boil.

That second square of sky, almost identical to the one visible from the bedroom, apart from the additional tip of a spire, is her favourite thing about the flat; what you might call its selling point, if it had needed a sell beyond the fact that she could afford it – just – and that it was both close enough to where she grew up and suitably removed from her previous routine to enable her to feel as if she is properly starting again, away from the memories and the temptations and the . . . well, she tries not to dwell on it.

If one thing was to change then everything had to change. And hasn't it just.

When Ramona sighs, the sound is accompanied by the bubbling of water starting to boil in the kettle behind her. Below, a train trundles past on the railway lines that separate one side of the street from the other, reminding her of all the places she doesn't need to be. With an aching in her bones, she imagines the news conference that will soon be taking place without her, her former colleagues revving up for the week ahead; the worker bees making their way to and from the office and the courthouses and the council buildings.

Looking up at the dusty wine rack that was here when she moved in, Ramona notes that it is empty. Not that she ever kept wine; Bells whisky was more her thing: a litre of the stuff purchased from the off-licence on Camden High Street if she was feeling flush; more likely a half, bought with scraped-together change and consumed almost as soon as her cash had hit the counter.

At the sound of the whistle, she takes down a cup and stirs two heaps of Nescafé into the oversized Sports Direct mug that had belonged to Si. Adding a third, she takes the coffee and sits at the tiny table in front of the window in the kitchen, using both hands to crank it open before lighting one of the fake Marlboros she gets in bulk for seven quid a packet from the Albanians outside the Nag's Head on Holloway Road. The flavour is of twigs and the slow approach of death, and she coughs at the first inhalation, taking another and waiting for her lungs to accept the welcome blanket of smoke.

Exhaling, Ramona starts up her computer. She is an anachronism; too young to be as resentful of technology as she is; too young to live without it. Still, she tries her hardest. Having spent her adult life until now as a reporter, Ramona understands too well how easy technology makes it to track another person's every movement, habit and relationship. So she avoids it where she can, and where she can't she has the best inbuilt anti-spyware technology that money – or a sweet word with Gareth – can buy.

Certain details and clues can only be found by watching, and talking to, people – not least when it comes to catching out those who might well be as technology averse as she is. But she is not too bloody-minded to know there are certain websites she needs right now.

Blowing onto her hands for warmth as she waits for the old laptop to start up, Ramona scrolls through Reddit and Twitter to see if anyone has responded to her latest advert.

No new messages.

Turns out social media is as averse to her as she is to it.

It is fine, she tells herself as she stands and moves to the sink, turning on the tap and reaching for a scouring pad that has seen better days. She has at least a month's rent saved up before she has to go pleading on hands and knees back to her old boss. Not that she will. Not that she could, even if she wanted to.

Blinking, she sees herself that morning, the man's face pressed up against hers; the wire hanging from her neck. A single trace of blood running from her nose, like a tear.

Fuck off, fuck off, fuck off.

Squeezing the dregs of washing-up liquid into the mug, she shakes her head, wrestling for another thought and landing on the image of Si the evening before; her ex-boyfriend's skin glistening in the rain under the floodlights at Market Road football pitches. For a moment, the image soothes her and she feels her face lift in a half-smile. He'd looked happy, in a way she hadn't seen since—

Shit.

The water is unexpectedly hot, scorching her skin so that her fingers lurch open and she drops the cup.

Turning the tap to cold, she holds her hand under the icy flow, enjoying the sensation as her skin finally turns numb. When she goes to resume her washing up, the handle of the mug comes away in her fingers. Great. Another thing she has broken, or maybe, as she has come to think of so much else, it was always destined to fall apart.

Picking up the remnants, Ramona chucks the cracked pieces into the bin as she passes on her way to the table and sits in front of her computer.

Why had she gone to Market Road last night? The moment she had seen Si's face, she had known it was a mistake. She is pretty sure he hadn't seen her, but still.

Looking up, she notes the time on the clock on the wall. 8.45 a.m.

Shit.

Her hair is short and home-bleached a dodgy shade of blonde, and she scrapes the bits that will be contained into the elastic band she wears on her wrist, and twists it into a ponytail. Drying her hands on the thighs of her tracksuit bottoms, she slaps down the lid of the computer and takes the two or so strides from one side of the studio flat to the other, sliding on her trainers, slipping on an old baseball cap and grabbing the denim jacket, with the hooded zip-up sweater still stuffed inside its sleeves from the day before.

If she runs, she will only be a few minutes late. In any case, she prefers to arrive last, avoiding having to mingle with the others, who tell their same stories on loop over Styrofoam cups at the back of the room before and after the session. The same stories she heard last week and the week before – narratives inside which the speakers have locked themselves, without any escape, reinforcing their perceived path to where they are now.

Not that she is one to talk, so she doesn't.

CHAPTER TWO

The needling of the alarm pierces through the gauze of a dream in which Madeleine Farrow is back in Hanoi, the air claggy; the cries of the city streets turning to screams.

Gasping, she sits up, slowly becoming aware of the familiar contours of the king-size bed and the shape of the mattress holding her somewhere between sleep and the day ahead.

It's OK. She is home, back in her flat on Marylebone High Street. The scent of mimosa wafts over from the diffuser, overpowering in its sweetness.

Attempting to lure open an eyelid still heavy with make-up, she focuses on the clock on the side-table as the numbers slowly come into focus.

7.20 a.m. Jesus fucking Christ, her head.

Jabbing at the sleep button, she lies back on the silk pillowcase, a world away from the mosquito nets and the thrumming fans of Vietnam, waiting for the throbbing in her temples to subside. She is home, for now at least. As always, the thought strikes her with an equal amount of relief and anticlimax.

Right now, her brain is still working at half-speed owing to the negronis in the Soho bar the night before, consumed to forget the events of the day. Faltering, she registers the lace bra hanging from the circular glass handle of the bedside table – too small to be one of hers. When she looks left, she notes the outline of a woman half-concealed beneath the sheet.

Christ.

Careful not to wake her, Madeleine sits up, her palm moving to her forehead as she studies the pool of silky blonde hair spilled out on the pillow. Reaching through the fug of her mind for the woman's name, she misses, picturing herself leaning in at the bar the previous evening, in an effort to hear the words being mouthed above the music.

Diana? Gaia?

Vaguely, she recalls herself making some reference to a Greek goddess.

Bloody hell, she'd been drunk. Tentatively, she sifts through any recollections of the night before, the way one might navigate one's way through a cave, nervous of what might leap out. The only thing she remembers with any clarity is the funeral in north-east London earlier that day, and the cab-ride back to Soho, the city a smudge of light and shadow through the rain-smeared window.

After that, her memory falls away, and not without reason.

She feels horrendous now – that much is painfully clear. What did she expect? Before yesterday, she had barely touched a drop in months, and any tolerance she might once have possessed has long since abandoned her.

Closing her eyes, she pushes against the wave of anxiety threatening to take hold. It felt wrong, to leave straight from the service, but staying any longer would have been rubbernecking. She hardly knew Jamie or the girls. Her relationship with Laura, however friendly, had been professional. And in any case, there will have been plenty of people heading back for the wake. Laura had always known how to draw a crowd.

No, Madeleine won't beat herself up for seeking comfort and oblivion, in the circumstances – and in the circumstances, neither had been hard to find.

The sleeping woman stirs and Madeleine holds her breath.

Once she is still again, Madeleine reaches for a glass of water, her gaze landing on the order of service beside it on the bedside table. From the cover, the young woman smiles back at her. Below the photograph, the words *Laura Tatchell: loved by all who knew her.*

Clearly not all, Madeleine thinks. Though perhaps that's the point: whoever did this didn't know – or care – who Laura really was.

God, she was so young; just forty-four. But her age is the least of it – the scale of loss in Laura's absence would be better measured by what the much-loved Shadow Minister had done in her brief time on earth; for her friends and colleagues and constituents, not to mention her family. Though Madeleine has no children of her own – never wanted them – she respects that, unlike some politicians, Laura Tatchell never attempted to hide the fact that she was a mother, or to diminish it. Her daughters were her world, and somehow, despite the demands of the job, she managed to hold in careful balance her commitment to her children and her husband, Jamie, while always making time for those she represented. Few people could live twice as long as she did and achieve half as much as Laura Tatchell had.

Swallowing the lump forming in her throat, Madeleine blinks away the mental image of the daughters, Tilly and Ruth, both now teenagers, watching on from the front row, in a state of shock, as their mother's coffin was paraded through the centre of their local church.

Given the manner of her killing, and her reputation, Madeleine imagines the late MP could have commanded a state funeral. But knowing Laura even as briefly as she did, she knows this would be the last thing Laura would have wanted. Unlike so many she worked opposite or alongside in Parliament, Laura was truly in her position as a representative of her constituency, and of wider society. She believed in democracy in its most literal sense: people power. In Laura's mind, there really was one rule for everyone, including herself.

Forcing thoughts of the previous day to the back of her mind, Madeleine stands and walks across the bedroom, pulling on the black satin robe hanging on the back of the door. Pausing to remove a plastic-sheathed suit and dry-cleaned shirt from the suitcase on the floor where she had left it before heading out last night, she walks quietly to the same built-in wardrobes that were here when she inherited the place and takes out a set of matching black underwear from the internal drawer.

Closing it as quietly as she can manage, she moves stealthily across the carpet to the bedroom door, bringing it to a close behind her. When Madeleine wanders through the blank walls of the hallway, tightening the belt of her robe, she is met by large sash windows, a light grey mid-winter London sky peering in as she enters the kitchen.

Monday. Despite her weeks away, the place is almost as if she had never left: the countertop gleaming, the plain white plates she'd had the sales assistant pick out in the Conran shop down the road, stacked neatly on the open shelves that the cleaner keeps pristine during her client's stints abroad.

She had been due to return from Vietnam imminently anyway, the news of Laura's death only hastening her return by a matter of days. But the transition from one world to another is always discombobulating. Even on the occasions when nothing has changed.

Outside, the city rattles to life, the sound of glass bottles being upended into the recycling van serving as punishment for last night's excesses. The evidence lies sprawled across the marble counter. Picking up a pair of knickers and the remnants of the kebab purchased at the Lebanese on Edgware Road on their way home, Madeleine throws the empty wrapper in the brushed metal pedal bin as she passes. Placing the two dirty crystal tumblers on the counter in the sink, she throws the underwear into the washing machine.

As she does so, there is a moment of recall: her new blonde friend, the previous evening, reprimanding Madeleine on the basis of the coffee machine's reliance on single plastic. Madeleine had silently marvelled at the hypocrisy of this coming from someone dressed head to toe in Zara, who works for a notoriously dubious bank and openly boasts about the quality of her dealer's cocaine.

But rather than feeling any real disdain, she had been prickled by a sort of envy. Necking one espresso and pressing the button for a second to brew, she walks back through the hallway, trying to imagine a life so simple that one's biggest concern for the future of humanity might be a non-reusable coffee pod.

That's not fair, though – she has no idea what other concerns the woman has or doesn't have. But life's not fair.

Looking up at the clock, she checks the time.

7.32 a.m.

Following her own warped rule about not looking at her phone before getting dressed once she is up – doomscrolling in bed in the small hours doesn't count – Madeleine heads to the bathroom. It is one of the few parts of the flat she has actually bothered renovating since inheriting the place from her parents a decade earlier, and she loves every inch of it. This flat is the closest thing they ever had to a family home, spending months here intermittently, between her father's various international postings with the Foreign Office. Just the three of them usually: herself, her father, Charles, and her mother, Juliet. Occasionally they would be joined by her older brother, Dominic, while on exeat from Eton and then Oxford.

Bristling at the thought of him, Madeleine closes the door to the bathroom and for a moment lets herself lean back against it. God, she has missed this. Of all the things she hankers for when she is away – of all the things that make her feel that maybe the apartment above the boutique on Marylebone High Street is home, after all – it is this bathroom with its scented toiletries and cool soft-tiled floor and soft thick towels and the promise of a high-pressure shower; a place where no matter the day or night she has the chance to wash it all away and start again.

Stepping out of her robe and into the cubicle, she sighs in relief as the heavy flow of the cascading water pummels her shoulders. After a minute or two, she lathers the shower-gel she doesn't remember buying onto her Vitamin D-deprived skin. Only one who has spent her entire stint abroad locked in a succession of windowless rooms, as she has, could come back from south-east Asia, in January, paler than when she left. Not that she cares for tanning; at her age she values the relative absence of skin damage, despite a childhood largely spent baking under the blistering skies of Africa and the Middle East.

Dabbing moisturiser on her forehead and rubbing it in, in smoothing strokes, Madeleine pulls away from the mirror and dries herself. Once dressed in the wool-cashmere blend suit she had made up at Minh Quang tailors while she waited for the raid, she pulls a comb through the dark shoulder-length hair, applying a hint of eyeliner and a slick of red lipstick to distract from the jet lag and everything else, before moving back into the kitchen.

Just as she downs the second coffee, she hears stirring in the bedroom, and freezes. Scribbling a note – *Juice is in the fridge. Take a taxi home* – she quickly removes a fifty-pound note from her bag and leaves the note and the money on the countertop.

Not that a woman who works in a bank needs Madeleine's cash, but what is she supposed to say? Help yourself to anything edible you can find, then please fuck off?

Registering the sound of the bedroom door opening, followed a moment later by the bathroom being shut, Madeleine breathes a sigh of relief and then disappears into the hall, picking up a pair of black loafers and quietly closing the front door behind her.

It is only once she passes the downstairs flat, which is empty as ever – the Saudis who own it presumably at one of their other residences in Jeddah or Mauritius – that she slips on the shoes and pulls out her phone to check her work email. The message at the top, from Paul Rittler, is subject-lined *Welcome back!* The contents simply read: *Headquarters. Briefing room, 9.00 a.m. Don't be late!*

Stepping out into the bracing central London air, Madeleine inhales.

Happy fiftieth birthday to me.

CHAPTER THREE

Ramona walks quickly, glancing over her shoulder as she heads down through the churchyard. The meeting is held in the crypt, which smells of disinfectant and soggy biscuits, with Vicky, the group leader, seated at the centre.

Wincing at the sound of the door creaking closed behind her, she scans the room before moving her eyes to the floor as she shuffles inside, taking a seat towards the back.

At the front, facing his audience, Ramona's sponsor, JJ, is deep in a monologue that Ramona can almost recite by heart, flanked on either side by boxes of plastic toys and half-size chairs that are brought out for the parent-toddler group that runs in the same space after the sessions.

'I went into care at the age of ten. My wife, Lorna, and I met at one of the pubs I drank at in Hoxton when we were both still practically kids. She was a barmaid.' JJ speaks with a softness that somehow commands attention. Presumably at some point he was thinner – smack is nothing if not great for shedding the pounds – but these days he is doughy as well as tall, with a thick red beard and freckled skin. His blue eyes are kind and intense, but you wouldn't want to take him on in a fight.

As he continues, Ramona's mind drifts. This is one of the few places where she has come to feel relatively safe. While Narcotics Anonymous meetings attract people from all walks of life – among them ex-gang members – meetings are a sacred space, and if anything was to kick off, Ramona knows everyone in this room would do what they can to protect her. But Ramona also knows that trouble is likely to bite when you are most comfortable.

When the door bangs open and closed, she turns sharply, her fingers curling around the edge of her skateboard. But it is just the wind. Her heartbeat takes a moment to settle as she focuses on what JJ is saying, keeping herself low in her seat. She has only known her sponsor for six months, though in real-world terms this might as well be a lifetime. Connections in NA are generally accelerated through their intensity. She knows the intimate details of most of the people in here, even if they, in turn – with the exception of JJ and Cindy – know fuck all about her. It is partly a choice, on her count. But even if Ramona had been able to tell, she is pretty certain she wouldn't. At least she tells herself this is why she never does.

Generally speaking, sharing in meetings is not so much about what JJ is doing now – delivering a sermon of sorts, on his own sobriety journey. Rather it is about working through the day-to-day challenges faced in the process of getting, and staying, sober. Secrets are what activate destructive behaviours; if you confess, it takes the power out of the surging thought, whatever it might be.

This is the theory – and in this sense, Ramona still has some work to do.

She focuses on JJ. In his early fifties with bright red hair, he is almost twice her age. On the face of it, they share little in common besides the area they live in and a fondness for getting out of their minds. Yet when she listens to him, something inside her twinges with recognition. Not just because of the kindness he has shown her, answering her calls in the middle of the night, being the one to talk her down when it felt too hard in the beginning, too pointless.

The truth is, Ramona has never heard a single life story in this room and not felt a slight pinch of connection. More often than not, this fact has made her cringe. But it is also what keeps her coming back, day after day.

Closing her eyes and then instinctively opening them again – wary of letting her guard down even for a second – she tunes back into JJ's words. His is a story that she knows too well involves a smack habit, a wife and a child that no longer wants to know; years spent on the streets; violence; self-loathing. And now, a grandchild that he is determined to do better by, though this detail Ramona only knows from their private conversations.

When Ramona compares her own addiction issues with JJ's, she feels like a fraud. Whisky, sleeping pills, party drugs consumed while successfully holding down a full-time job is hardly stashing heroin in your kid's dolls. Thank God.

For fuck's sake JJ, she had thought, the first time she heard that detail. *What kind of person—*

Drawing breath, she stops herself, as if even thinking it now is some sort of betrayal of her sponsor, who has been nothing but good to her. Any sort of judgement isn't tolerated here. No doubt if she were to 'share' her own sorry past, there would be the same noises of affirmation rippling through the crowd that rise now; the same sympathetic nods and smiles from other users; the same encouraging applause that moves through the room as JJ takes his seat.

There is so much self-indulgent bullshit that surrounds this process. It was this that had kept her away for a full six months after Cindy suggested she join. But over time Ramona has come to appreciate the bullshit as part of what makes this a safe space for everyone, even the most naturally hardened cynics, such as herself. She can mock it, or she can shut up and get on with it.

Belatedly joining in the clapping, albeit a little less enthusiastically than others in the crowd, Ramona looks up and feels Vicky's eyes on her. As always, the group leader wears neon-green eyeliner drawn in Amy Winehouse-style flicks. Attempting to coax Ramona forward, she gives a gentle smile that reveals a single gold tooth in a row of white. 'Does anyone else have anything they'd like to share?'

Vicky holds Ramona's gaze until she looks away.

'OK, maybe next time.'

Maybe not, Ramona thinks.

'Right, Cindy. You're up.' Vicky moves towards another familiar face in the crowd.

At the sight of her friend, Ramona smiles and leans back in her chair with a sense of pride, relaxing ever so slightly as Cindy gathers an inner strength that is at odds with her tiny frame, in order to tell her story.

Catching Ramona's eye, Cindy winks and Ramona nods back in mutual recognition.

Clearing her throat, she speaks.

* * *

As soon as it is over, Ramona watches as Cindy slips away. She knows, counter-intuitively, that Mondays are a busy day in her line of work and she will have clients before collecting Sonny from school. Watching her disappear into the hubbub of Dalston, Ramona stands and follows suit before the group leader can catch her eye again. Not today, Vicky. Not today.

Outside, Ramona pulls her cigarettes from the top pocket of her denim jacket and lights one. As she turns, she bumps straight into JJ.

'Alright?' His smile wavers as he clocks the packet of extra-large silver Rizla sticking out of her open pocket, which ordinarily would be obscured by a packet of Marlboro.

'Ramona—'

Before he can lecture her on the pitfalls of continuing to smoke weed, she makes a face. 'Sorry JJ, I've got to go.'

Placing the spongey headphones over her ears in an unsubtle attempt to muffle out the sound of her sponsor kissing his teeth in disapproval, she continues onwards.

The morning is bright and fresh, and at this time of day Ramona finds it easy to keep her attention diverted away from the bars and pubs that line Kingsland High Street.

Wincing at the thought of JJ's disappointed expression as she reaches the corner of Crossway, Ramona enters the Turkish grocers and nods at the young man behind the till.

'Alright, beautiful. Listen, why aren't you working? I'm looking for your name every day in the paper, but I'm not seeing it,' Sami calls out after her as she heads through the store, scanning the prices of the items on the shelves.

Basmati rice, tinned beans, pistachio baklava laid out on a polystyrene tray wrapped in cling film.

'You know I don't work there any more, Sami,' Ramona calls back, totting up the prices in her head, picking out a loaf of sliced white bread, a tub of hummus and a can of tinned soup before heading to the till. She holds her breath as she counts out her change.

'Not working?' Sami kisses his teeth. 'What, have you won the lottery or something? You gonna buy me one of them big houses on London Fields for my birthday, yeah?'

'Yeah, no worries.' Ramona laughs, pointing to a row of cards behind his head, ignoring the bottles of spirits. 'Can I get ten pounds of phone credit, too?'

'Phone credit, what is this, the year 2000? What do you need a burner for— Wait, you're not shotting drugs now, are you? Is that why—'

'Sami, please.' Ramona rolls her eyes at her old school friend.

Friend is perhaps a bit of a stretch but they were both part of the same group that smoked weed together at break time in sixth form, and she can't help but feel a fondness for Sami, even if he does render every single interaction a surreal minor interrogation. She is also quietly grateful for how willingly he has accepted her new name, though she can't help but worry that he is one of those people who might well be indiscreet when overexcited. She has no choice but to trust him – and for now, she has nowhere else to go.

Besides, he claims to understand the need, even if not the reason, for silence. *Snitches get stitches, I know how it goes, girl. You can trust me not to say nothing*, he had reassured her after she bumped into him at his uncles' shop, only a London borough away but far enough from where they grew up that she had been surprised to see him there, in the days after she moved into her new place. She had been hard-pressed not to point out the double negative but concedes that what Sami makes up for in enthusiasm, he lacks in a basic grasp of most other things – grammar included – and so saves her breath.

'You know I'm messing with you,' Sami grins as she places her money on the counter. 'I know you're not a dealer. If you were, you wouldn't be paying me with shrapnel.' He tuts as he scrapes the coins into his hands. 'But seriously, you're the only one who knows what goes on around these ends. All those other writers, it's bullshit. You had your ear to the streets, girl. It's a loss.'

Smiling despite herself, Ramona shrugs. 'Yeah well, I'm doing my own thing now.'

Making a thumbs-up signal, she backs out of the door, feeling herself blush at her own grandiosity.

Doing her own thing. Yeah, like going to meetings with names like *Staying Clean in Bethnal Green* and *Euston, We Have a Problem*. Although admittedly that last name was pretty good. Good enough that when Cindy mentioned it, Ramona had finally consented to going to Narcotics Anonymous with her, despite her initial reservations about the evangelical nature of the program.

Stepping out onto the junction, Ramona's thoughts are interrupted by a loud ringing coming from the pocket of her hoodie, the sound partially muffled below a denim jacket.

Pulling out her Nokia, she studies the screen a moment, scrutinising the number before answering. 'Hello?'

'Hi—' There is silence before the voice continues. 'Is that Ramona Chang?' The caller is young and female. Something about her tone makes Ramona stop in her tracks, putting a finger in the ear exposed to the street, to block out the sound of the car horns and the drill beat thumping from an open window.

'I saw your advert online; I'm looking for a private detective.'

CHAPTER FOUR

The briefing room is on the first floor.

Madeleine knocks, not waiting for an answer before pushing it open. Inside, her direct boss, Paul Rittler, is seated at the head of a conference-style table, leaning back in his chair – one of six people in the room, including herself. The way he is positioned, his hands held behind his neck, it is more as if he is reclining on a sun lounger in Marbella than in a faceless government building at the arse end of the River Thames.

It looks as if Madeleine isn't the only one who got some last night. Or perhaps he is just overjoyed to have been given a day-pass to head-quarters, and a chance to play with the big boys, for once. For Rittler, the headquarters of the organisation for which they work will only ever be a brief reprieve from his own department's eccentric outpost; and here he is in the company of the top dog, Gerald Okoduwa, himself. No doubt, this is the stuff Paul Rittler's wet dreams are made of.

Madeleine steps inside. Here at HQ, everything is uniform and clean, in the loosest sense of the word. No scope for personalisation or interpretation; no room for manoeuvre. Dressed in a pinstripe suit, Gerald Okoduwa adjusts his horn-rimmed spectacles, his attention moving pointedly to the clock on the wall, which reads three minutes past nine.

'Madeleine Farrow. The wanderer returns!' Rittler says, making a show for his superior officer, though what message he is trying to convey isn't exactly clear. If by wanderer you mean one barely sleeping for four months, working night and day with international agencies to close in on a ring of paedophiles, reliant on the ever-diminishing resources of the UK's answer to the FBI, Madeleine silently responds, then sure. Call me Forrest bloody Gump.

Smiling tightly, she closes the door behind her, surveying the room.

One of the strangers seated at the table is tall, thin and blond, with one of his legs crossed over the other, filing his nails with a black emery board.

MI6, presumably.

Naturally suspicious of men more groomed than herself, Madeleine eyes the stranger warily, as she takes a seat.

'Rittler. Gerald.' She greets the two colleagues she already knows with a courteous nod. Rittler, never Paul. A moniker he himself insisted on, as though he were bloody Madonna.

'This is Jamal Brown,' Gerald Okoduwa says, indicating towards one of the younger surveillance officers who looks more like a semi-pro footballer than a policeman. 'As well as Arabic, Jamal also speaks Russian, which may or may not prove useful.'

Jamal smiles, bashfully, and Madeleine takes an immediate liking to him based on her gut feeling – a method she finds as reliable as it is unscientific. 'Jamal will be assisting Amol Fernandez, who is . . .' Gerald Okoduwa looks at his watch, 'late.'

His attention moves to the young woman at the centre of the table, with poker-straight posture. She is armed with a pencil and logbook – recording what, exactly?

'And this is Sadie Mackintosh, a trainee investigator who joined us a couple of weeks ago, from the Met,' he continues.

Madeleine smiles knowingly to herself. She has seen Sadie Mackintosh's type before. She has, no doubt, watched every episode of *Line of Duty* and imagines it somehow qualifies her to be a detective. She probably also hopes to keep an anonymous kiss-and-tell policing blog that will one day be transformed into a million-pound book deal. And on the last matter, good for her.

'Last but by no means least, this is Fionn Edwardes, our new FI,' Gerald says, pointing towards the impeccably presented middle-aged blond man who will be working as the financial investigator on whatever new case it is that Madeleine is being pulled onto.

Fionn Edwardes? She rolls the name around her head, trying to place why it sounds familiar. When the penny drops, she inwardly groans. Surely fucking not.

'Not had the pleasure – but I've heard of you,' Madeleine manages, her apparently casual tone not matching the implication of her words. Which is to say: you thieving bastard.

'Well, you'll all know each other soon,' Rittler interjects, attempting to distract from the point they all know she is making.

Who does he remind her of, to look at? Julian Assange, that is it. As first impressions go, this is not going well.

'And here's Jonny . . .' Rittler adds, doing his usual *The Shining* voice, as the team's dedicated surveillance officer – and Madeleine's firm favourite, Jonny Robertson – enters the room.

'Alright, hen? I was beginning to think you'd done a bunk,' he calls over to Madeleine in his Glaswegian brogue, and she winks back at him.

This is exactly what she needs – familiar faces. Already she feels her spirits lighten.

'Luckily for you, you're not as late as Amol,' Gerald comments, disapprovingly, as Jonny steps inside.

Both Jonny and Amol are in their fifties, but this is where the similarities between the two men end. Even at the best of times, Amol Fernandez has been a lazy sod; now that he is nearing early retirement, with a filthy rich Spanish heir for a husband to pay his way, he is becoming lazier with every moment that passes. For surveillance manager Jonny to be held up, on the other hand, something must have happened; Madeleine's first bet would be an altercation with a traffic warden, one of Jonny's personal nemeses, along with aphids and the Scottish Labour Party.

'To catch you up, I was just introducing Madeleine to Fionn, who you've already met,' Gerald Okoduwa says. 'As I was explaining, we've brought Fionn in on a freelance basis from Strategic Intelligence Services to help with a new case.'

Gerald's voice catches only slightly as he references the name of one of the private investigation firms the organisation seems intent on haemorrhaging cash on, having been stripped of its own resources. 'Fionn has a finance background – he was an in-house lawyer at a major Japanese bank, until the corporate intelligence service lured him away.'

Until he tried to rob the bank blind, and got off with a slapped wrist and the anonymity granted by a non-disclosure agreement to protect the firm from spooked investors, and moved on to the only company shady enough to have him, Madeleine silently corrects her superior, clicking the lid of her pen.

Catching her eye, Jonny gives her a knowing look.

'Fionn will be working as the financial investigator on a new case that has come into our possession concerning the jailed businessman, Amir Zhatchanov.'

How is this even possible, Madeleine wonders. But of course, because of the cover-up following the banking scandal, Fionn Edwardes was never charged. In the eyes of the law, he is clean. There is no reason why he can't retrain as a financial investigator in law enforcement and pass the necessary vetting – even the more advanced Developed Vetting (DV) clearance level required for a unit like theirs, which sometimes involves liaising with MI5 and MI6.

Edwardes would hardly be the first wrong'un to slip through the net – and at least this way, they will get the benefit of his considerable experience, Madeleine muses.

She is nothing if not pragmatic.

'I don't know how much you've kept on top of the news while you were away?' Gerald continues, drawing Madeleine's mind back to the briefing.

'I've been a bit busy, actually,' she replies, unable to stop herself, and Rittler chips in again.

21

'Of course – and what a result! Twenty-six men rounded up, wasn't it?'

She has missed this: watching Rittler spin on his head in front of his superiors, in an effort to protect her against any accusations of insolence; an effort that is in fact about Rittler effectively protecting himself. Christ knows how much more work he would have to do if he didn't have Madeleine on the team, but clearly he has done the maths.

In order to have Madeleine on board, Rittler needs her to keep his boss on her side. The slightest hint of insurgency and Gerald the top-dog will pull rank and have Madeleine tugged across into head-quarters where he can keep an eye on her, by the scruff of her perfectly moisturised neck. Not trusting Madeleine to do the necessary arse-licking herself, this part of the job – if nothing else – falls to Rittler. If Gerald's motto is keep your friends close and your enemies closer, then Rittler's is keep your friends close and your colleagues who do most of your work for you, within touching distance at all times.

Though this is a rule that has to be suspended on the occasions when Madeleine is seconded on specialist cases, like the one in Vietnam, from which she has just returned.

'Twenty-seven men,' Madeleine replies, unable to match her boss's enthusiasm as she pictures the harrowed faces of the boys they had freed, their stony-faced captors walking behind already mentally working up their respective legal defences.

Twenty-seven men. Someone's father, someone's grandfather, some-one's son. Twenty-seven men and not even the tip of the iceberg – not even close.

If she had her way, they would castrate the lot of them. She would do it herself.

'Madeleine's one of our finest officers.' Rittler appears to address the new recruits directly, but Madeleine knows he is stating this for Gerald's benefit. 'Highly experienced. She was at the Foreign Office before joining the agency, though that was long enough ago now that we've forgiven her. Ha! She's just come back from Hanoi where, as you know, she has been working with great success with our own international partners to bring down a network of paedophiles, including British citizens. She will be joining us on this case for a while—'

Rittler cuts himself short and Madeleine hears in her mind's eye the words he doesn't need to say. *She needs a break before jumping into all that again, after what she's seen.*

And on this occasion Rittler is right. Madeleine is long enough in the tooth to understand the value of taking time on the home front to restore, and dig deep into her day job as Detective Sergeant. While being a DS in a unit such as theirs entails dealing with serious and complex investigations, uncovering the truth and analysing evidence on cases – ranging from undertaking search warrants to making arrests to pushing a case through the courts – Madeleine knows that Rittler will have her on some soft job, for now.

It is a form of mandatory therapy, really; she is still officially working but at a distance, removed from the darkest recesses of humanity; a place from which it becomes harder and harder to fully re-emerge, the older she gets.

In her experience, you can't unsee it, but you can try to look at something else for a while, until the image fades.

'Amir Zhatchanov: fill me in . . .' Madeleine says, clearing her throat.

'Amir Zhatchanov is a former businessman and British national, currently serving time in his home country of Kazakhstan for swindling the state bank there out of the equivalent of two billion pounds,' Gerald Okoduwa says. 'As you might have heard, the country's former leader – a peasant who joined the Soviet Communist Party in his twenties and rose through the ranks – expanded the constitution during his almost two-decade reign to protect himself and his inner circle from scrutiny. Under his leadership, a tight circle of businessmen were able to amass fortunes and political influence.'

Madeleine flinches, an image of Laura Tatchell rearing up in her mind.

Making the connection, Rittler looks over at her, his expression suddenly nervous. He knows Madeleine and Laura's paths have crossed over the years and it is impossible not to make a link between the case she is being briefed on now and the late MP, who called out a group of Kazakh mining tycoons in Parliament, under parliamentary privilege, weeks before she was killed by persons unknown.

On this matter, and others, Laura was a dog with a bone. Despite the self-confessed bleeding heart, which made her a divisive figure, politically speaking, she had a directness and a personable quality that could endear even the most hardened Tories to her cause. But she was happy to rub them up the wrong way, too. She was a people person but not a people-pleaser.

Salt of the earth was the expression that had been used repeatedly in the press, swiftly followed by the fact that she was *the first person in her family to go to university* – a form of shorthand used mainly by posh people as bywords for 'working class'; a means to characterise a woman who in so many ways defied convention.

Warm, dedicated. A loving mother.

Laura was all of these things, but Madeleine knows, from the times they had worked together and the MP's notable public profile, that she was also outspoken and unapologetic, a pit bull when the occasion called for it. The treatment of workers in the mineral-rich Central Asian country of Kazakhstan, and the British government's refusal to crack down on those who benefited from it, was one of Laura's bugbears. It had been so, ever since Madeleine first met the ambitious young MP while working at the Foreign Office.

Madeleine had listened to her rant in private about the UK not doing enough to bring sanctions against individuals connected to the Kazakh regime laundering and spending its dirty money, without repercussions, here in London – and she had heard the details of the questions Laura had raised in PMQs, shortly before she died.

'Amir is part of a group of allies of the former president, who have been targeted in recent years by the current regime,' Gerald Okoduwa continues. 'Hence his imprisonment, over there. And while Amir is locked up in Kazakhstan, his wife, Ingrid, is over here, spending the proceeds of his crimes with impunity.'

You've got to be fucking joking. Madeleine bites her lip, barely suppressing a snide laugh. Now she understands why Fionn Edwardes, specifically, has been brought on board for this case; talk about having access to an inside mind.

'We're talking weekly trips to Cartier, private island in the Caribbean, a golf course—' Rittler continues.

'Are we thinking this Amir Zhatchanov is linked to Laura Tatchell's death?' Jonny asks, verbalising the question Madeleine has not yet found the words to ask.

'No,' Rittler says resolutely, glancing at Madeleine. 'Amir Zhatchanov wasn't one of the mining tycoons Tatchell was referring to in her statement.'

'Sorry, Tatchell was the MP who was run over, right, on her way to work?' Jamal interrupts.

'A hit-and-run, just days after she called out, in Parliament, the names of certain oligarchs washing their dirty money in British banks, and received death threats as a consequence,' Jonny responds. 'They mowed her down in front of her two girls, just outside her home. The vehicle was found burnt out a while later. They never traced the driver. A fucking travesty.'

'Allegedly,' Rittler interjects.

'Allegedly a fucking travesty,' Jonny replies.

'Laura Tatchell's hit-and-run is a separate case, which is being handled by the Met,' Okoduwa says, pausing for emphasis. 'But, following her death and the public outcry that ensued, enough feathers have been sufficiently ruffled to wage war on those Kazakhs using London as their personal laundry. And unfortunately for them, Amir Zhatchanov and his wife have made obvious targets of themselves.'

Easy targets, more like, Madeleine scoffs. She can't imagine this belated effort to clamp down on a few big spenders will be of much comfort to the teenage girls who have lost their mother. Especially when the police are no closer to bringing to account those responsible for her death.

Gerald Okoduwa interjects before anyone else can, an expression of pride moving over his face as he turns to the new financial investigator – most likely a personal connection. 'Fionn has been doing some excellent groundwork on background. Perhaps you'd like to do the honours?'

'Surely.' The corporate shoo-in nods and Madeleine can't help but wonder how much he is getting paid for his time, compared to her; not that it matters on anything more than principle. After winning the brief tussle with Dominic over her inheritance of their parents' flat, Madeleine is set for life. More than that: she is rich. It is a fact she neither relishes nor resents. She has no children of her own – though she loves her niece, Bella, like a daughter; no outgoings besides the stuff she increasingly buys to fill the hole left by every case.

She has always had money, and if it's taught her one thing it's that it can't buy inner peace. But it can buy you most other things.

'We're going to make use of the relatively new Unexplained Wealth Orders the so-called "McMafia" legislation designed to combat the funnelling of illegally obtained money through the British system.'

'McMafia?' Madeleine frowns.

'You know, after the TV show,' Sadie chips in, clearly thrilled to have a role in the conversation.

'It was a book, originally,' Edwardes corrects her, and Madeleine looks between Fionn and Sadie in composed silence.

It is a point of pride for Madeleine that she doesn't watch any of the endless crime shows she knows from Rittler's unsolicited domestic updates that he and his significantly younger wife, Julie, use to while away the hours on weekends. Nor does she read the sort of crime-as-entertainment dressed up as serious non-fiction, which adorns the windows of the Daunt Books opposite her flat; the kind of books that men in spectacles and red chinos make a show of reading on the tube, presumably until they are safely at home where they are free to watch porn.

She has neither the time nor the interest. Not when she could be doing any number of other things, like buying things she doesn't need on the internet or staring into the meaningless void of her own existence. If she did ever stop to wonder why she is so averse to being immersed in other people's made-up stories, she might reason it is because there is only so much a person can take. Or maybe it is simply that she doesn't like the false sense of hope and resolution offered, when she knows that in truth ends are rarely so neatly tied up.

'As I'm sure we're all keenly aware, upward of one hundred billion pounds is laundered through the UK every year by corrupt officials, rogue states, and transnational organised crime networks,' Fionn continues.

'Do we have a working definition for money laundering?' Sadie asks, her pen poised above her notepad.

He pauses, the disdain evident in his voice. 'Simply put, it is the concealment of illegally obtained money, usually by means of transfers using foreign banks and or legitimate businesses. Essentially, it's about a group or individual taking money generated by illegal activity, and attempting to make it appear legitimate. There are plenty of ways to do this, of course – some highly complex, some more basic.

'A popular method is to use a legitimate, cash-based business as a front. This could be anything from a grocers to a nail bar, where daily cash records are doctored to look like the business is taking more money than it is. Illegally gained money is then funnelled into the business's bank accounts – presented as genuine takings – and withdrawn again, at leisure.'

Madeleine thinks of the number of such premises that line high streets across Britain. Talk about hiding in plain sight. Often 'front' businesses also employ, in the loosest sense of the word, victims of modern slavery. She has encountered plenty in her time, working in human trafficking. All roads may lead to Rome, but plenty also lead straight back to car washes and nail bars that have become part of the fabric of British society.

'Other common methods include the use of shell companies, which are businesses that only really exist on paper; and "smurfing" or "structuring", where criminals spread money over multiple bank accounts to avoid detection,' Okoduwa adds. 'Currency exchanges, wire transfers and cash smugglers – so-called "mules" – who sneak large sums of cash across borders and hide them in bank accounts in countries where money-laundering enforcement is less strict, are also popular.'

Madeleine scans through the printed pages Gerald passes to her as he talks, outlining the most recent points of law relating to the Criminal Finance Act 2017. The printout might have been extracted from *Law Enforcement: A Manual for Dummies*, Madeleine thinks as she works through it. In fact, it is lifted from the agency's remarkably unsexy latest strategic assessment of serious and organised crime, which it defines as 'individuals or groups planning, coordinating and committing serious offences, whether individually, in groups, or as part of transnational networks'.

Unexplained Wealth Orders are part of the UK's attempt to reduce its appeal as a prime money laundering destination. Under the order, a judge can require suspected corrupt foreign officials, or their families, to prove they acquired their property by legitimate means. If unable, the law gives the organisation the power to confiscate it.

'So that's our plan?' she asks, rhetorically. 'In lieu of actually finding out who killed Laura Tatchell, we're going to go after some other Kazakh billionaire who has nothing to do with it. For what, optics? Bit cheap, even by our standards, isn't it?'

Of course, she is all in – something is better than nothing, and this is exactly the kind of crackdown Tatchell had been campaigning for. But now her friend is dead and Madeleine isn't going to make it easy for any of them – including herself – to imagine they have done enough.

Rittler squirms in his seat and Fionn Edwardes takes up the baton again in a slightly bored-sounding tone, seemingly oblivious to the second part of Madeleine's question. 'One of the simplest methods

to launder money is to invest in valuable items, like cars and properties. It is also one of the easiest to trace, and prove.'

He runs a hand through his thick blond hair. 'The legislation we're
looking at allows us to apply for a freezing order on a suspect's
accounts. Once we have what we're looking for, we can apply to be
appointed as a "receiver" – under that power we would be able to
seize property.'

'What sort of property?' Madeleine asks.

'Anything over the value of fifty thousand pounds. It doesn't matter
if it's jointly owned. It just matters that we can prove the suspect
bought it, and that the money they used for the purchase is linked
to criminal proceeds. According to the legislation, for an Unexplained
Wealth Order to be sanctioned, the High Court must be satisfied
that there are "reasonable grounds for suspecting that the known
sources of the respondent's lawfully obtained income would have
been insufficient for the purposes of enabling the respondent to obtain
the property"; that "the respondent is a politically exposed person,
or has been involved in serious crime (whether in a part of the United
Kingdom or elsewhere), or that a person connected with the
respondent is, or has been, so involved."'

'So, in English,' Madeleine says, 'we're using the wife to fuck the
husband.'

Rittler beams and looks over at Gerald. 'Told you she was one of
our best.'

CHAPTER FIVE

Hey, it's me. I— Si's voice cuts out as the National Express coach service pulls away from Victoria coach station.

Thought I saw you the other— football— I— work— later. The recording continues and breaks up again.

Looking down at the cracked screen of her Nokia, noting it has full reception, Ramona places the receiver once again to her ear and attempts, in vain, to hear the message as Si's voice lurches in and out of range.

The fault must be at his end. Well, that would make a change.

Pressing delete, she lets the handset drop back into her rucksack and takes a cigarette from the pocket of her denim jacket, rolling it between her forefinger and thumb. Shaking away the image of him and the stab of envy she feels when she pictures him rushing between assignments for her old paper on the other side of London, she lets her left cheek press up against the glass and closes her eyes, the familiar rush of adrenaline building as she thinks of the phone call she received the previous afternoon.

There isn't a lot to go on but already the scant details of what she has been told by her new potential client are enough to know, after a year of inane assignments, that this one could be something. Something more meaningful than the succession of infidelity cases and the single suspected arson that have so far defined her glittering career as a private eye. Something worth jumping on a coach for, at the very least. Something that will make the switch from journalism, where she spent her days covering murders and gang warfare, fronting up criminals with the weight of a multi-million-pound corporation behind her, seem less misguided.

The honking of the horn cuts through her thoughts as the National Express coach pushes through traffic somewhere near Kensington, a Porsche cutting in front of it. Leaning forward, Ramona spots a mobile phone pinned to the passenger's ear as her driver jumps the light.

These fucking people, Ramona thinks as the car pulls left, with a total disregard for the people they are inconveniencing, if not putting in actual danger with their recklessness. In moments like this, Ramona wishes she had accepted the invitation to join law enforcement when it had been presented to her – not that people like that got their comeuppance through legitimate channels. It is a bullshit simplification to say that all coppers are bastards, but even the good ones are hard-pushed to make a difference from within the constraints of a legal system designed by, and with the express intention of protecting, the privileged few.

And let's be honest, plenty are bastards.

* * *

It is turning dark by the time they close in on Bristol, the outlines of the city coming into view below the pink and blue streaks of a West Country sky.

Checking her watch, Ramona sees it has been three and a half hours since they set off. The seat beside her is empty and she stretches out her legs. Watching the silhouette of the Somerset hills give way to tower blocks, bathed in a winter blood-moon, she feels her soul righten.

After everything, Ramona had considered leaving London in search of a bold new start. She understands the lure of the countryside, in the abstract, or at least the lure of something simpler. But the truth is she doesn't want simplicity, she doesn't want safety. She wants adventure. She wants this: heading into the unknown in pursuit of a proper case.

Taking out her notebook, Ramona reads the few notes she had made under the heading Time for Tuition. *Lucy. 5.00 p.m., the Gallimaufry, Gloucester Road.*

Gathering her bag and skateboard as the coach pulls around the Bearpit and towards the bus station, she glances at the words CHEERS DRIVE emblazoned on the overhead wall in the arrivals area, pulling out her packet of cigarettes.

* * *

The pub is a half-hour walk from the coach station, directly along a main road that leads from Bristol centre to the north of the city. It feels good to be out of London, somewhere where she has no connections and little chance of being followed.

Still, old habits die hard and Ramona finds herself hunching as she walks, keeping watch for nearby silhouettes in the windows of buildings as she passes, turning every so often to scan for a familiar face.

Her iPod is one of the few concessions to the wonders of modern technology that she will allow herself, though 'modern' is perhaps mislabelling a technology from two decades ago. She isn't going to give in to getting a smartphone for the sake of having a music app that, just like social media, is an industry selling surveillance, harvesting its users' personal data for cynical commercial gain. But if anything was to persuade her the trade-off is worth it, an application giving her access to endless music might have been it.

When Ramona was thirteen, she found an old Walkman at the car boot sale on Holloway Road. After quizzing her briefly on her non-existent musical preferences, the guy who sold it to her pulled out an old trainer box filled with cassette tapes he could no longer make use of, and insisted on throwing them in for free.

'The best hip-hop collection in N19,' he told her proudly. 'Consider it an education.'

As she discovered later, once she returned to her gran's house in the suburbs of Brighton, the titles and artists were neatly handwritten on the cassette sleeve: A Tribe Called Quest, Kool Keith, De La Soul, Souls of Mischief, Mos Def and Talib Kweli. Over the following months and years, she listened to those tapes on repeat until she knew the lyrics to each of the songs. The more she learnt about eighties and nineties hip-hop, the more she appreciated the DIY values: the jazz sampling and introspection and consciousness of the lyrics. But sometimes, like now, she just wants a beat.

Turning the dial to Wu-Tang, Ramona braces herself as she touches on the title *Liquid Swords* and waits for the drop.

'Got a spare fag, Miss?' A man seated cross-legged on the pavement at the foot of a tree outside an off-licence signals to her and she pulls off her headphones, fiddling in her pocket and taking out a cigarette which she passes to him, waiting while he uses her lighter.

Moving off again, she thinks of the young woman she is due to meet. Lucy, if that is her real name, had sounded both traumatised and wary enough on the phone that Ramona hadn't faltered before offering to visit her in her home city. If any obstacle, distance or otherwise, stood in the way of their conversation for too long there was a strong chance the girl would lose her nerve, or decide the case wasn't worth pursuing after all. Experience has taught Ramona this much.

Since she stopped drinking, and almost everything else, Ramona has given bars of any sort a wide berth, but she can't avoid them forever; and if she is going to put Lucy at ease enough to talk, she wants to take her somewhere where she feels safe.

Following the directions she had memorised before setting off, Ramona crosses the underpass and onto a stretch leading into the area known affectionately as the People's Republic of Stokes Croft.

Passing vintage record stores and cooperative vegan cafés, she watches a crackhead waltzing with his Staffy in front of a bonfire on the pavement alongside endless graffiti-daubed hoardings. The words *IN THE ASYLUM WE ARE ALL LUNATICS* leap out at her and she feels herself instantly soothed.

She will never be so at peace as when lost within the walls of a city.

At the crossroads beneath a railway bridge, Cheltenham Road turns into Gloucester Road. The chaos of Stokes Croft and Montpelier gives way to proper pubs and independent shops that remind her of Kentish Town when she was growing up; before the media set took over, rebranding selected enclaves of North London as 'villages' in an effort to legitimise charging five pounds for a loaf of bread in a converted corner shop – and the prices they in turn hoped to inflate for their perfectly turned out terraced homes with the uniform plantation blinds and Instagram-ready front doors.

Passing a sticker reading HELL IS OTHER PEOPLE, Ramona smiles as she waits at the zebra crossing. When she senses a flurry of movement behind, she jumps left, her fingers tightening around her skateboard.

But it is just a group of students swaggering towards the traffic lights, oblivious to those around them.

The lyrics in her ears rage, and she turns the volume up louder. Pulling her cap low over her face and tightening her hood, she presses on, her heartbeat refusing to slow.

Forwards. Turning back is not an option.

CHAPTER SIX

Both ends of Kensington Palace Gardens are buttressed by a security checkpoint manned by Diplomatic Protection Group police.

Madeleine scrutinises the stuccoed veneers and mega-basements of the diplomats and super-rich on billionaires' row, from behind her sunglasses. Amir and Ingrid Zhatchanov might as well live in Fort Knox – or rather the United States Bullion Depository with which it is often confused, Madeleine reminds herself, in a tone that is worryingly reminiscent of her father. Although Amir, of course, is currently serving time in a very different type of compound in a medium-sized prison in Kazakhstan, leaving his wife, Ingrid, in charge of their affairs – and the seemingly full-time business of spending their ill-gotten gains.

Nice work if you can get it.

Madeleine's jaw tenses and she forces her mind to change gear, thinking of her final words to Rittler – *Remind me why I'm doing your donkey work?* – as she gathered her things in the office a while earlier, following their meeting at headquarters. They had travelled back together by tube from the briefing at HQ to the old mews terrace where the Serious Crime Investigations Department is located, a stone's throw from Charing Cross. The patter of his small-talk distracted her from the image of Laura's daughters in the pew at the church, their faces pale and disbelieving.

'Donkey work? Do you mind, you're our finest show pony. And that's why we don't want you in the knacker's yard just yet,' Rittler had replied with a forced jollity that they both appreciated. For a moment, Madeleine wondered if he was going to say something more. But then he stopped, and Madeleine pulled on her coat in order to head back out to meet Jonny for surveillance of the house.

Now, on Kensington's Billionaires' Row, she takes a deep breath.

They both knew that her small display of resistance to street surveillance was little more than a dance – one they have performed countless times before; a tacit agreement that allows them both to stick to their roles without any discomfort – Madeleine below Rittler in the official pecking order, with him as Detective Inspector, the lead officer and senior investigator to her Detective Sergeant. They are both part of a small team appointed to assist in investigations carried out for the organisation, sometimes in collaboration with the security services, either governmental or corporate, and Rittler understands her need to push back, slightly, just as they both understand that she needs this time to readjust, after Vietnam; after all of it.

He also knows that she is far brighter, more formidable than he is, and that if she wanted it, Madeleine could easily have his job. Although for this to happen, she would have to learn to kowtow to management in a way that they both know she can't – or won't. And so they work together: Madeleine, the front-line warrior quietly running Paul Rittler, the yes-man who steadily rose up the ladder at the Met before joining the Serious Organised Crime Agency – RIP – and finding himself in the right place at the right time when SOCA was disbanded and another agency was created to replace it.

All in all, it is a relationship made in collegiate heaven, and on this morning's journey back to the office from HQ, Madeleine had been grateful for the company, a distraction from renewed thoughts of Laura, or rather of her daughters, the eldest of whom, Tilly, has her GCSEs coming up in a few months' time.

Taking a look around her at the diplomatic flags and ornamental flourishes on the high gates that protect the mansions along one side

of the street, Madeleine focuses on what lies ahead. Her hands are
laden with shopping bags from Calzedonia and Space NK. Dressed
in an oyster-coloured silk shirt and tailored trousers, she takes out
her phone and speaks to an imaginary husband in performative
French. Adjusting the oversized sunglasses that don't warrant a second
look around here, even in the midst of an English winter, she takes
in the garish architecture, so 'new-money' it would have given her
father a heart attack.

For this reason alone, she loves it.

'Still no sign of her?' Jonny asks from his station a few streets
away. Madeleine recognises the unmistakable crunching of crisps
through the earpiece of her phone, and pictures her colleague parked
up on Kensington Court, a road where red-brick mansion-flats brim
with matching hanging baskets, mainlining fistfuls of Golden Wonder.
She supposes the munching sound is preferable to that of him sipping
from a hip flask, though it's been a while since Jonny was that bad.
And God knows he had reason to be as bad as he liked, and worse.

Jonny Robertson's legend is sufficiently well known for Madeleine
– long before he had confided in her over several pints at the Theodore
Bullfrog on John Adam Street – to have heard the story of how the
former detective had worked his way down the career ladder, through
no fault of his own. Of how, after years spent serving as a squaddie and
sniper in the army, in his late twenties Jonny had joined the police,
quickly making detective. Of how he was all set for an illustrious career,
until one balmy afternoon in June – having survived tours of duty in
Helmand, physically unscathed – he attended what should have been
a routine call-out to a perfectly middle-class terrace in Tufnell Park.
Uniform were already on their way but Jonny happened to be passing
so he took the call. Minutes before he got to the scene, the husband
– an English teacher with no previous convictions, the newspapers would
go on to stress – stabbed his wife and young daughter eleven times
between them, before attacking the detective as he arrived in the after-
math.

Madeleine was still working for the Foreign Office at the time, but she remembered the case. Specifically, she remembers the tabloid headlines revelling in the moment the 'scorned husband' had 'taken revenge' on the mother of his two children after she threatened to leave him.

It had been a shitshow, in so many ways.

For Jonny, who still struggled to hold back tears as he described the events of that day to Madeleine, years later, this was the beginning of his own slide towards the place he affectionately nicknamed SCID Row, after his own mental state – via a period of severe PTSD, and comfort sought in junk food and gallons of after-work beer, which graduated to lunchtime spirits. Though who is Madeleine to judge, on either count? They have both done their fair share of stints at the police rehabilitation centre known as Flint House.

As for Jonny's remaining coping mechanisms . . . If ungodly quantities of heavily salted snacks help him get through the day, and don't get in the way of the job he is assigned to do as surveillance manager, then it is fine by her.

Still, she does wish he wouldn't munch so loudly in her ear, for fuck's sake.

Scanning the detached mansions along one side, the other backing onto Kensington Palace, Madeleine's eyes settle on the Zhatchanov's home – one of only a handful of private residences on the street.

According to Zoopla, the Zhatchanovs bought theirs for a mere £38 million, in 2018. Well, she hopes they had their mortgage rate fixed.

As she passes, Madeleine peers casually through iron gates and sees there are two parked cars in the drive: a gold Porsche and a red Bugatti with the registration number: CRYPTO1.

'The wife's car is still here. So unless she left on foot . . .' Madeleine speaks under her breath as she turns left under one of the plane trees that line the street, towards the cut-through to Hyde Park.

'Yeah, maybe she's just nipped out to Tesco for a pint of milk,' Jonny replies.

'I'm going to hang around for a bit longer, until it's time for Matilda to finish school,' Madeleine says, reverting to French for the benefit of the dog walker who passes as she steps into the park. Two cockapoos, a Great Dane and a Shih Tzu as props would admittedly make an elaborate disguise for private security, but if the Zhatchanovs, or any of the other billionaires and political targets around here, wanted additional eyes and ears about their domain, then surely a few overpriced mutts as accessories would hardly be considered pushing the boat out.

'You know I can't understand a word you're saying, right?' Jonny replies in a heavy Glaswegian brogue as Madeleine follows the path, taking a seat on the bench with a view through to Palace Gardens.

Et voilà. With a bristle of anticipation, she sits forward on the bench, honing in on the gap in the hedge which reveals a flash of gold as the Porsche Carrera GT reaches the gate.

'Actually, I think I'm going to go and get some of that tea you like,' she says pointedly, reverting to English and issuing the code.

Standing, she follows the path in the other direction, back towards the main road.

'She's coming out of the gate now, on your side.'

'Roger,' Jonny replies.

'Roger,' Amol chips in, from his own position a street away from Jonny.

'You're with Amol,' Jonny tells Madeleine. 'I'll be up front.'

Her expression hardening, she summons the mental image of Tilly and Ruth, their fingers clinging to one another's as the hymn swelled through the vestibule, and walks.

* * *

'Standby, standby. Known vehicle exiting property and turning left left left towards the Royal Albert Hall notable landmark. Positive ID subject Pearl is in the back seat, wearing sunglasses, black jacket and a fur scarf. Eight two has the eyeball.'

The covert black taxi is driven by Amol, dressed in his trademark undercover get-up: blue shirt, undone one button too many, and sunglasses with lenses like oil slicks.

From the back of the cab, Madeleine listens carefully as Jonny fires out instructions from his car, positioned just two vehicles behind Zhatchanova's chauffeur-driven Porsche.

Jamal had been listening to pundits discussing yet another imminent Cabinet reshuffle on Radio 5 Live when she jumped in. Now, though, as they chug along Kensington Gore the only sound is Jonny issuing directions.

'It's a right right right onto Trevor Street,' he continues, as Madeleine's ride passes Prince of Wales Gate, where tourists are gathered with the inevitable Pac a Macs and selfie sticks.

Knightsbridge at this hour is a hum of unnecessary 4x4s, designer trainers and laminated eyebrows.

Christ, what has happened to this city? Every generation believes theirs was the last of the good times – and with her inherited wealth and preference for the finer things, Madeleine is hardly part of the revolution. But even she remembers when London had soul. Now everywhere she looks, all she sees is the corruption, the hollowing out of humanity. Maybe this is simply what happens when you spend your days and nights chasing depravity, you end up finding it everywhere you look.

'Target Pearl is entering the car park on Brompton Place. I'll wait on the double yellow outside the exit,' Jonny says, and Madeleine signals for Amol to follow suit.

There are five cars in total stationed in the vicinity, and Madeleine manages to spot them all in turn. She can only hope Ingrid Zhatchanova and her driver are less intuitive.

'Good plan,' she replies. If there is one thing you can say for Knightsbridge, it's that obnoxious parking will never make one stand out.

'I'll get out here,' Madeleine tells Jamal before stepping onto Brompton Road, grimacing at the crowds of tourists flocking into Harrods. At the top of the steps, shoppers whose arms are heaving with newly purchased items step over a young man hunched on the pavement, wrapped in a sleeping bag. Reaching into her pocket, Madeleine pulls out her purse and removes a crisp ten-pound note which she slides into his hand as she passes, meeting his slightly shocked eyes before continuing on.

'Do-gooder. You know he's just going to go and spend that on crack, don't yer, pal?' Jonny says in her earpiece.

'Really, I thought he might spend it on Pokémon cards,' she replies.

What business is it of hers? Whatever helps him get through the day.

'She's coming out and heading towards the entrance on Hans Road,' Jonny reports, through her earpiece.

'I see her.' Madeleine moves briskly towards one of three entrances into Harrods, her skin prickling with anticipation as she moves under the famous green awning and onto the tail of the oligarch's wife. Anywhere else in the world, Ingrid Zhatchanova would stand out like a beacon with her surgically enhanced face framed by Swarovski earrings and a mink scarf. Here, it is as though she is dressed in camouflage as she moves ahead through the crowd, blending in with customers and mannequins alike.

The extreme artificiality of the light and the bass-driven pop music blaring from the speakers add an extra element of drama Madeleine could do without. Even for one as wholeheartedly committed as she is to overpriced consumerist tat, this store is a bricks and mortar manifestation of a panic attack: a hall of mirrors sprawled over six seemingly windowless floors, each more confusing than the last.

Shit. Where is she?

Approaching the lifts, Madeleine looks around for a second sighting of the wife.

Ahead, an index of the various departments reads like the results of the random word generator she uses to create her password for her various identities on the so-called dark web: *luxury piercing, wellness, toy concierge*. Pushing against the tide of images that rear up at the thought – of children as young as two or three, listed one after the other – Madeleine feels her stomach turn, as though she might throw up. That is no longer her case, she reminds herself. Though are any of them that different, when you boiled it down? Human suffering is her business. And however many forms it might take, the basic shape is still the same.

If she wanted to, Madeleine need only scratch the surface and she would be able to find a line linking Amir Zhatchanov's criminal activity with the men she just arrested in Vietnam – be it through some dodgy shipping company they used to transport the boys, or the lawyer they employ to attempt to get them off. If there is one thing Madeleine has learnt it's that the roots of corruption run deep, and shoot off in unpredictable directions.

Walking faster, she scans the area, her teeth biting against her lip. *Fuck.*

She texts Jonny, who she can only presume is still parked a street away: *Lost her.*

His reply is instant: *Driver just returned to the car park, he's having a cigarette by the entrance. Shall I stay put?* They had been briefed to know that Ingrid's driver has bladder cancer, and as a result secretly leaves the car every time he drops her off, to pee. 'I've got eyeball,' Sadie says through Madeleine's earpiece, interrupting her thoughts, and Madeleine exhales in relief. Jonny is best off where he is: he might be one of five cars now positioned around the building as part of the wider surveillance team, but there is only one man she truly trusts.

'Wait— It's not her,' Sadie clarifies.

Stay put. Madeleine texts Jonny again, her fingers moving furiously over the screen.

When she looks up, she almost steps on her target. Taking a step back, Madeleine notes the woman's shoes – a pair of Aquazzura Bow Tie 85 suede pumps she recognises from a recent late-night scoping out on Net-a-Porter, and has the briefest flash of respect.

In a world of dualisms, it should be possible to separate out a corrupt oligarch's wife from her fashion choices.

When the lift doors open, Ingrid steps inside and Madeleine follows. If the ground floor of Harrods is intense, the fifth is like a first-class airport lounge reworked by MC Escher after a night on meth. Slipping sideways to pass a man in a white thobe, Madeleine pauses to admire a Dior dress embellished by a display of uplit dried grasses as Ingrid dithers a little ahead.

Taking out her phone, she casually composes a message to Jonny as she walks.

I'm on her.

Looking up, she follows and finds herself in the hair salon at the end of the hall. Ahead, Ingrid is followed by Sadie less than a metre away, in a baseball cap and dark glasses. She might as well have a sign on her head reading: UNDERCOVER OFFICER AT WORK.

'Can I help?' the salon assistant asks, and Madeleine clears her throat, turning her attention to the woman in front of her.

'I haven't actually booked but I don't suppose you could fit me in? I have to meet my daughter later and I look a *fright.*'

'You look great.' The girl smiles back, her face unnaturally blemish-free, beautiful green eyes obscured by false eyelashes. 'If you follow me over to reception I can check if we have any space.'

'Sure,' Madeleine says as the young woman swipes systematically at the screen of her iPad.

Glancing back, signalling with her face for Sadie to back off, Madeleine watches as another employee rushes forward, holding out her arms to the incoming customer. 'Mrs Zee, let me take your coat. What are we doing today – the usual?'

'Darling, work your magic. I've had the most stressful morning. Can you be quick? I have food shopping to do. One moment.'

Indicating to her phone, Ingrid speaks into the receiver. In the split-second silence that follows, Madeleine switches her own phone to video mode, and presses record.

'*Sälemetsiz be, Habibi. Ol qalay dawıstadı?*' Ingrid Zhatchanova speaks a moment more before hanging up.

Frowning apologetically, the woman behind the counter shakes her head at Madeleine. 'We're fully booked. The Blow Bar downstairs might have a spot?'

CHAPTER SEVEN

Lucy is sitting on an area of raised platform at the back of the pub, as far away as physically possible from the bar and the other drinkers, her expression that of someone waiting for the most uncomfortable blind date in history.

Picking up the pint of cider on the table in front of her as Ramona approaches, Lucy takes a large swig and the Pavlovian dog inside Ramona lurches at the familiar sway and smell of being back in a pub. Righting herself, she places her rucksack and skateboard on the floor and takes a seat on the stool opposite. It would be so easy to go up there and order herself a single whisky, even just a half of beer. There is literally nothing stopping her, except herself. And when it comes to letting herself down, Ramona has form.

The girl before her looks younger than Ramona had expected, but then Lucy is only in her first year at university, which makes her just eighteen or nineteen years old.

It had crossed Ramona's mind that she might be walking into a trap set up by Michael O'Keegan's men to lure Ramona somewhere she would be vulnerable. But if they had found out what she was doing now, they could have hunted her down in London. Besides, she can't think this way about every potential case or she will never do anything again.

'Lucy?' The girl smiles tightly, by way of confirmation. Her hair is dyed platinum blonde with thick roots that are almost certainly intentional, cut into a bob with a severe fringe. The black eyeliner is reminiscent of a young Courtney Love.

'Can I get you a drink?'

Ramona shakes her head. 'I'm good.'

'Thanks for coming all this way.' Lucy fiddles with the vape pen on the table in front of her, her expression one of wary defiance.

'It's not a problem,' Ramona replies. After a pause, she takes out her own cigarettes and places the packet on the table. 'Do you want to go outside so we can smoke?'

'That would be good.' There is relief in the girl's voice, possibly at the prospect of getting up and shaking away some of the energy that has built up in anticipation of this meeting rather than at the thought of nicotine itself.

She walks ahead, dressed in dark wide-leg jeans and a hoodie not dissimilar to Ramona's own.

'It's a cool city,' Ramona says, dumping her stuff at her feet before sitting again.

'I suppose. I don't actually live in this bit,' Lucy replies, as they take a seat under one of the heaters in a sheltered section of outside seating, cordoned off with scrappy wooden planters, on the edge of the main road. 'I wanted to come somewhere I could talk without bumping into my parents, or my friend—'

'She doesn't know you contacted me?'

'I wanted to speak to you first.' Lucy shivers and Ramona makes an encouraging expression.

'That makes sense.'

'I didn't expect you to look so—' The girl struggles to find the words.

'I'm older than I look.' Ramona lights her cigarette.

'That's not what I meant.'

'How did you hear about me?' The rhetorical question is designed to draw the conversation naturally around to the matter at hand, while giving the impression that Lucy might have heard of her through word-of-mouth, implying this wasn't Ramona's first proper case.

'I liked the fact that you were a woman.' She pauses. 'And not too expensive.'

As compliments go, this is broad but she will take it.

'So your friend didn't go to the police, after the—'

'Fuck the police,' the girl cuts in, her tone surprisingly sharp, though her eyes, as they briefly hold Ramona's, shine with tears. 'Do you know the conviction rate for sexual assault?'

'Yes I do, and it's shamefully low.' Ramona returns her gaze, evenly.

'I mean, I don't even know what this is, if it is even considered an offence. I looked it up—' Lucy's voice drifts off and she looks down, scraping with her thumbnail at something on the table Ramona can't see.

'It's not illegal for escort agencies to make lawful introductions between clients and sex workers, but that's not exactly what you're saying happened in this instance, right?' Ramona replies. 'Do you think you could tell me more about what happened? It would really help to start at the very beginning, and be as detailed as possible. If that's not too—'

'It's fine.' Lucy inhales, and then breathes out a cloud of saccharine-sweet vapour that hangs in the air between them. 'A friend of mine found this website called Time for Tuition. In the blurb it says it's a premium service matching eligible female students with older men willing to pay the girls' university fees in return for "companionship".

'She thought it would just be some low-level escort work. Like you take some rich older guy out for the night, act as his arm candy, and in return he gives you cash. No big deal. Plenty of students do it.'

'Sure.' Ramona nods, waiting silently for Lucy to continue. Many do plenty more, too. She thinks of Cindy with her baby face and her room above the club on Dalston Lane. She is twenty-five now, but she had been younger than Lucy is now, when she started. Plenty of the girls Cindy works with at the clubs are paying their way through an education system that will leave them with the sort of debt that takes a lifetime to pay back, presuming there is a job awaiting them at the end of it. And they're doing a lot more than acting as arm candy.

'Seriously, I get it.' Ramona nods reassuringly.

'So, my mate emailed the website and she got a response straight away saying "cool come and have an interview". The person she initially spoke to said that because of the "calibre of their clients", they are very particular about who they take on. So they gave her an address and she turns up and—' Lucy clears her throat, steadying herself for a moment before continuing. 'It was like this office block in the middle of nowhere. There was a bottle of cava on the table and this man who was "conducting the interview" . . .' Lucy makes the same speech marks with her fingers.

'He told my friend that he was going to simulate how a potential pairing might go. It started with him asking about her course and more about herself, and then he asked if she would be "willing to be intimate in return for what will be a substantial amount of money".' Lucy shakes her head and takes another puff on her vape. 'By this point my friend had already spent like a hundred pounds or whatever on her ticket to London from Manchester, and she didn't want to risk not being taken on by the agency, so she said what she thought he wanted to hear.'

Ramona inhales, wishing to God there was a drink on the table in front of her, imagining the soothing whisky burning the back of her throat. 'Take your time.'

Lucy stops, her voice trembling when she finally starts again.

'He told her he believed she was the right fit for the role but that in order to be taken on by such an elite service, she would have to be able to prove to him that she was willing to do the things she said she would do. He didn't want to risk presenting someone to a client only to discover she was a time-waster.'

'Right.' Ramona's stomach turns. 'And she had sex with him in the office?'

'She didn't know what else—'

'I get it. You don't have to justify anything. I just need the facts.' Ramona takes a final drag of her cigarette. 'So what happened afterwards?'

'By the time she got back to Manchester, where she's studying, there was already an email from his secretary.' Lucy pulls on her vape pen. 'She said that they were sorry but that she hadn't made the grade this time around. Can you imagine how insulting that is, on top of everything?'

Ramona watches the girl's fists clench.

'That's when she called me. She was— She didn't want to go to the police. Even if she had, what would she say? Because she agreed to it, chances are there is nothing that can be done. But that can't be right, can it?' Lucy's voice wobbles again. 'And now she's terrified her parents will find out, and other people. The guy's like fifty or something, and he was so . . .'

Ramona lets Lucy's slip of the tongue go unremarked. Moving on, she asks calmly, 'Have you told anyone else about this?'

Lucy shakes her head.

'And you . . .' She pauses. 'Your friend really won't call the police?'

'No way. Not unless it's certain that he will go down. Even then—'

'OK.' Ramona thinks for a moment.

'The truth is, I don't even know what I'm looking for—'

What Lucy is looking for is justice. Ramona recognises this instantly, even if the girl herself doesn't. She wants this man not to get away with what he has done. If, in the absence of proper legal process, her best bet is a private individual with the registered authority to check public records and interrogate court documents and legal records, then so be it. Ultimately, Ramona knows that what Lucy wants is for the bastard to suffer by whatever means are available to her. In the absence of a just world, she wants justice of some sort.

A legal vigilante. Wasn't that the term Si had used when Ramona told him her new career plan? It had sounded alright to her – though in reality that's not her job. Ramona's job is to give people the information and answers they crave. It's up to them what they do with it after that.

'I can't believe they can get away with this,' Lucy says, as though she has been eavesdropping on Ramona's thoughts. 'My friend— Why would they not take her on? Nothing about this makes any sense. Something just feels . . .'

Ramona nods. 'Did they say why she hadn't "made the grade"?'

'No. Look, I should be straight with you: I don't have much money. Your advert said you would only charge if you solved the case, or whatever. But even then, I'm not—'

'How much can you afford?'

'I don't know, a couple of hundred quid?'

Ramona stares back at her. Two hundred pounds? Is she—

Licking her lips, she clears her throat. 'OK, look, the first thing I'm going to do is contact the website. Then we're going to take it from there. Right? I want to help you—' Ramona doesn't add that she also needs to eat; that she has already forked out the cost of the coach and the room in the Airbnb she has booked for the night.

But she knows there is no going back, now that she has had the first scent of blood.

The girl nods. 'Look, I haven't been straight with you. It wasn't a friend—'

Ramona smiles, kindly. 'I get it.'

Lucy smiles, biting her lip as though to stop herself falling apart. 'Thank you, for everything. For being so nice, and for coming here, and . . .'

Ramona reaches out and touches her arm.

'By the way, my real name's Ottilie,' the girl says. 'Not Lucy.'

Pausing, as though she is about to say something more, Ramona pauses and then changes her mind, holding out her hand. 'Ottilie. It's good to meet you.'

CHAPTER EIGHT

Madeleine gets out at the Strand, leaving Amol to drive straight back to the office, along with Jonny and Sadie who travel together from the Harrods stake-out in a separate car.

Madeleine is already salivating as she ducks into the old school Italian café on one of the side roads, where she picks out the ingredients of her favourite panini from a selection of tubs behind the Perspex counter: mozzarella, Parma ham, olives, sundried tomatoes, basil, salt and a healthy splash of olive oil.

Yes, fucking please.

This is another thing she has missed, along with the overhead shower and decent towels, and access to Net-a-Porter. She audibly groans as she eats her sandwich from the waxed paper wrapper.

God, that tasted good – all the better for how long she had waited for it.

It had been a torturous period between Madeleine leaving Ingrid Zhatchanova in the salon upstairs in Harrods, and her target re-emerging several floors down in the food hall, her silky dark hair swishing as she perused aisles of obscurely flavoured teas.

To pass the time, Madeleine had made herself inconspicuous as she wandered between rows of exotic fruit, reminded of the bustle of the night market in the area around her station on Ta Hien Street;

the putrid-smelling durian, spiky jackfruit and pink lychee, which, like the boys in the room over the road, had been brought up in boats along the Mekong Delta. Thinking of it, she had been tempted to fire off an email to her partners in Hanoi to check on any progress with the men they arrested two weeks earlier. The British man involved owns an important construction company in Vietnam and will already be lawyered up to the hilt, no doubt. Madeleine's stomach clenched at the thought, demonstrating abdominal muscles she didn't know she had.

But she knew she shouldn't follow up: this way madness lies. What happens now isn't her concern, and she can't allow it to be – she has learnt that the hard way. The boys are safe, for the moment; at least those boys they managed to save will be. She doesn't let herself think of all the ones they were too late for.

For her own survival she knows she must blot out the mental image of the countless faces on the computer monitor as Madeleine and the international team in Hanoi trawled through the listings of children for sale on Tor, the uncontrolled part of the internet that more than earns its nickname as the dark web, in the weeks building up to the arrest.

Not forget them – you can never forget. Just focus on what she is doing now.

Placing the memory of the boys back in one of the boxes in her mind, next to the one labelled Laura Tatchell MP, as she wandered through Harrods food hall, Madeleine focused instead on her annoyance with her new colleague, Sadie, who had apparently misread her *back off* gesture, upstairs in the salon, for *fuck off*, and retreated to sit in the car with Jonny.

But she was so hungry it was hard to focus on anything else at all. In Hanoi it would be ten at night, she reasoned. While Madeleine's head might have been able to adapt to the sudden lurching from one continent to another, her stomach was less submissive.

The sign on the pillar next to her when she next looked up – NO EATING OR DRINKING – felt like a cruel test. But any sense of her own hunger had instantly fallen away as she spotted Ingrid stationed at the specialist tea counter.

And her patience had paid off, she reminds herself, as she returns to SCID Row on foot, taking the final bite of her sandwich in the doorway and dropping the paper in the bin as she steps inside. In more ways than one. Sadie is running papers off on the printer, looking up and then quickly away again as Madeleine steps through the door, taking her coat off and heading upstairs without a backwards glance.

What was the point of having a go? The girl had fucked up. There was no use reprimanding her. It was useful, in a way, to get such a clear sense of who the new recruit was, so early on. Madeleine liked to know what she was dealing with, and then adjust her expectations accordingly. Besides, Sadie is young and inexperienced – and time will tell. Though she doesn't hold out much hope: experience is one thing, instinct quite another.

Madeleine tucks her shopping bags into the footwell of her desk and calls over to her colleagues to gather round for a debrief.

Pulling out her phone and placing it on her desk, she waits while Rittler, Fionn, Amol, Jamal and Sadie take their places.

Giving herself a moment to consider the photo she had surreptitiously taken while queuing at the loose tea counter, she hones in on Ingrid Zhatchanova's purse with its rainbow spread of loyalty and credit cards, before passing the phone to Jonny first.

'She's splitting payments between different credit and in-store loyalty cards,' Madeleine announces, and waits while Jonny considers the image before passing it on to Rittler.

'What are we looking at?' Rittler asks.

'Flick through the images. The first is of her paying for tea at one till: four hundred and ninety-six pounds, no less.'

Jonny splutters. 'You can't be serious.'

'It was speciality strains.' Madeleine shrugs. 'Some of the tins in there are more than sixty quid a pop, adds up quite quickly. The point is, when she goes to pay, you can see from the picture she takes out a white credit card and loyalty card. They are both in the name Ingrid Zhatchanova.'

'Right,' Jamal says, taking the phone from Jonny and studying it.

'Flick to the next picture,' Madeleine instructs. 'That was taken minutes later in the chocolate room, where she racked up a separate bill of five hundred and thirty-five pounds. Again, we're looking at some Godiva selection boxes costing two hundred pounds each, so easy enough to do. Now if you zoom into the purse, you can see she pulls out two different cards to pay with.

'You see, these cards are in a slightly different name. I. S. Zhatchanova. She does it again later, in the beauty department – this time the credit and loyalty cards she uses are in the name Zatchanova, spelt without the first H.'

'So she's splitting the payments in order that the money can't all be traced back to her,' Jamal surmises.

'Exactly. She was talking to each of the cashiers like they were her friends, she's clearly there all the time,' Madeleine confirms. 'It might as well be her local convenience store, as well as her own personal launderette.'

'Surely we can't use footage taken in this way—' Sadie pipes up, quick to flag the lack of protocol, and Madeleine studies her.

Is she for real?

Moving her gaze disdainfully towards the notebook Sadie is holding, her pencil poised above the page, Madeleine sighs calmly, as though dealing with a child. 'Obviously we can't use the photos.'

Taking the phone back, once everyone has had a look, Madeleine places it face down on her desk. 'The point is that we now know what she is doing – haemorrhaging the proceeds of her husband's illegally acquired fortune and covering her tracks by spreading the payments for a range of goods over a series of different cards, registered in slightly different names.'

'Nice,' Rittler replies. 'So what we need now is to prove it was she who was doing the spending, rather than her card being used by someone else, which is obviously what she will try to claim. This will involve obtaining CCTV and ideally tapping up staff members to ID and formally identify our suspect. Most of the evidence we need will be obtainable via bank material, including credit checks, which should be easy enough to get hold of. And the department store has its own police liaison team whom we can contact to provide live data in relation to the use of the rewards cards . . . Fionn, you get onto that.'

'I know the liaison officer,' Jonny pipes up casually, from where he is spritzing a leaf of a rubber plant that stands seven-foot high against the wall. 'We used to work together in the Met. She was fired after being arrested for fornicating in a public fountain in Benidorm, if you can believe it.'

'I've met her, and I can,' Amol says.

Madeleine narrows her eyes. 'And you're only telling us this now?'

'I'm no gossip, DS Farrow.' Madeleine rolls her eyes and Jonny moves to his desk. 'I'll give her a call. She's a good lass – even better after eight shots of Jägermeister.'

Amol chuckles, wheeling his chair back to his station.

'Ask for an evidential package showing her rewards card usage and receipts.

'If we can get her to produce data relating to the different loyalty cards over several months and we can show they were all being used at the same time, then this, combined with cell-site data which will put her in the vicinity – added to the real-time surveillance – begins to build a picture,' Madeleine says, thinking this is what police work really is: throwing paint at a canvas and seeing what sticks.

'Also, there's a video recording here. It might be nothing. She was talking to someone on the phone in the salon, the audio is terrible but I'm sure someone can clean it up for us. It's not Russian, so I assume they're speaking Kazakh,' Madeleine adds, addressing Jamal. She doesn't speak much Russian, but she knows enough to recognise that this isn't it.

'Send it over,' Jamal says.

'Have you seen who their son is?' Sadie pipes up again from her seat, where she is tapping at her keyboard. 'Look.'

Leaning in, Madeleine reads aloud from an article in the *Guardian*.

"'Zhatchanov Junior is CEO of AlterRon, one of the biggest cryptomines in the world, which takes advantage of the cheap electricity in his home country of Kazakhstan. Sergey – son of Amir – is one of a number of high-profile players lobbying against new rules set to regulate the industry with a new corporate tax as well as impose restrictions on the industry's energy consumption nationwide.'"

Taking control of the mouse and clicking a link to a generic piece on Kazakhstan and mining, in an international news platform Madeleine respects, she reads on.

"'In its crudest form, cryptocurrency is a digital peer-to-peer currency that doesn't rely on banks to verify its transactions. It requires a huge amount of electricity, which was both abundant and cheap in Kazakhstan, making it an attractive base for foreign-owned cryptomines.

"'Following the collapse of the Soviet Union and the subsequent disintegration of industrial production in the area where AlterRon is based, investors flocked to the coal-abundant region in order to take advantage of a surplus of electricity and unused warehouses that were a hangover from the Soviet era, where they could house their equipment.

"'But implosion was as inevitable as it was catastrophic as excessive mining tipped the country's national grid from a surplus of electricity to a deficit.

"'By the end of 2021, the crypto industry was consuming seven per cent of the entire generating capacity of Kazakhstan. There were blackouts caused by power shortages, leading to heightened tensions over corruption, the rising cost of fuel and perceived nepotism. When the government cut miners from the national grid, in January 2022, international investors fled. The Kazakhstan government continues to try to draw back crypto exchanges and investors, but it seems unlikely.

"'AlterRon – owned by Sergey Zhatchanov and Nurislam Sultanov – is one of the country's surviving operators, though its output is not what it once was . . .'"

Poor darlings, Madeleine thinks, clicking off the page, standing tall and strolling back to her desk as her personal phone beeps.

Looking down at the screen, she doesn't recognise the number.

Hey, it's Daphne. You left early this morning. Wondered if you were about tonight.

Daphne. That was her name. Of course – Daphne, the nymph who was turned into a tree after rejecting every one of her potential lovers. Oh, the irony.

'Right, everyone, bugger off. I want you in bright and early tomorrow,' Rittler says.

Deleting the message, Madeleine pulls on her coat.

'Off anywhere nice?'

'Night all,' she says, without looking back.

Heading out, she steps onto the street and reaches into the gold Godiva box in her handbag, pulling out a chocolate.

Well, when in Rome.

* * *

The house stands opposite the Pipe and Slippers, a swell of laughter and drum and bass rising from the tiny fenced-off forecourt as the pub door opens and shuts again.

Turning away from the call of the bar, Ramona keeps her attention fixed instead on the incongruous Victorian villa perched at the top of a steep flight of steps, set back from the main road. The wrought-iron veranda heaves with ivy and one of the windows is boarded up with a graffitied panel of wood.

From behind a set of curtains, she sees a light glowing on the right-hand side of the house. She fiddles with the gate, keeping her back to the street as she works her way up a series of chipped stone steps through the front garden, which is matted with bindweed, beer cans overflowing from broken recycling bins.

There had been no photos of the place when she booked it online and it's not hard to see why, though it has a certain charm. Particularly if you're into crack dens or horror movies.

Inputting the access code into a box attached to the crumbling wall, she pulls out the key and her mind returns to Lucy – or, rather, to Ottilie – as she walked away half an hour earlier, leaving Ramona at the traffic lights on Gloucester Road.

It was a ten-minute walk back the way she came, to the house in front of which she now stands on Cheltenham Road, and once again she finds herself opposite another pub.

Welcome to England.

Using the key from the box, she lets herself in and flicks the light switch to the left of the front door.

'Who the fuck are you?' a young man in boxer shorts greets Ramona, stepping into the hall from the door on the right, a foppish lock of blond hair hanging down in front of his face.

'I'm renting a room for the night, from Jemima.'

'Joker.' The man-boy shakes his head, whether in reference to his absent flatmate or to Ramona herself, Ramona neither knows nor cares, and she holds her ground, waiting for him to say more.

'Hope you brought your own toilet roll. And don't touch the milk in the fridge,' he adds after a beat, before continuing through the door on the right and closing it behind him.

Flicking her middle finger towards the housemate's back, Ramona turns to the door on the left, as per the instructions on the Airbnb listing, and turns the handle. Inside, Jemima's room is surprisingly neat; there is something touching about the tray set out on a small desk with a kettle, a mug and two teabags, and the handwritten note reading *Please help yourself.*

Jemima – a student apparently looking to make some cash by illegally subletting her room – had seemed almost surprised that anyone had responded to the half-hearted advert for a bed in a shared house in the heart of 'lively' Stokes Croft, in her message regarding Ramona's booking.

In hindsight, Ramona probably didn't need the room, she could have got away with taking the coach straight back to London, after all. But she hadn't been sure how much the client would have to offer, in terms of information, and whether there was any digging that could only be done from here. Turns out, there wasn't much at all.

Besides some deeply immoral behaviour on the part of a man old enough to know better, it's unlikely that a crime has even been committed. Strictly speaking, the woman had consented. Still, Ramona thinks, picturing Ottilie's forlorn expression as she dredged through the details of the assault, she will do her best to bring the bastard to justice in whatever way she can.

In any case, Ramona is here now and it's good to be somewhere new. More importantly, according to the advert, there is Wi-Fi and power, and at twenty-eight pounds a night, she will simply make the most of it.

Reminding herself to add money to the key for her own electricity meter when she gets home, Ramona places her rucksack on the floor and sits on the bed, taking out her computer and powering it up. Inserting the words 'Time for Tuition' into the search engine, she waits for the page to load. Standing while the old laptop whirrs on the bed, she walks to the door, slipping the lock across before turning back towards the room.

Scanning the spines of several ring binders that line the IKEA bookcase, Ramona's attention alights on one that reads 'uni admin', and she pulls it out.

Flicking through the pages until she finds the one least likely to be missed, dated weeks earlier with the university address in the top right-hand corner along with the name J. Watters, she removes it and replaces the file.

Cheers, Jemima.

Heading back to the bed, she finds the website she is looking for and hits the link.

'*Time for Tuition offers financial rewards to students in return for intimacy. Please contact us directly.*'

Spurred on by a rush of adrenaline, she starts to type into the contact form. 'Hi there, I found your website online and would love to be considered for the role. I'm a student based in Bristol. I look forward to hearing from you. Jenny Watters.'

The mention of the city shouldn't ring alarm bells; Ottilie is studying in Manchester and Ramona doubts she will have mentioned where she grew up.

Adding one of her email addresses – a generic Gmail incorporating random words instead of names – Ramona pauses a moment before pressing send. Once it is done, she reaches into her pocket for her cigarettes and removes a small block of hash and a single silver Rizla. It is the one concession to her old life that she allows herself these days: one spliff before bed, to take the edge off.

It is an almost ritualistic process. Crumbling the tobacco and hash into the smoking paper, Ramona enjoys the way the powder feels against the tips of her fingers. The smell reminds her of summers on the Heath, looking up at the clouds as she lay on her back on the grass; and of winter nights pulling together the threads of a story in the flat on Camden High Street.

She has barely finished skinning up when her computer pings with a message alert.

Her heartbeat picking up, Ramona reads the reply.

Dear Jenny, Thank you for your message. In order to consider your application there will need to be a formal interview process. We are inundated with applications but we're pleased to say we have a slot available tomorrow afternoon.
    Best wishes,
    Gail Mitford
    Secretary to James Harvey, Principal Assessor

Bloody hell, that was quick.

Reading the address provided for the proposed meeting, Ramona smiles and licks the line of glue along the top of the smoking paper.

Typing her response, once she has signed off, she unplugs her computer and places it in her rucksack and props the spliff behind her ear.

Looks like she's going straight back to London, after all.

Leaving the only money in her purse – a tenner – on the table as unofficial payment for the stolen letter, Ramona heads out. In the hallway, she pauses, her vision resting on the flatmate's door. Turning, she walks back towards the kitchen and over to the fridge.

Opening it quietly, she takes out the only pint of milk and moves to the sink. Carefully, she removes the lid and turns the bottle upside down, watching with satisfaction as the milk cascades into the plughole.

Leaving the empty container on the counter and walking back towards the hall, she blows a kiss to the closed door as she passes the flatmate's room, and slams the front door shut behind her.

CHAPTER NINE

Madeleine can't bring herself to go straight home. At work, it's easy enough to keep her mind off the thoughts that lurk just below the surface, but at the flat there is no distraction.

Instead, she flags down a black cab and instructs the driver to head west.

The patter of the rain taps against the window as her taxi weaves through the streets of London, and Madeleine's mind is briefly soothed, though she knows the ghosts that await her at the other end of the drive.

Samantha's stands off one of Soho's main thoroughfares.

Twenty years later, every inch of it still rings with memories of Catrin: the spot where they first kissed and left holding hands, wandering back through streets Madeleine had known most of her life but which suddenly took on new meaning.

Even now, as she steps out of the cab, careful to avoid the puddles that have mounted in the gutter, she pictures them as they were that first night: Catrin waving her arms around madly to Girls Aloud amidst the strobe lights; the cheap standing tables sticky with the residue of rounds of sambuca, as Madeleine leaned in to watch, a smile growing over her face.

Back then, this bar became their place; their secret haunt away from the stuffy corridors of power at the FCO, where they felt compelled to keep their relationship a secret.

Tonight, the air inside is thick with heat and perfume.

'Same as usual?' the woman behind the counter asks.

'Make it a double,' Madeleine winks, accepting the plastic pint glass of Coke and sipping it, looking around at the flashing strobe and unchanged decor and wondering what her design-obsessed sister-in-law would make of this place. Closing her eyes, she takes a sip of the slightly flat but reassuringly sweet soda and pushes away the image of Dominic's wife. She won't let the thoughts of Amber ruin this evening.

Half a century old. How is that even possible? When she imagines a fifty-year-old woman she thinks of . . . what? Not a person in particular but, well, a decade away from sixty. Two decades from seventy.

Fucking hell.

Two decades ago, Madeleine was working at the Foreign Office, dating Catrin, with her whole life stretched out ahead of her. That feels like less than a minute ago. It is unfathomable that in the same time again she will be seventy – older than her own mother was when she died.

Well, how's that for a cheery birthday thought?

Turning her back to the bar, Madeleine surveys the room as she slips off the camel-coloured wool coat she bought the day she joined the organisation, and walks towards one of the circular standing tables, taking her bags with her and tucking them under her stool as she slides herself onto her seat.

It is not long after seven o'clock, but down here it could be any time of day or night; Madeleine could be in any bar in any city in the world, which, if she was prone to bouts of introspection, she might suppose is part of its appeal.

At this hour, the bar is relatively quiet, men and women in pairs leaning in to be heard above the music.

Pulling out her phone, she remembers the message from Daphne and falters just for a second. No. She won't fall into that trap. One night of a good thing is enough. Madeleine is in no place to start a relationship. She spends too much time abroad, and when she is in London her mind has to be half somewhere else, at all times. She isn't so much married to her job as resigned to the fact that she and her career are both hardened spinsters destined to spend the rest of their lives sharing a bed, with only slightly begrudging resignation.

Still, there is a lot of power in the space between where an attraction starts and reality begins.

From the little she remembers of Daphne, she knows she is beautiful, and Madeleine also knows from experience how a certain kind of beauty can be mistaken for something more. But no; the woman is a banker, for heaven's sake.

Besides, Madeleine already has enough to think about.

Leaning back in her seat, she swipes away from her messages and types the name 'Sergey Zhatchanov' into Google.

The 4G signal down here isn't great and she waits while the results load, and a variety of images of Amir and Ingrid Zhatchanov's son fill her screen. When they do, she clicks on a film dated from January of two years ago, and turns the volume up. Sergey speaks in English, though helpfully there are additional subtitles – presumably owing to the intense whirring noise in the building at the time of recording.

Recognising the logo in the corner of the screen, Madeleine sees that the film is part of a report for a renowned international news outlet. In it, Zhatchanov Junior – in his late twenties and dressed in a flat cap that is at odds with the deep tan and tight T-shirt – stands against the backdrop of the inside of a large warehouse.

On either side, he is flanked by armed guards carrying machine guns.

'I am Sergey Zhatchanov. Welcome to the beating heart of AlterRon, the second largest crypto-mining company in the world, and the biggest in all of Kazakhstan.'

He addresses the camera with a practised look that Madeleine imagines is supposed to convey the sense of natural authority he clearly feels.

'Here, across seven warehouses, fifty-thousand machines operate day and night. These machines are working to solve complex mathematical problems in order to make cryptocurrency transactions possible and thus ensuring the true democratisation of global wealth. Further to this, we at AlterRon are offering a new career path to our native Kazakhs.

'Of course, this puts us at odds with those who seek to profit from our system, those who seek to regulate the industry and shift the balance of power back into the hands of the few—'

The film freezes, presumably due to the lack of internet, and Madeleine clicks it off, having heard enough. Vive la révolution. Oh please. Does he really believe he is part of the solution rather than the problem?

So much for taking her mind off things. But that was never really an option. Taking another sip of Coke, Madeleine flicks back to the search engine and hits 'image search'. Scrolling through photographs of the son until she reaches one taken at an event at the House of Lords, a couple of years earlier, she notices that the photograph is watermarked with the name of a photographer renowned for capturing incongruous celebrities in unexpected clinches.

Not disappointing, in this one, Sergey Zhatchanov is shaking hands with the then-Chancellor of the Exchequer, now Prime Minister.

Briefly, Madeleine's mind slips to Dominic. Her brother, the Minister for Transport. Taking another, final sip of her drink, she clears her mind of the picture of him. Not now, thank you.

Clicking onto the next photo, she shakes her foot impatiently as the image emerges: Sergey and his father standing side by side at a conference.

She has barely swallowed her mouthful when her phone beeps, the message flashing on her screen.

Daphne, again. *Can I see you tonight?*

She freezes. Wait – how does Daphne have her number? Despite the patchiness of the previous evening, it seems unlikely that Madeleine would have given her unexpected date her number, given that they were already going home together.

Then she remembers that Daphne had briefly lost her mobile and asked to call it from Madeleine's, as they walked home. It had been in Daphne's handbag all along, and now Madeleine wonders if her misplacing the phone had been a ruse, a way to get her number without directly asking for it.

So what if it was?

Sighing, Madeleine flicks the message away. She really shouldn't see her again. She knows the pattern; one night is one thing, but two nights in a row with the same woman – especially one as beautiful as Daphne – is a slippery slope. She can't trust herself, much as she'd like the company right now.

Flicking back to the tab she was last looking at, she considers another image of Amir Zhatchanov and his son, the name of the event on a board behind them.

International Industry Conference 2022.

With a shiver, Madeleine thinks of Laura Tatchell the first time they met. It had been a similarly titled event, with a segment on human trafficking, that same summer and the Labour MP was speaking about one of the charitable projects to which she had become attached, as was her style, via a constituent.

The constituent in question had been trafficked from Kazakhstan for sexual exploitation in Europe, before escaping to England. Her home country – Laura had explained on the woman's behalf in a moving and impassioned speech, in which the MP flagged her own apparent white saviour syndrome, justified in this instance by the fact that the woman was scared to speak out herself – was a source, place of transit and a destination for victims of human trafficking.

Tatchell had been keen to use her platform to flag other issues at play in Kazakhstan, including the exploitation of migrant workers from neighbouring countries in the Kazakh oil-infused economy, as well as their construction and domestic services. According to a personal plea by Tatchell's anonymous contact, whose father died as a result of the exploitative labour he faced as a worker in a mine there, repeated protests by employees in the country have culminated in security forces opening fire on protestors.

For she's a jolly good fellow—

When Madeleine looks up, she sees Rittler and Jonny walking towards her, pissed as farts. Rittler's tie is loose, a telltale glint in his eyes.

'Didn't think we'd let you slink off without a drink, did you, on your birthday?' Jonny calls out, and Madeleine notes the unzipped zipper on his trousers, which she only hopes is the result of a lavatory malfunction, trying not to think about any alternative explanation.

'We haven't had a proper debrief since 'Nam,' Rittler adds, pronouncing the abbreviation of Vietnam like he's Marlon Brando in *Apocalypse Now*.

Madeleine winces. She can't think which fills her with more dread: the prospect of celebrating her significant birthday with these two, as drunk as they clearly are, or having to dredge through the details of one of the most haunting cases she's been a part of. Was it more haunting than the others, or is she just more easily haunted these days?

Maybe she would stay if it was Jonny on his own – but even that is a step too far across the line between colleague and friend. A few pints at the Theodore Bullfrog is one thing . . .

'How did you find me?'

'We're detectives, for fuck's sake,' Jonny snorts, looking around with a vaguely baffled expression. 'What the feck is this place?'

'It's one of two bars you ever go to, and you weren't in the other one—' Rittler clarifies, picking up the plastic-laminated drinks menu. 'What you drinking, the good stuff?'

Exhaling, Madeleine shakes her head, shimmying herself off the seat and clutching her shopping. 'Such a shame, chaps, you should have asked – I'm meeting my parents for dinner.'

Before they can reply, she slips on her coat and gives a small wave, pulling out her phone and composing a message to Daphne as she walks towards the exit. *My place. 20 mins.*

Rittler's voice carries through the door as Madeleine steps outside. 'But I thought your parents were dead?'

* * *

Madeleine makes the journey home on foot, the bars of Soho giving way to the silent shops, their windows eerily illuminated despite their being closed for the night.

Drawing the belt of her coat more tightly around herself, she is grateful for the cold night air as she traverses Oxford Circus, cutting through the back streets towards Cavendish Square where the garden is quiet and dimly lit.

Despite being just a few streets away, this part of Marylebone is a different world from the one she just left behind; the smart stucco-fronted buildings along Harley Street and Upper Wimpole Street famously occupied by plastic surgeons. Madeleine had read an article recently, about the rise of Botox and fillers in women in their twenties and thirties, and had been indignant. A little panicked, too, if she is honest. What fresh hell is this when women half her own age consider themselves in need of preservation?

The thought conjures an image of Ingrid Zhatchanova in the photographs taken the day her husband was arrested. It was the same series of shots they use in the newspapers whenever the case is mentioned, snapped outside one of the town houses turned overpriced butchers that line this stretch: the wife striding towards the gold Porsche double-parked on the kerb, her phone pressed to her ear, oversized sunglasses intended to cover whatever nipping and tucking she has had done.

A thought occurs to her, but it is superseded by the sight of Daphne, waiting outside the apartment. Madeleine can't help but smile. Making a mental note, she pushes the thought of Mrs Zhatchanova aside.

Tomorrow she can think about all that, she reminds herself. Before tomorrow, there is tonight.

CHAPTER TEN

When she awakes the following morning, Daphne has already left.

For a moment, as Madeleine turns in the soft cotton sheets, her mind takes a while to distinguish where she is. Lying there, in that hinterland between wakefulness and sleep, listening to the usual muted sounds, through the sash windows, of the city coming to, she can't be sure whether she had dreamt the feeling of Daphne's soft body pressed against hers.

But the other woman had been there, for sure, when Madeleine awoke with nightmares at 4.00 a.m., overheating despite the fact that it was February and she had already turned off the radiators. There had been something comforting about there being another person in the bed beside her, making quietly soothing hushing sounds.

Now, though, at 7.21 a.m., she is relieved to be alone. Relieved and a little mortified to have seen her two nights running. This is very much against the rules.

Well, she never has to see the woman again. And she won't. Last night was a blip – besides, you only turn half a century once in your life.

* * *

Jonny calls Madeleine as she makes her way to the office, and she pictures him, about to take his position a stone's throw from the exit of Kensington Palace Gardens – the road Amir and Ingrid Zhatchanov share with the Russian Embassy, among a number of other diplomatic residences – dressed in the silent protestor gear that makes a change from Jonny's usual street disguise, as an overweight homeless man.

Typecasting, as he has been known to complain.

'Should I not just present myself to the territorial support unit? It might be easier—' Jonny's voice wails through her earpiece, as she strides along the Strand.

'No way,' she replies, without hesitation.

'You can't write off a whole section of the Met because of one rotten apple—'

'It's not a bad apple, Jonny, it's the whole fucking tree that's rotten—' Madeleine snaps back at him. She makes no bones about the fact that she is instinctively wary of the diplomatic police, and the types it sometimes attracts, given that it is the easiest route to getting a gun.

With less skill or training required than for the dedicated proactive and response firearms units, there is also less stringent vetting than for counterterrorism.

Sure, things might finally be beginning to change thanks to the report that followed revelations about Wayne Couzens, but change is a slow process. And that it took a young woman being murdered by a police officer to get there . . .

'I get it, hen, I'm sorry.' His voice is contrite, and only mildly bruised by the hangover from the drinks he and Rittler had put away the night before.

She knows that he, too, understands the problems the force faces as an institution, but unlike Madeleine, Jonny doesn't believe in stereotypes, or tarnishing a group of people with the same brush, and it's too complex an argument to get into now, so she doesn't bother.

'I don't want to risk involving territorial support at this stage,' Madeleine says instead, attempting to hide her mirth. 'You never know who talks to whom and this is sensitive.'

'I have no idea about who is talking to whom, but what will I say if someone tries to talk to me in Ukrainian?'

'You're a silent protestor, Jonny. It's all in the name,' she replies. 'Call me if she leaves the house, and if she does, follow her.'

* * *

Ramona reaches for the shirt inside her bag as she approaches Hatton Garden, a road best known for its jewellers, in the historic area of Farringdon.

Tuesday, two o'clock, exactly as arranged. Following the curve of the pavement, she turns right into a mews street that reminds her of a different life.

It had been Si who had first brought her here, not long after they first got together, stopping briefly in front of the inconspicuous entrance, knocking twice and waiting for an overweight man in a Metallica T-shirt – part off-duty Viking, part central casting spyware nerd – to receive them.

Seconds before the door opened, Si had leaned in to kiss her and Ramona had let him, despite not being one for public displays of affection even at the best of times – and this was not Ramona at her best. She had been putting in long hours, determined to work her way up from covering traffic accidents and town planning meetings to covering crime, which in Camden was nothing if not ample. Spending evenings and weekends linking the dots in a spate of violence connected to Camden's notorious Somers Town – thanks to the kind of contacts you only really get from having gone to school in an area – meant that Ramona hadn't been getting much sleep.

She had recently started taking prescription pills to switch off and these, mixed with booze, had the after-effect of making her feel both groggy and anxious, as she waited that first time on the doorstep.

Still, she tingled with excitement, knowing that she was doing exactly what she had wanted to do for as long as she could remember.

This was the first time the news editor had agreed to let her go undercover in a case that she had no way of knowing would go on to dominate three years of her life, and Ramona had been gleeful as Gareth the Viking led her and Si up a narrow flight of steps into his shop.

Sometimes, recently, she finds herself wondering whether she ever really loved Si or whether she just associated him with moments like this, which made her feel alive.

Pressing the buzzer now, she reprimands herself. This is not a fair assessment of their relationship, and she knows it. She had loved Si. She loved that he was sweet but serious, never more so than when it came to his work or Arsenal's position in the league.

Her thoughts are interrupted by the sight of Gareth, answering the door in a black T-shirt with a *Seinfeld* logo; instantly Ramona pictures the oversized *Reservoir Dogs* T-shirt, so large that she uses it as a nightie.

Of course: this is where it had come from. She had picked it up from Gareth, the night O'Keegan's men had finally busted her for wearing a wire.

She will never forget the look on Gareth's face when he opened the door to her that morning, visibly shaking, blood streaking her face and the remains of the white shirt she had arrived in the evening before, still with part of the buttonhole camera lodged inside it. How had she forgotten that it had been him who had given her one of his tops to replace the stained one? In answer, a lot from that time in her life was hazy. Some of the haziness was a result of the booze and the pills, the rest an act of self-preservation.

She had once read that the brain is a deletion machine – getting rid of what it doesn't need so as to make space for new information – and she imagines in the same way that it also self-censors the parts it can't handle.

'Alright—' Gareth cuts himself off before saying her name. His breezy tone isn't matched by the look in his eye as he continues. 'What are we calling you these days? I can't keep up. "Still alive, then?" has a certain ring to it.'

Inside, the beige decor in the narrow hallway is indicative of a shared student house, not unlike the one she spent approximately ten minutes inside the previous evening, in Bristol. Following Gareth up a steep flight of steps which winds round to the right, Ramona follows him into a room stocked with floor-to-ceiling shelves, each showcasing a different form of hidden camera.

'What can I do you for?' he asks as he turns to face her.

'One of your buttonholes, please,' Ramona says, removing from her bag the shirt she picked up at Leather Lane market, on her way in. 'Could you make it quick?'

He pauses, and then turns away. 'On the condition you promise not to nearly die on me this time. Last time you said that I lost one of my favourite T-shirts.'

CHAPTER ELEVEN

The office is quiet when Madeleine arrives, but for Fionn Edwardes, who barely acknowledges her arrival, and Jamal who is already seated in the corner of the room.

Jamal looks up and smiles as she settles at her desk.

Rittler's chair is empty. He had sent a message via Jonny to say that he would be in late, and that Madeleine was to stay put at her desk until he was back. A doctor's appointment, apparently. A likely story, Madeleine thinks, imagining him holed up at a greasy spoon along the road trying to soak up the previous night's booze. He will be pissed off with her, no doubt, for walking out on them in the bar. Rittler is a needy soul, unlike Jonny who has barely acknowledged the previous night's events.

Making her stay put is Rittler's attempt to punish her.

The child. What does he care if Madeleine buggered off on her own birthday? Jonny, by way of contrast, had never held a grudge in his life, other than perhaps against the man who stabbed him. Even that was held not so much for himself but for the child and the wife whose lives he took that horrific summer's afternoon.

It is raining, and as Madeleine looks around the office, her spirits briefly lift, thinking of her colleague dressed in his silent protestor gear, stationed on foot instead of in the car, for once, on the corner of the newly renamed Kyiv Road, holding a Ukrainian flag and a sign reading STOP PUTIN. Even in his absence, Jonny's presence looms in the shape of the plants that surround her – the beloved prize orchids that he cares for with an attentiveness that is as touching as it is unlikely.

'*Is this a PTSD thing?*' Rittler had asked with characteristic tact, the day they found him wheezing on the stairs, halfway through heaving a series of oversized tropical plants and delicate orchids up to the first floor.

'*Are you trying to recreate the jungle where you shot all those bastard insurgents?*'

Jonny had been stationed in Afghanistan, not known for its lush vegetation, Madeleine had pointed out when Jonny didn't immediately reply. But Rittler was never one to let the truth get in the way of a deeply offensive, not very funny, joke.

It transpired later that the former squaddie-turned-sniper-turned-detective-turned amateur botanist had inherited a hoarder's greenhouse worth of indoor plants after his elderly neighbour died, and Jonny – loyal to a fault – didn't have space in his one-bed flat to store them all, so had lugged them here instead. He'd had no choice, he reasoned, when Madeleine questioned him on how he had kept them all alive, despite the rickety windows that means the dilapidated mews house is always – blessedly, for Madeleine – several degrees below whatever temperature it is outside. The old man who left them to him had spent years nurturing his beloved, occasionally prize-winning, flora, and Jonny wasn't going to have them dying on his watch.

Jamal's voice interrupts her thoughts. 'I've managed to pick out some of what Mrs Zhatchanova was saying in the call that you recorded in the queue at Harrods.'

'Excellent.' Looking over, Madeleine stands, picking up the box of Godiva chocolates on her desk and bringing them with her.

She offers him one, and he takes it.

'Fionn?' As an afterthought, she holds the box in the general direction of the new financial investigator, who shakes his head.

'Anything interesting?' Madeleine asks, returning her attention to Jamal.

'You were right, they are speaking in Kazakh. The audio quality is terrible but I got the words "and how did he seem?"'

'Anything else? Did you get a sense of who she was talking to?'

'I can say for definite that it was a man, or a boy,' Jamal replies. 'She signs off Habibi, which is an Arabic expression meaning "my love", addressed to a male. To a female, she would have said Habibti.'

Placing a hand on his shoulder by way of congratulation, Madeleine removes it again and picks out a dark chocolate, placing it in her mouth and enjoying the bitterness as she holds it against her tongue.

Moving over to Fionn's desk, she mulls over the words. *And how did he seem?* Who would Ingrid Zhatchanova address as 'my love', other than her husband or one of her children? Unless she is having an affair.

'Fionn, did you get anything more on the son?' she asks.

'You were right about the son having the ear of the Conservative government,' he replies. 'He personally donated twenty million pounds, last year alone. It's right here.'

Leaning over his shoulder so that she can see his computer screen, Madeleine scans a report on the state of lobbying in the UK in the wake of the cash-for-peerages scandal.

It would explain the photo of Sergey and the PM looking so pally. It is not what you know, after all.

Flicking through the accompanying series of images, she scans them on autopilot until stopped dead by the face staring out from the background of a single image. There, deep in apparently meaningful conversation with a woman, is Laura Tatchell.

Zooming in, Madeleine considers the woman she is talking to. From the jacket and slender wrist, she can be sure this isn't the wife. For one thing, this woman is smaller than Laura, who was only five foot four or so.

Scrolling on, Madeleine is met with a family photograph taken at the same event. To Amir's right, the wife, Ingrid, stands poised and unreadable in a red satin cocktail dress. To the left stands his son, Sergey, beaming, with his arm fixed firmly around his father's shoulder. Set slightly away from the rest of them is the woman who was talking to Laura in the previous shot.

Madeleine reads the caption: *Amir and Ingrid Zhatchanov with their children, Sergey and Shyrailym.*

Her heartbeat picking up pace, Madeleine focuses in on the younger woman, noting her uncomfortable demeanour, the eyes set away from the photographer. Their daughter? Studying her, Madeleine is reminded of how at formal events with her parents when she herself was younger, Madeleine would sometimes close her eyes, imagining that if she couldn't see anyone they, in turn, might not see her; that her father might be so overcome with fear that he had lost his only daughter that he might begin to love her more.

'I've found the address for the son,' Fionn calls out from his chair, and Madeleine looks up, struggling to compute for a moment as he reads out the location.

'Say that again.' Grabbing her phone, she makes a note of the number and the street name, along with the name Shyrailym Zhatchanova.

Pocketing her phone and picking her jacket and bag off the back of her chair, she stands and heads for the door.

* * *

Madeleine walks with an air of belonging through Mayfair, wondering idly about the secrets that lie behind the sparkling exterior walls, so perfect they appear like something from a stage set.

It is funny, she thinks, as she crosses Berkeley Square towards the street where Sergey Zhatchanov's London residence stands: having spent her childhood being tugged between international postings and her family's apartment in central London, she is never quite at home anywhere. Yet, here in the dark streets of Mayfair, slowing down as she reaches the address provided by Fionn back in the office, she realises she is as at ease as it is possible for her to be. Comfortable? Certainly not. But comfort is a trick.

What she feels now is a confidence that makes her stand tall as she approaches number eighteen, a three-storey townhouse with a veranda and an ornate portico, polished stone steps leading up to the front door. From ground level, there is no sign of the sort of subterranean basement and car-stacker lifts, which are famously favoured by the types of billionaires who consider London's banking system their own personal launderette; the type triggering spats between residents that are recorded with relish in the pages of certain newspapers.

Mounting the steps, she considers the enormous brass knocker which is cold to the touch as she takes it in her right hand, and bangs.

Immediately, she senses the presence of a figure behind the matt-black door and composes herself as she waits for it to open. When it does, the woman in front of her is dressed in a black and white maid's outfit. Filipino, Madeleine hazards a guess, and immediately she thinks of Laura Tatchell's speech on corruption at the conference where they first met, her mention of migrant workers in Kazakhstan – specifically from China, the Philippines, and Ukraine – drawn into appalling conditions in industries including domestic service.

But she is jumping to conclusions, even she knows this.

Forcing herself to slow down and take a breath, Madeleine smiles, scrutinising the maid's face and reading a thousand possible meanings into her slight bristle when she pulls out her formal identification.

'Good afternoon. I'm looking for the owner of the house, Mr Sergey Zhatchanov.' Madeleine holds the woman's eye.

There is a pause and the maid's expression tightens. 'Mr Zhatchanov is not here.'

When she nudges the door as if to close it, Madeleine casually rests her hand against it, resisting the gesture.

'Any idea what time he'll be back?'

'Mr Zhatchanov is not in the country.'

The woman is hard to age, though Madeleine guesses that she is a little older than herself. Fifty, she remembers with a jolt. OK, maybe not.

'Of course. He's in Kazakhstan?'

Madeleine doesn't move, her eyes idling over the inside of the hall.

The entrance is pristine, not a discarded coat or hat to belie its owner's presence, Madeleine thinks, picturing Amir's son with the incongruous flat cap she had seen him wear in the video online.

'Mr Zhatchanov is not here. You can send a message to his assistant, or lawyer.'

Noting the maid's expression shift as she glances over Madeleine's shoulder, Madeleine follows her gaze to the branded van advertising an overpriced florist, with bases at various sites around the city, pulled up on the opposite side of the road.

'Sorry we're so late today.' A young woman in a branded apron bustles up the steps with armfuls of flowers Madeleine could not name. 'I'll bring the rest straight through.'

'Right then.' Madeleine stands back, letting the florist pass before making her own way down the steps.

Glancing at her watch, she sees it is almost half past five.

The maid waits for Madeleine to cross the road and then disappears back into the house, leaving the door ajar for the flower delivery. Peering into the back of the open van as she passes, she notes the elaborate bouquets standing in bunches secured in plastic bags filled with water and tied with expensive-looking twine. How many flowers does one man need, when he's not at home? Who does Sergey Zhatchanov think he is, Elton John?

Stepping out of the path of the florist as she returns to the van in her *Robbins & Ribbons* apron to collect another load, Madeleine crosses back onto the square. Already, the sky is beginning to turn dark. She struggles to imagine the streets outside her station in Hanoi, bathed in a thick heat, even through the night.

If Amir and Ingrid Zhatchanov's son is in Kazakhstan, then chances are it will have been him who his mother was talking to on the phone yesterday, asking after her husband, who Sergey must have visited while he was there. But isn't Sergey, along with the rest of his family, persona non grata in his home country, thanks to links with the past leader?

Madeleine feels a chill as she continues on her way back through the square gardens, where tourists sit on park benches, bags of shopping gathered at their sides, and office workers walk with their eyes set on the pavement.

When her phone rings, she sees Jonny's number flashing on the screen.

'What's up?'

'Aren't you supposed to be at the office?' When she doesn't answer, he continues. 'So I got a call back from my mate, splashy Kate, who works at Harrods . . . She's had a look at the records for the various loyalty cards our friend Ingrid is using in store, to split her payments, and it turns out the wife's steep tea and coffee habit is just the tip of the iceberg. The records confirm that cumulatively she is spending tens of thousands of pounds a month in store, and covering any trail by using cards registered to different names and addresses.

'As well as buying beauty products and spending a considerable amount on jewellery, the wife is investing in products through the interior design service, buying art through the gallery . . . Looks like it's not going to be hard to prove that she is funnelling her husband's dodgy cash through British businesses . . .'

Madeleine feels a burst of confidence as she heads back towards the office, the phone pressed to her ear. 'This is excellent.'

'It's unofficial for now. Helping out a mate, kind of thing.' Jonny's clarification only slightly dampens her spirits. 'If we want to produce the records evidentially, with an accompanying witness statement, then we will likely require a Special Procedure Court Order, which will have to be authorised by a crown court judge.'

'How long will that take?'

'Depends,' Jonny sniffs.

'Right,' Madeleine replies. 'Let's go for it. I'll get hold of Rittler. Actually, do you think you could call him? I think he's giving me the silent treatment.'

'What are you doing now?'

She looks behind her shoulder before continuing. 'Did you know Amir and Ingrid Zhatchanov have a daughter?'

'Right?'

'She's a professor at the London School of Economics.' Madeleine takes her phone away from her ear and clicks back on the toolbar to display a headshot of a smartly dressed young woman with intelligent eyes and a slight smile, on the LSE's staff page. Reading aloud from the text below it, she says, '"Professor Shyrailym Zhatchanova. Department of Philosophy, Logic and Scientific Method. Professor Zhatchanova specialises in ethics and public policy evaluation."'

'That's one black sheep,' Jonny retorts. 'Have you been to see her?'

'Not yet,' Madeleine says, holding out her hand and waving down a cab. 'I'm going back to the office, I want to do a bit more digging first. It seems like she knew—'

Before she can say Laura's name, Madeleine stops herself, as though scared that by verbalising the thought she might curse it.

Instead, she says, 'I'm going to start making some calls.'

* * *

Hatton Garden has fallen dark by the time Ramona steps back outside, leaving Gareth with the address where she is headed, in return for his agreement to let her go alone.

'What's the point in me giving you an address?' she had asked, secretly relieved for reasons she won't let herself think of now, and he had shrugged as she scribbled down the name of the café and the suburban postcode.

'This way I'll know where to start looking for a body. It will also make it easier to claim on insurance, if they bury you in the kit.'

Taking the Piccadilly line to a far corner of north-east London, Ramona listens to Mos Def, standing with her back to the carriage, her hood pulled up around her face. At her stop, she is greeted by dull, run-down residential streets truncated by a dual carriageway.

Moving briskly along the pavement, she notes the sickly yellow pallor of the dim street lamps and pulls the denim jacket more tightly around herself. Already, she feels something inside her build. Perhaps it is desperation. For the first time since starting the business, twelve months previously, Ramona has the prospect of a proper case. Despite herself, the feeling that bubbles inside as she follows the route she memorised before setting out, is one she recognises as the thrill that comes with the scent of a story.

The address of the building James Harvey had suggested for their meeting had struck her as odd as soon as she received it, remembering, with a wave of unease, Ottilie's description of where she had found herself after setting out from Manchester to this secluded spot near the end of the tube line.

In this city it is rare to feel physically removed from other people but, as civilisation gives way to a scraggy patch of green and the motorway beyond, the sense of isolation is palpable.

Shivering, Ramona scans the shop fronts. A Greek bakery with lavish wedding cakes and pastries displayed in the unlit window is already closed up for the day. In an empty launderette, a single drum turns, the suds frothing like a raging ocean.

Scouring the windows for a second silhouette in the reflection, or any other sign that she is being followed, Ramona tries to push aside the niggling feeling that she is being watched. Turning suddenly, she notes, with an exhalation of breath, that the stretch of road behind her is clear. She is being paranoid, there is no one there. Still, she wishes she had asked for somewhere more public for this meeting – even if the location is a definite improvement on the private offices that Gail, the Time for Tuition secretary, had originally suggested.

The final building is the kind of café that stays open all times of day and night; sparsely furnished with a laminated menu advertising

six-pound fry-ups, tea, and two types of coffee – white or black.
Aside from an older man who sits, magisterial, in one corner – regular
customer or the café's proprietor, it is hard to tell – there is only one
other customer. Looking up from his phone with mild contempt that
slips into a smile as Ramona enters, the younger of the two men
nods pleasantly as she walks through the room, towards where he
sits at the booth furthest away from the window.

His manner as she approaches is one of total ease.

In his mid-forties with a receding hairline and a blue shirt slightly
rumpled under a plain M&S jacket, he sits with his hands crossed
on the table in front of him, shamelessly revealing a wedding ring.

Pleased by the clarity of the lighting and the lack of background
noise, Ramona pulls self-consciously at the hem of the black miniskirt
she wears over black tights, along with an old pair of Nike Air Max,
as she takes her seat. Trying not to stare, she takes in the person
opposite. On closer inspection, she decides he is a textbook example
of the rule that not every pervert looks like a pervert, presenting like
a mild-mannered uncle or teacher at a community college.

For all she knows, he might well be either, or both. These days
everyone has a side hustle.

'What can I get you, love?' the waitress asks, her expression simultaneously harried and bored, and Ramona finds herself taken off
guard by the incongruousness of the situation. She doesn't know what
she had expected from her first meeting with a man offering to pimp
her out to wealthy elders, but this isn't it.

'Erm, tea please. White, no sugar,' Ramona says, meeting the eyes
of the man opposite her. 'If that's OK?' she adds, making sure he
recognises the reverence in her expression. She needs him to believe
that he is in charge.

'Of course.' Beaming confidently back at her, James Harvey remains
poised, repeating the order to the waitress who disappears back towards
the kitchen.

'Thanks for coming all this way, Jenny.'

'Not at all.' Ramona smiles, reaching into her pocket and pulling out the paper with the university letterhead. 'Did you need this, as proof of my status?'

'Not yet.' He gives little more than a cursory glance at the paper with Jemima's initials and the University of Bristol logo in the corner. 'We can work out the paperwork later, if—' His look is plain, just a flicker in his eye giving a hint at the implication. *If* she gets accepted.

'Right.' Ramona smiles weakly as the waitress returns to deliver her drink, adjusting the cup so that it doesn't obscure the hidden camera's line of vision.

'Sorry, I'm a bit nervous,' she adds, once she is sure the waitress is out of earshot.

'That's OK.' The man's tone is casually reassuring. 'Don't worry, it's perfectly normal.'

'Is it? OK, good.' She attempts a laugh. 'I'm sorry for not agreeing to meet at the office straight away. I suppose I just wanted to meet somewhere a bit more public . . . Meeting a complete stranger – I just, you know, wanted to be clear about who you are.'

'Of course,' the man jokes. 'I totally understand – you have to be sure you're not meeting a serial killer, right?'

She stalls, briefly wrong-footed. 'Yeah. I'm sorry if that seems a bit silly. I mean, I didn't think you were, I just had a few questions. Like what if I met one of the guys I was paired with but then he didn't pay? How can I be sure—' Pausing, she giggles nervously. 'Sorry, I am probably rushing ahead. I'm just—'

'Of course.' James Harvey shakes his head, in a manner she assumes is meant to be reassuring. 'So the way we work is that ahead of the first meeting we take the money off the sponsor to make sure they've got the funds they have promised – then once we've heard back from both of you – that is the sponsor and the student – that it's all gone fine, then we release those funds to the student. That becomes your first payment for your first term . . . Then the payments generally happen around the start of each term.'

He looks down at the skateboard propped against the table. 'So you skate?'

She winces, self-effacing. 'Not really, but I'm learning. Trying to . . .'

Pausing, Ramona takes a sip of her tea before continuing, her tone tentative. 'So it's quite vague on the site, what I have to do. How do I know what I'm expected . . .' She lets the words trail off, hoping the creeping sense of revulsion she feels towards this man is translating as nothing more than a blush.

He makes a gesture, then replies.

'There's a standard questionnaire we'll go through together, which helps us form your profile, covering the sort of things that you're comfortable doing so there's no awkwardness about unfulfilled expectations, or one person wanting something different. We cut out any possible misunderstandings upfront.'

'Oh good, OK. Phew.' Ramona laughs along.

'And then, as long as you're happy to go through with those things that you said you would do, then that's fine.'

The fingers of her right hand ball into a fist at her side, the other clutching the handle of the white plastic cup. When Ramona replies, her voice is quieter. 'And, sorry if I'm being dense, but what sort of things would I actually have to do?'

After a moment's pause, Harvey sits back, resting his left ankle on his right thigh. Ramona's stomach turns as an image reappears, of Ottilie. Quietening the memory of how she had sounded as she recalled what this man had made her do, Ramona feels her jaw set.

'The thing is, Jenny, there is no right and wrong here.' He goes on: 'There are no rules, as such. Obviously, what you're trying to do is to attract a certain level of sponsorship, right? So you don't want to go in there saying you know you're not even going to hold hands or whatever, because you're not going to attract any interest at all. So you've got to kind of . . .' He thinks before continuing. 'My advice is this: the more you're prepared to do, the more interest you're going to get – and the more sponsorship you're going to end up with. So obviously you don't want to commit with more than you're happy to do, because then you'll be anxious about it and all the rest of it. But equally, you do want to get the opportunity to have those introductory meetings.'

'Right.' Ramona nods, clearing her throat, willing her voice to unclench itself. 'So how many other girls are already doing it?'

James Harvey screws his face in an expression of thoughtful recall. His skin is relatively free of wrinkles, his hands smooth as though he has never done a real day's work in his life.

Who the fuck are you? Ramona wonders, as intrigued as she is unsettled by the man in front of her.

'I think we currently have just over four hundred women actively searchable on our site, ready to go into . . .' he says.

Go into. Really? Nice turn of phrase.

'That many?' Ramona holds his eye a beat too long and then looks away. 'Wow.'

If he senses the brief shift in tone, then he doesn't show it. 'Look, ultimately these guys are businessmen. The thing is they get a tax break for offering sponsorship to students but obviously they're having a bit of fun, you know, into the bargain, and they're genuinely nice guys.'

'Really?'

'Oh, yeah. I've got some sample profiles printed out.'

'Brilliant,' Ramona says. 'That would be really reassuring, actually. Can I see them?'

'Of course. I've left them at the office, so I can show them to you when we get there.'

Again, she hesitates. 'I'm really sorry for not wanting to meet there – I just wanted to be sure you weren't . . . You know.'

His expression is clearly intended to be reassuring. 'Don't worry, it's just around the corner, anyway. We can go for the practical interview now, if you're finished with your tea?'

'Oh.' Ramona instinctively touches the nose of her skateboard. 'So what exactly do we have to do in the "practical" interview?'

His posture stiffens only slightly, but she senses his patience wearing thin. Righting himself, Harvey replies: 'Well, we'll go through the questionnaire, like I said. And then we'll go through whatever you put down as what you want to do: a sort of assessment to make sure that you're comfortable to do the things that you said you'll do, and to get an idea of what your first meeting with the sponsor will be.'

'What – like now?'

He cocks his head, subtly. 'I mean these are important clients to us, they trust and respect us and they're paying a lot of money. So we have to be sure that when we put you in front of your sponsor, you're confident in doing the things you said you would do. You understand that, don't you?'

'I'm sorry, of course. That makes sense.'

'Good.' Relieved, he laughs. 'So, shall we go?'

'And so, do the guys have health checks or anything?' Ramona asks, stalling for time.

James Harvey's expression is growing, if not wary exactly, then impatient. He has looked at his watch three times in the past two minutes.

'Shall we?' Ignoring her final question, Harvey makes to stand, to lead the way towards the office where Ramona is expected to perform sexual acts on this man who reminds her of an old music teacher she once had with bad breath, and a tendency to sit too close when he spoke to his female pupils.

'In a minute,' Ramona replies, more assertively than she had intended.

'You're incredibly thorough, and here was I thinking it was me who was conducting the interview,' Harvey says, considering her a moment.

Feeling the wire brushing against her bra strap and lodging itself awkwardly so that if she moves again, the whole shirt will skew and her cover will be blown, Ramona stays perfectly still.

Before she can respond, he sits down again. 'We do invite our clients to have health checks. Not all of them choose to – but you can choose to wear protection or not wear protection, on that basis.'

'I'm sorry for asking so many questions, it's just that I've never done anything like this and it just feels like a big step.' Ramona back-pedals, sitting forward ever so slightly so as to avoid the risk of her shirt straightening too much and revealing the wire taped to her skin beneath.

'I mean that's sort of the service we're offering, and which you have willingly applied to be part of,' Harvey responds, with an almost disdainful laugh. 'We're not attracting people who are used to this kind of lifestyle . . . That's why these men come to us, because we are offering students rather than common—'

He doesn't finish his sentence – doesn't have to. The missing word rings clearly in Ramona's ears, though he must not notice her expression hardening as he carries on, unfazed. 'It's an elite service, which is why we have to make sure you're willing to do what you say you're going to do, by performing the practical part of the interview before we can take you on.' There is a slight desperation in his voice now.

'But is it totally confidential?' Replacing the cup slowly, so as not to further agitate the spy-cam, Ramona feels her skin tingle with beads of sweat. She regrets not taking off her jacket when she first arrived at the café. She had imagined this way she could better disguise the equipment under her blouse, but now she pictures the tape holding the wire in place peeling away, dislodged by her perspiration.

Studying her a moment, James Harvey continues. 'In the photos we use on our site, we can obscure your face; we can cut them from here, if that's what you're worried about.' He mimes chopping off the top part of her body. 'Whenever you decide to leave us, everything is securely erased, wiped, there is no record at all. Any sponsors that you take out an agreement with will only know you by a nickname . . . Once you've left, there's no way for them to contact you again.'

'Do you think I could have a moment to think about it?'

Blinking, Harvey responds, evenly: 'Sure. Do you want another cup of tea—'

'I mean, can I go home and think about it? I'm sorry, I don't want to mess you around, I just . . .'

His expression narrows as he studies her face. Aware of her heartbeat growing faster, Ramona pushes back her chair, pulling closed her jacket to obscure the slight lump of the camera that she can't be sure she imagined his eyes lingering on, just a beat too long.

For a moment, a darkness shadows his features, but then his tone shifts.

When he speaks again his voice is light. 'Well, obviously I can't force you. Like we said in our original email, the application process closes in a couple of days so don't take too long making your decision.'

'Right.' Ramona nods, feeling a droplet of sweat running down her hairline. 'I will, I'm sure, I just . . . I'm going to go to the toilet so you don't have to wait for me. I can make my own way.'

Reaching into her pocket, she pulls out two pounds in change for her tea and he doesn't stop her when she places it on the table. Tight bastard.

Who are you? she wonders again.

'Right then.' Curtly, James Harvey smiles. Standing, he considers her a moment. 'Like I said, don't wait too long.'

Welded to the spot, Ramona remains silent, waiting for him to say something else. But then his face changes again and he walks towards the exit.

Ramona remains where she is, half-expecting him to turn and look at her.

Even when he steps out into the night, she imagines he might glance back through the window. But he doesn't so much as slow down. It is as though she no longer exists.

Turning towards the toilet cubicle visible through an open door at the back of the room, she walks quickly, locking the door behind her.

Meeting her own reflection in the mirror, she opens the button of her shirt and pulls out the recording device. Slipping it into her bag, she walks back out into the café, briskly heading for the exit through which James Harvey had walked moments earlier.

* * *

The man is barely visible at the corner of the next road junction as Ramona steps out onto the street and turns right.

Away from the main strip, if you can call it that, the lamps that line the residential street are sparse and dimly lit. Watching him from a distance, his phone raised to his ear, Ramona finds that James Harvey is far enough ahead on the dark suburban street that she can't hear a word he says to whoever it is at the end of the line.

Pushing against the desperate urge to find out, she holds back, keeping to the shadows as she follows from a safe distance.

He reaches the end of the road ahead of her, and Ramona watches as he turns right into the outdoor car park of a nondescript commercial building where, inside, the lights are off.

With a shiver, she stays low so as not to be seen, a feeling she recognises creeping over her. It isn't fear, exactly. The fact that Ramona doesn't experience fear in the same way as other people was one that had been commented on time and again, with a mixture of reverence and frustration by her ex-boyfriend, Si, and their former boss at the paper, Ben. As well as being uninhibited and capable of an emotional detachment that borders on psychopathic – their words, also duly noted – her ability to push through when others might instinctively pull back is what makes her succeed where others fail. It is the one trait inherited from her mother that she is grateful for.

But she is not immune to the sense of danger.

Stopping suddenly, Ramona feels the hairs on her arms spike further as she scans the area for signs of her target. Scopaesthesia. That is it; the term for when a person knows, by some extrasensory force, that they are being watched. The so-called psychic staring effect.

Yet, as Ramona crouches down and peers below the parked cars ahead for signs of shoes or any other kind of movement, and then behind her at the dimly lit street, she sees that there is no one else around.

Uneasy now, she stands and searches for James Harvey, looking right and left across the car park. The building is still unlit, suggesting he didn't go inside. How is it possible that he has just vanished? Watching her breath form in front of her mouth, Ramona blows into her fingers for warmth as she turns. Out of the corner of her eye, she sees a shadow but when she takes a step forward, it disappears.

Aside from the occasional rush of traffic from the motorway, somewhere beyond, the car park is silent. Still convinced that a pair of eyes is on her, though unable to work out the direction from which it is coming, Ramona makes herself small again, sinking back against the wall that separates the car park from the road she has just come along. In her pocket, her phone vibrates, the sudden motion making her jump, and she closes her eyes, imagining the sound carrying across the night air to wherever James Harvey now waits.

Shit.

A few metres away, a pair of headlights suddenly flick on and Ramona curses, jumping back to avoid the glare of their beam. As she does, she feels a hand grab her arm.

Turning, she lashes out as the figure takes her by the wrist with one hand, and with the other grabs her skateboard before she can raise it as a form of defence.

Hissing, Ramona kicks the man in the balls, hard enough that he doubles up in front of her.

Kicking him again, in the shoulder this time, she braces herself for potential retaliation, but he falls back onto the pavement. When he lands, the hood of his sweatshirt falls back, revealing a pair of eyes that she knows at once.

What the—

'Stop. Fucking hell, stop. It's me—'

The sound of his voice makes her stop dead.

'Si?' Taking a step forward, she struggles to compute what she is seeing, cocking her head as her ex-boyfriend winces on the ground in front of her.

Both of them are now struggling for breath, for different reasons. Taking a step forward, Ramona waits while Si sits up, slowly, attempting to alleviate the pain in his groin. The sound is eclipsed by that of an engine starting up in the near distance.

Ducking down next to him, Ramona recognises the smell of the aftershave she always claimed to hate, and her stomach does a flip. Si makes a groaning noise.

'Shut up,' she whispers, as the car – a silver mid-range Audi – slips past.

Once she is sure it is gone, Ramona stands and takes a step back.

'Was that him?' Si pulls himself into a sitting position.

'Who?' she asks, her mind fracturing with questions before landing on the most important one. 'What the fuck are you doing here? Jesus!'

Recovering slowly, Si stands, leaning against the wall. 'I was keeping an eye out.'

Ramona blinks. The outrage that previously laced her voice is replaced by something quieter, more unsettled. 'How did you even know where I was?'

'I asked Gareth to let me know next time you came to him for undercover work. After last time . . .'

Gareth? Ramona thinks of him at the suite in Hatton Garden, how he had asked for the address of where she was headed, *just in case*. The snake. All along, he had been in cahoots with Si.

And yet, Ramona had felt relieved, hadn't she, to know that someone had her back? But this is different. This is—

'What the hell, Si, are you mad? You can't . . . You're not my boyfriend any more, and even if you were . . . this is not OK! For fuck's sake.'

'Oh right, so you can come and watch me playing a match and hang around, where Holly might see you. But I can't look out for you when—'

At the mention of the name Holly, Ramona's stomach tightens.

'Oh fuck off . . . It's not the same, and you know it,' she spits.

'Not the same? No, it's not the same – what I am doing is protecting you . . . What's your excuse?'

Stalling for words, Ramona searches his face and finds it almost unrecognisable. She thinks of him on the press benches in court, the day she first realised she loved him. The way his eyes narrowed in concentration as he listened to the judge's verdict, the buttons of his shirt paired up to the wrong holes. The quiet intensity on his face before delivering the most cutting question with the softness of a polite guest asking where he might find the loo.

That was her Si. The Si she had known before.

If one thing is to change then everything has to change.

She shakes her head to clear the cloud of thoughts.

Why had she gone to the pitches? Because she wanted to see him, from a distance, to remember how he looked when he was happy, running around in the rain, his skin glistening. She wanted to feel connected to something in her past that was solid and concrete. To remember, briefly.

'I was just passing Market Road.' She feels her cheeks burn as she looks away to avoid his gaze.

'Just passing?' He laughs, the laughter falling away as he shakes his head. '*Ramona*. It's not even your real name . . . I can't even call you by your real name because you put yourself in such a dangerous position that someone tried to have you killed, and yet if I try to—'

'Don't.' Her tone is firm this time, her whole body tense with threat. 'Can't you see? This . . .' She throws her hands up to indicate everything that stands between them. '*This* is part of the reason I could never be with you. You want me to need you, but I don't.'

The words slice through the air like a grenade and she watches the force of them knock him back. The impact takes its toll on her, too. Biting her lip, she continues more quietly.

'You know what? Just leave me alone, and I promise I will never come near you again.'

'Why are you reacting like this? Please . . . I'm worried about you. And it's not just me—'

Without looking up, she speaks evenly. 'Si, just fuck off.' And then she walks away.

* * *

Ramona is still shaking by the time she returns to the flat, sometime after nine. The combination of relief, fury and trepidation rushes through her as she powers up her laptop, the effect intoxicating in a way that she relishes.

It was Si who had been following her, causing her skin to goose-pimple.

Running the tap, she imagines herself pouring a glass of whisky instead. It would be so easy. When she leans across to the draining board and picks up a tumbler, she holds it under the tap and watches as the water flows into it. Yes, it would be easy, but in a way it's just as easy not to. Glancing over at the Post-it covering the camera lens of her laptop, she reads the four letters written on it in capital letters, aloud, and considers their meaning. NQTD. *Never quit the decision.*

The acronym is one of the few parts of the rhetoric around the business of sobriety that Ramona respects as well as tolerates. She is nothing if not stubborn. As far as she is concerned, there is no point expending any more time and energy on debating a choice that has already been made.

Taking her glass of water, she moves across the room, picking up her laptop and throwing herself on the brown corduroy sofa that was here when she moved in – a brown corduroy thing with sharp springs. Taking several gulps and then placing the glass on the thinning carpet by her feet, she rearranges herself on the cushions to avoid the sharp edge of one of the springs, and checks the time – 9.20 p.m. Pulling out her Nokia, she texts Ottilie: *Cn u speak?*

The trade-off between the process involved in typing a single text on such an outdated device versus retaining as much privacy as she can in these Big Brother times is worth the effort; still, right now she resents the strength it takes to push down each button, and the piercing sound the phone makes when she does.

Once she has finished, she sets the device down and opens her laptop. Clicking onto Companies House, the government-sponsored agency that registers company information and makes it available to the public. She inputs the name of the company – Time for Tuition – and her search comes up empty.

So, officially, Time for Tuition doesn't exist. It isn't unusual for a company to be registered under a different name. Clicking back to the agency's website, Ramona scours the page for the company number and VAT number.

The site is a slick, if opaque, affair consisting of little more than a landing page and a contact box. Scrolling down until she finds what she is looking for, she copies the information into a text box and then clicks again on the tab for Companies House.

This time, a result immediately comes back. Sitting forward, she clicks through to the address and name of the company: *Experiences Enterprise Ltd* [EEL] and its responsible officer: Leon Wimalasundera. The address is registered as a residential street in Brixton.

Yes.

Her phone rings as Ramona copies the name of the company's listed director and the word Brixton and pastes it into Google.

Answering, she hears the buzz of a busy street in the background.

'So did you meet him?' Ottilie sounds breathless.

'I don't have anything yet, but listen, I have a question: do you remember the address of the office you went to, or any signage that might indicate the website being owned by a larger company?'

Ottilie pauses. 'There were definitely no signs – the office was basically just an empty room apart from a desk, no company signs or anything. I can look up the address in my emails, now. Also, I found this forum with girls sharing their experiences of having applied to the agency . . . You have to create a profile to join . . .'

As Ottilie recalls the name of the site, Ramona types it straight into the search bar and presses enter.

'Send the address to me. I'll be in touch as soon as I have something.' Ramona hangs up and spends the intervening minutes creating a profile that will gain her access to a forum on which users share horror stories involving the website. There are slight variations in detail of each woman's experience – including how far they went with their assessor, the range spanning from oral sex to full penetration – but each one shares a narrative line: they saw the vague notice advertising sexual encounters in exchange for payment towards their university fees, they went along to apply at a so-called practical assessment, and were subsequently sent an apologetic email explaining that they hadn't passed the assessment but could reapply at a later date.

Ramona shivers, thinking of the man sitting opposite her earlier this evening.

The sound of her phone pinging interrupts her thoughts.

As suspected, the address Ottilie relays is that of the same faceless office building to which Ramona had followed James Harvey earlier this evening, in the forecourt of which he had evidently parked the mid-range Audi that somehow didn't fit his overall presentation.

What car would he have? It was hard to say. Not least given that she knew fuck-all about cars. But a Skoda, perhaps.

Picturing the characterless navy jacket and the thin gold band on his wedding finger across the café table, Ramona's mind automatically moves from James Harvey to an image of Si, recoiling in pain in the shadows. As quickly as they had emerged, the pictures recede as Ramona focuses her mind on the profile of the man loading in front of her on the university staff page. Mixed race, with soft eyes and a brown suit. Professor Leon Wimalasundera.

Leaning in closer, she reaches for a cigarette, feeling another shift that she recognises as a step forwards. But towards what, she is not yet sure.

Her eyes sharpening, she stares at the LSE professor and takes a lighter from her pocket.

Right, so who the fuck are you?

CHAPTER TWELVE

Madeleine keeps a stream of commuters between herself and her target as she follows Shyrailym Zhatchanova along Kensington High Street, watching her through the lenses of the Saint Laurent D-frame sunglasses she had treated herself to as an early birthday present at Bangkok airport during her transit home to London from Hanoi, days earlier.

It is Wednesday morning, and she had hardly slept again the previous night – increasingly convinced that what she had first put down to jet lag is in fact just the reality of who and what she is, now that she is fifty years old. For hours, thoughts of Laura and Vietnam had circled one another as she tried to zone out, occasionally eclipsed by the image of Amir and Ingrid's daughter, who walks a little ahead of her as they approach the ticket barriers at High Street Ken tube station.

In the flesh, the young woman before her now – pulling the Oyster card from her coat pocket and continuing briskly towards the platform as Madeleine reaches for her purse – is hard to reconcile with the image of the young professor she had studied on her phone screen, in the small hours. There, her gaze had been averted from the camera, as though wishing herself somewhere different. She had looked younger, yes, but fearful, too.

With that image as her only reference, beside the equally incongruous profile photograph on the LSE staff page, Madeleine had done a double-take when she spotted her target emerging from the front doorway of her mansion flat off Kensington Square, fifteen minutes earlier. Despite her slight size, Madeleine had noted how the young professor actively took up space, as the young people say, as she passed the row of patisseries and high-end launderettes that line the curved road opposite her impeccably positioned mansion flat. She recognises in the younger woman the sort of innate confidence that comes with believing that you deserve what you have; the self-entitlement she has seen in those she rubbed alongside at school and university, and every other institution she had belonged to.

People who believed that what they have can never be taken away from them.

People like herself, Madeleine muses. Except that despite being one of them in almost every sense, Madeleine has never belonged. She is an outlier for reasons it is impossible to put her finger on – though she doesn't need a shrink to tell her that the expensive schools and material comforts of her childhood are things she would have traded in at the drop of a hat in exchange for the love of her father. Another poor little rich girl with daddy issues. Good God, could she be any more of a cliché?

But at least Madeleine understands who and what she is. Ingrid and Sergey's daughter? She is not yet sure.

It had been unnecessary, following Shyrailym all the way from her flat to the offices of her university, where the lecturing schedule she had pulled up from the LSE's website suggests she is heading to now. Madeleine could just as well have intercepted her at work. But who knows who she might meet, or call, on her way in?

Pausing a moment, she watches from the top of the steps overlooking the railway platform, as Shyrailym takes her place. She wears a neatly pressed taupe-coloured headscarf, held in place with two tiny diamante clips, scanning the crowd for a space to stand through clear, watchful eyes.

Reaching into her bag and swallowing a second paracetamol without need for water, Madeleine briefly imagines Jonny and Jamal in another part of London, tailing the wife.

The departures board shows that the next train will arrive at the platform in one minute. There is no need to break a sweat, though she can already feel the heat radiating on the surface of her skin. She seems to spend half her time these days feeling as if she is trapped inside a furnace. It has been a creeping, gradual shift. The *change*. Even the coyness of the term makes her wince: a wry, knowing smile of a word for what is nothing less than a screaming sucker punch. The etymology, traced back to Ancient Greece, is just as misleading. *Men*, meaning month; *pausis* meaning pause. Menopause: the end of the monthly cycle.

It always sounded so simple – restful, even. Especially for a woman like Madeleine, who has never wanted children; who never had to face the internal battle others might have as they crept towards the final window of opportunity. And this was how she always imagined it: a quiet falling away of something that has never served her anyway; a period – literally – that had only ever brought discomfort and inconvenience.

Yet, now that she is at the coalface – quite literally, it feels some days – Madeleine experiences the fast approach of the next phase of her life as an unbalancing acceleration towards something for which she is totally unprepared: night sweats giving way to day sweats; brain fog so profound and so out of kilter with her essential nature it is as though something fundamental inside her has broken; mood swings and flickers of self-doubt appearing where once there were none.

Had her mother felt the same at her age? Casting back through memories of Juliet, she sees the Ambassador's wife – softly curled hair cascading around her face – as she works the room. Always with such elegance, such poise, Juliet was so completely at home in her own skin that, no matter which continent they were in or which embassy was hosting the party, it was as though the whole room was there for her.

No, it is impossible for Madeleine to believe that her mother ever felt anything short of completely sure of herself. Only one who wholly loves themselves can be capable of loving others as abundantly as Juliet had.

Shaking her head to clear it of the sort of distracting thoughts Madeleine would never have countenanced a year ago, her attention returns to the here and now, scanning the headline of the free news-paper she had accepted on the high street a few minutes earlier, to protect her hair from the rain.

Bailed drug lord and Interpol's most wanted Michael O'Keegan awaiting extradition to the UK, ahead of trial.

Wait, isn't that— But the thought is cut off by the arrival of the train.

As it approaches, she stands back to let the crowd pass, waiting for Shyrailym to step inside the carriage, one door up, before boarding the Circle Line towards Victoria, and onwards to Temple.

* * *

The three-mile walk from Dalston takes just over an hour, a relent-less morning drizzle dampening the air as Ramona heads south.

Noting the time on one of the electronic bus displays – nearly half past seven – she ties the frayed drawstrings of her hoodie at her chin, chewing the end of one as she disappears into the bustle of the morning cityscape.

There is nothing more cathartic than taking in London on foot. Within the crowd, she is blissfully removed from those whom she passes, tuning in and out again to the hum of the traffic as she makes her way along Upper Street.

Her city. The one her mother had chosen for herself after leaving Brighton at the age of sixteen, and one that is steeped in Ramona's bones like a form of DNA, despite being ushered between Kentish Town and the suburbs of Brighton for much of her childhood.

There is a connection she has to London that means no matter which corner of it she is in, she feels rather than navigates her way through its streets. This morning, she barely looks up as she weaves through the huddles of impatient office workers and teenagers vying for space at the bus stops that intermittently punctuate one of Islington's main thoroughfares. Avoiding the CCTV camera that stares out from the Business Design Centre as she passes, she lights a cigarette, letting her thoughts move between her meeting with James Harvey the previous evening, and the day ahead.

She shivers as her memory catches on the image of Si staring back at her in the dark street at the edge of the car park.

His words: I want to protect you.

Ramona can almost hear the voice in her head telling her she is overreacting, reminding her that some people might find it touching to have someone who cares about their safety. Is it so surprising, given all that has happened in the past year, to think that Si might urge Ramona to take extra caution; that after all that has passed between them Si might still feel concerned, invested even, in her wellbeing?

She crosses the road before the lights turn red, knowing by heart the time it will take for the oncoming bus to reach the yellow box where Upper Street is truncated by Chapel Street.

The answer is no.

Still, there is a world of difference between him caring, like a normal person, and Si taking it upon himself to have an alert system with a mutual associate when his ex-girlfriend sets off on a job – and then following her without permission, nearly giving her a fucking heart attack when he jumps her. He is lucky she didn't crack him over the head with her skateboard. What if she had?

Fucking Si.

Pushing thoughts of her ex aside, Ramona focuses her mind on the profile of the man she is on her way to see now – the person listed on Companies House as the director of Experiences Enterprise Ltd.

Leon Wimalasundera.

From her subsequent online research, Ramona couldn't find a bad word said about the notably handsome psychology professor. She had also discovered that he has children, and rather than front him up at home in Finsbury Park, she had chosen to head to his work instead.

It makes no sense that a man of such standing in his chosen profession would risk his reputation in this way, even in the age of the unlikely portfolio-career. But nothing about this makes sense – and if there is one thing Ramona knows for certain, it's that you can't judge a book by its cover, or expect to understand why other people behave the way they do.

It is another reason why there is no substitute for getting out and talking to people, even if you have no idea what you're going to say. Even if in doing so, you never know whose path you will be stepping into.

Lighting a cigarette, Ramona lets her thoughts clear as she emerges on Arundel Street. The rain has stopped, leaving her denim jacket soaked through to the black hooded zip-up sweater beneath. Finishing her cigarette, she folds her arm in front of her chest and marches towards the entrance of the university building, grinding her cigarette butt under the heel of her trainer.

9.05 a.m. As good a time as any.

* * *

Despite the empty tube seat in front of her when she enters the carriage, Shyrailym doesn't sit, moving aside a little to make space for an older gentleman, holding onto the rail with one hand while still browsing her phone with the other.

Taking a seat, Madeleine scans the front page of the free newspaper, and the story relating to the warrant issued for the arrest of the gang leader wanted by Interpol on counts of international drug-running to the tune of a billion pounds. Some days she thinks it would be easier if this were her regular patch, chasing career criminals rather than spending months at a time infiltrating the depraved world of paedophiles and trafficking. But she didn't choose easy. She chose to compensate in what small way she can for the disparity of a world in which she lives as she does, and others live . . .

Well, she doesn't want to think about that now.

Taking in her target, surreptitiously, over the top of her copy of *Metro*, Madeleine notes the casual suit jacket, trousers and expensive white trainers.

Looking away again, she turns the page and spots a picture of Dominic, suitcase under his arm, wearing the same fixed, capable smile he wears whenever cameras are close by, as he marches towards number ten. A bad taste forming in her mouth, she closes the page.

Fucking Dominic. He is ten years older than her, and yet whenever she pictures him, she still imagines him seated next to their father in the house in Beirut on one of his exeats from Eton, Charles laughing as the cherished prodigal son regales him with tales of one of the masters who had been there when their father himself was a boy. Back then, the only comforting thought Madeleine could muster as she watched her father looking at her brother in a way she knew she would never be looked at by him, was that one day she would be able to get away from the golden child, once and for all.

Of course, at the time, she hadn't wagered on her brother becoming one of the most media-friendly MPs in the fucking Cabinet. Though, in hindsight, she should have.

The train brakes slightly, causing those standing to sway to one side. In the space between the passengers, Madeleine catches a glimpse of herself in the reflection of the window and sits straighter, dismissing thoughts of her brother.

Placing the paper on the seat beside her, she pushes back the wings of her hair on either side of her face, to frame it, and exhales, approving of what she sees.

Feeling like death, increasingly often, but dressed to kill, always.

Madeleine misses the days when she could see what someone was reading from the cover of the newspaper, book or magazine in which they were engrossed. What does she imagine Shyrailym is reading on her phone this morning? Picturing the details of her psychology specialism on the university homepage, she makes the obvious conclusion.

The *Economist*, the *Lancet*?

Emails, most likely. Amir's daughter has no social media profiles that Madeleine can find. Unlike her click-happy brother, whose Instagram, of all things, had confirmed that he had indeed been in Kazakhstan on Monday when Ingrid made the call in Harrods, addressing the male on the other end of the line as 'My love'. Had he been to see his father in prison? If so, he certainly hadn't posted about that. Surely it is as politically contentious as it is unlikely, Madeleine thinks, given that the father is in state prison on charges brought against him by the current government, who are targeting those linked to the previous regime, and the son is a vocal campaigner against state controls targeting the crypto community.

But what does she know? The person she would ordinarily have reached out to for advice on this increasingly complicated question, is dead.

Madeleine shivers as the train pulls into an area of signal and her personal phone pings in her handbag. Taking it out, she glances at the screen and spots a Facebook friend request from a Daphne King.

Her eyes narrowing, she logs into her account for the first time in months. Her profile is little more than her name Madeleine Farrow, and a photograph of a sunset.

Tapping on friend requests, she sees an image of the woman she had taken home two nights running, in a pair of sunglasses, against the backdrop of a sunset so perfect it might have been a green screen, and her stomach turns.

Had Madeleine really given Daphne her full name?

The train is now arriving at Embankment. Please stand back from the parting doors—

An irritated voice over the tannoy interrupts her thoughts and

Madeleine clicks off the site without responding to the request, slipping the phone back into her handbag.

* * *

It is a ten to fifteen-minute walk from the tube station to the university. The rain has stopped but a dampness clings to the air as Madeleine walks parallel to the Thames, the Royal Festival Hall on the other side of the water, gulls calling above the fray of river life.

A Facebook friend request? The move strikes her simultaneously as a peril of modern life and thoroughly passé. Despite the fact that Madeleine spends her time prying into other people's existences, the thought of her own name being placed in a search engine feels horribly intrusive. It serves her right, of course, for using her real name on her profile – and for having an account in the first place. In her defence, she had still been at the FCO when she set it up, long ago enough that she could hardly have imagined what social media would become. These days, she only uses it for occasional work-related snooping, and cat memes.

At this point, the account feels so irrelevant she barely remembered she had it – until now.

She passes the obelisk, Shyrailym walking a few metres ahead. Madeleine lets her attention drift briefly to the stationed restaurants and commuter boats which set sail from the Festival pier. She never tires of this view, despite her time at the Foreign Office at King Charles Street, just a couple of streets parallel, and then the past eight years at the Serious Crimes Investigations Department.

As cities go, there are certainly worse.

Buses trundle along Waterloo pier above Madeleine's head as she turns left onto Savoy Street and then right onto the Strand, following the daughter at a distance through the heart of theatreland onto Aldwych.

They are almost at LSE's Old Building, when Madeleine's thoughts are curtailed by the ringing of her phone.

Christ, these devices. Reaching into her bag, she sees Rittler's number flashing on the screen.

So he is alive, after all.

'Boss?'

'Where are you?' Rittler's tone is sharp and Madeleine surmises that he still hasn't forgiven her for running out on him and Jonny in the bar on Monday night. Or perhaps he is simply passing down the punishment that would have been meted out by Julie when he got home, roaring drunk. Rittler would have insisted on matching Jonny pint-for-pint for the rest of the night after Madeleine abandoned them – a mistake one will always live to regret, presuming one doesn't drop dead of liver poisoning beforehand.

'I'm just a few minutes away from the office, actually,' Madeleine says. When she pictures Rittler, she imagines him feet up on the desk next to one of Jonny's miraculous orchids.

Love, Jonny had replied when Madeleine questioned him on the trick to the delicate plants' survival, given the wind that blows in, day and night, through the cracks in the old safe house's ancient windows. *They thrive because I love them.*

'Great to know you're in the area, but do you think you could get in here at some point?' Rittler growls at the end of the line. 'I told you to stay put.'

Temper, temper. Madeleine makes a face, holding back a little as Shyrailym turns the corner.

'That was yesterday, and I haven't heard a peep from you since,' she retorts, evenly.

Monday's hangover must have been bad for him to be holding on to a grudge, two days later. Maybe he had woken up one of the children again, on his way into the house. Or, worse still, hadn't made it further than the hall before passing out. Madeleine clearly recalls Julie's unamused expression as she lambasted her husband's colleagues with the details of how little Teddy and Freddy (truly) had found their father comatose at the bottom of the stairs on their way down to breakfast the morning after the office's last Christmas party.

Poor woman, but honestly it's hard not to believe that she brought it on herself. What had she been thinking, getting knocked up by Paul Rittler?

Stripping her voice of any amusement, Madeleine replies: 'I'm tailing the daughter to work. Something tells me she's our way into the family.'

'Didn't think to run it by me first?'

Madeleine makes a face. Men. Did they never grow out of the constant need for validation? How exhausting it would be to have to live with one. 'We're a man down. Woman, actually. One of the trainees, Sadie, broke her ankle on the way home last night. She's on medical.'

'You're joking.'

'Do I sound like I'm having a laugh?'

'Right,' Madeleine replies. 'There's a packet of paracetamol on my desk. Take two, I'll see you later.'

Shit. Madeleine curses Sadie as she turns into Houghton Street, and is met by Shyrailym, standing square to meet her on the pavement of the side road.

'Why are you following me?'

'My name is Madeleine Farrow, I'm from the Serious Crime Investigations Department. Do you have a minute to talk?' Madeleine replies, without missing a beat.

'No.'

The younger woman's curtness is not wholly unexpected and Madeleine's eyes flicker. She hasn't even asked why Madeleine is at her place of work, so presumably she knows. 'That's a shame. I'm—'

'You're working to discredit my family and you assumed I was your best option, because I live a different lifestyle to my parents and earn my own money rather than taking from them.'

Madeleine hadn't been privy to this detail and she instantly doubts it – who ever heard of a person living in a mansion flat off High Street Kensington on a teaching salary alone? But the overall implication is accurate. She had expected some contrition, at least, if not an immediate offer of help.

If it is true that Shyrailym is removed from the family business, that she doesn't gain from its proceeds, then what has she got to be contrite about? It is impossible to know at this stage whether the young woman's boldness is the result of a genuine sense of detachment from her family, or simply a case of the lady protesting too much.

'You don't miss a trick,' Madeleine says.

'I'm busy. If I have done something wrong, come back with a warrant or—' Shyrailym turns away.

'Wait – please. We're getting off on the wrong foot. Five minutes.' Madeleine reaches for her arm. The younger woman flinches, and then stops.

Turning back to face her, coolly, Shyrailym considers Madeleine a moment: the wool suit and Louboutin leather loafers. Perhaps recognising something in Madeleine, or maybe just curious as to the figure standing in front of her, she concedes with a quick glance at her Apple watch.

'It's five to nine – I can give you four minutes, if you walk with me.'

CHAPTER THIRTEEN

The main door to Connaught House, where the university's international development department is based, is on Aldwych. Stopping just inside and taking an exercise book from her rucksack, to buy herself time to scope out the entrance, Ramona does an immediate about-turn as she finds herself met by security gates.

Shit.

Back outside, she surveys the street and spots a Chinese student standing on the pavement, making a call. Signalling for his attention, she makes an apologetic face.

'I'm so sorry, I'm new and I'm really late to a meeting with my professor but I've forgotten my pass. Do you know if there's another way—' Ramona looks about herself helplessly, and the boy says something into the handset in Cantonese.

She recognises the word 'mother' – one of the few she remembers from her grandmother's teachings – and presumes he is talking to his parents back in Hong Kong.

'Have you tried reception in the Old Building? They might be able to help.' The boy covers the mouthpiece and indicates towards Houghton Street, where the entrance to the adjoining university building is located.

'Thank you so much! Of course,' Ramona replies, following his gesture. 'I'll try there.'

Approaching the side street she notices a small group of students gathered outside Wright's Bar, at the foot of the stone steps leading to the Old Building, their university lanyards hanging around their necks. The young women laugh as they suck on their vape pens.

Silently considering her next move, Ramona spots a group of young women heading towards security. Taking a few long strides, she catches them up and adds herself to the end of the chain, leaning in as though she is part of the group who stepped out briefly for a smoke, and holding her head high, marching alongside them through the entrance.

A woman on reception calls out to them. 'Excuse me, girls? Passes—'

'We were using the dance room, we just popped out—' the one nearest reception replies, unapologetically.

The phone on the desk rings and the woman at the desk bats a hand as she leans in to answer it. 'Yeah yeah, I remember.'

As they pass the lifts, the girl next to Ramona turns, confused, towards the overfamiliar newcomer and Ramona breaks away from the group, making for the stairs, before anyone can question her. Following the signs for the walkway that links the Old Building and Connaught House, she spots a man in his forties, who appears to be a member of staff, and calls across. 'Sorry, do you know which one Professor Wimalasundera's office is? This place is like a maze!'

'Next corridor, on the left.'

Ramona follows his directions and finds herself outside a blue door helpfully adorned with the words PROFESSOR LEON WIMALASUNDERA: INTERNATIONAL DEVELOPMENT.

Knocking twice, she waits. When there is no answer, she tries the handle and finds it locked.

Shit. The university listing specifically stated that he would be in by 9.00 a.m.

'Can I help you?' The voice behind Ramona is gravelly in its depth, the eyes the same soft intensity she recognises from the photograph on the staff page, when she turns to meet them in the hallway.

'Professor Wimalasundera?'

'Yes?'

'Can I talk to you for five minutes, please?'

He is dressed more like a graphic designer than a professor, in a Patagonia fleece and black Adidas Gazelles. When he pauses, she continues. 'It's about Time for Tuition.'

Holding up his hands, he makes a confused gesture. 'I'm sorry, am I supposed to know—'

'The website you run.' She keeps her volume raised as two students pass. 'The one promising to connect young women with men who will pay for sex.'

'Excuse me?' He reacts more urgently now, his face shifting into an expression of alarm as he takes a step forward, speaking quietly. 'Is this some sort of joke?'

'You tell me.'

Fiddling with the key to his office, he glances back towards the students whispering as they pass, opening the door and indicating to Ramona to step inside.

'Right, you have five minutes to explain what the hell is going on.'

* * *

Madeleine stands back a little, watching as the young psychology professor reaches for the key to her office door and unlocks it with a deft turn of the wrist. Stepping inside, Shyrailym Zhatchanova leaves the door ajar for Madeleine to follow, placing her handbag on the desk and removing her coat, without looking up.

Does she look like her mother? Given the amount of work Ingrid has clearly had done, it is hard to say for sure. The daughter is certainly less buxom, less glossy than the woman Madeleine trailed two days earlier, but there is a similarity. An energy, Madeleine thinks, though this is the kind of nondescriptor she generally dislikes.

Beyond an unmistakable air of self-belief, there is little Madeleine can say about Shyrailym. Generally, people give themselves away, even without knowing they're doing it. Leave enough space in conversations or even in silent interactions, and people tend to fill in the gaps with words, with gestures and body language – or with the things they don't say. It is the same with people's homes. Though Madeleine herself has no interest in expressing herself through design – not like her sister-in-law Amber with her interior mood boards and subscriptions to magazines that advise on how best to haemorrhage thousands of pounds on landscaping a garden she will never sit in – she knows that anyone entering her own apartment would be able to pick up details of her life, even just through their absence.

The lack of novels or a television; the single family photograph of herself and her parents, taken one summer in Istanbul, framed in the plain white hallway she has no interest in repainting; the extortionately priced frozen microwave meals from the organic deli down the road.

Madeleine's attention sharpens, ready to seize on some small detail hinting at who the daughter of Amir Zhatchanov really is.

Until a few days ago, the little Madeleine had known about Kazakhstan was limited to what she has read around its disgraced former leader, and its natural resources. And it seems that both these roads – the disgraced MP, and the country's resources, specifically electricity – lead back to the Zhatchanov family.

Looking around, Madeleine finds Shyrailym's office almost deliberate in its lack of self-expression; as if someone had designed it to be as unrevealing as possible.

Aside from the certificates plainly framed on the right-hand wall, and the textbooks lined up in the glass cabinet that stands behind the walnut desk, there is not a trinket or framed photograph pointing to any kind of private life. Even the furniture – a coat-stand, a single chair, and double-pedestal desk with a pot of pens – feels intentionally nondescript.

'You can get paranoid, when you come from a family like mine. It's easy to wonder how many students are genuinely interested in taking an additional course in Darwin's theory of evolutionary psychology, and how many are actually just here because they're intrigued by my family history.' Shyrailym's intuitive answer to the question Madeleine hasn't verbalised catches her off guard.

Evolutionary psychology. Yes. She had read up on the subject in the small hours of the morning in that famously accurate scientific bible, Wikipedia. According to which, Shyrailym's specialism is 'a theoretical approach to psychology that attempts to explain useful mental and psychological traits – such as memory, perception, or language – as adaptations, i.e., as the functional products of natural selection'.

'I understand. That must be . . . hard,' Madeleine replies, genuinely.

'It's not hard. I just refuse to participate. If someone is here to find out more about my family, to pick up gossip, then they'll soon learn they're in the wrong place.'

'I'm not here for gossip.' Madeleine meets Shyrailym's eye.

'No.' Shyrailym looks thoughtful. 'You're here to try to persuade me to help you strip my family of their wealth and social standing, and perhaps you think I'll happily go along with it because you read somewhere that I am morally opposed to my father's business activities. And now you're analysing my academic specialism, imagining that my entire career is dedicated to trying to prove or disprove my inherited nature.'

'I read an article by you online.' Madeleine clears her throat, shifting the subject towards an interview she had found in the *Telegraph*. 'In the piece, you wrote—'

'I was ambushed at an academic conference by a journalist who made promises and then wrote that article, quoting me out of context.' There is a flutter of emotion in Shyrailym's eye, which Madeleine isn't sure whether to read as fear or frustration or something else. But then it is gone, replaced by the same cool expression. 'Look, all you need to know is that I will never help you. The fact that you think you can win against him is touching, but—'

She cuts herself off, leaving one word hanging in the air.

Him.

Shyrailym's eyes scan Madeleine's face, her look shifting again. When she continues, her voice is quieter. 'You have no idea what you're dealing with.'

'Go on . . .' Madeleine says, willing her to continue. 'By "him", you mean your father?'

When Shyrailym doesn't reply, Madeleine takes a deep breath. 'How did you know the MP Laura Tatchell?'

'Excuse me?'

Her expression falters so subtly it's hard to be sure, but Madeleine is pretty certain she doesn't imagine it.

'It's a simple question.'

Madeleine thinks she can almost see the panic running through the young woman's mind, though her face soon resumes its composure. There is no trace of the fear Madeleine is certain she spotted a moment earlier.

'I'd like you to leave now.' Shyrailym Zhatchanova's voice changes so that it is businesslike once more. 'I said you could have four minutes and I've given you six. I have nothing to do with any of them. I have nothing to tell you.'

Desperate to push further but knowing it will only be detrimental, Madeleine turns and reaches for the door handle. 'Thank you for your time. Look, I'm going to leave you my business card. If you ever want to talk . . .'

'Hey?' Shyrailym responds as Madeleine opens the door.

When Madeleine looks up, the young woman suddenly looks more like a student than a teacher. 'Yes?'

'Be careful, I mean that.'

'This is my job,' Madeleine says simply.

Shyrailym clicks open her briefcase. 'And this is my life. Please – I'm begging you – do not come here again.'

* * *

'OK, hold on, let me get this straight: you're saying a man has stolen my identity and is using it to pose as the director of an escort agency?' Professor Leon Wimalasundera stares at Ramona, as they sit opposite one another in his office.

His demeanour suggests he isn't sure whether or not this is an elaborate prank; either he is a bloody good actor or his ignorance is genuine.

'And you didn't think to ask me privately before making accusations in the hallway to my office?'

Ramona shrugs. Admittedly, her approach hadn't exactly been professional, but it had got her the result she needed – and that is the nature of her job: results-driven.

Besides, the handsome young professor isn't her client, and in the ten minutes or so since they first met, she hasn't warmed to him, showing as he did, so little empathy for the young women whose plight Ramona has described, by way of context. Women like his own students, who were being taken in – by what, a fake escort agency?

As far as Ramona could see, any concern Professor Wimalasundera has is merely for his own potential involvement. Not that he has reason to worry about that. There is no reason to believe that anyone else, besides her, has made the connection between the company and the name stated under its listed directors, searchable when one inputs the VAT and company numbers from the bottom of the website into the Companies House register.

'The police are onto it. They've requested that we don't make any contact with the owners of the site in case they go underground,' Ramona lies. She can't afford for him to stir things up by going public and pushing whoever is behind the site into hiding before she has a plan in place.

'What's your role in this?' The professor's tone undulates between defensive and angry, and lands on accusatory.

'My client is a private individual.' She stands, looking the man straight in the eye.

'I mean, you can't just come in here and tell me something like this without more information . . . My professional reputation is at stake.'

Any empathy Ramona had originally felt – which is arguably less than she might have – is fading fast.

Pausing, she stands and heads for the door. 'We'll be in touch. I'll see myself out.'

* * *

Ramona curses as she steps back out onto Houghton Street, returning the cap to her head. It had been a long shot.

Just as the bemused and then furious professor had pointed out, he would have to be an idiot, or at least remarkably arrogant, to put his real name and address on a website connecting female students and paying clients, if he had actually been the person behind it. Well, the arrogant part seemed to fit – but the rest . . .

Pulling out a cigarette from the packet in her top pocket, Ramona sighs with frustration.

She had already known that Companies House is far from a fool-proof resource. Without internal investigators to hold users to account, there is little to stop fraudsters inputting fake names, VAT numbers and addresses as their own company details.

Throw into the mix the capacity for shell companies and shady lawyers willing to act as guarantors, and Ramona can think of numerous ways in which information gleaned from the official business listings forum might be far from reliable.

Of course, in hindsight it makes sense for whoever really runs the website to adopt the persona of a respected academic, with the joint purpose of hiding their own identity while creating an illusion of credibility within the higher education realm, should any potential applicants think to check. Still, Ramona can't help but take it as a blow. Hers is a game of angles and circles, of two steps forward, and six steps back.

Right now, she feels little further along than when she started.

All she has for certain is Ottilie's personal statement of what happened to her, as well as the online accounts of other young women suggesting she wasn't the only one who went through the practical assessment only to be rejected and invited to reapply another time. Last – and by no means least – Ramona has the recording she made of the man she met last night, outlining his expectations of his would-be employees.

It's not nothing. But it is a long way from something she can use.

Ramona still has no idea who the man who calls himself James Harvey really is, or any way of knowing how to get in touch with either his existing or previous clients – or the girls he employs to work for him.

If only she had someone to talk it through with, though it had been a considered choice to set up on her own. Working with others comes at a cost. Right now, isolation is preferable to the compromises that have to be made when operating within an organisation. Except she will be more than isolated if she doesn't make some money soon – and how will she do that if she can't even solve the first proper case she has been presented with?

Not that this one will actually pay any sort of bill, either way.

Lighting up, Ramona takes a drag of her cigarette. Enough of the self-pity. The only thing she can do now, is go fishing. Picturing her laptop on the table in her kitchen, she starts to draft in her head the email she needs to send as soon as she gets home.

Moving towards Aldwych, she feels the smoke catch in her throat, a chill running up her neck along with the familiar feeling that she is being watched.

* * *

Madeleine checks her phone as she walks down the steps of the Old Building and onto Houghton Street, checking her messages. Only one is of interest, from Jonny stating that he and Amol had followed the wife to an unknown address off the King's Road, and watched as she used a key to let herself in.

Taking a moment, Madeleine calls Fionn and instructs him to make financial enquiries at the address, through the multinational credit reporting agency Equifax, before turning her attention to the here and now.

It had been worth a try, but it had also been a long shot to imagine the daughter would give her father up so easily, regardless of the fragility of their relationship. Of course, it is impossible to know whether Shyrailym is protecting her family or whether, as Madeleine suspects, she is genuinely fearful.

It's possible that the daughter and Laura had met just once, at that event. Laura would talk to anyone. Perhaps Shyrailym reacted the way she did because she was fearful of being caught up in any investigations into the MP's death. The theory of what was to blame for her hit-and-run – along with the names of the mining tycoons called out in Laura's speech – had been doing the rounds on Twitter.

As Rittler had originally said, the Zhatchanovs weren't on the list. Madeleine accepts that Laura's murder is not her investigation. But even if Amir Zhatchanov is not directly responsible for Laura Tatchell's death, it is impossible in Madeleine's mind to fully separate out the behaviour of men like them, who operate in businesses that profit from other people's suffering, and the plight of those individuals whose stories Laura was trying to bring to light.

That may well be. Still, Madeleine is not arrogant enough to think that she can make inroads on the case relating to Laura's death without being so much as party to the current investigation – and she has to believe that one is meaningfully ongoing. She couldn't do her job if she didn't have the slightest faith in the institution she works for, even if it is increasingly stretched to breaking point.

Stopping outside Wright's Bar, Madeleine considers her next step. She is not yet ready to return to the office, with Rittler in his current mood.

Shyrailym would have every right to be wary of a police officer arriving at her place of work and asking about any relationship between herself and a woman who is believed to have been murdered by someone operating in a similar area to her family – especially a circle of corrupt businessmen as tight as the one to which Laura had been referring in her speech.

Despite her instinct that the daughter is genuine, Madeleine can't dismiss the possibility that her chief interest is in protecting herself, and securing her own inheritance. Judging by the postcode of her flat, Madeleine has to assume Shyrailym's claims of being financially independent are dubious.

She sighs. If they can't get someone who is already inside the family to help let them in, then they will have to find their own ways to infiltrate them from the outside.

Madeleine walks in the opposite direction of the office and catches the faint scent of cheap tobacco trailing through the air. Turning towards it, her attention settles on a young woman standing a little along the pavement. Even from a distance, with her hood pulled up, Madeleine knows the figure instantly – perhaps by the fingers of her left hand which hang by her side, clicking out of nervous habit.

'Hey.' Walking towards her, Madeleine smiles.

* * *

Ramona starts at the sound of her old name being called across the pavement, and looks about her nervously. Despite herself, at the sight of Madeleine Farrow walking towards her, she breaks into a smile.

'I thought it was you.' Madeleine beams. 'What are you doing here?'

'Work,' Ramona replies, trying to remember how long it has been since they last met.

'You're teaching journalism now?'

'No.' Cagily, Ramona takes a step closer, aware of how exposed she is here in the middle of town. She has just been recognised, for God's sake – though she can only hope that CCTV, with its specific measurements for facial recognition, will be easier to trick.

Adjusting her hood, she positions herself away from the lens of the university's security system, before continuing. 'I'm freelance these days.'

'I thought you'd had enough of the media. That's what you said last time I saw you.'

Ramona tries to remember when exactly that was. She had been covering a story and Madeleine had been in court, sitting in the public gallery. Privately, she had admitted to Ramona that she had been one of the investigating officers on the case, and had wanted to look the defendants in the eyes as they received their sentences. A rare perk of the job, she had called it.

It was over a year ago – not long after Ramona had decided to leave the local paper for a national. Ramona had been briefly flattered when Madeleine tried to tempt her to join the agency instead. But it was never going to happen – even if Ramona had got through the background check.

Ramona was more a lone wolf than a pack animal – besides, she believed in rules, but not necessarily those of the law.

'I left the paper,' Ramona says, simply. 'I'm not a journalist, any more. I'm— It's a long story.'

Madeleine looks at her watch, which Ramona senses will have cost more than she herself has earned in the past year. Not that she begrudges Madeleine for it. Despite all the things that set them apart, she feels a connection to the woman – even if she is old enough to be her mother. Maybe, in part, because of that.

'Freelance? How modern. Well then, freelancer . . .' Madeleine says, reaching out to accept Ramona's lighter, 'I assume you have time for a coffee?'

CHAPTER FOURTEEN

Madeleine guides Ramona to her favourite seat in the old Italian café on High Holborn, which is one of the few things she can rely on to remain as she left it every time she returns from a stint abroad. In a city of change, the laminated menu, and red and green awning at Papa Luigi, are a constant.

'Who are they?' Ramona motions towards a wall of framed photographs immortalising various celebrities who have dined at the establishment over the years – a fair few of whom have since been discredited by the fallout of #MeToo, though Madeleine doesn't dare tell Luigi Junior this – and no doubt if challenged, he would argue that times had been different then. But had they? Not much has changed, as far as Madeleine can tell.

'Seriously?' She frowns, pointing to two of the more incongruous images hanging side by side in separate frames. 'That's Frank Sinatra and that's Oswald the Ostrich. I like to think they ate here together.' After a pause, she adds, 'I like your new hair cut – and you've dyed it, too, I see.'

Considering the young woman in front of her, Madeleine continues more cautiously. 'I saw the news about Michael O'Keegan.'

Ramona's eyes flick up at her. 'What about him?'

'That he is being been transferred to custody in the UK.'

Ramona nods. 'Yeah.'

'I assume this is what the change of name is about,' Madeleine says.

Ramona leans back in her chair without answering, looking around the restaurant.

They have only met a handful of times over the years but, despite Ramona's spikiness, Madeleine had instantly warmed to the maverick reporter whose lack of inhibition she found endearing, even before she learnt about the challenges of the younger woman's upbringing.

Not that she pities her. She respects her, and in a way she envies her too, for the freedom that comes with operating outside the system.

Despite the obvious differences between them, they are the same deep down, Madeleine likes to think: outliers, destined to love no one and nothing as much as their work. Work that, they both know – and readily accept – will never love them back.

'Ramona is my middle name and Chang was my grandmother's maiden name,' Ramona finally replies. 'My gran looked after me when I was young.'

Quietly triumphant, Madeleine nods. Unlike most people her age, Ramona is hesitant to serve up personal details about her life, and – irrespective of the fact that Madeleine already secretly knows this particular detail about the girl's grandmother – she takes her confidence as a sign of trust.

'What will you have?' she asks, as the waitress approaches to take their order. 'A cappuccino and a cannoli for me.'

'Coffee,' Ramona says. 'Black.'

'And to eat?'

'Just coffee.'

'Two cannolis, and get her a coffee and a fresh orange juice,' Madeleine addresses the waitress and hands back the menus. 'It's on me, and you're looking too thin.'

'You're not supposed to comment on women's bodies these days. Didn't you hear?' Ramona replies, deadpan.

Madeleine shakes her head. 'I'm still sorry I couldn't tempt you to join us.'

121

The truth is she isn't sorry, not really; she wants to revel in Ramona's refusal to conform. She wants to live vicariously through her, not to see her tied down by the same shackles as she is – even if the ties of the Serious Crime Investigations Department are markedly slack. That is the upside of being out on a limb as they are in SCID Row: as long as you deliver on the evidence most of the time, and don't spectacularly – or at least obviously – fuck up, then you're largely left to your own devices.

Or maybe there just aren't the resources any more to keep an eye on them. Either way, it works for Madeleine. Though it would help if they had proper staff. *Bloody* Sadie.

Ramona shrugs diplomatically. 'I prefer to work to my own schedule.'

Madeleine considers the young woman in front of her, a thought crystallising in her mind. 'How busy are you right now?'

The waitress returns with their pastries and drinks, setting the tray down between them.

'Busy-ish,' Ramona replies, unconvincingly, taking a bite and wiping away the flakes of pastry with her sleeve.

'Look, tell me to fuck off if you like but if you're freelance, I might have something for you.'

'Like what?' Ramona stops chewing.

'Like there's a case I'm working on involving a rich billionaire who is laundering his money in the UK, and I need someone to watch the wife. I don't suppose you'd be interested? It's a good day rate.' The little Madeleine knows about Ramona personally, she is sure she isn't motivated by money. But moral purpose alone won't pay the rent.

'The man involved is reprehensible scum. The wife, too, it would seem,' Madeleine adds, for good measure.

'I'm working another case actually,' Ramona says.

'What kind?'

'I'm not sure yet. It's complicated.'

Madeleine notices a flicker and pauses, momentarily, before she continues. 'OK, so maybe we can help each other.'

CHAPTER FIFTEEN

'We have the financial reports,' Fionn Edwardes announces from behind his computer screen, back at the office.

Looking up, Madeleine catches a glimpse of blond hair above the monitor in the corner of the room.

Does Fionn ever leave his chair, she wonders? When does he wash or iron his rotation of perfectly pressed shirts? Does he have midnight manicures at his desk while the rest of them sleep or shag, or simply lie staring at the ceiling waiting for the apocalypse?

When the robots finally take over, Madeleine imagines they will look exactly like Fionn Edwardes.

'Great, and what did they say?' she asks, standing and brushing off the crumbs of the croissant from her skirt before walking over to his desk.

'It is indicated that some of the bills are in the name of the subject . . .' Fionn says and Madeleine leans in to read the words he is pointing to.

Yes.

'Nice work,' she says, heading back towards her desk.

It is the day after her chance encounter with Ramona and she feels her hope renewed when she thinks of her new ally, followed by a twinge of guilt.

The truth is, it had been a lie when she claimed not to have known about Ramona's new name. Madeleine had kept tabs on her briefly, after the attack by one of O'Keegan's men. It wasn't Madeleine's case, but she had heard about it. Even before they first crossed paths on a human trafficking case that Ramona was covering for the paper – ultimately bringing Madeleine's office information they themselves had failed to obtain – Madeleine had known of the journalist. She had ruffled feathers while making a name for herself as a reporter at the *Camden News*, where she was instrumental in bringing down a global gang operating out of North London – a gang run by one Michael O'Keegan.

Without her, the case would never have come to trial.

Preceded by a reputation for being ruthless and not always orthodox in her methods, Ramona's dogged investigation into Somers Town's drug network, which ran across county lines – and beyond, to Bolivia and back again – helped the police bring down an operation of heroin and cocaine imports worth billions. More impressive still, Madeleine had thought when she finally met the journalist who had been so instrumental, she looked like a bloody child; the least threatening person in the room. Perhaps that was part of her power. After their first meeting and then subsequent ones, Madeleine had become curious and then fascinated by the young reporter.

When she did a background check, partly as a precursor to the job offer, partly out of nosiness, she became more intrigued still.

Born in London in the late nineties, Ramona was the only child of Emma, a revered foreign correspondent who Madeleine also knew by reputation; a mother largely conspicuous by her absence.

Admittedly, Madeleine's sniffing around went well beyond what she needed – or had any right – to want to know. But she was an investigator, what did one expect? Putting aside what she knew of Ramona, and has no right to know, Madeleine returns to her desk, clicking the lid of her pen as the computer whirrs.

Taking up her mouse, she moves between the image of the wife in the photo the papers used to accompany their stories about Amir

Zhatchanov's arrest, and zooms in on the name of the plastic surgeon's she is walking away from.

Arise Health Clinic.

Arise? Good God. She does hope they specialise in erectile dysfunction.

Inputting the name into the search engine, she waits a moment for the number to load on her computer screen.

Madeleine had checked in on Ramona intermittently, after the attack, and was relieved to discover that she had left the area and the paper she had moved to, and was living in a new area under a new name. Not long after that, Madeleine had gone abroad on a job and had lost touch with what was happening. She was good at that: placing something in a box and choosing when to open it. Now that she has, there is no option but to examine the contents of what is inside.

It was too much of a coincidence, both of them being at the university making enquiries at the same time, and so she had been compelled to do some more digging. It isn't that she doesn't trust Ramona, but she has to be sure.

The more recent details of her life had been harder to find, but not as hard as Ramona presumably likes to think.

Following her enquiries, Madeleine is satisfied that bumping into her again like that was just a coincidence – more than that, it was a gift. Ramona is an anomaly in many respects, Madeleine thinks as she scrolls through the Arise website on the computer in front of her, dialling the contact number for the plastic surgeon on her phone, and pressing call. She feels an almost maternal instinct towards her, in the same way that she does with her niece Bella. Though with Bella, there is the complication of having to deal with the girl's actual mother.

'Good morning, Arise Health Clinic, this is Coco speaking, how can I help?' The secretary answers her call after two rings.

'Oh good morning, I'm calling on behalf of my employer, Mrs Ingrid Zhatchanova. Gosh, this is embarrassing but I've made an error and wiped her entire schedule from our joint calendar. We made an appointment for Mrs Zhatchanova to see Dr Imerman but I cannot for the life of me remember the date. So . . .' Madeleine continues, 'I was just wondering if you could check for me?'

'Of course. Let me just look that up for you. What's Mrs Zhatchanova's birthday, please?' Coco says in a clipped South African accent.

Shit.

Madeleine stalls. She should have been prepared for some sort of security question.

'I'm so sorry, just give me two seconds. I'm just slipping out of a meeting.'

Putting the call on mute, she signals to Fionn. 'Psst, do we have a date of birth on the wife?'

'Thirtieth of October 1970,' he replies without looking up.

Did he just recite that from memory?

'You sure?'

Clearing his throat, he continues looking at his screen and Madeleine narrows her eyes before pressing the unmute button on the handset.

'Thirty, ten, seventy,' Madeleine says tentatively, and there is a moment's hesitation before the secretary responds.

'Okey dokey. So Mrs Zhatchanova is due for her fortnightly appointment tomorrow, at 11.00 a.m.'

'Tomorrow? Thank you,' Madeleine hangs up. 'Fionn, when you have a minute, could you look into who owns another property? It's the flat where the daughter lives, in Kensington.' If they can prove that the parents own that, Madeleine thinks . . .

'I'll ping you the address now,' Fionn replies instantly, and Madeleine's gaze narrows.

Maybe the robots are already here.

* * *

A flurry of toddlers screech past as Ramona reaches home following her meeting with Madeleine.

She uses a practised kicking motion to open the gate, which hangs precariously on its hinges, a spring in her step as she takes the stairs to her flat two at a time.

Once an imposing four-storey townhouse, the shared hallway of Ramona's home on Mildmay Grove North is now defined by magnolia Artex walls and stained carpets that speak of the various generations that have occupied it since its glory days. From the middle floor, the sound of the TV blasts from behind the closed door as she passes up the stairs, taking comfort from the familiar theme tune.

In an era of streaming and box sets, it's nice somehow to know that afternoon game shows like the ones her grandmother was so devoted to, still exist. She is less moved by the overwhelming stench of cat piss, and the bags of newspaper that spill out from the doorway of Jeffrey's flat into the shared space, but she would take the hoarding sitting tenant over so many other varieties of Hackney-ites she has encountered, not least the ones recently imported from the home counties, with their linen tote bags stuffed with thirty-pound bottles of organic wine and I LOVE DALSTON badges.

She thinks of how Si berated her for her cynicism one night as they sat in Clissold Park, Ramona laying into the various tribes who passed.

'How can you so clearly give a shit about society but be so scathing towards individuals?' he had asked, genuinely inquisitive as he took a drag of the spliff she passed him.

Not just any individuals, she had countered, snatching back the joint. Only the pretentious pricks.

'Why does it bother you so much? You hate change, that's your problem. You're too nostalgic.'

She doesn't hate change. What she hates is corrupt landlords and social injustice, and the fact that every time she nearly has something worked out, the world reinvents itself yet again and the goalposts shift. She hates how difficult it is to decide who she is within the psychogeography of where she spent much of her childhood, when the layout keeps changing.

Also, she really hates pretentious pricks.

The sound of buzzers and a studio audience erupting into applause fades into silence as Ramona reaches her own front door, at the very top of the building. It's a fire hazard up here, but she will take the risk for the sense of seclusion, and the view.

The key sticks in the lock and Ramona pauses before turning it sharply with the necessary well-placed last-minute kick. Dumping her skateboard by the door and her rucksack on the table, which is pushed up against the single stud wall that separates the living room-slash-kitchen-slash-almost-everything-else from the bedroom, she takes out a box of cigarettes from the top pocket of her denim jacket and lights one.

Madeleine Farrow. Well, that was a surprise. Ramona had been conflicted when she said no to the older woman's offer of joining the organisation, choosing to opt for the newspaper instead. The parameters of the law were always going to be too tight for Ramona, but she had liked her personally – more importantly, she respected her. Unlike others she could think of, Madeleine had been generous with her time, and quick to attribute to the reporter the work that Ramona had done on the case Madeleine's team had been building, rather than taking the glory for herself.

Better still, she hadn't been too bothered about how or where Ramona had come up with the information.

But, to Ramona, joining the broadsheet at that time had felt like an opportunity she simply couldn't let slide. The culmination of years of hard graft, working at a major paper might be considered a life goal if she were prone to thinking about things in such terms, which she is most definitely not. A therapist might have surmised that in forging a path in journalism she was trying to impress the mother who never seemed to notice her, by meeting her in her own field. But it was more than that. Investigating was steeped in Ramona's bones. She wanted answers, be it for herself or for others.

Which is for the best, given that no matter what Ramona did, Emma still never gave a fuck.

Settling in front of her laptop, Ramona opens the lid and is greeted by a new email from Time for Tuition, signed off by someone claiming to be Gail, the company secretary. The message reiterates Harvey's claim that she only has a couple of days to fulfil the practical element of her assessment. Jesus, how desperate are these people?

These people. But who, exactly? Nothing about the direct contact she has had with them so far – that is a meeting at a café in the sticks, and a couple of slightly desperate sounding emails – has persuaded her of their credibility or scale.

Logging on to the Time for Tuition website, Ramona opens the contact form and starts to type the email she had started mentally composing the moment Madeleine accosted her outside LSE.

Dear Sir or Madam,

I am a high net worth individual interested in becoming a benefactor of your services. Please let me know how to proceed.

Best wishes,

Mr Faisal Farhat.

Reading it over once, she presses send, and then she heads out.

* * *

The entrance to the crypt of the church is ajar and Ramona winces as she pushes it open, feeling several pairs of eyes from the front of the room landing on her.

Lurking in the back row, she surveys the crowd, noting a couple of faces she has not seen before.

Taking in every one in turn, scanning for potential threats, Ramona notes that her sponsor, JJ, is conspicuous by his absence, and she cranes to catch sight of him. He is never not here. The only time he had missed a meeting since she started coming here was on his granddaughter's birthday, though he had not been formally invited to the party. Instead, he had hung around outside to catch a glimpse of her, leaving a present with no name or note before slipping away again.

But Ramona had missed a meeting, hadn't she? With a sense of pride, she realises that she hadn't been here the day before and she hadn't even noticed, which means a full twenty-four hours must have passed without her having thought about drinking.

With a pang of guilt, she realises she is relieved by JJ's absence, dreading the words he will no doubt want to have with her about the dangers of continuing to smoke hash. She knows he means well, but she can do without it.

Is there a chance that he hadn't noticed the Rizla in her pocket? No. JJ doesn't miss a beat, and he would never be able to stop himself from saying something about it. It is just the kind of person he is, always as ready to call someone out on bad behaviour, as he is to point out the good.

Studying her hands, she sits in silence throughout the session, letting the words of the other members of the group wash over her as they share their stories, remaining quiet when the inevitable question comes up as to whether anyone else would like to share.

When she is leaving, Cindy catches her at the door. Ramona hugs her friend and drinks in the smell of coconut hair product and the same honey and almond perfume she always wears.

'Where you running off to?' Cindy asks, pushing a streak of baby pink behind her ear.

'Just got some work on.'

'Gwan, you.' Cindy smiles. 'Which way you walking?'

'Doesn't matter, I'll go whichever way you are,' Ramona replies.

It is an unspoken rule between them that neither woman probes the other in any detail about their work, unless they bring it up themselves, and so they walk for a while arm in arm, twos-ing a cigarette in companionable silence. At Dalston Kingsland overground, a man with mangy dreadlocks and a sleeping bag dragging over his shoulder approaches them.

Ramona spots him first and rolls her eyes, elbowing Cindy gently. 'Look who it is.'

'Baby girl!' he says, his smile revealing several missing teeth.

'Alright, Maxy.' Cindy nods gently. 'Not today, mate.'

'Come on, just a pound. You know I'm good for it.'

'Yeah yeah, I know.' Cindy laughs and Maxy kisses his teeth.

'Come now . . .'

'I have no money for you. Our son—'

The words catch him like a blow to the face, and he takes a step back, holding up his hands. 'Don't do me like that, Cind. You know I would help if—'

'Yeah, yeah. Later, Maxy.' Cindy rolls her eyes and turns her attention back to Ramona. 'Don't,' she adds as they walk away, before Ramona can pass comment, silently doing the maths. Sonny is nine years old now, which means it has been a long time since Cindy and Max— She doesn't allow the image to form.

'I swear to God he was gorgeous at school.' Cindy laughs, reading her friend's thoughts. 'Listen, I'm really, really sorry to ask, and you know I wouldn't if there was any other way, but there's another teacher's strike day tomorrow and now I have to work. Is there any chance—'

Without a second thought, Ramona nods. 'I'll pick him up at 8.30. Sound OK?'

'Sounds like I owe you.'

'Nah.' Ramona shrugs. 'You know I love Sonny. It'll be fun.'

Checking her phone as she and Cindy part ways, Ramona sees that there are no new text messages. Not that she would necessarily expect anything material by now. It's only been a night since they bumped into one another outside LSE and she doesn't want to put too much importance on anything particularly useful coming of Madeleine's promise to poke around on her behalf.

Obviously, she had been pushing her luck with the proviso that

Madeleine helps her in return for Ramona agreeing to work freelance for SCID. She is hardly in a position to turn down proper money. But neither can she afford to get distracted from building her new career. Besides, if their brief encounters in the past have shown her anything it's that Madeleine is as averse to injustice as Ramona is; if some pervert is running a racket exploiting young women, then Madeleine Farrow is going to give a shit about it.

Shivering, Ramona pulls her hood more tightly around her face as she turns onto her street.

Suddenly, behind her, she hears a scuffle of feet. Instinctively, she turns. Noting the silhouette of the man moving towards her, she takes a step back, her fingers curling around her skateboard as she raises it up, ready to slam it back down.

'Ramona?'

On second take, she exhales, letting the board drop gently back down by her side.

'Fucking hell, JJ!'

Her heart beats furiously in her chest. She hadn't recognised her sponsor, his red hair concealed under a beanie, which he wears at a jaunty angle that is somewhere between start-up tech entrepreneur and the short-term labourers who gather on the street corners just north of here at 6.00 a.m., shivering their tits off as they wait hopefully to be picked up by passing builders.

JJ, of course, is neither of these things.

Since getting clean, JJ has worked at the local fishmonger where the pay, as he told her over a cup of tea in the local café during their first get-together, is almost as bad as the smell. But he likes the accountability of having to be somewhere at a certain time each day – apart from Sundays when he volunteers at the same church where their NA meetings are held. He also likes having a reason to go to bed early and to get up again at the crack of dawn – the time when, if it's going to, his craving for brown usually kicks in.

'Have time for a cuppa?' JJ scratches his beard.

She winces. She really can't be arsed with a lecture but she knows it is coming, one way or another, just as he knows where to get her where she can't bolt.

He certainly looks as if he needs a tea. He will have just come off an early shift, which he usually avoids on days like today when he attends morning meetings.

'Only if you wash your hands as soon as we get inside,' Ramona says, pushing past him and heaving open the dodgy iron gate with her hip.

Licking his lips, he scratches his beard again, opening his mouth to speak.

'JJ, look—' Ramona begins her practised recital about hash never having been the problem for her, when her phone rings.

Brightening at the sight of Madeleine's number, she answers. 'Yeah?'

'Lovely greeting,' Madeleine says. 'Listen, are you free? We've had clearance, you're good to start. I just need to chat something through with you. Are you OK to come to the office if I text you the address?'

'Now?' Glancing up at JJ, Ramona nods. 'Yes.'

'If you're busy . . .' Madeleine adds.

'I'm not. You're central, right? Give me forty-five minutes.' Hanging up, she pats JJ on the arm. 'Sorry, I've got to work.'

'Ro, I really need to talk to you. It's important.'

'I'm sorry,' she shrugs.

'Will you be around later?'

'Yeah, come over this evening.' She can deal with it then, not now.

'OK.' He nods. 'You'll be here? This is serious—'

'I said I will.' She smiles reassuringly, and puts out her fist for him to bump. When he responds, she notices a mark on his lower arm.

Her phone beeps. *John Adam Street.* Registering the address and working out in her head which route will be quickest, she looks up again.

'You'll be here?'

'Yes, JJ. I promise. Seven o'clock – I'll be here . . .'

133

'OK,' he sighs. 'I'll see you then.'

And then she walks away, without a backwards glance.

* * *

'Welcome to SCID Row,' Madeleine says, greeting Ramona at the door. It is always amusing, seeing the office through the eyes of a first-timer: the dilapidated picturesque mews house with its rising damp, curved bay windows and an array of pot plants placed at precarious points, off one of central London's main thoroughfares.

'I thought you lot were in some shithole over in Vauxhall?' Ramona says, seemingly impressed, taking in the William Morris wallpaper that peels at the edges of original cornicing.

'We're an outpost. Like Gibraltar, but with fewer monkeys and less of a chip on our shoulder about Spain,' Madeleine replies as she ushers Ramona upstairs, noting the young woman's usual uniform of faded black drainpipe jeans and equally scuffed Converse.

'Did you ride that thing here?' she asks.

Ramona shakes her head. 'I don't skate.'

Madeleine processes the statement as she guides her visitor upstairs; she is so easily baffled by the world these days.

'Seriously, what is this place?'

'No one really knows. There was a rumour that it had been owned by a prominent MP – one of several homes paid for on expenses; when the newspaper investigation started, it was hurriedly transformed into a legitimate government office before a scandal could erupt. The wheels of justice in action. Others say it was an old safe house. Either way, it's a three-minute walk to the river, a five-second hop to the Adelphi theatre if you like that kind of thing, and a thirty-second stroll to Charing Cross, with plenty of bars between here and there.'

Madeleine points to the kettle, remembering her mistake but not acknowledging it. Ramona had already given up the booze the last time their paths crossed. It isn't something Madeleine is going to bring up again. 'Tea?'

'No, I'm good.'

'Excellent.' Clapping her hands together, she takes a seat in front of her desk and indicates for Ramona to do the same. Instead she half-perches on the corner and Madeleine watches her scanning the papers piled neatly either side of her computer.

Following her gaze, Madeleine fills her in. 'Background on the family. Amir and Ingrid were childhood sweethearts who grew up in the once bustling fish port of Aralsk, now a dusty desert town a thousand kilometres from the capital of Kazakhstan. Can't say I'd heard of it.' Reading aloud from her notes, she continues. 'Once the fourth largest lake in the world, the Aral has shrunk after being exploited in the Soviet era to provide irrigation . . .'

'Quite the rags to riches story, then, your couple,' Ramona says, once she has finished listening to the background of the case.

'Isn't it touching?' Madeleine replies.

'What did you make of the daughter?' Ramona chews the end of her pen.

'Not sure,' Madeleine replies. 'She seemed to be angry or fearful, maybe both. Her brother is a piece of work: unsubstantiated allegations of abuse of workers in his factories. Nothing proven, of course.' She pauses. 'So, tomorrow, are you free?'

CHAPTER SIXTEEN

Ramona struggles to sleep. Sometime around two in the morning, the moon keeping her company through the window, she fills the kettle and briefly casts around for Si's old Sports Direct mug before remembering it is broken.

From the back of the cupboard, she pulls out one of her grandmother's commemorative teacups instead, with an image of Queen Elizabeth imprinted on the side. Making an instant coffee – she won't be able to sleep now, in any case – she takes it to the table and turns on the side-light, watching the moon bathe the rooftops opposite.

JJ hadn't showed up at seven o'clock, or any time after that, and Ramona had been relieved, lighting up her ritualistic evening spliff at nine, once it was clear he wasn't coming after all. Since then, she has sat at the kitchen table. Something will have come up, or perhaps he had a change of heart about having it out with her over the hash. JJ is a diligent sponsor but sometimes he oversteps. She is a big girl, she knows what she is doing. Smoking weed has never been her problem. The problem was the alcohol and the Xanax, and whatever other sleeping pills she could get her hands on.

Whatever the reason for the no-show, she is relieved not to have been made to have the conversation, hoping the matter will be dropped by the time their paths next cross.

It is chilly and she zips her hoodie over the oversized T-shirt, tucking her legs under her on the chair. Turning on her computer, she imagines the various encryption software, which she had Gareth put on the computer to stop her being tracked, loading as she listens to the machine's whirring.

The lights in here are off and she looks at a window on the street the other side of the railway tracks, which is illuminated. With the window closed, she can't hear the music as she watches figures laughing and dancing, oblivious to the extra set of eyes.

How long has it been since she last went to a party? Long enough ago that she can't remember. Not that she ever really enjoyed them, anyway, besides the element of getting trashed. And even that was more about a way to get through a social situation that came unnaturally.

Once the computer is ready, Ramona types in 'Kazakhstan oligarchs' and waits for the pages to load.

* * *

The morning, when it properly comes, is bright and promising.

Waking to her alarm at 7.30 a.m., Ramona dresses in an outfit she wore for court in her reporter days: a plain white shirt, black trousers and the same penny loafers she had at school, which appeared to have made a comeback.

Three hours' sleep is almost worse than none at all and she yawns as she brushes her hair into a ponytail, necking a coffee and cleaning her teeth. With a final glance back at the doorway to the bedroom, which held so little appeal in the small hours but which now seems to call to her, she grabs her denim jacket with the hoodie tucked inside.

Stopping to light a cigarette, she steps out of her front gate and into the path of a tiny child in a yellow raincoat and wellington boots, careering towards her on a bike with no pedals. The girl's mother, wielding a coffee in one hand and two bags in the other, chases after her, and Ramona can still hear her desperate pleas for the child to slow down as Ramona turns onto Newington Green Road.

Loosening the hood around her jaw so as to let the sun touch her cheeks, Ramona keeps half an eye out for a flash of JJ's familiar red hair as she passes the Alma pub. Placing on her headphones, she turns the iPod to shuffle mode and waits to see what loads. When an Angie Stone song that reminds her of Si comes on, she presses the forward button and keeps skipping until Sleaford Mods kicks in. The name of the band reminds her of her grandfather.

Turning left towards Cindy's estate, Ramona thinks of Roger, an original mod who would no doubt turn in his grave at the punk duo screaming blue murder over austerity and Brexit. She hardly remembers her grandfather, but when she thinks of him she thinks of The Who and The Yardbirds records and the correlating suits neatly stacked in her grandmother, Ai's, modest but immaculate Brighton home – a proper two-up two-down on the housing estate in Moulsecoomb, which the council had offered Ramona's grandparents after they started clearing the inner city slums. Ramona had almost cancelled her promise to look after Sonny once she got the call from Madeleine asking her to work today, but she can't do that to Cindy. If her friend doesn't work, then she can't pay the rent; and with social services already involved, despite the fact that you couldn't hope for a more attentive or loyal mother, the slightest slip could mean Sonny being taken away.

What a system.

Cindy's flat is on the first floor of a four-storey block. Despite this being the same estate she grew up on, Cindy doesn't have a lot of people round here – or anywhere – to call on, besides the girls she works with. She was disowned by her Catholic parents long before Sonny was born. In any case, her father, an Irish parishioner of the same church where Cindy and Ramona now attend meetings, is dead, and her mother moved back to Nigeria a few years ago, leaving Cindy with no family to speak of other than Sonny.

Most of her old friends have moved on – and, from what Ramona infers, there was plenty of love lost during the heroin years between those who remained. Aside from the family in the flat to the left of Cindy's, who have four children of their own but still insist on delivering parcels of food to their neighbours at Eid time, Ramona is the most reliable friend Cindy has.

Inhaling a whiff of skunk floating down from one of the balconies, as she crosses the forecourt of the flats and buzzes for Cindy to let her up, Ramona tells herself it will be fine. It will be better than fine, it will be fun.

* * *

Madeleine sleeps well for once, waking before her alarm. It is almost 8.00 a.m. when she steps out onto Marylebone High Street, into a rare bout of February sunshine, dressed for work in a navy suit, pearl-coloured shirt and square-toed black Acne boots.

Feeling remarkably human, she takes a lungful of biting city air as she passes a handful of schoolgirls in uniform heading in early.

Madeleine always imagines that she hates winter in London, but perhaps she is wrong – or perhaps she has changed.

Opening her emails as she walks, she reads the single, poorly punctuated line from Jonny: waiting at car park Cavendish Square when you need me. Picturing her colleague just a couple of streets away, Madeleine wonders if this is a coded request for coffee and carbs. It is just under three hours until Ingrid Zhatchanova is due for her Botox and whatever-the-Lord-else appointment on Wigmore Street, but Jonny, being the diligent team member that he is, will have got to site early, just in case.

If Madeleine knows him as well as she thinks she does, he will also be mentally preparing for potential conflicts with any actual bonafide traffic wardens in case one should show up and challenge his authority. There hadn't been time to apply for a residential parking permit and their department's relationship with Westminster council is fragile, at best.

If all goes to plan, Jonny will tow the Porsche away to do the necessary, before delivering it to the official tow-ground where it can be collected by Zhatchanova's driver at the stated time. Well, fine, she will pick him up a coffee and a croissant and deliver it personally; the walk from home to the office takes her directly past the Arise Health Clinic, the underground car park less than a five-metre detour.

The second email is from Fionn confirming that the address off the King's Road to which Jonny and Jamal followed Ingrid Zhatchanova the day before, matches the registered address of one of the loyalty cards the wife used in Harrods.

Yes.

Today is going to be a good day, Madeleine tells herself, taking a detour and stopping at the Arôme Bakery and ordering two croissants and a cappuccino.

Imagining Jonny's delighted face when she arrives with this – most likely second or third – breakfast she absentmindedly scrolls to the homepage of *The Times*.

Reading the headline, she stops dead, as though a fist has hit her stomach.

Madeleine stares at the headline for what might have been seconds or minutes before the sound of horns on the road in front of her brings her to.

Another Cabinet reshuffle comes out of the woodwork.

What. The. Fuck.

Scanning down, and then rereading more slowly, she grabs the lamp post just to be sure she isn't still dreaming.

The Prime Minister has announced the results of a reshuffle of some of the Government's key members, including the promotion of former Transport Minister Dominic Farrow to Home Secretary—

Ahead of her, the taxis and cyclists and pedestrians continue their journeys through central London, as though nothing has changed. For a moment, looking around her, she wonders if she is in a parallel universe looking down at herself, marooned on the corner of Upper Wimpole Street.

Fucking Dominic.

When was the last time she had seen her brother? A year ago, picking up Bella for their annual afternoon of aunt-and-niece time. As usual, Madeleine had parked on the street outside when she arrived to collect Dominic and Amber's daughter, choosing not to pull up inside the large gates that separated the reservoir side of Highgate Village from her brother and sister-in-law's enormous detached home.

This way, Madeleine reasoned, she would have had clear reason to slip away if they invited her in. Not that this was a likely prospect. Madeleine inheriting their parents' flat was a source of ongoing bitterness between herself and Dominic – and his wife. This, despite the fact that her brother inherited two foreign properties when their parents died within months of one another, on top of already owning outright the North London colossus he and Amber loved to note they had 'bought for a song' in the nineties. Rather than softening, the bitterness between them seems to have grown sharper over the years, regardless of the fact that they both know that Madeleine intends to leave the apartment to her niece – Dominic's bloody daughter! – when the time comes.

Not bloody, Madeleine reprimands herself. Bella is an angel. How this can be, given her gene pool, is one of life's mysteries, but she is.

Having given it more consideration than is healthy over the intervening decade, Madeleine is pretty sure her brother and sister-in-law only gave up their threatened legal contest to the will without turning to lawyers for fear of what the tabloids might say about their favourite backbench MP acquiring a fourth property. Or perhaps they had totted up the tax implications and simply determined it wasn't worth the effort.

Where is she going with this? Madeleine's head is fuzzy as she searches for the thread of her thoughts.

Dominic, now her boss. That was it.

Silently screaming, she reaches for the lamp post and grips it. How is this happening? And why? Why, of all the politicians in all the fucking land, does it have to be him?

Mind you, with the rate of government reshuffles these days, it's a wonder Madeleine herself hasn't yet been offered the role – or any other poor bastard who happened to be strolling within a mile radius of Parliament at the time.

Her phone beeps with a text from Ramona.

On way.

Grateful for the distraction, Madeleine texts back with a thumbs up and then remembers her Nokia won't recognise the emoji.

A Nokia, in this day and age. Why can't Madeleine get away with being so aloof as to not have a smartphone? She wants a Nokia. Actually, she doesn't. But why doesn't she? When did she get so . . . chained in? It's not as if she has children of her own to worry about, she is supposed to be footloose and fancy-free.

As she steps out onto Oxford Street, a taxi turns without warning and the driver gesticulates as it swerves to avoid her.

Oh, fuck you too. Madeleine steps back onto the pavement.

Steadying herself against the traffic light, still slightly surprised to find it real and not the figment of some vivid nightmare in which she is somehow trapped, she hears her phone ring and pulls it out, noting Rittler's number flashing on the screen. Gathering herself, she waits.

Madeleine has no idea how to play this. Having a tantrum is not her style. But why hadn't her boss given her a heads-up about Dominic's new position? He must have known.

Clearing her throat, she answers, circumspect, waiting to gauge Rittler's tone before saying her piece. 'Hello.'

'Listen, I won't be in for another hour or two. Give me the lowdown. Where's Jonny?'

'I beg your pardon?' Madeleine falters. There is something about

Rittler's voice that isn't right. He never calls them by their proper names. Madeleine is Mads or Mad-for-it and Jonny is Jon-Boy, or – mood dependent – that fat fucker.

'His phone's going to voicemail. Have you spoken to him?'

Madeleine's brain scrambles. Reaching for the top button of her shirt, she opens it. 'Jonny's already at the car park. He's waiting for the signal that the Porsche is ready to tow and then, once the listening device is implanted in the car, we'll be able to hear all the conversations taking place inside.'

Rittler is silent at the other end of the line. None of his usual quips: *Big Brother House, you are now live, please do not swear!*

Listening intently, she tries to make out where he might be. Perhaps he is at HQ, and there is someone else in the room with him, preventing him from mentioning Dominic's promotion. Or perhaps he is, for reasons quite unfathomable, simply unaware that the news has dropped.

Why hadn't he warned her? It is impossible that the man notionally in charge of the subsection of a major police agency would not have been privy to the appointment of a new head of the government department in charge of the whole of law enforcement.

'Is there anything else?' Madeleine asks.

After a moment's silence, Rittler responds. 'No.'

'Right. Well, I'll see you.' Madeleine hangs up and frowns at how odd her boss is being, waiting a beat before calling Amol.

'Everything set?' he asks.

'Yes,' Madeleine replies, crossing the road towards the car park. 'Jonny's already in situ.'

'And what about your girl?'

Madeleine checks her watch automatically. 'She'll be there soon.'

* * *

'Where are you even taking me?' Sonny asks as they take the bus down Balls Pond Road, towards the tube station.

143

'Oxford Circus,' Ramona says, and the boy's eyes widen. 'Really? Can we go Nike Town!'

Nike Town? Jesus. She could swear it was only yesterday that Sonny was begging her to buy him a sticker album. It was probably eighteen months ago, but time seems to warp when kids are involved.

The leap from seven and a half to nine years old is significant. Still, Nike Town? How fucking depressing.

'You're coming to work with me.' Ramona ruffles the boy's hair.

'What work?' He keeps his eyes peeled as they pass the crossing at Essex Road.

'You ask a lot of questions, you know that?'

'My teacher says it's good to ask questions,' Sonny replies.

'Well then, ask your teacher.' Ramona laughs. 'Come, this is our stop.'

Ringing the bell, she stands, putting a hand on the child's shoulder and letting him lead downstairs from the top deck of the bus.

'Where's your skateboard? I wanted a ride on it.'

'Didn't bring it. We'll go to the park later,' Ramona replies, picturing the board in the front room.

'After Nike Town?'

'Maybe. After we've done this one thing.'

'What thing?'

'Do I look like your teacher, Son? Please, no more questions.'

* * *

The tube from Highbury and Islington to Oxford Circus takes less than twenty minutes.

At this time of the morning, the escalators and platform are logjammed with commuters. By the time Ramona and Sonny reach Euston, two stops later, tourists begin to pile on and off the carriage, instantly identifiable by the backpacks and the slight hesitation in their movements. When they reach their final stop, Ramona leads Sonny towards the exit for Regent Street where the steps lead up onto an intersection of main roads.

Weaving expertly between the swarms of people, she keeps her hand on the boy's shoulder as they walk north towards Cavendish Square.

At the first Costa, she stops. If she had more time, they could walk up to the Greggs on Great Portland Street and save themselves a few quid, but that would be an additional twenty minutes – longer with the kid in tow – and she can't afford to be late.

'What are we doing?' Sonny looks back hopefully towards Oxford Street, where in store after store the lights and music are already blazing.

'I just need to wait for someone, near here. We can take a hot chocolate with us,' Ramona replies, as she pushes open the door to the café and steers the boy inside, reaching for the five-pound note she had taken from the dwindling stash in the shoebox under her bed.

'A hot chocolate? I'm nine years old, not five.'

'Jesus, Sonny . . .' Ramona rolls her eyes. 'What d'you want, a beer?'

'I told them to put a shot of rum in it for you,' she says, a minute or two later, handing him the takeaway cup loaded with hot chocolate, cream and marshmallows as they exit by the same door.

'Well, you can't have any, then,' Sonny quips, taking a sip and licking away the residual blob of cream from his upper lip.

Batting him playfully around the back of the head, Ramona laughs. Addict jokes at her expense, from a nine-year-old? A new low.

'Why are you not having anything?' Sonny asks, following her out onto the street.

'Wait for it to cool down, I'm not taking you to A&E again,' Ramona warns, ignoring his question as they cross diagonally through Cavendish Square towards Harley Street. When the memory dawns on him, Sonny starts to giggle. He had been in year one when Ramona got a call from his school asking for her to come and pick him up after he got a Hama bead stuck in the gap between two of his baby teeth.

At first, the two of them giggled as Ramona – the child's emergency

145

contact, for when his mother couldn't be reached – tugged at the plastic bead with a pair of blunt tweezers in the bathroom of her old flat on Camden High Street. It had been a tall order, even if Ramona is less squeamish than most. She had only slept for two hours the night before and had run out of a council meeting in order to collect her friend's son, when the school called.

Gradually her hangover, combined with her growing unease over the threats she had begun to receive in connection with her work on the Somers Town gang, meant the nervous laughter turned to panic. This was set off nicely by the theme tune of *Paw Patrol*, which Sonny was glued to on her computer, and Ramona found herself bundling the child onto the twenty-nine bus to UCLH, holding his hand as they sat in the children's A&E department, feeling more ridiculous with every moment that passed, and every genuine emergency that arrived through the doors.

Pulling herself together, Ramona had summoned Sonny into the hospital bathroom and used her fingers to dislodge the bead before discharging the boy and taking him back to hers via the sweet shop.

Cindy had been endlessly grateful and racked with guilt when she arrived at Ramona's flat above the kebab shop, having belatedly picked up messages from both Ramona and the school. By then, seven-year-old Sonny was back to his old self, drinking orange squash on the sofa. But Cindy's gratitude had turned to something else as she looked around, noting the empty bottles and overflowing ashtrays, which Ramona no longer even noticed.

'Big night?' Cindy had asked.

Not particularly, the look on Ramona's face conveyed, and a penny had dropped for each of them. In that moment, seeing the flat through Cindy's eyes – Sonny enraptured by Marshall and Chase on the sofa next to a discarded bottle of whisky and empty packet of pills – Ramona felt something inside herself shift.

That wasn't her rock bottom, as such, but it was a step towards it.

'So what do we do now?' Sonny asks in the present, interrupting Ramona's thoughts as they take a seat on a park bench, conveniently located overlooking the corner of Harley Street and Wigmore Street, where the Arise Health Clinic stands on the corner.

'We wait,' Ramona replies.

Looking around, Ramona considers the faces of the office workers who huddle outside buildings, for a cigarette or a vape or to simply stand on the pavement and stare at their phones. At moments like this, the slightest part of her wishes she had a smartphone. She would check her emails to see if there had been any response to her email to Madeleine about the estate agency who rents out the Time for Tuition offices. But the truth is, it can wait.

'Can I play Snake on your phone?' Sonny asks from the seat beside her.

Even just the name of the game alone summons the distinctive, penetrating sound – beep, beep, beep – and Ramona inwardly weeps.

'Fine,' she concedes, sparing the child her usual lecture on the power of allowing yourself to get bored. 'You can play once you've finished your drink.'

Picking up a discarded newspaper, Ramona reads the headline.

Home Secretary? Dominic Farrow . . . Wait, isn't that—

Studying the picture, she knows it is him. Part of Ramona's job as a reporter had been to know the names and (ever-changing) roles of Cabinet members, as well as noteworthy back-benchers. Madeleine's brother – who as of today has been made head of the department that oversees law enforcement as well as the security services – included.

As Home Secretary, Dominic Farrow is also now the person reported to by the Secret Investigation Authority, which regulates private investigators like herself, as well as other services within the private security industry, including security guards and – groan – CCTV operators.

Dominic Farrow, though. Ramona makes a face. From their brief interactions, she never liked him. He was a smarmy prick, always way too friendly in press conferences.

Composing a text to Madeleine telling her she is in position in

Cavendish Square, Ramona presses send, wondering if she has heard the news.

Turning back to Sonny, Ramona narrows her gaze as the boy prods with his finger at the whipped cream at the edge of his cup. 'That's disgusting, we've just been on a bus. Do you know what people do with their fingers before they put them all over the railings on buses?'

'If you know this person isn't coming until eleven, then why have we been sitting here for the past hour?' the child responds sulkily, though it's a fair point.

'Because we don't want to miss her.'

'Who is she anyway?'

'None of your business. Now, you remember the plan? When I say so, you turn around and face the other direction and whatever you do, you stay exactly where you are. Do you hear me?'

'Yes.' His voice perks up. 'So how much are you gonna give me?'

'You what?'

'For not telling my mum.'

'Sonny . . .' Ramona is about to remark about there not being anything to keep secret from Cindy, but instead she sighs. 'Fine. A fiver, but look—'

'A fiver?' Sonny kisses his teeth. 'This isn't the nineties, Ebenezer. Tenner.'

'You're a joker.' She laughs. 'Fine, a tenner. But no more of your lip.'

* * *

At ten fifty-nine, on the dot, the gold Porsche pulls up on the pavement opposite.

'Rah—' Sonny's jaw drops at the sight of the car.

'Right, turn around.' Taking off her cap and adjusting her hair to look slightly less dishevelled, Ramona straightens out her denim jacket – worn briefly without the hood – as the car stops on the double yellow lines at the edge of Cavendish Square.

'What you doing all that for?' Sonny asks, confounded at her sudden relatively tidy appearance.

She hushes him. 'Never you mind.'

When Ingrid Zhatchanova's driver steps out, he vaguely surveys the area before walking to the back passenger door to open it for his charge. The wife exits the car. Wearing oversized sunglasses, she carries a quilted black leather handbag with a Chanel insignia so distinctive that even fashion-averse Ramona recognises it.

The woman's driver-slash-minder follows behind as Ingrid walks towards the clinic. From the intelligence she has been provided with, Ramona knows she has around a minute from the time the driver escorts his charge to the door, until he returns. There isn't a lot to be said for bladder cancer, but in this instance it makes for a useful ally for the SCID.

Letting the six-inch long nail she has stashed up her sleeve drop into her palm, Ramona turns to Sonny for the final time. 'Don't move a muscle, understand?'

'Fifteen pounds,' he says, looking at her deadpan.

Little bastard.

'Stay,' she reiterates, crossing the road towards the illegally parked Porsche. Keeping one eye on the door of the plastic surgeon's and the other on the car as she approaches the back wheel, Ramona stays low. Pausing for a second, she lifts the nail and rams it as hard as she can into the back right tyre.

'What are you doing?' At the sound of Sonny's voice, she looks and finds him crossing behind her on the empty road. Pulling her hand away from the wheel, she ushers the child onto the pavement, her cheeks burning.

'What the fuck, Sonny? I told you—'

'Can I help?' When Ramona turns, the driver is standing in front of them, his eyes narrowing in suspicion at the sight of the young woman and child arguing next to his car.

Lost for words, Ramona opens her mouth but it's Sonny's voice she hears.

'Is this yours?'

'Yes,' the man replies simply, in a thick Middle Eastern accent.

'Sick car. You've got a nasty puncture, though – you should be careful, that could be really dangerous,' Sonny says, making a face.

'My son and I were just admiring your car – I hope you don't mind – and he spotted that nail in the tyre. Looks pretty deep,' Ramona cuts in, taking Sonny's hand and squeezing it hard.

Cursing in Arabic, the man studies the hole, the tyre growing slowly flat around it.

'Good luck,' Ramona calls behind her, pulling the child away and disappearing back towards the corner, just as Jonny ascends the ramp in the tow-truck.

* * *

Back at her desk, Madeleine wills herself to be distracted from thoughts of Dominic settling in at his new office along the river on Marsham Street.

She checks her watch. Right now, Jonny is less than a mile away, posing as a council officer intent on towing away Ingrid Zhatchanova's illegally parked Porsche.

It is a fact that in London, you are never more than six feet from a rat or a traffic warden; this part of the city, in particular, is teeming with them. Not that this matters to people like Zhatchanova who treat fines like a down payment for priority parking; what is seventy pounds for an hour's convenience to a billionaire?

Unless your beloved car is actually towed . . . That is likely to incur a blaspheme or two.

'I've had an answer on the flat off Kensington Square,' Fionn calls across to Madeleine from his desk. 'It is owned by Shyrailym Zhatchanova. Her name is on the deeds, looks like she bought it for cash about a year ago.'

Madeleine nods thoughtfully, heading towards Fionn Edwardes' desk, which is as immaculate as one might expect from someone who doesn't seem to function as a human being but rather as a machine.

The fact that Shyrailym's property isn't in her parents' name or that of a shell company, neither proves nor disproves Madeleine's question over whether the daughter is financially independent from her family. If she is, then where did she get the money to pay for a mansion flat in Kensington?

'Thanks, Fionn,' she says. 'Actually, if you have a spare minute, there's something else I need you to look into for me. A man named James Harvey . . .'

By the time she has finished outlining the case of the student escort agency, thirty minutes later, Madeleine's phone pings. She smiles as she opens the text from Jonny.

Got the car. Big man not happy. Our guys doing their job now – see you in a coupla hours.

Yes. Madeleine closes her eyes in relief. Perhaps there will be some reprieve in today, after all.

When her phone alerts her to another message, a little while later, this time it is from her brother.

Assume you've seen the news. Can we chat? Gordon's, 4.30 p.m.?
Or maybe not.

* * *

'Who was that man with the car?'

'No one,' Ramona tells Sonny as they cross at the lights at Oxford Circus towards Nike Town. 'I told you to stay put.'

'You nearly got caught – I saved you!'

Ramona struggles for the right words as they reach the pavement in front of the store Sonny had been so keen to visit. What the hell had she been thinking, taking him along on a job? And was she really now trying to make up for what she had done by giving in and taking him to Nike Town?

'What were you doing, messing with his car? That was dark.'

151

Sonny says, his voice drowned out by grime music as they enter the huge doors that lead inside the building on the corner of Oxford Street and Regent Street.

Fucking hell, it is loud. Ramona feels as if she has been stabbed with a shot of adrenaline in her eyeballs as they move through the atrium. Still, she is grateful for the distraction; there is no way she can be expected to defend herself above this level of noise.

'Where we going then?' she mouths over the music to Sonny, who looks almost as bewildered as she is.

'I dunno,' he shrugs, his eyes lighting up at the spectacle of it all. Leading her past a set of decks, at the base of the escalator, where a DJ is setting up his table, he indicates towards the next level up.

On the first floor, nonchalant young men with complicated hairstyles and pristine tracksuits stand around holding walkie-talkies. Glancing at the price tag of a basic-looking T-shirt as she passes, Ramona stares in amazement.

'Can I look at the football shirts?'

'Sure, wait a sec,' Ramona replies as her phone pings with a response from Madeleine to her message. *Jonny has the car. Good work.*

Smiling to herself, she relaxes a little as she follows the direction of Sonny's pleas.

'They're just there.'

'Fine.' Watching Sonny jog off, she turns back towards the displays.

Bringing a child with her and nearly getting them caught sabotaging Ingrid Zhatchanova's car was definitely not how this morning was supposed to go, but the end result is good and she smiles at the thought of the driver's face as Jonny rocked up to tow away the car.

Guiltily, she thinks of Cindy and what she might say if she knew what Ramona had embroiled her child in, but she pushes the thought away, concentrating instead on finding something for Sonny. Preferably something under five pounds. Like what, a plastic bag? If she had more money, she would spend it; Sonny is worth a splurge, not least given his help today, but she doesn't have the cash upfront.

When she is a bit more flush, she will treat him to whatever football shirt he wants.

Casting her eyes around the rails of clothing, she can't find any sign of anything in children's sizes, or anything that might be suitable . . . Like what? She thinks back for inspiration to Si's football kit, which he lugged into the office three times a week. Si would know what to buy for an Arsenal-mad nine-year-old. For a moment she considers texting her ex to ask his advice. Si was good at this stuff. He had met Sonny a couple of times and they had got on – bonding over their mutual love of the Gunners. Remembering the way her boyfriend had commented afterwards on how much he liked Sonny and how much the kid clearly liked Ramona – on how good she was with him and what a good mum she herself would make one day – Ramona bristles. Of course, she can't text him.

How could the same man for whom she'd had so much respect, be the one who was now, just a year after they split up, not just shagging Holly, but living with her in his flat?

Turning, she decides to go looking for Sonny. She can't afford anything here, but maybe they will find something in the newsagent on the way home. Cindy was always complaining about him demanding the latest issue of *Match of the Day* magazine. She will get him one of those instead.

Three pounds ninety-nine: job done.

The DJ who had been setting up downstairs is beginning his set as Ramona crosses the shop floor. Whoever he is, he has attracted quite a crowd and when Ramona looks down through the escalator towards the ground floor, she sees a gathering of onlookers, holding their phones in the air, cameras on.

For fuck's sake, is it impossible not to be recorded, ever?

Pulling up her hood defiantly, and continuing to glance about for Sonny, she reaches the far side of the store where the football tops are kept. Not finding him, she turns and looks behind the wall of shirts, but he isn't there either. Feeling her heartbeat quicken, she walks a little faster, glancing back the way she came.

No sign.

Doing a figure of eight between the racks in case he is too short to be seen, Ramona calls out, quietly, not wanting to attract the attention of the other shoppers but hoping the child will be alert to the sound of her voice. But there is nothing.

'Sonny?' she tries again, louder this time.

There is a whooping from downstairs as an MC starts rapping over the beats, which is now the sort of drill music she hates, its insistent bass echoing the increasing churning sensation in her stomach. Walking back across the room, Ramona feels the rising panic.

She had assumed the driver hadn't connected them with the damage to the tyre, but—

Suddenly, she thinks of O'Keegan. What if—

Forcing herself to stop, she takes a deep breath. She can't let herself think like this. She has been standing here, right next to the escalator, the whole time. If Sonny had been snatched, Ramona would have seen them pass.

There is no other way up or down. So where is he?

'Excuse me, have you seen a boy?' Grabbing the arm of a passing employee, Ramona hears the panic in her own voice. 'He's black, light-skinned, has brown eyes and short hair. He's about this big—' She places a hand on her own ribcage to indicate his height.

'What's he wearing?' the man replies.

Racking her brains, Ramona struggles to recall. What was he wearing? How can she not remember? And then the image forms: Sonny grinning at her in the doorway of the flat, dressed in immaculate black jeans and a cream-coloured T-shirt with the *Among Us* graphics. Picturing Cindy's face as she stood proudly next to him, Ramona feels bile rise in her stomach.

'Black jeans and a light top with a character—'

Her chest tightens, and an image presents itself – a memory, experienced as though she is outside herself, looking down: her torn, bloodied top hanging off, reflected in the shop window, not yet open for business; the sound of her own heartbeat thundering above the slapping sound of her trainers striking against tarmac.

Her legs buckle slightly.

'Miss, are you alright? Do you need to—'

How had she not thought about the danger she would be putting Sonny in, just by having him with her? The air is thick in her chest. Struggling to breathe, she stops, forcing herself to think rather than feel. If they had grabbed him, they would have taken him down there.

Leaning against the barrier of the escalator, she stares down into the crowd, her eyes flitting from one side to the other.

'I can do a shout-out on the radio. What did you say his name is?'

'His name is Sonny. He's nine years old—'

'Ah, this place is dead. Arsenal is Adidas, innit. I forgot.'

At the sound of his voice, Ramona turns. 'You're—'

The end of her sentence won't form and she reaches out and touches his face with her fingers as if expecting the soft lines of his features to disappear, mirage-like.

He leans back awkwardly, as if concerned she might be having a stroke. 'You OK? Are you crying or something?'

'This is him, yeah?' the attendant interjects, and Ramona nods, too overcome with gratitude to be embarrassed.

Wiping her cheeks with her sleeve, she turns to Sonny, suddenly filling with rage. 'You ran off!'

'I just went to chat to that man . . .' The child points across the room to another employee with a radio, dressed in uniform head to toe in Nike, and now carrying a pair of trainers to a customer. 'I wanted to know why there aren't any Arsenal tops. It's 'cause Arsenal is Adidas. Tottenham is Nike.'

Recovering herself, Ramona closes her eyes and tips her head back, allowing her heart rate to slow. Of course Sonny didn't realise. Why would he worry about being kidnapped in a shop in broad daylight, in central London?

155

'I thought you'd gone,' Ramona utters, so quietly he doesn't hear.

'Can we go now?' Sonny asks. '*We hate Tottenham—*'

He makes a face, chanting the rest of the song under his breath, substituting the swear word for a beep. When he stops, his eyes light up. 'Anyway, you owe me fifteen pounds.'

* * *

Of all the politicians in the land. Of all the *people*.

Madeleine inwardly rages as she marches from the office towards Charing Cross, turning left onto Villiers Street.

At 4.30 p.m., the vaulted cellar of Gordon's Wine Bar is a muted hum of collegiate after-work drinkers and loved-up couples nursing glasses of prosecco and Chablis at tables fashioned from upturned wooden barrels. A roar of laughter emanates from the small gathering of men in suits as Madeleine descends the stone steps that lead into the nineteenth-century cellar.

Ordinarily, Madeleine would wager a bet with herself as to how long her brother will keep her waiting. But today she is too incensed for any deviation from a single taunting question: *Why?*

'Table for one?' the waitress asks.

Madeleine loves it down here, in the windowless cellar of London's oldest wine bar, with its Dickensian candles and dank earthy smell. But today, she feels a rising sense of panic threatening to eclipse the rage that has been flooding through her veins ever since she read the morning news.

Former transport secretary Dominic Farrow promoted to Home Secretary.

How can this be happening?

'Actually, I'll sit outside.' She turns, making her way back out onto the pedestrianised street. The sky is turning dark and it has begun to drizzle. So much for the promising sky this morning.

She takes a seat at one of the larger tables on the far side, under a large awning. When the waitress offers to turn on the heating

156

Madeleine shakes her head, grateful for the cooling rain in the air.

'I'll have a bottle of Coke, with ice and lemon.' The wine menu is tempting but she can't afford to lose her head around her brother.

Wishing she still smoked – anything to take the edge off – she feels herself tighten at the sight of him striding towards her, on his phone. He is ten years older than Madeleine but still has skin like a baby. His narrow head and thinning hair have done little to dent the confidence that was imbued at birth and built on with every year that passed, brick by brick and term by term, at school and then university.

'Your drink—' The waitress arrives at the same moment, setting it down and looking up again as Dominic approaches, clearly recognising the politician whose face has been on the front of all the papers for the past twenty-four hours.

Flustered, the young woman struggles to meet his beaming gaze.

'Champagne, surely?' Dominic says, turning to Madeleine. 'We're celebrating.'

'Are we?' she mutters through gritted teeth. 'I have to go back to the office in a minute. Surely you have work to do, too?'

'This is work, now – meeting my people on the ground. Or haven't you heard?'

Picking up the Coke, Madeleine resists the urge to douse him with it.

'One glass of Pol, then.' Dominic gives the waitress a wink and hands back the menu. 'Thank you so much.'

Waiting for the waitress to leave, Madeleine turns on her brother, unable to hold back any longer. 'Why, Dom?'

'I'm sorry, I don't—' His expression is inscrutable.

'My job is the one thing I have that has nothing to do with you or our parents—'

'Oh come on, grow up, Madeleine.'

'Me grow up? How old are you – sixty? Even now, you can't bear to let me have my own—'

'Sorry, wait. You're saying that you think that I took the job of Home Secretary – that is, one of the most prominent jobs in British politics – just to piss you off?'

'Ab-so-fucking-lutely, I do.'

Taking a large swig of her drink and regretting not having ordered vodka instead, Madeleine feels her cheeks burn despite the damp air.

They are interrupted by the waitress returning with his champagne. 'You're Dominic Farrow, right?' she asks, with a nervous laugh. 'I'm actually studying politics and I just wondered—'

'Piss off,' Madeleine says, more harshly than she intends, and the young woman blanches.

'I am so sorry, another time? This is rather sensitive business,' Dominic interjects, placing a hand apologetically on the woman's forearm.

Waiting for the waitress to back off, Dominic sighs. 'Good God, you really are a narcissist. And that temper—' He tuts. 'Not a good look.'

Realising what a mistake this meeting was, Madeleine stands and pushes back her chair.

'Oh don't leave, Madeleine, for God's sake, you're being incredibly childish.'

'This is my job. If you try to—' She cuts herself off. Anything she says now will sound irrational. Madeleine knows she is over-reacting. But it is impossible to explain. Unless you have a sibling like Dominic, it's impossible to understand. Since childhood, he has taken pleasure in commandeering or sabotaging anything that was rightfully hers – and he had never stopped.

Standing, she fixes her hair.

'Madeleine. Sit down, please, you're making a scene. At least come over soon. Amber would love to see you, and so would Bella.'

The mention of her niece's name stings. Madeleine hasn't even bothered to call her since she got back. Christ, what is wrong with her? Dominic was right, she is a narcissist.

Stepping away from the table, she turns to leave, furious with herself for letting her brother continue to appear to be the rational onc. She isn't sure who she is more angry with: Dominic, for intruding on her life – or with herself for letting him get to her like this.

Christ, why is it so bloody *hot*?

Over her shoulder, Madeleine calls back to the table as she steps into the rain. 'I'll leave you to get the drinks, I imagine you'll expense it.'

* * *

Ramona can tell the moment Cindy opens the door that something is wrong.

'What's going on?' she asks shiftily, as Sonny steps inside and peels off his coat. There is no way, surely, that her friend could already know what she has embroiled her child in.

Pushing down the rising guilt, Ramona watches Cindy as she waits for her son to disappear into the kitchen. When she doesn't call after the boy to remind him to thank Ramona for having him for the day, she knows that whatever is bothering her must be serious. Cindy is relentless about instilling manners in her boy.

'It's JJ.' She scratches her forehead with pale purple gel nails filed into a soft point.

'What about him?'

'I'm sorry, Ro.' Cindy meets her gaze, and nods almost imperceptibly.

'What?' Ramona shakes her head, understanding what somehow doesn't need to be articulated in words. 'No.'

Cindy exhales. 'I thought he was doing good, but—'

JJ? How is this possible?

'*Shit*.' Ramona kicks the base of the door to Cindy's flat and then apologises. As well as being the politest and most moral person Ramona knows, Cindy is also the most house-proud.

'I'm so sorry, Ro. Come in, have a cup of tea.' She stands back to make space in the narrow but immaculate hallway for Ramona to pass inside, but her friend stays put.

'What happened?' she asks, unsure that she wants to hear the answer.

'They found him in the canal.'

Blinking, she tries not to picture it: JJ's bloated body being dredged from the water. Her mind flips and she pictures the granddaughter she had seen him with once, on one of the rare days when he was allowed access. They had been walking together, hand in hand, into the Rio cinema, carrying a bag of sweets. It wasn't that long ago.

JJ? Closing her eyes, the world around her turns dark. How is this possible? JJ, of all people? JJ was doing good. If it wasn't for him, Ramona doesn't know if she would have stayed clean. But things can change quickly, and old habits die hard.

Isn't that what was often said after someone relapsed, or worse? It came out of the blue, that they had seemed fine.

Fuck.

'I only saw him yesterday,' Ramona says, scraping around to make sense of it.

Fleetingly, she pictures the mark on his wrists. It is impossible from the quick glimpse she had to know if they were track marks. But she should have questioned it at the time, just as JJ would have done, if the tables had been turned. Ramona had assumed he was coming to have it out with her about the large Rizla he had seen in her pocket – but what if he had needed her help?

Quietening her thoughts, she takes a breath. There is no point in speculating now. 'Where did they find him?'

'Near Camden Lock.'

Shaking away the image before it forms once more, Ramona reaches for her cigarettes. For once, Cindy doesn't pass comment.

Taking one out of the packet and rolling it between her forefinger and thumb, Ramona reaches for her lighter and takes a step away from the doorstep, sparking up and turning away so that she exhales the smoke over the balcony. Looking out at the main road, Ramona quickly works through what she will say about today's events on Cavendish Square and what she had embroiled her son in, suddenly desperate to be clear of any secrets between herself and her friend.

How could she have done that to Sonny? It wasn't intentional and nothing had actually happened to him, but the fact remains that she had put him in harm's way.

'Cindy, I—' she starts, turning back towards the entrance.

'What's for tea?' Sonny re-emerges in the hall, his attention moving seamlessly from his mother to Ramona, and back again. Letting the cigarette drop over the side of the balcony to the pavement below, Ramona rights herself.

'I'm making soup.' Cindy ruffles the boy's hair, putting on appearances for his sake. 'So what did you two get up to today?'

Sonny meets Ramona's eye and holds it a second before grinning. 'Ramona took me to Nike Town!'

'Nike Town? Goodness . . .' Cindy's parents had been heavily religious, and still she can't bring herself to take the Lord's name in vain. 'And did you say thank you?'

'Thank you, Ro. You're the best.'

A lump forming in her throat, Ramona nods. After the drama of thinking she had lost him, she had forgotten to get him the copy of *Match of the Day* magazine, as intended. She will remember to do that later. 'It's a pleasure, Sonny. We didn't buy anything, by the way. Arsenal is Adidas, apparently.'

'Obviously.' Cindy makes a face for Sonny's benefit and then returns her attention to her friend.

'I'm going to get back,' Ramona says. 'I've got stuff to catch up on.'

'Right. Take it easy, yeah? And Ro—' Cindy nods. 'I'm sorry about JJ. But listen, there's nothing anyone could have done. This weren't your fault. You hear me?'

The breath catches in Ramona's throat, and she nods. 'Right.'

CHAPTER SEVENTEEN

Traffic fumes hit Madeleine as soon as she exits the station. With Highbury at one end, with its specialist cheese shops and multi-million-pound terrace houses overlooking 'The Fields', and the more recently gentrified Archway at the other, it is a marvel that the section of the A1 known as Holloway Road, which connects the two, remains so perfectly urban. Taking out her phone, Madeleine checks the time. 8.55 a.m. – five minutes until she is due to meet Ramona.

Waiting on the pedestrianised area outside the entrance hall, she scrolls through her contacts until she finds HARRIET – LAURA TATCHELL'S OFFICE, and presses call. When Harriet doesn't answer, Madeleine follows up with an email.

When she checks the time again, it is 9.05 a.m. Still no sign of Ramona.

Pinging her a text, she instantly receives a reply: *L8 Srry.*

Really, for a meeting Ramona had requested?

Madeleine sighs and types her reply: *I'm here, will do it myself – meet me in King's Cross. Will message when I'm leaving.*

* * *

The lettings agency stands between a nail bar and a newsagents, a way along the Holloway Road.

'How can I help?' the man behind the desk asks, clearly struck by the presence of the impeccably dressed woman in his office. Madeleine Farrow is not his usual breed of client, and with a quick glance around her, it's not hard to see why.

'I'm from SCID.' She pulls her badge from her pocket, enjoying the ripple of unease that courses over him as he spots the badge. 'Serious Crime Investigations Department,' she adds, for clarification, as if it clarifies anything at all.

'Right, and how can we—'

'You rent out a space in Oldfield Retail Park, which we have reason to believe is linked to unlawful prostitution. Among other things . . .'

The man sits up straighter in his swivel chair. 'Look—'

Holding up a hand by way of placating him, Madeleine goes on: 'Look, you're not in any trouble at the moment, but I am going to need you to give me as much information as you have about the company leasing the property.'

* * *

London at night is a different world from London by day, but the city at dawn is Ramona's own special hinterland.

It doesn't matter what route she takes this morning. She could be anywhere in the city – all she needs is the feeling of the pavement beneath her feet, something to push down against, crushing the swell of thoughts that threaten to overwhelm her; the call of the bottles in every newsagent she passes.

It would be so easy to succumb, to drown out the image of JJ in the oblivion that she knows so well. But she can't do that to JJ, never mind to herself.

Fucking heroin. It's like Cindy said: once you smack you can't go back. Except Cindy had got clean, hadn't she? If nothing else, what happened to JJ is a reminder that we are all susceptible.

Ramona should have known, she should have picked up on the signs. Even now, looking back, she can't fathom it. She really hadn't seen any hint of JJ relapsing. How had it happened so quickly?

Taking the A1 north and passing under suicide bridge, Ramona's mind floods with thoughts. Stopping, she turns back the way she came so that she can admire the view, feeling the rest of the world melt away.

From here, the Shard and St Paul's are visible in the space between the tower blocks at Archway, further down the hill. As she sees the space stretched out, her thoughts fill with memories; the pieces of the jigsaw of her life slotting into place.

When her phone beeps, she starts.

Where are you?

Shit. Tapping out her response, she turns and heads back the way she came.

Instantly, she remembers where she is supposed to be. She doesn't remember when they made the arrangement, but she knows they did.

Maybe she really is losing her mind.

* * *

'You were right, the lease for the offices is made out to an individual, not to any company.' Madeleine fills Ramona in on her update on Time for Tuition as they walk side by side along a series of escalators and walkways towards the platform at King's Cross.

Ramona looks even paler and more drawn than usual, and instantly any resentment Madeleine felt towards her for being late falls away.

'I *knew* it,' she replies as they step onto the eastbound platform, the wind picking up as their train approaches.

'Are you alright?'

Inside the carriage, Madeleine takes a seat, pulling from her handbag a traditional Vietnamese bamboo and paper hand-fan and waving it back and forth in front of her face. Ramona remains standing, keeping her back to the door. She looks more like a teenager than a twenty-eight-year-old woman, Madeleine thinks. Watching her now, she is reminded of a group of stray dogs she spotted on the shore on Ha Long Bay. It was on an overnight stakeout at a beach bar four or so hours away from the capital city, and leading the pack on a stretch of sand, ahead of several bigger dogs, was a terrier; of all the dogs on the beach, Madeleine instantly knew by its manner that, despite its size and appearance, this was the one who wouldn't hesitate before taking off her hand, if necessary.

'You OK? You're very quiet.' Madeleine tries again as they reach their stop.

Ramona adjusts her cap and the hood of the zip-up sweater she always seems to wear with the denim jacket over the top, as they step out onto the platform. They are almost at the end of the line and there is just one other person left in their carriage as they take the exit. 'I would have paid money to see the driver's face when he saw Jonny rock up with the tow-truck,' Ramona says, changing the subject to the events of the previous day, in Cavendish Square.

Madeleine pauses and then smiles as she recounts what has happened, as relayed by Jonny. The bottom line was that the job had been done – the Porsche was now fully mic'ed up, with every word that the wife uttered in the back seat live-streaming to the listeners at SCID.

'Apparently the wife's driver wasn't too happy about it but what could he say? He was illegally parked and the car had a puncture. Even the owners of Porsches need to operate within the law. And of course there was no way any council enforcement officer worth his salt could let him drive it away. It would be more than his job's worth.'

Ramona raises an eyebrow in agreement.

'By the time he arrived at the pick-up destination Jonny had given him, our surveillance guys had gone in and rigged the vehicle up like the Royal Albert Hall. I can't imagine Ingrid Zhatchanova was too pleased at having to get a common taxi home.'

At the barrier at the top of the escalator, Madeleine taps out with her Oyster card and waits as Ramona puts her paper ticket in the slot machine to exit the tube station.

'Don't you ever feel you're fighting a losing battle?' she asks, out of genuine interest, nodding towards the old-style ticket as they continue, side by side. 'No Oyster card or smartphone, only paying in cash . . .'

Ramona shrugs. 'The harder they make it, the more important it is that we resist.'

Somehow, when she says it, it doesn't sound as pretentious or naïve as it should do. And she is right, Madeleine knows this. The convenience of modern technology is a small trade-off for what is being stripped away with every electronic transaction, every new satellite image. Human rights and freedom being stripped away, one by one, along with jobs.

But God, it's also a luxury in this day and age to be able to live without devices in the way Ramona does. Madeleine certainly wouldn't be able to do her job without being constantly connected.

The future is coming, whether or not we embrace it.

As if the universe is leaning in to remind her that yes, she will never not be answerable to someone, her phone pings as they emerge from the tube station. Bracing herself, Madeleine recognises the distinctive beep of her answerphone, knowing only one person who loves the sound of his own voice enough to still leave a voicemail message.

Madeleine. It's Dominic, we need to talk. It's about—

Does he never give up?

Pressing delete before hearing the end of the sentence, Madeleine turns to Ramona with a brisk smile. 'So you met the guy near here?'

'A café on that strip of shops.' Ramona leads the way along a nondescript street that connects the station with the entrance to the motorway, and points towards the dingy row where she had met James Harvey two nights earlier.

'Do you think it's connected to the business?'

'Probably not, but who knows?' Ramona shrugs. 'Maybe. Thanks for coming with me.'

'Like you said, if our guy is there, then we don't want him recognising you and putting the pieces together.'

Madeleine had hardly taken much persuading once Ramona had shared her suspicions about what the website really was: the work of a lone predator. After all, Jonny was right – you can't help everyone, but you can do what you can do. And she feels a duty to help Ramona; not least as she knows how much for her, personally and professionally, rests on this case. Though she would never say so, Madeleine has seen the reports from the initial interview after the assault by O'Keegan's men, and she knows about the attempted rape at the hands of one of his men.

She also knows Ramona chose not to pursue the case, for reasons Madeleine can guess at: she knows too well the secondary trauma that the legal process can create, and how few cases result in the perpetrators being brought to justice.

Sometimes reparation takes unexpected forms.

'So what's the skateboard about, if you don't actually skate?' Madeleine asks, indicating towards Ramona's permanent accessory.

'Useful prop,' Ramona replies, and with that it is plain that the conversation is over.

* * *

'You wait here,' Madeleine instructs, as they approach a low wall bordering the outdoor car park at the entrance to Oldfield Retail Park. 'Stay out of sight.'

Walking on, towards the single door that leads inside the building, Madeleine pauses and considers it. It is depressingly ordinary: the kind of faceless office block that can be found on the edge of cities, the world over; so unremarkable that it would be the perfect place to hide an illegitimate business.

Turning to the list of names of the various companies occupying the space, hanging behind a plastic-fronted panel to the right of the door, she works through them. There is no mention of Time for Tuition. This is not surprising, given that Ramona said herself the company is not listed as such at Companies House but registered under a different name: Experiences Enterprise Ltd.

There is no mention of that either, but three of the slots on the board where office names should be, are empty.

The security guard on the front desk barely glances up as Madeleine enters the building. When he does, he sits a little straighter.

'Hi. I have an appointment on the third floor.' Madeleine smiles brightly, allowing her expression to shift as she gives him a pointed look and then indicates towards the leaflet for a small women's HIV support charity, piled up next to his bunch of keys.

The guard is in his early sixties, with a greying afro. He pauses momentarily, before giving a courteous nod. 'The stairs are on your left.'

Jeez. Madeleine reprimands herself as she makes her way towards the staircase. The HIV clinic: that's where your mind chose to go? But how could the guard argue with that, she reminds herself, the heels of her Acne boots clacking against the cheap metal treads as she heads upstairs.

If the end justifies the means . . .

According to Ramona's contact, the office James Harvey took her to on the night of the physical assessment is on the second floor. Scanning the walls and ceilings, she is reassured to see that there are no obvious cameras. There hadn't been a monitoring screen on the security guard's desk, either. This is, of course, unusual in any type of public space these days, but the absence of recording equipment had been one of the specific points mentioned on the building's listing, along with the promise: *Offering total privacy.*

Madeleine hasn't decided, yet, what she will do when she gets upstairs, but she will work that out when it comes to it. The important thing now is to get through the door.

On the second floor, Madeleine finds as she enters the hallway, there are three doors. The first has the name of an accountancy firm on the outside. The second is for a double-glazing company. The third has no sign outside.

Composing herself, she knocks twice.

* * *

Ramona is sitting on a low wall, keeping watch, when her phone rings.

'What's up?'

'You were right, no one's here.'

Before she can respond, Madeleine continues.

'I've got a plan, are you listening?'

* * *

The security guard is sitting at the desk when Madeleine walks back downstairs. 'I'm sorry to bother you – I just saw from the back window that some kid with a skateboard is graffitiing on the back of the building. I thought you might—'

Lurching forward to lean against the security desk, Madeleine winces, placing a hand on her lower back. With the other hand, she puts her handbag on the counter in front of him and continues to lean up against the side of the desk.

'Sorry, it's my—' Raising her palm again to show that she is fine, Madeleine contracts her mouth into a forced smile. 'I'm fine, it happens all the time. You go! Don't let them get away—'

Dithering slightly, torn between the plight of the smartly dressed woman propped up against the counter and the report of a kid spraying paint on the back of the building, the guard moves swiftly for a man of his age around to the front of the reception area and towards the door.

'Honestly, I'm fine,' she confirms when he pauses at the exit, giving a small nod, before setting off again at surprising speed.

Waiting until he is outside before standing straight, Madeleine removes her handbag and slips the guard's keys from under it. Lingering a moment in case he notices he has left them and decides to turn back, she counts to five and makes a bolt for the stairs. From the determination on the guard's face, she reasons she has a few minutes until he returns.

She takes the steps two at a time, noting how her breath becomes instantly tighter. She had never been particularly fit but this is ridiculous.

'Have Monica look into it . . .' A disembodied voice along the hall catches Madeleine off guard as she arrives at the second floor.

As she passes, a man in a cheap suit comes out of the door to the accountancy firm. Barely noticing her, he continues talking on his phone as he makes his way to the stairs. She waits until she can't hear him any more and then, keeping her hand steady, she tries the various keys.

The first is not a fit, nor is the second. Third time lucky.

Guessing that no more than a minute has passed since the guard went outside, Madeleine pushes open the door and stops stock still.

The room is empty, just as Ramona had said it would be, but for a single desk and chair on one side. On the other, there is a bookshelf with a few disparate titles. Moving towards them, she picks up the only hardback on the shelf and opens it.

And there it is. Dirty motherfucker.

* * *

Ramona glances over her shoulder as she crosses a strip of wasteland towards the motorway, where cars and lorries roar past, and spots the security guard rounding in on her.

She hadn't anticipated that he might actually be able to run – not that Madeleine had given her much time to consider her options. The old boy is wearing loafers, for fuck's sake. And Ramona is what, half his age? It might have helped if she hadn't been smoking a cigarette when he'd started to give chase.

Still, it's good that he keeps up. The closer he gets to catching her, the more likely he is to continue after her, thereby allowing Madeleine more time to do whatever it is she is doing in there.

Approaching the wire fence that is now the only thing between herself and the man chasing her, and the North Circular, Ramona tears off her hooded jumper and denim jacket and throws them over the top. Having created a cushioned area along the edge of the wire fence, over which to climb, she levers herself up with her hands and feet, grateful for the narrow toes of her Converse boots, which lodge perfectly in the criss-cross space between the wires.

She is also grateful for having stashed her skateboard moments after Madeleine rang with her instructions. For once, Ramona doesn't need a weapon. She could hardly hit an old man with it; at any age, he is surely not paid enough to be dealing with this shit. But what can she do?

'You little bastard,' the guard spits, as she pulls herself over the top of the fence, one of the spikes catching on her thigh.

From this vantage point, the fence suddenly seems much higher than it had on the way up – and the motorway on the other side of a low metal barrier much closer. When Ramona lets herself drop, she has to be careful not to fall too far from the fence. If she does, she will land on the barrier itself or, worse still, in the road.

A car beeps its horn as it passes, perhaps in solidarity with the guard, or maybe warning her not to jump. Probably both. Wavering for a moment, Ramona holds onto the fence beneath her jumper and jacket, preparing to lower herself carefully and drag her clothing down with her.

'What are you doing?' the guard calls out, looking worried now. 'Come down, don't be stupid.'

Warily, Ramona considers the distance. One millimetre too far and she will land on the metal barrier between herself and the roar of traffic. But it's not so far down. Breathing in, preparing her position for optimum landing, she adjusts her footing, but at the last second she slips.

The sharpness of the jagged edge of the wire piercing her skin causes her to cry out. Instinctively, she lurches away from the source of the pain, but the sudden movement causes her toe to slip from its hold.

'No!'

She can't be sure if it's his voice or hers that cries out as she tips forwards towards the road.

After that, there is darkness.

* * *

Where is she?

Madeleine is loath to walk back upstairs where there is phone reception to try calling once more, especially given that Ramona's phone is clearly off. The plan was to meet here, not that Ramona is averse to making her own rules.

Her mind moves to the headline in the paper, a couple of days ago: *Bailed drug lord and Interpol's most wanted Michael O'Keegan to be extradited to the UK, awaiting trial.*

On the platform, there is a whistling sound as the wind picks up and Madeleine feels the platform start to gently tremble in expectation of the train rumbling towards them.

Surely they would have bigger fish to fry than Ramona? How many enemies did a man like O'Keegan have? His lawyers would be working night and day to lower his sentence, and would surely have stressed to their client the potential damage that would be caused by any reprisals against the journalist who helped bring him down?

Madeleine hasn't asked if Ramona would be giving evidence at the trial, but she is pretty clear on the answer already. Without her, the police might never have got what they needed.

And O'Keegan, and his men, know it.

Sound gathers as the train arrives with a clatter of wheels and brakes.

Where the hell is she?

* * *

A minute or a split second, Ramona can't say. When she opens her eyes again, the space in front of her bulges. From her position on the pavement, between the concrete ground and the gap under the barrier, she becomes gradually aware of the wheels of cars passing by on the motorway just a couple of metres away. She isn't able to turn and look back to the other side of the fence, but she can hear the guard speaking. To himself or someone else?

There is a moment of blessed nothingness, and then she feels the pain.

Her head.

Lifting a hand to the base of her skull, Ramona touches the lump. Wincing, she pulls her fingers away and sees the blood. Her chest aches as she lies there a moment on the cold pavement, catching her breath. The sensation of her heart pounding forms a wave in her chest, sloshing against the shore on the beach in Brighton.

She closes her eyes, and again the world is peaceful.

'Hey! Do you need an ambulance?'

When she opens them again, she uses her hands to pull herself around and look at the guard. Separated only by a mesh of wire fence, he is close enough that she can hear his wheezing.

The movement of turning to look at him causes her head to pound harder, as if someone has turned up the volume on the world. Around her, Ramona becomes aware of roaring traffic.

Focus, she tells herself. Wake the fuck up.

Using both hands to lever herself up, she uses the wire fence for support.

'Where are you going?' the guard asks. He appears to be searching for a way to get to the other side of the fence to meet her; one that doesn't involve traversing a wall of sorts and dropping down twelve feet onto a concrete path next to a motorway.

He hasn't called an ambulance yet, so she still has time to get away.

'I'm OK,' she says. Holding the back of her head, she turns and limps away from him, following the line of the fence in the direction she hopes will lead back to the tube station.

'I see you around here again, and I'm calling the police,' the guard calls after her, but she hears the concern in his voice.

Sorry, she wants to tell him. You don't deserve to be embroiled in this, but what can she do? He's not the only one.

* * *

Walking helps. Ramona feels the pain in the base of her skull subside a little as she follows the line of the fence, assured that the guard is no longer following her.

Keeping as close to the fence as possible, to avoid the cars and the cameras, Ramona moves as quickly as she can. She doesn't think the old man will call the police but she can't be sure.

In the end, he had seemed as shaken as she was. It was only a bit of graffiti, after all – not worth chasing a young woman into oncoming traffic for. Still, she knows from her reporting days the toll that seemingly innocuous acts like this can have on people who feel besieged by petty crime – yet another hallmark of a society they no longer understand; a place where people no longer respect their neighbours.

In any case, she wants to get out of here; and she wants to know whatever it is that Madeleine had found. Maybe nothing.

A little further along, the fence gives way to a scraggy patch of grass. Beyond it, the same row of shops where Ramona had met James Harvey on Tuesday night, at the café.

What day is it? Thursday. OK, so she's not concussed. But her head . . .

Her legs are sore, too, she realises now. She doesn't remember the landing but she must only have been out cold for a couple of seconds, as the guard would surely either have called someone, or panicked and bolted. Stopping a moment, she closes her eyes and winces at the pain. Opening them again, she moves across the grass.

There is a small alleyway between the end of the fence and whatever area runs behind it, and the beginning of the shops. In her peripheral vision she sees a figure and she turns towards it, her fight or flight mechanism kicking in. If the guard is back, she will have to bolt.

Preparing to run, she watches as he stops ahead of her. Definitely a man, she can tell even in the darkness of the alley, from the height and shape of him. Not her security guard at all, but a younger guy. He is dressed in a hoodie a little like her own, and tracksuit bottoms that seem familiar.

Si?

Taking a step forward, she calls out his name.

At the back of the launderette, a door opens onto the alley and the person who had been facing her turns and runs off in the other direction.

Starting up after him, Ramona feels her head pound again.

'Excuse me,' she says as she stumbles past the worker who has stepped outside to smoke a cigarette. Ahead of her, the man disappears around the corner.

'Si?' she calls again, louder, but he is gone. When she rounds the corner a moment later, she looks left and right but on either side the street is empty.

CHAPTER EIGHTEEN

'Hey.'

At the sound of Ramona's voice, Madeleine swivels on her heels. 'Christ, I was beginning to wonder if he might have called the police. Good God—'

She gasps, taking in Ramona's jacket, torn at the sleeve, her hair even more dishevelled than usual. At the top of her thigh, her jeans are stained with blood.

'What happened?'

'I'm fine, it looks worse than it is,' Ramona says, unconvincingly, wincing as she lifts a hand to the back of her head. 'Might have been a bit awkward if he had called them. What happened?'

Madeleine pauses, about to push further, but then she stops. Instead, she gives a knowing smile as a warm wind picks up on the platform, signalling the imminent arrival of the train.

'Hidden cameras. The bastard is filming them.'

* * *

This time when they step on board the train, Madeleine insists that Ramona sits. 'That cut looks painful, I'm not risking you passing out on me. Also, I'm not shouting the sensitive details of a case across the carriage.'

'So you think it's an actual case now?' Ramona replies, doing as she is told for once.

'Did you ever hear back from the website in response to those emails you sent, pretending to be interested in acting as a sponsor?' Madeleine asks, ignoring the question.

'Nope. I've had nothing in response to that message, but I've had several reminding me to book a follow-up appointment with my "assessor". It makes no sense. Why would they not want more clients?'

'Unless there are no girls and there are no clients,' Madeleine responds, simply. 'There is no agency; there are no rich men willing to pay for time with students. It's all just a con.'

'Fuck. Fucking pervert.' Ramona leans back in her seat, her head resting against the window as the train trundles along its tracks. 'Of course. It's such a complicated ploy, though, just to get laid. I mean, the guy wasn't exactly Kano but he didn't have two heads. So you think he's been making porn and selling it.'

'Maybe.' Madeleine exhales. 'Sex, money, power. It's always one of the three, if not a combination. My guess is, in this instance it's primarily about the power.'

Ramona touches the back of her head. 'Do you think we have enough to arrest him?'

Madeleine considers the evidence. They have a witness, and online testimonials – once they track the women down.

That, together with the fact that the company and VAT numbers are registered to a business entitled Experiences Enterprise Ltd, the director of which, as per the information given at Companies House, is a professor who seems to have no genuine connection to it, makes Madeleine hopeful.

'I can't say anything for definite but based on what we have, we're getting there.' She thinks for a moment. 'I'm not even sure if he is selling the tapes. This doesn't feel like a slick operation, in any sense of the word. It's ambitious, in a way, but . . . One thing I do know for certain is the lengths some men will go to fulfil their perversions – and I would bet that our man is a voyeur.'

Ramona exhales loudly, and then the women sit in silence.

Staring at her own distorted reflection in the window, Madeleine thinks of one of the T-shirts of the women manning the stall outside the Hanoi market as the boys filed out after the raid, the logo reading 'Same Same But Different'.

Madeleine could make her own: 'New country, new day, same old fucking perverts'.

* * *

The Northern Line runs straight from King's Cross to Camden Town, but once she and Madeleine have parted ways, Ramona decides she needs to walk the rest of the way.

She hadn't mentioned the figure she had seen in the alleyway, in their debrief on the train. This was partly because there had been other, more pressing things to discuss; partly because Ramona had worried she was tripping out after the blow to her head.

Yet, the more she thinks back on it, the more she is sure there was someone there. A man – tall, in a tracksuit just like the one Si wears for football training.

Leaving the station, she heads into a pub on the corner, making a beeline for the toilets.

Inside the cubicle, she pulls out a dark wig from her rucksack, adjusting the fringe so that it lies low over her forehead. Once in place, she takes out a compact and a brown lip liner and uses the mirror to draw over the contours of her mouth, adjusting it slightly so that when she is finished her lips appear narrower, more pursed.

Finally, using the same pencil, she lightly draws on a scar, from above her left eyebrow to the bridge of her nose.

With a final glimpse in the handheld mirror, she heads out again, walking north-west and cutting through Coal Drops Yard, the old railway arches that have been transformed into a series of high-end shops glittering with neon signs and sedums hanging in macrame holders.

Around her, shoppers and fashion students from nearby St Martin's sip overpriced coffee outside cafés and on a couple of stone benches overlooking the public fountains.

Pulling her hood around her face so that it obscures her nose and mouth, Ramona imagines the cameras turning, their lenses tightening as she passes.

The disguise is reserved only for special occasions, just like this one. She knows it is impossible in a city like London to avoid being caught on CCTV. She also knows she isn't being paranoid – especially here – in imagining her image could end up in the wrong hands. This area of King's Cross is now private land and, as with so much previously public space, its owners use facial recognition technology to map people's faces in crowds. As a private company, what they do with that information once it is harvested isn't subject to the usual data laws.

Ramona herself had covered the story of how police had secretly handed images of individuals to private land owners, for comparison. Is it such a stretch to imagine that an operation as powerful and far-reaching as Michael O'Keegan's might not persuade owners of private surveillance to feed back any trace of certain individuals to them?

Heading up a set of steps and along the raised walkway framed with flower beds, towards the exit by Camley Street, Ramona crosses the street and heads into a discreet alley, where another set of steps leads into the gardens that surround the Vestry of St Pancras.

She has spent countless hours here, over the years, listening to inquests at the coroner's court that stands to the west. But today, it feels like another world.

At this time of year, the trees are bare and the wind bites as she crosses past the statue at the centre of the park, where an old ash tree grows around a circle of overlapping gravestones.

At the edge of the gardens, where the gate leads out onto Pancras Road, Ramona adjusts her wig and pulls her hoodie as low as it will go, as she emerges at the bottom of Somers Town.

Shivering, she thinks of the figure in the alley. Could it really have been Si, having followed her to the same spot that he had two nights earlier? It was dark and she could barely make out the colour of the tracksuit he had been wearing, let alone the man's features. But she could have sworn it was him. Couldn't she?

Her hands are cold, but she keeps them by her side rather than tucking them into the pouch of her hoodie, as she moves along Crowndale Road, past the working men's college, turning left at Oakley Square where the branches of the trees seem to bear down with the weight of all they have seen.

Pushing against the voice in her head that tells her – screams at her – to run, she cuts through the gardens. On one side of the street, there are huge houses with Roman colonnades. Some gleam with layers of newly applied paint, their window boxes brimming with bright reds and greens, against restored wooden shutters; the facades of others are worn and tired, with bins spilling over from the porch onto the pavement.

Opposite, the estate runs the length of the street.

Heading along the paths that cut through Oakley Square Gardens, Ramona can't help but look up, wondering if she can spot, from this side of the flats, the window belonging to the room she was held in.

Halfway down the square, three older men sit on a bench with their backs to her, sharing a joke in a language she can't understand. A bouquet of flowers and an ageing piece of paper inside a plastic sheath pinned to the railings memorialises a face Ramona doesn't recognise.

As she picks up speed, the space around her grows quiet, apart from the quickening of her own heartbeat, the sound contorted as though she is underwater, looking up; the light on the surface glistening like shattered glass.

A passing ambulance, its blue lights flashing, pierces through the film of consciousness, and she starts. Perhaps she has spoken out loud, as an old lady with a dog – a Yorkshire terrier as weathered as she is – takes a step sideways.

Placing a hand on her chest to remind herself that she is in one piece, Ramona feels the fingers of her other hand curl around the weapon she is carrying, out of some sort of muscle memory – except nothing is there.

Just thin air, so that instead her fingers ball into a fist.

Shit. Her skateboard. In the confusion after she fell, she had failed to go back to where she had stashed it by the car park.

Walking faster as she approaches Mornington Crescent tube station, she keeps her head as low as she can.

What the fuck is she doing here? They say that perpetrators often return to the scene of their crimes, as a way of reliving it, and Ramona recognises that she is acting on a similar impulse. But why – in order to reclaim in some small way the narrative of what happened to her? No doubt that is how she would have been encouraged to frame it in one of those women-mining-their-personal-experience pieces that her editors at *The Times* had so desperately encouraged her to write, in their endless pursuit of personal horror stories dressed up as meaningful 'authentic *lived experience*'.

Ramona's lack of ambition to be anything other than simply a reporter – a columnist, perhaps, or a leader writer – had been met with astonishment by her colleagues and superiors, alike. Didn't she want to find her voice? Her *voice*, she had wondered: what was this, the school choir? When did everyone become so obsessed with telling their own story, their own *truth*? Were male reporters encouraged to deviate from straight reportage, in the same way? Not in her 'lived experience'. The men on the desk were allowed to tell stories in objective, unemotional ways.

As she reaches the bottom of Camden High Street, her heartbeat fluttering against her ribcage, Ramona recalls the daily conference in the editor's office the day she decided to leave journalism. Verity from the Saturday magazine had been selling a piece her team had worked up about personality types crudely based on the Myers-Briggs method, with the working title: *Narcissist or empath: find your inner you.* The peg for the article was a new book by a TikTok psychologist.

'Love, love, *love*! So relatable,' Maya, the deputy editor, had chirruped, and Ramona felt her own soul leave her body.

'Hasn't it been proven that the Myers-Briggs test is unscientific and ultimately lacks any rigour?' Ramona had asked, ignoring the many other problems with the pitch, and Verity had looked at her as though she had hurled dog shit across the table.

'We're in the business of selling papers,' Maya retorted, and Ramona genuinely wondered, Weren't they in the business of telling the truth?

It isn't as though, for her, becoming a journalist was an act of righteousness. She hadn't chosen to spend six years as a local reporter before moving to one of the biggest broadsheets in the UK in order to right the wrongs of the world, or to speak for the disaffected. She isn't naïve enough to believe she would ever hold that much power.

Ramona had been chasing the escapism that comes with immersing herself in other people's stories, and she had wanted adventure. But she was also driven towards journalism because she wants answers.

Perhaps in a way, by coming back to where it happened, Ramona is confronting her fears. But it is also the most convenient route from King's Cross to the place where she would most likely find Si – or learn where he might be.

Passing by her old flat, above the kebab shop on Camden High Street, and Belushi's and the World's End, she feels a pang of nostalgia. For so long, the small perimeter of Camden Town had been her world.

In the end, it isn't even the things she knew she valued that she misses. Rather, it is the shopkeepers who know her preferred brand of drink, and would give her credit despite their policy not to, despite not even knowing her name. It is the binmen she nodded to every morning for so long; the old man she walked home from the pub when he'd had too much and couldn't manage the stairs to his flat.

When you work a patch as a local reporter, you get to know every inch of it. Now, Ramona is an outsider. But much as there are things she misses, she enjoys being on the periphery of society, as invisible as it is possible to be in this day and age. In many ways, she is a ghost.

Slipping into McDonald's and heading for the bathroom, she removes her disguise and places the wig back in her bag, wiping the scar with a wet tissue.

Catching a glimpse of herself in the mirror, she notes the blood-stain on her thigh, from where the wire had snagged her jeans, and the flesh beneath. Well, there's not much she can do about that now.

* * *

The exterior of the offices of *Camden News* is exactly as it had been the day she left, the worn paintwork peeling at the edges.

How long had it been – fourteen months? After six years – a large part of her adult life – this had come to feel like a second home, like the dysfunctional, bustling family she never had. Looking at it now, she feels strangely detached from the place, as though it is someone else whose life she is remembering.

In a way, she had been a different person, then.

It is the first time she has been back since she left and Moira, the secretary, buzzes her through from reception with a wink and only the slightest hint of surprise, while deftly handling a nuisance caller with her characteristically no-nonsense manner.

Ramona's old news editor, Ben, looks perplexed to see her, standing and putting on his glasses as though a better clarity of vision might reveal someone else entirely.

'Hi—'

He greets her by her old name. At the sound, a couple of faces she recognises – and a couple more she doesn't – look up from their desks.

'It's good to see you.' Walking around to greet her, he stops short of a hug – thank God – and instead offers an awkward tap on the arm. 'You should have said you were coming by . . .'

'I was just passing,' Ramona lies, feeling a tug of envy as she looks around the bulging desks, the stacks of well-thumbed newspapers, press releases and court documents.

'Is Si here?' she asks, as casually as she can muster. The lump on the back of her head aches and she raises a hand, absentmindedly, to soothe it.

'Are you alright? You look—' Ben struggles to find the right word.

'I just need to speak to Simon.'

'He's in court. Has been all morning.'

'Which one?'

'Look—'

'It doesn't matter,' Ramona says.

'Do you want a cup of tea?'

'I've got stuff to do, I was just passing.'

'Right, well—' Ben looks almost relieved. She understands. In all the time they worked together, she can't remember once speaking about anything more personal than a council meeting. And without the job to talk about, Ben will have been alarmed at the prospect of his old employee popping in for a chat; as much as she would be if the tables were turned.

'Good to see you,' she says, turning back towards the door, giving a small salute to the art director, Giovanni, who waves from his desk, his phone pinned to his ear.

Ben calls after her. 'Hey, your head – I think it's bleeding.'

CHAPTER NINETEEN

There is a second message from Dominic as Madeleine emerges at Charing Cross station, having parted ways with Ramona at King's Cross.

She doesn't have time to listen to it now, and presses delete as his voicemail kicks in. She is late as it is – not that anyone appears to have noticed.

Turning onto John Adam Street, Madeleine feels a surge of adrenaline as she buzzes herself into the curved mews townhouse. SCID Row is precisely the kind of home she had envisaged herself living in when she was growing up, rather than the reality, moving from compound to compound on various continents. The SCID is its own dysfunctional family: no one who works there ever chose each other, and probably never would, but there is a strange sense of affinity simply because they're on the same team. And right now, Madeleine is as furious as a child. The feeling of rage is eclipsed, as she opens the door and is met by a tangible energy she recognises as one that comes with a breakthrough of one form or another.

'What's going on?' Madeleine asks as she steps inside.

'We've caught a fish.' Jonny looks up from Fionn's desk, where he and Amol are huddled.

'I beg your pardon?' Madeleine replies, slipping off her coat.

'The line in the car . . .' Amol clarifies. 'Ingrid Zhatchanova has made an appointment to have a selection of jewellery repaired.'

She moves over to where the men are standing.

'A diamond necklace, earrings, a few bracelets . . .' Jonny's eyes glisten as he talks. 'She detailed the whole lot over the phone – very generous of her to be so indiscreet. And our colleague, Mr Calculator over here, did the sums.' He motions towards Fionn. 'Reckons we're looking at upwards of fifty thousand pounds' worth.'

Madeleine straightens. 'The lower limit of value for seizure.'

'We can use the Criminal Finance Act to seize the jewellery,' Amol says. 'We'll need a separate search warrant to enter the premises in the first place. Then we will need to go in front of a magistrate within forty-eight hours to apply to keep the jewellery. After that, we will have to reapply to keep it for a further six months until application for confiscation is approved.'

'How easy will that be?'

Amol shrugs.

'There's another thing . . .' Jonny says. 'Fionn, you can do the honours.'

Fionn makes a face, clearly displeased to be embroiled in such amateur dramatics, and then rallies. 'It is about the property Jonny and Amol followed Mrs Zhatchanova to, in Hampstead – the address that is the same as one linked to one of her Harrods loyalty cards. We've looked into it and the Land Registry shows the property is owned by a shell company, registered in the Virgin Islands. Here, the date of purchase is listed . . .'

Madeleine looks at the date on Fionn's screen, as indicated. 'Very nice.'

'Open-source checks on the street just prior to the property being purchased have picked up the estate agency's advert . . . It was on for ten million pounds,' Fionn says.

'Great. Let's put a Production Order on the estate agent, for details of the correspondence with the buyer, and work out from there if it's Amir or Ingrid Zhatchanov. Great work – thank you, gentlemen.'

Turning to Jonny, Madeleine continues. 'We'll need an independent to sign off on the production orders for the estate agent—'

'Rittler's looking into that now,' Jonny replies.

'He's here?' Madeleine asks, feeling herself tense.

'Is who here?' Rittler's voice beams from the doorway. When Madeleine turns, his expression is unreadable.

She feels a ripple of unease at the change in his demeanour. She hasn't so much as seen Rittler since he accosted her at the bar on her birthday, three days earlier, and now it is as though she is faced with a different person entirely.

'Nice of you to join us,' Madeleine says, her voice tight. 'Been busy catching up with your new boss?'

'You've heard the news, then?' he replies, after a beat, not meeting her eye.

So he had known about her brother. Of course he had, how could she ever doubt it? 'Why didn't you tell me?'

'I wasn't given much notice.' His tone is dismissive and Madeleine feels her jaw clench.

'You should have told me.'

'I didn't have a chance. Anyway, who the head of MoJ is doesn't make a difference to us, day to day. We still answer to HQ. Your brother has always been in politics, it can't have come as too much of a shock.'

'Transport minister! Yes. Home fucking Secretary? Come on, Paul, don't give me that shit.'

He flinches. To Rittler, being addressed by his first name is a grave show of disrespect.

The energy between them is febrile. Jonny and Amol barely move, possibly for fear that they might become a target if they do.

'You should have told me,' Madeleine manages, finally. When her phone pings with the sound of a WhatsApp message, she whips it out furiously and sees Dominic's name and a single sentence. *You missed Bella's birthday.*

Staring at her phone screen on the pavement outside SCID Row, Madeleine takes a deep breath and swears at full volume.

Fuck fuck fuck fuck!

The room falls into total silence, as though even the traffic through the window has ground to a halt. Staring hopelessly at her phone screen, Madeleine resists the urge to smash it on the floor. It was Bella's thirteenth birthday, the same day as her own fiftieth – and Madeleine had forgotten.

Leaning back against the wall of the building, she closes her eyes. She hadn't even been away this year. Madeleine was here, and still she had forgotten.

How? Madeleine had been planning to do something extra special for her thirteenth, after last year's debacle.

They had even discussed it, briefly. Madeleine turning half a century the same day that Bella became a teenager had been the perfect excuse to deviate from their usual afternoon tea. Despite everything that had passed between herself and Dominic, Madeleine had never forgotten his daughter's birthday. It is her one concession to being the kind of aunt she wishes to be. Every year, whenever she has been in England – or sometime close to it, if she had been away for work on the actual date itself – Madeleine had taken Bella for afternoon tea at the Savoy. It was their private joint birthday celebration, and one of the highlights of both their calendars.

Why hadn't her own birthday triggered a memory of Bella's? Usually, the two events are conjoined in her head. When Madeleine originally heard that Dominic's wife, Amber, had given birth on Madeleine's birthday she had hooted with appalled laughter. Of course, her brother claimed for himself the one date that was Madeleine's own: her birthday. But the moment she met newborn Bella, any resentment for the child had instantly fallen away. It was hours before Madeleine was due to fly out to Krakow for a stint there, back when she was in the trafficking unit, and the moment she saw her niece, swaddled in a pale pink blanket at the private hospital on Great Portland Street, she had fallen hopelessly in love.

Since then, their connection has only strengthened, even if their time together is not always as much as it should be. For all their many faults, Dominic and Amber have never prevented Madeleine having a relationship with her niece. If anything, they encouraged it. But Madeleine is always so busy with her job and, if she's honest, a little self-absorbed. Much as she adores Bella – truly, adores her – she had barely found time during her brief windows in the country to hang around in playgrounds or in the fresh hell that is soft-play – as she discovered on one horrifying and never to be repeated occasion.

Nevertheless, small children are easy – or at least Bella had been. Their afternoons together, though rare, were a delight. Madeleine still smiles when she pictures Bella looking like a doll in a Rachel Riley dress or, later, in a Boden two-piece, wide-eyed as she worked her way diligently through a silver tower of triangular sandwiches and perfect little cakes. There was never any hesitation or awkwardness despite the lapse of time. Madeleine was there and then she wasn't; this was simply a fact Bella had come to accept. Perhaps she was well practised, given the carousel of au pairs.

Over the past years, though, Madeleine has increasingly been doing stints abroad and the gaps between their meetings have grown longer, and the changes in Bella in the intervening months more obvious. Never more so than last year, when – having turned twelve and recently graduated from the arm-and-a-leg-job prep to a prestigious girls' secondary school, well-known for instilling academic excellence in its pupils along with a generous dash of self-hatred – Madeleine arrived to collect Bella and found her niece a shadow of the girl she had been.

Over tea, she had barely touched a thing, cutting a tiny sandwich into pieces and pushing it around her plate. Despite Madeleine's best attempts to encourage her niece to open up about the problems that skited over the surface of the girl's eyes as they sat opposite one another in that grand tea room under the high glassed dome, too much time had elapsed. She had a tummy ache, Bella said, not meeting Madeleine's eye when she questioned why she wasn't touching her food.

What had Madeleine expected, that after months of no contact her niece would suddenly open up? That she, the bi-annual aunt, would be the one to fix her, in an hour-long interval over an incongruous selection of finger foods? Suddenly the whole thing felt farcical.

In the end they had left early, walking arm in arm in companionable but tainted silence through the streets of London, the evening lights reflected in the puddles.

Amber was defensive when Madeleine tentatively mentioned the lack of eating to her sister-in-law, as she dropped Bella off that evening, waving goodbye from the door as she watched her niece heading up the wide staircase towards her bedroom to finish her homework.

'Maybe she doesn't want to spend the afternoon gorging on carbs. Maybe if you made an effort to see her more regularly. Perhaps if you asked her what *she* wanted to do—'

Even Amber had known to stop there, presumably seeing the rush of hurt that must have spread over Madeleine's face. This wasn't something she foisted on her niece. This had been their tradition, hadn't it? Every year since Bella was five years old.

Every year, except this one – because Madeleine had forgotten.

Fuck.

She can't call her niece now: Bella will still be at school.

Madeleine dials her brother's number instead. He answers after four rings.

'Madeleine. Good of you to call me back.'

'Why didn't you say something?'

There is a pause. In the background Madeleine hears laughter growing distant and imagines him at his offices in Westminster, winking amiably at one of his colleagues as he makes his way somewhere more private.

'I'm sorry, I missed that.'

He speaks with an infuriating calm; that practised, condescending air he had perfected over years in the Cabinet.

'Why didn't you say anything about Bella's birthday yesterday, when we were at Gordon's?'

'I thought you might have texted her already. How was I to know that you'd forgotten?' He snorts. 'Besides, as I remember it, you ran off before I could so much as take a sip of my drink.'

A wave of afternoon theatregoers head past on their way to the Adelphi and Madeleine inhales deeply in an effort to control the flood of rage.

'We're having a party at the house. I realise you wouldn't ordinarily bother coming, but given that she is turning thirteen, and—' Dominic continues, casually, affecting an awkward laugh. 'Given you forgot the actual event . . .'

A bus hisses loudly on the main road and Madeleine again resists the urge to throw her phone onto the pavement.

'Bella has asked if you will come. If you're free tomorrow evening, then an invitation will follow, but I wanted to be sure that you could be relied upon to make it before sending it out. We would hate her to be disappointed again.'

Relied upon? Tomorrow evening? The bastard. Bastard bastarding *fuck*.

Silently screaming, Madeleine leans back against the wall of John Adam Street.

'Madeleine?'

Righting herself, she walks away from the office towards the Theodore Bullfrog. How can she say no? She can't, and her prick of a brother knows it.

'Send the invitation,' she tells him, and without another word, hangs up, grappling briefly with the weight of the pub door as she throws her weight behind it, and marches towards the bar.

The barman seems to sense the rage coming off her and takes a defensive stance.

'Whisky, large. Please,' she says, waiting for the drink, downing the glass in one and tapping her card against the payment machine in a single movement before turning around and walking back towards the office.

* * *

Through the window of her flat, Ramona watches the sky turn from grey to black. She had been tempted to head straight to Si's place and confront him directly after leaving *Camden News*, but she knows that tonight, as is usual every Thursday, he will head straight from court to Market Road pitches, and Ramona doesn't want to confront him there. She wants to be away from Camden, away from memories of her old life.

Going back there today had been a mistake. More than that, it had been reckless.

In her flat in Hackney, she feels as if she is in another universe to the one she revisited this afternoon. In reality, her new home is less than a twenty-minute drive away from her old one, but London is a series of villages. You can go your whole life without bumping into someone who lives just down the road. And then, when you least expect them, there they are . . .

She glances behind out of habit. Without a name or a route to Ramona Chang, Michael O'Keegan's men are hardly likely to track her down. They will assume, she imagines, that she has moved south of the river, which might as well be another country – or to another city altogether. In Hackney, she is hiding in plain sight.

Why hadn't she gone further afield? She had considered it, of course, but where would she go? This way, she is somewhere she vaguely knows, with enough contacts within running distance to stay afloat. Besides, O'Keegan has plenty of enemies. She imagines that on the list of people he wants to get back at, she is low down in the pecking order. Surely? In many ways, the move was about starting again, for her own sake.

If one thing is to change then everything must change.

Those had been JJ's words, interpreting her reasons for moving after breaking up with Si and handing in her notice at the paper, after she stopped drinking. Of course, she hadn't mentioned O'Keegan or the change of name, or which paper she had worked for. He knows that she is a private investigator now. *Knew.* Past tense.

Thrumming her fingertips against the countertop where she is perched in her kitchen, her legs tucked up beneath her, Ramona notes that the pain at the back of her head has faded from a light throbbing to a faint hum.

Returning her thoughts to earlier in the day, she considers calling Ottilie. Presumably, her client would be interested to learn that the official Time for Tuition headquarters was rigged with at least three sets of insultingly basic hidden cameras. One, it had been explained, implanted in the spine of a fake book; another crudely lodged in a single piece of generic ready-to-buy 'art' on the wall (in the nostril of a photo of a cow taken with a fish-eye lens). The third, in a lamp.

But she doesn't want to worry the girl, or get her hopes up, prematurely. Madeleine hadn't been certain that they could bring charges of voyeurism, or anything else.

The site has been taken down – one of the IT nerds at SCID had reported it to Madeleine. Perhaps this means that James Harvey, whoever he really is, knows he is being traced and is attempting to go to ground. Or perhaps he dropped dead and his server payment failed.

Either way, they can still trace the owner and check for any connection to tapes being sold for porn. It might just take longer than originally hoped.

Ramona shivers, recalling the young woman's haunted expression, the evening they met.

Please, she pleads to a God she doesn't believe in – don't let him have distributed images of the girl. Spare her that violation, at least.

Outside, there is a wave of laughter as a crowd passes by, and then the room falls quiet again. In the silence, the occasional sound of the television from the flat below is vaguely comforting. For want of anything else to do, Ramona lights a cigarette and finds it gives her no pleasure, but she persists with it nevertheless.

When her mind inevitably moves to JJ, she shoves the thought away, not trusting herself to cope with this right now. She needs to focus on things she can change, not tragedies over which she can have no effect.

The discarded wig on the kitchen counter, where she left it after returning from Camden, catches her eye, and she exhales.

Does she believe Ben, that Si was in court all afternoon? She believes that Ben thinks it's true. Ramona's old boss would never lie to her. Certainly not in order to hide the fact that one of his reporters was on the other side of London, stalking his former employee.

Si could have lied to him about where he was going, although this seems unlikely. While it isn't ideal that a news editor doesn't know which court one of his reporters is in, it is hardly suspicious. For a local rag, the remit of their Camden borough is far-ranging, with related cases tried in a number of magistrates' and crown courts nearby. Ben trusts Si implicitly, just as he had trusted Ramona, and he was a good delegator, happy to leave his employees to get on with their jobs. So good that he hadn't known how far Ramona had got herself with the Somers Town lot until she was in too deep.

Had he blamed himself, in part, for what happened? He definitely had an air of guilt about him this afternoon. Or maybe he is just even more awkward than Ramona remembers.

Frustrated by the lack of answers, Ramona strains to pull out any details from the memory of the man in the alleyway. Was she simply seeing what she had wanted, or expected, to see?

Why would she want Si to be following her?

Out of nowhere, she thinks of her ex and his new girlfriend locked in a kiss, and bites her lip so hard she winces in pain. The throbbing in her head has only slightly receded. How long has it been since she last had sex? The thought occurs to her as an abstract question rather than one born of any real desire. There had been a couple of guys since her and Si; desperate, demoralising encounters not to be repeated.

Where would she meet anyone worth meeting? Other than the NA, and work, she doesn't go anywhere or do anything.

She imagines the Tinder profile she might make for herself, if anyone still uses Tinder: *Scruffy young woman with trust issues, a predilection for exposing violent crime, and a lingering addiction problem seeks attractive, unneedy male who loves her unconditionally, and knows when to fuck off and leave her alone.*

Catching her own reflection in the dirty kitchen window, she looks beyond to the spire piercing the soft grey of the sky, as night falls.

Why does it sting so much? She was the one who had ended their relationship. Yet it hurts that Si, for all his wild proclamations of love, has moved on so easily. And to Holly, of all people? Meek, pious Holly.

Forcing herself to think of something else, Ramona glances at the clock and sees it is already 8.00 p.m. In twelve or so hours she can legitimately follow up with Madeleine on the case.

For now, she rolls a spliff. As she smokes, she feels a wave of exhaustion pull at her. Leaving the roach in the ashtray on the kitchen table, she kicks off her jeans and moves to the bedroom where she lies on the unmade bed, and feels herself falling into a deep, reviving sleep.

CHAPTER TWENTY

The morning of Bella's party, Madeleine casts hopelessly through her wardrobe, wishing she had so much as a dress code to work from. The invitation, for all Dominic's pomp and ceremony in his initial call, was merely a message via Paperless Post, arriving with the address and time. As if she, as well as half the country, doesn't already know the location of the house Amber had insisted on showcasing in a sycophantic feature in *World of Interiors*, after she announced her new career as an interior designer.

Informal dress, surely? It is a thirteen-year-old's birthday party, not a Cabinet get-together.

But Madeleine needs to get this right; she doesn't want to turn up looking like she's just left the office. Neither does she want to look like she's off to a swingers' do, she reasons, pulling out the foiled silver dress with a plunged neckline that, like so much in here, she can't remember ever having worn. Or having bought, for that matter.

What does she even wear for socialising in London, any more? Madeleine is so used to going straight out from the office, gliding from her desk to the bar in a variation of the well-cut Fortela or Max Mara suit that has become her staple. Not that she's knocking it . . .

What would she wear if she was going undercover as the fun but newly reliable aunt at a teenager's birthday? She shudders, knowing not what she would wear but that she would certainly give herself, by that description, a wide berth. Sighing, she lifts out an oversized black satin Jil Sander shirt-dress and lays it out on the bed to take to the dry-cleaner on her way into the office.

Oh God, she really doesn't want to do this.

Pipe down. She's doing it for Bella, she reminds herself. Two hours in and out and she can be home and dry. How hard can it be?

* * *

Fionn Edwardes is the only person in the office when Madeleine arrives, having dropped her outfit at the dry-cleaner's on her way in.

Hearing the phone ring on Fionn's desk, she settles herself in her chair, reaching into the drawer for one of her Godiva chocolates, as quietly as she can – the better to eavesdrop – and finds the box empty.

By the time she looks up again, Fionn has finished his call. She hadn't heard him utter a single word. Christ, had he been using Morse code?

'It's been authorised,' he says, as though reading her mind. His voice is its usual monotone and, for a moment, it is impossible to know whether he is delivering good or bad news.

'Sorry?'

'The Unexplained Wealth Order. They're seizing the jewellery today.'

'Today?'

Madeleine blinks, irritably. Why hadn't she been informed? It is a redundant question; this is Fionn's role, not hers. And she was informed, just now, by Fionn himself.

Still, something doesn't feel right. Why is she suddenly always the last to know?

'Was that Rittler?'

'No,' Fionn responds, monosyllabic again.

Focusing on the thought of Ingrid Zhatchanova's face when she learns her jewellery has been seized and will be held by the police until she can prove how she came by the funds she used to purchase it, Madeleine feels her irritation subside.

'OK,' she nods. 'When are they picking it up?'

'This afternoon.'

Lifting the receiver of the office phone, she calls her colleague in human trafficking over in Vauxhall, leaving a message when there is no answer.

'Tim, it's Madeleine. I'm at the office – could you give me a call when you have a moment? I have a question I need to pick your brain on.'

She hesitates before walking over to Fionn Edwardes. Can she trust him to keep this to himself? She doesn't have much choice.

'That other thing I mentioned to you before . . . the website . . . Have you found anything?'

'Not yet,' Fionn replies, but she senses from the slightest inflection that there is something he is not telling her.

Pausing, she nods. 'Right. Well, you'll keep me posted?'

His response is a wordless clacking of his keyboard.

Brilliant. Great talking to you, too.

A message pings on Madeleine's phone and she smiles and stands, reaching for her coat.

* * *

After the first proper night's sleep in as long as she can remember, Ramona awakes feeling almost revived. If the type of uninterrupted rest she experienced last night is the consequence of a blow to the head, then maybe she should take one more often.

The sensation of being well-slept is so peculiar that she is almost panicky with hyper-alertness as she listens to the usual morning goings-on from the street below. Logging onto her PI email, Reddit and Twitter, in turn, she finds another enquiry about a suspected case of adultery and a separate message from a disgruntled man wanting someone to set up a camera to capture a neighbour he suspects is dumping their rubbish in his bins.

She likes to think this is how Jack Palladino started out.

Picking up her coat, iPod, cash, phone and keys and placing them in her rucksack, she puts on her cap and coat and heads for the door.

This could be a long day.

* * *

The sky rolls grey above the River Thames. Madeleine spots the woman she is due to meet, already seated on the bench overlooking the water. She wears a pink jacket and a scarf pulled protectively around her neck.

Looking up at Madeleine's approach, the woman attempts a smile.

'Harriet, thank you so much for seeing me,' Madeleine says, taking a seat beside her and leaning in to kiss the woman on the cheek.

An almost maternal figure, Harriet had worked for Laura Tatchell ever since she became an MP, and Madeleine has never seen her before without Laura by her side. The absence of their mutual friend and colleague haunts the space between them.

'Of course, I was happy to hear from you,' Harriet replies. As Laura's devoted and equally straight-talking assistant, if something concerned Laura, then it had always concerned Harriet too, and apparently that hadn't changed, even in death.

'How are the girls?' Madeleine asks, remembering their glassy eyes at the funeral, where Harriet had bolstered them on one side, their father on the other.

She shakes her head. 'They're strong, like their mother. But . . .' Her voice drifts off. She doesn't need to finish the sentence. Their mother had been killed, in cold blood, and no one has yet been held accountable.

'Listen, I know how busy you are and I don't want to hold you up, but I wondered if you could tell me if you recognise this woman?' Madeleine hands Harriet a printout of Shyrailym's photograph.

'Shyrailym?' Harriet smiles. 'Of course.'

Madeleine sits a little more forward in her seat.

'Shyrailym and Laura met via a charity they both supported. Originally, Shyrailym acted as a translator for the women Laura represented.' After a moment's consideration, she continues. 'Come to think of it, I haven't seen her for a while. Perhaps she no longer works for the charity. I don't know . . .' Harriet looks down at her lap, her tone turning tremulous. 'All of this line of questioning. The police . . . I—'

'You're what?' Madeleine repeats, once it's clear she doesn't plan to continue. 'Harriet, what were you going to say?'

Shaking her head, she lifts her bag from her side and stands. 'I'm sorry, I have to go.'

'Harriet?'

'I'm sorry,' she says again, and moves hurriedly away, disappearing into the city, the crowds closing around her once more, as though she was never there.

* * *

Ramona pulls the wig low as she retraces her steps from the tube station on the Piccadilly Line to Oldfield House Retail Park.

Keeping track of every sound as she walks, she doesn't wear her headphones. Instead, she remains tuned into the quiet roar of the cars on the motorway, a few streets away; the in-and-out of her own breath as she glances left and right for any sign of a tail.

The skateboard is exactly where she left it, and she grips it to herself as though reunited with an old friend. Crouching down where she is, she settles in, her gaze fixed on the door of Oldfield House Retail Park, and prepares to wait.

CHAPTER TWENTY-ONE

The matter of what to wear to a thirteen-year-old's birthday party is problematic – but the question of what to *buy* a teenager is infinitely more so.

When Madeleine pictured herself arriving at the party, at the time of her RSVP to Dominic, which she followed up with a gushing text message to her niece – accompanied by far too many heart emojis, she realised only in hindsight – Madeleine had pictured herself carrying a beautifully wrapped box with a red velvet bow. Over the past twenty-four hours, though, she has failed to give any thought as to what that present might be.

Last year, Bella had been given an iPhone by her parents – a gift that Madeleine wholeheartedly embraced after a brief moment of disapproval, once she recognised it as a means to communicate with her niece without having to talk to the girl's parents. Following a blunt lecture on the dangers of online predators, the afternoon of their subsequent annual tea at the Savoy – the tea which this year had completely fallen from Madeleine's mind – she and Bella had spent a fortune in the Apple shop, picking out a baby-pink shatter-proof case and AirPods she could wear when running.

It wasn't until later that Madeleine realised that her niece's newfound interest in exercise was part of an ongoing effort to shed non-existent weight – and that the phone itself would become an instrument of self-torture, with Bella joining slimming apps and hero-worshipping all manner of toxic influencers masquerading as wellness experts.

Subsequently, the politics of present-buying has escalated into a new realm. This year, every potential choice is laced with uncertainty.

At 5.00 p.m. on a Friday afternoon, central London is a hubbub of after-work drinkers and shoppers. The New Year sales have long since finished and spring-inspired displays have started to grace shop windows, incongruous against the grey backdrop of what the papers are describing as another eternal winter. Not that Madeleine would know about that, ping-ponging as she does between different weather patterns in far-flung corners of the world.

Liberty is almost a halfway mark between the office and home; as she pulls open its heavy doors, she feels a wave of comfort. She loves this place. The difference between Harrods and this department store, with its natural lightwell and wooden beams, is chalk and cheese.

Moving expertly through a corridor of scented candles, she inhales deeply and feels herself reset.

Gift-wise, something personalised is Madeleine's instinct. If she had time, she might have commissioned a gold chain with Bella's name on it.

Urgh, why hadn't she remembered? There is no excuse. Chastising herself, she heads towards the lift.

Bella, of course, had been characteristically sweet and self-effacing in her reply to Madeleine's message apologising profusely for her absolute fuck-up. *It was nothing, I'm just so happy I'll get to see you.* Her niece typed with a diligence that is unusual in people her age.

Are you excited? Madeleine had responded, trying to ignore the weight in her gut when she thought of setting foot inside her brother's house. There had been three moving dots on the screen, indicating that Bella was typing, but no response had followed.

Clothes? Squeezing into the lift along with five others, Madeleine presses the button for the first floor. Theoretically, clothing feels like

a good choice for a thirteenth birthday, but everything Madeleine
sees as she moves through contemporary womenswear is either too
buttoned-up or too flamboyant or too whimsical for Bella. She ums
and ahs over a crochet crop-top with toucans on the front, but then
stalls at the sizes stated on the label. What if she buys it too small
– though this seems unlikely, given her niece's frame – and Bella is
hurt; worse still, what if she buys a size too big and she infers that
her aunt believes she is larger than she is?

Christ, when did the world become so complicated? Not that it
wasn't ever thus. And yet things just feel more—

Her thoughts are interrupted by the ringing of her phone.

'Jonny?' she answers, sticking a finger in her other ear to hear
better as she passes through the gift section.

'The wife's been blabbing again, in the car.'

'To who?'

'Her daughter.'

Her stomach tightening, Madeleine turns and makes her way back
towards the stairs.

'I'll be right there.'

* * *

Madeleine sits cross-legged at the edge of Jonny's desk as she listens
to the recording taken through the wire in Ingrid Zhatchanova's car
for the third time since she arrived at SCID Row, straight from
Liberty.

Pressing pause on the recording, she lets her gaze roam around
the room. Through the curved first-floor window, winter sun casts
lines of light across the surface of the old double-pedestal desk that
was here when SCID arrived, bearing mug-stains indicating some
past life she surmises she would rather not know about; something
involving spooks, no doubt – a world she has worked hard to keep
as far away from as she can.

She had been tapped up herself by their friends along the river;

naturally, given her heritage combined with her personal background at the FCO. And Madeleine had taken great pleasure in politely telling them to go fuck themselves. Or maybe it wasn't that politely, come to think of it.

'How long until the translation is through?' Madeleine asks, impatient now.

'It's being processed as we speak,' Jonny replies.

Pressing play, she tries to read between the lines. The mother and daughter are clearly arguing, with Shyrailym mentioning Sergey by name several times. Besides that, it is impossible to make out a word of what they are saying, given that neither Madeleine nor her surveillance manager speak Kazakh.

Turning her wrist to look at her watch, she notes the time. She has some wiggle room before Bella's party but not much. In the end, Madeleine had opted for a hundred-pound gift voucher and a starter set of beauty products, which she had picked out hastily on her way out of the store, and now worries will be interpreted by her niece as a sign that Madeleine doesn't think she is beautiful enough already.

'I have to go – send it to me as soon as it's in?'

* * *

It is 8.00 p.m. and all the lights in the offices of Oldfield House Retail Park are off by the time Ramona abandons her post.

He hadn't shown up. She had known he most likely wouldn't, now that the website has been taken down. Unless he has a number of sites, each designed to draw in young women. Thinking of the wedding ring – possibly another ruse, to reassure the girls he meets that he is a nice guy, a businessman – she pictures him curled up on the sofa, at home, with his wife.

Perhaps he's stopped; had a change of heart, for one of countless reasons that she has no interest in considering. Because that doesn't mean he can be allowed to get away with it. Or maybe he's in another part of the city, right now, abusing other young women.

Her expression hardening, she stands, tucking the skateboard under her arm, and heads back towards the tube.

* * *

Ramona gets off the bus just over an hour later, having taken the tube to Manor House and jumped on the 253, east.

Early Friday evening, Upper Clapton Road is an assault on the senses. Car lights skid past reflecting on the tarmac, music blaring from an open window.

The few square metres around the Overground station remains comfortingly scruffy. The same betting shops and chicken shops and newsagents, the same Turkish and Jamaican barber shops where men and children call to each other from leather-backed chairs. Ramona likes to think that she could come back to this spot a year or a decade from now and it will be the same.

Though she knows, as much as she and others might resist it, that change – even if relatively slow – is as inevitable as death.

Si's flat is in an old converted fire station on a road otherwise inhabited by Orthodox Jewish families where Upper Clapton straddles Stamford Hill – a labyrinth of substantial terraced homes, kosher shops and synagogues.

From her side of the street as she heads north, Ramona watches various scenes play out, finding some comfort in the familiarity of it all.

At this juncture, crossing from one street to another can feel like stepping back in time, or even into another world. Ramona had loved this about the place when she first visited, marvelling at the different kinds of hats and outfits worn on different days of the week, each slightly different according to which region the wearer's branch of Judaism hailed from.

She feels the ghost of a smile on her lips as she approaches his front door, picturing Si's bemused face as Ramona regaled him with the intricacies of some of the religion's cultural variations, which she had looked up in the days after she first came here and found herself fascinated by. Any trace of warmth in the memory turns cold, though, as she looks at the doorbell and sees the words *Si and Holly* written next to his buzzer in girlish script.

Pressing the button hard, Ramona waits for the intercom to cut in. When it does, there is first the tail-end of laughter before a sing-song voice answers, 'Hello!'

'I need to speak to Si,' Ramona says, wishing to God it had been him, not Holly, who had answered.

With one hand she grips her skateboard and with the other she removes her cap and rubs her soggy hair in an attempt to tame it.

There is a confounded silence and then Holly speaks again. 'Erm, who is it?'

'It's the Dalai Lama,' Ramona replies, her voice tight as she holds back the emotion. As if Holly doesn't know her voice. As if they hadn't all worked together before Holly fucked off to work in PR for a charity while Si and Ramona carried on at the newspaper.

The intercom goes dead. For a moment, she thinks she has been intentionally cut off, but a moment later Si takes over. 'What do you want?'

'Can you let me in, please? It's freezing out here.'

'You—' There is a frustrated intake of breath and a pause, followed by the sound of the external buzzer as he lets her into the hall.

'Wait there,' Si calls down from outside his flat as Ramona pushes open the door. Brushing away the strands from her face, she waits as the door to the flat above bangs shut, followed by the sound of Si's footsteps as he makes his way downstairs.

'What are you doing here?' he asks in a stage whisper, his pace slowing at the sight of her. 'Holly doesn't want—'

'Holly can go fuck herself, Si,' Ramona replies, at a normal volume.

Looking him straight in the eye, she tries to recognise in him the man she once loved, before pushing the thought aside.

'Why are you here? Two days ago you told me not to come anywhere near you.'

'Oh, so you do remember that?' Ramona replies, pointedly.

'What is this about? I'm about to eat a takeaway and watch a film—'

'How inspiring.' She rolls her eyes. 'What were you doing earlier today?'

'Excuse me?'

'I saw you.'

'What are you talking about?' Si lowers his voice again. He looks genuinely confused, or nervous.

Still, Ramona makes no attempt to be quiet. 'I saw you in the alley next to the industrial estate, the same place you were the other night.'

Glancing back towards the staircase, Si pauses before his eye meets hers. 'What are you on about?'

'You're denying it?'

'Denying what?' He moves from foot to foot, in agitation. 'Do you know what? I'm so through with you. You're—' He struggles to find the words, running his hands back through his hair.

'Good, then you promise to stop stalking me?'

'I wasn't there yesterday, got it? The other night, I was trying to *protect* you.' He bites his lip. For a horrifying moment, she wonders if he might cry, but then he takes a step forward to study her. 'Look, I've learnt my lesson. I don't know how it took me so long. And while we're on the subject of stalking . . . Who was it who came to watch me play football, earlier this week, and then turned up at my work today looking for me, and is now here, in my girlfriend's home and mine, looking like—'

He looks her up in a way that makes her flinch.

His words trail away and Ramona stands her ground, the throbbing starting up again at the back of her head.

'I saw you, Si,' she says, more quietly this time. Because she had seen him. Hadn't she? If not him, then who?

'You're losing it. You are fucking losing it. And do you know how I know? Because I wasn't there.' He enunciates each word carefully.

'I was at the coroner's court, you can check it out for yourself if you don't believe me. A body—' He cuts himself off. 'You know what? I'm done.'

He turns and walks away from her. 'You know where the door is.'

* * *

On a cold winter's evening, the street lamps reflect warm gold against the tarmac as the taxi glides through Highgate village. Through the windows of the bars and restaurants that line the hill leading to a tiny roundabout that ushers Madeleine towards her brother's house, she watches families and couples gathered at tables and feels completely disconnected from the world they inhabit, her thoughts preoccupied by the conversation she had heard between Shyrailym and her mother, Ingrid.

The familiar clicking from the front of the cab as the driver indicates left is followed by a voice over the microphone. 'This is Grove End. Just here alright for you, love?'

The house stands between a set of white pillars. Tonight, the entrance is guarded by the kind of understated security fit for a new Home Secretary who likes to be seen as a man of the people, but who would also prefer not to be disturbed by the riff-raff while at home in his mansion in this desirable spot, associated with old money and the bohemia of a London long since vanished.

This will be the first time in as long as Madeleine can remember that she will have stepped inside the hallway of her brother's home, rather than dropping Bella off at the door and making her excuses to leave. She has to push against the urge to turn and run away.

A stream of cars blocks the driveway to her brother's home. Taking a moment, Madeleine gathers herself. Inside the gates, a marquee has been erected on the grass to the right of the main entrance, leaving access to the front door via the gravel path. Strings of tiny lanterns emit a soft hue as she approaches the gates, met by the swell of voices from beyond.

Looking down at her wrist and her mother's favourite watch, which she has picked out for the occasion as a special fuck-you to Dominic, Madeleine sees the time is 8.18 p.m. Her stomach growls and she wishes she had eaten something more substantial than some macaroons and the handful of crisps she had pulled from her cupboard on the way out, as an afterthought, leaving the rest of the packet on the kitchen counter.

'Can I have your name?' The lady on the front door holds up a clipboard and meets the new arrival's gaze with a directness that makes Madeleine stand tall.

'Mads!'

At the sight of Dominic, approaching with an enthusiasm that makes her want to turn on her heels and bolt, Madeleine notes how the younger woman lowers her list, her smile tightening as she steps aside.

'So pleased you made it. We had begun to wonder if you'd forgotten—' Dominic leans forward and kisses his younger sister on the cheek and Madeleine bristles, aware of several pairs of eyes on them as he steers her through a break in the crowd.

Willing herself to follow him, she notes that the music emanating from the large front garden isn't the synthetic pop Bella had favoured last time they met, but the sort of tastefully inoffensive background noise that probably came from a request from Amber to the Alexa rigged up to their sound system for the most popular classical music tracks of all time.

'Let me take your coat—' Another young woman emerges and reaches for Madeleine's trench coat.

Grateful to peel off the layers, under the roar of the outdoor heaters, Madeleine hands it over after just a moment's resistance. While her instinct tells her to hold on to her possessions to allow for a swift exit, she will not let herself scarper; this is her niece's party, after all – and yet, where are all the young people?

Looking around, Madeleine recognises a couple of journalists and politicians and looks away before making eye contact. The only people under the age of forty appear to be the staff. The teenagers must be inside, she reasons, cursing herself for wearing such an unnatural fibre. Even without her coat, she is roasting hot. Holding her arms out slightly, she tries to keep a flow of air to her armpits.

'Where's Bella?' Madeleine asks, finding her voice.

'Hmm? She's around. What are you drinking?' Dominic replies.

'I'll go and have a look for her. I want to give her this.' Madeleine signals to the present in the bag she is holding. *And get the fuck away from you*, she thinks, lifting a champagne flute from a tray as she passes one of the waitresses, and heads inside.

She hasn't been in the house since the great renovation, though she has seen the staged domestic press shots and gushing magazine spreads. Stepping over the threshold, Madeleine feels as if she is peering around the edge of a folly, that one foot further through the doorway and the entire world might fall away.

Instead, she finds herself in an admittedly breathtaking entrance hall, with green walls framed by perfectly hung works of art. Ahead of her, the wide staircase is painted a deep charcoal with striped runners.

Still no sign of Bella.

Taking a more deliberate step forward, Madeleine notes that on one side a set of steps leads down into an enormous open-plan kitchen. To her right is the drawing room. The walls, she recalls from the *World of Interiors* spread, had been painted a Tory-appropriate Hague blue. One wall, she notices straight off, is covered floor to ceiling with books – first editions of novels, she imagines, Dominic won't have read. Holding court at the centre of the room is an old thespian Madeleine vaguely recognises, with a group of guests gathered around.

'Madeleine?'

The hairs on the back of her neck bristle at the sound of the familiar voice. She takes a second to compose herself, hoping her face doesn't give her away, as she turns and finds herself opposite Catrin. Struggling for words, Madeleine feels her cheeks flush and wishes that of all the places to find herself face to face with her ex-girlfriend, she wasn't in such a well-lit spot.

'Catrin? What are you—' She stops herself. 'Sorry. Hi.'

'Hello.' Catrin's smile is disarming in its gentleness. The Welsh lilt Madeleine remembers from those early days at the FCO has softened, or hardened, depending on your point of view. But Madeleine's ex-girlfriend looks almost the same, her pale impish features a little more lined but no less lovely for it.

Looking into those familiar blue eyes, for a moment Madeleine is stumped and then she recovers. 'I didn't know you and Bella were friends.'

Catrin laughs. 'And I always forget how hilarious you are.'

Glancing over Catrin's shoulder, Madeleine sees her brother hovering at the other side of the hall, in conversation with a journalist Madeleine recognises from the BBC's coverage of the last election.

'Dominic mentioned you were coming—' Catrin says.

Madeleine's gaze narrows. Since when were her brother and her ex-girlfriend close? Of course, they are now colleagues in the same department, him as Minister and her as civil servant. How bloody cosy.

'I can't say the same,' Madeleine replies, more sharply than she meant to. 'How is the Ministry of Justice?'

Catrin shrugs. 'Same as ever. But how about you, you're back in London. How long for?'

'I'm not sure.' Willing Bella to walk down the stairs this very minute and save her, Madeleine clutches her glass.

'What are you working on at the moment? If I'm allowed to ask.'

Madeleine makes a face. 'You're allowed. Nothing much.'

'Hardly.' Catrin laughs. 'It sounds like you've been busy.'

'What?' It had become a joke between them, Madeleine being so posh that she deemed it ruder to say 'pardon?' than 'what?'; another of those ridiculous English upper-class rules that Catrin would never understand. But Madeleine isn't joking now. Why is Catrin interested in what Madeleine is working on? Or maybe it is just something to say.

Her expression softens as she continues. 'I saw you at Laura's funeral last week. I'm sorry, I know you were friends.'

Clearing her throat, Madeleine takes a step sideways. 'I'm going to get some water.'

She had half-expected to spot Catrin there, but the church was bursting with mourners and, not in the mood to socialise, Madeleine had lingered at the back, keeping her head down for most of the service.

Inevitably, she had crossed paths with her ex over the years, as Madeleine moved from the FCO to the agency and Catrin worked her way through the halls of power in Whitehall. In this respect, events like funerals were another hazard of the job. But these could be prepared for and precautions taken. Unlike this sudden ambush, where Madeleine finds herself with no excuse to leave.

'I thought the idea was for you to ease up a little while you're here?' Catrin asks, subtly blocking her path.

Feeling the heat rise in her cheeks, Madeleine stops. When she replies, her voice is dry. 'I'm sorry, I'm struggling to understand what it is that you're trying to imply, or why the sudden interest—'

'OK.' Catrin holds up her hands and Madeleine spots a plain gold band on her left hand. Swallowing hard, she looks away. She takes a sip of the champagne; it is too sweet and only makes her feel more thirsty.

Reluctant to leave too abruptly, Madeleine takes another sip and wills for it to quench her thirst. In the circumstances a drink or two might help in more ways than one.

'I'm not implying anything.' There is a flicker in Catrin's expression as she studies her that Madeleine struggles to read. 'Are you OK, Madeleine? You seem—'

'Like someone who is being grilled by their ex-partner at a party she was told was being held for a niece who doesn't even seem to be here?' Christ, why does she sound so brittle? She holds her glass against her cheeks, trying to cool them. Trust Dominic to have the radiators turned up to three thousand degrees.

'Partner?' Catrin's tone sharpens. 'Come now, Madeleine, I think we both know we were never really that.'

Christ, is this really happening? Madeleine takes another slurp. Is Catrin still really so bitter? It was shit of Madeleine, of course it was. But Catrin is hardly the first person in the world to be cheated on. Besides, when it came to being a pain in the arse, Catrin knew how to hold her own. And here, of all places . . . Of all the ambushes—

'Madeleine!'

The sound of her name being called out is followed by a thundering of footsteps on the stairs. Oh, thank God. When Madeleine turns towards the direction of the stairs, Bella is standing in front of her, her gaunt face lit up at the sight of her aunt.

'You *are* here – I thought they'd locked you in the cellar!' Madeleine says, flooded with relief as she embraces her niece, ignoring how frail the girl feels and instead focusing on the obvious delight on Bella's face as she notices the plush purple Liberty bag Madeleine is holding.

'Well, I'll see you, then—' Catrin says quietly, and Madeleine turns briefly to watch her ex walk away before returning her attention to her niece.

'Thirteen! God, I'm so sorry I didn't—'

'It's fine. I didn't even notice. But you're fifty.' Bella makes a face.

'Hey, less of that, thank you.'

'Is that for me?' Bella indicates towards the present.

'This?' Madeleine holds out the Liberty bag to inspect it. 'No, sorry – this is for my taxi driver. I forgot to give it to him.'

'Can I open it now?' Bella arches her eyebrow, grinning as she reaches for the bag.

'Obviously.' Madeleine smiles ruefully as she watches her niece unpackaging the tissue paper, revealing the floral-print cosmetic bag, rummaging through the goodies inside with genuine delight. Why had she not been around for her more? The answer is simple: because her job isn't here. And because Dominic is.

'I love it, thank you so much,' Bella says, carefully repacking the cosmetics inside the silk bag and zipping it closed. 'And what's this?'

She reaches into the bottom of the bag and picks out the envelope, genuinely confounded by there being another gift. For all her privilege, Bella never expects anything, and is never anything other than completely grateful for what she is given.

How is she related to Dominic and Amber – or to Madeleine, for that matter?

'Vouchers. So you can choose something.'

'How thoughtful.' Amber's voice cuts in behind them, and Madeleine notices Bella's face fall slightly. 'It must be so convenient for shopping, being so central.' Amber leans in to kiss her, and Madeleine stays where she is, trying to smile for the sake of her niece.

'Yes, it must be hell up here in the wilds of Highgate,' Madeleine counters, giving Bella a wink and then swapping her empty glass for a full one as another young waitress passes.

Moving too fast, Madeleine stumbles slightly and rights herself. Christ, she really needs to eat.

'Steady on.' Amber blinks, wholly composed in a long green dress with a halterneck that somehow accentuates her exquisite bone structure. Her sister-in-law never drinks more than half a glass, as averse to any lack of control as she is to what Madeleine had once heard her refer to as the 'empty calories'.

'Marie, have you met Dominic's sister?' Ushering in a passing blonde who might be anywhere between forty and ninety-two, judging by her unnaturally rigid features, Amber continues. 'Madeleine lives in Dominic's childhood home.'

'If you'll excuse me, I am going to find the loo. Bella – will you remind me where it is? Amber, it's been a treat, as always.' Madeleine turns and takes her niece's arm.

'Sure.' Bella bites her lip, apparently holding in a laugh, not meeting her mother's eye as she lets herself be pulled back towards the hall.

'This is a terrible birthday party,' Madeleine whispers as they walk away. 'Where are all your friends, anyway?'

'It's not really a party for me. It was always going to be about—' Bella stops herself before saying the words. *My father.* Even now, she is too loyal for that. Instead, she makes a gesture suggesting it doesn't matter and Madeleine walks towards her, taking her niece in her arms. How is she so bloody lovely?

'Right – this is shit,' Madeleine says, pulling herself upright. 'Let's get out of here. Where do you want to go?'

'What?'

'Name the spot. We'll jump in a cab.'

'Erm . . .' Bella's eyes widen with possibility. 'I don't know . . . I mean, there's a film I quite want to see at the Everyman?'

The cinema, really – of all the places she could choose? Still, it's not Madeleine's call – and what had she expected her to say, a strip club?

'Right then. Go and grab a coat. I'll secure the area . . . We'll wait until your parents are both distracted and then we'll run for it.'

'They're always distracted.'

'I know.' Madeleine nods. 'But they love you really. Now run and get your coat.'

'OK.' Bella turns halfway up the staircase and smiles. 'I'm glad you came.'

CHAPTER TWENTY-TWO

Weekend meetings always have a slightly different energy, partly owing to the demographic, partly because of the increased sense of desperation at a time that others still reserve for letting off steam; their vibrations almost palpable through the doors of the pubs and clubs that line the high street.

But this Saturday is particularly subdued.

'We'll be holding a special meeting to remember JJ, next week,' Vicky announces at the front of the room. 'I know a lot of people here were close to him. It is perfectly understandable to feel upset or angry. If anyone wants to talk about JJ, or how losing him has affected them . . . It'll be a sort of informal memorial.'

Catching Ramona's eye, Vicky makes a meaningful face and Ramona looks away, her cheeks burning with various emotions as the session is wrapped up.

It can't end quickly enough, as far as Ramona is concerned. JJ's absence is too much of a reminder of what has happened, and of what she had failed to notice.

Once it is over, she waits a minute, surrounded by the scuffle of feet and the scraping of chairs, followed by a murmuring of voices as she looks around for Cindy, in case she has been sitting somewhere out of view. When she doesn't appear, Ramona heads for the door

216

along with the final stragglers. It's not the first time Cindy has missed a meeting in recent months, and Ramona wonders whether her days of attending these sessions are coming to a natural end.

She isn't sure exactly how long her friend has been coming here – she worries that to ask would be to somehow imply that Cindy should have moved on – but she knows that it's for almost as long as Sonny has been alive. There had been some concern among the health professionals that the baby would be affected by the heroin his mother had taken when pregnant, or that it might cause the child to develop problems later on in life. This revelation, combined with the arrival of social services not long after Cindy stared into her son's eyes for the first time, had terrified the seventeen-year-old into action.

Since then, Cindy has stayed clean and held down a job, a flat and the various demands of motherhood, with these meetings the only other constant in her life, besides her child.

But maybe now that Sonny is getting older and Cindy knows herself better, as a mother and as a woman, she no longer has the same need of them. Selfishly, Ramona would prefer if she kept coming so that she doesn't have to do them alone. Especially without JJ.

* * *

Sami's shop is one of a number that sells phone credit on this stretch and Ramona almost walks onto the next one, unable to face his chirpy chit-chat after the meeting she has just come from. But she needn't have worried. When he sees her come in, he grows quiet, giving her a nod and waiting for her to walk around the shop and collect a few supplies before requesting her phone credit.

As well as the *Sun* and a Turkish paper Ramona doesn't know the name of, the shop stocks the local paper and Ramona does a double-take when she sees the sidebar on the front page along with the headline: **Canal death.** Next to it, there is a blurry CCTV image of JJ in the hours before he died.

Picking it up, she starts to read the article.

The body of fifty-two-year-old JJ Turner was found in the Camden Lock area of the canal in the early hours of Thursday morning.

'Did you know him or something?' Sami asks. Ramona looks up and blinks, only now realising that she is crying.

'Yeah.' Embarrassed, she wipes away a tear.

'That's dark. Sorry to hear it.' Sami rings the pitta bread, hummus and a bunch of bananas into the till, and reaches to the shelf behind him for the phone credit without passing comment.

Ramona scans the bottles of whisky and vodka, and looks away, licking her lips.

'So was he like a friend, or what?'

'Yeah, he was a friend,' she says. Taking a fiver from her pocket, she searches for more cash but sees that she is all out. 'Actually, I'll leave the phone credit.'

Placing five pounds on the counter, her thoughts spin as Sami counts out her change.

'Take care, yeah?'

Ramona nods. 'You too.'

* * *

The fishmonger's is halfway up Stoke Newington High Street and Ramona holds her breath as she steps inside the beaded curtain that separates the shop from the street.

'How can I help you, darling?' the man behind the counter asks, gutting a fish with a precision that is almost mesmerising.

'I'm a friend of JJ's,' Ramona replies, and instantly he stops what he is doing.

'I'm sorry for your loss.'

The old woman beside her in the queue glances up at them, clearly keen to hear whatever is said next.

'I just wondered if you . . .' Ramona pauses. She hadn't thought through what she was going to say once she got here. She just wanted to speak to someone besides herself who had seen him that day. Why?

218

To absolve herself of the guilt she feels that she didn't realise something was wrong, in the moments leading up to it, she supposes.

'JJ came to see me on Wednesday and I thought he might have been trying to tell me something. I was busy and he said he would come by later, but he never did,' she continues, after a beat.

'Who are you?' It is hard to know if the man is suspicious of her or trying to show compassion.

'I'm just a friend,' Ramona replies.

The fishmonger shrugs. 'I don't know what to tell you . . . He was his usual self. I can't—' He sniffs, as though holding back tears, and then he clears his throat.

'He was good. I saw him on Wednesday morning, he did an early shift and he was planning to go to his meeting later, and then come to work on Thursday. But he never did.'

'He was here on Wednesday morning?'

'Popped in on his way to buy cigarettes.' The man sighs. 'I can't tell you more than that 'cause I just don't know. There is no way he was back on the gear, though – I'd have known if he was. I'm sorry. He was a good guy, everyone loved him.'

The comfort she feels, that JJ's employer hadn't noticed anything either, is followed by a twinge of unease.

Cigarettes? But hadn't JJ asked for one of hers outside the flat? For whatever reason, he must have been distracted from buying his own.

'What time was that?'

'About ten.'

At least an hour before Ramona saw him, then. What was it that had stopped him from going about his business, as planned? If he was using again, maybe JJ had decided to buy gear instead. Except he wasn't high when she spoke to him. That much, she would have known.

* * *

Madeleine wakes up screaming in a fug of heat.

For a moment, lying in the darkness with the sheets damp beneath her, she believes she is still there. In her mind's eye, she can see them as clearly as though they are before her now: the boys silently cowering in the corner, each one no older than six years old.

Gasping for breath, she catches the scent of mimosa from the Jo Malone diffuser, and her outbreath softens. The shapes of the room coming into focus, she concentrates on the frame of the windows overlooking central London and the softness of the lines of her pristine white duvet and the oatmeal-coloured throw strewn around the end, where she had kicked it off in a fit of nightmares.

Her chest loosening a little more, she turns her attention inward, becoming aware of the cold sweat on her back and chest, where the silk nightdress clings to her skin. Looking down, the dark reds and blues of the abstract floral design appear like bruises in the shadows of the street light that trickles in between the cracks in the curtains.

Leaning over to click on the sidelamp, Madeleine takes a sip of water from the glass beside her bed.

She is OK. She is home.

Ordinarily on Saturdays when she is in London, Madeleine likes to read the weekend papers with breakfast in bed.

But not today.

With the assistance of two double espressos, she brings herself to life, taking her time to apply pea-sized droplets of face cream to her skin before curling her eyelashes and applying her make-up. As she does, she thinks of the party that was in fact held for Dominic – an intimate celebration of his promotion – not for Bella's birthday, as pitched to her.

Why had Dominic invited her if it was never about his daughter in the first place? Perhaps he had wanted his sister there as a show for the other guests. He didn't want a family rift spoiling his reputation. Presumably this is also why he refused to make a scene, outwardly, when Madeleine and Bella returned from their French exit.

After that, she certainly won't be invited again. That is some consolation, at least.

Dominic had done a double take when she and Bella returned sometime after midnight. Neither he nor Amber had even noticed that their daughter had left, and Madeleine savoured the flustered look on her brother's face as she and Bella arrived at the gates, giddy with the thrill of disappearing for several hours. Bella texted this morning to thank Madeleine again for the presents and for the spontaneous outing to see a bleak indie film with subtitles, which her aunt had snoozed through, having gorged a bowl of chips in her seat.

Reading the subtext in Bella's characteristically diplomatic message, it was clear that Dominic is also livid. So livid that he hasn't even tried to contact Madeleine to bollock her personally. Despite the fact that she had texted him as they left – *Bella and I have buggered off for a bit*. Well, it serves him right for lying about the purpose of the party. More to the point, Bella had deserved a celebration of her own, and of her own choosing. If he or his wife weren't going to give it to her, then Madeleine would. How's that for sanctimonious?

Standing, Madeleine pushes thoughts of her brother aside and picks up her phone.

The translated transcript of the wiretap had landed in her inbox around 9.00. the previous evening, around the same time she was being given the third degree by Catrin. She had read it for the first time on the way home, around 12.30 a.m., bleary-eyed. Instantly she had found herself awake.

Shyrailym: You need to distance yourself from the business.

Ingrid: I'm nothing to do with it, they could never—

S: I'm serious, Mother. You have no idea. It's about so much more than money, there is so much at stake. Sergey is—

I: I don't want to know.

S: This is so much bigger than you realise. You have to—

I: I don't have to do anything.

After that, according to the notes, the car pulls up and the daughter gets out. Even with the conversation translated into English, the meaning of it is hard to interpret.

Shyrailym had been warning her mother to extricate herself from her father's business, but why? And for whose benefit? Was she protecting the business itself, or warning her mother against the potential fallout of whatever she knows is at risk of being exposed?

Taking her handbag and coat, Madeleine heads for the hall.

The taxi takes twenty minutes, door to door. Trying the buzzer outside Shyrailym's mansion block for a second time, she stands back and looks up at the window of the flat.

For a moment she could swear she sees the curtain move, but then everything falls still again, and she can't be sure whether she saw it at all.

Reluctantly, she turns away.

As she does so, she hears the daughter's voice calling after her. 'What do you want?'

'Thank you for letting me in,' Madeleine says, once Shyrailym has led her upstairs. Unlike the young professor's office, her flat feels warm and personal – the furnishings practical but not clinical; a small wooden dining table and corresponding chairs; unflashy fabrics in muted greens, greys and oranges.

Only one item, propped on the counter, stands out. Madeleine falters at the sight of it and then immediately rights herself.

'I asked you very specifically not to come and see me again,' Shyrailym says, turning to face Madeleine.

'So why did you answer the door?'

Shyrailym scrutinises her uninvited guest before shaking her head. 'I asked you why you are here.'

'You never answered my question about how you know Laura Tatchell?' Madeleine waits for the words to sink in. When no response is forthcoming, she continues. 'Harriet, Laura's secretary, says you two were close.' Madeleine stops and considers the other woman for several seconds, in silence. 'You worked together.'

Shyrailym wells up, turning away so that Madeleine won't see her cry. 'Not exactly. I work for a charity, supporting people in my home country. Laura and I met a few times, through that. She had a few . . . causes, I guess you'd call them. I knew people from my country who needed their voices to be heard, and Laura was able to give them that platform.'

'It was you who introduced her to the women on whose behalf she was speaking, the day—'

'She asked me to help and—' Shyrailym cuts herself off, her voice cracking with emotion. 'We weren't close. But I'm so sorry about what happened. Those girls—'

'You were close enough to have attended her funeral.' Madeleine glances meaningfully at the order of service on the side table. There had been so many people there, it's hardly surprising Madeleine hadn't seen her.

With her back turned to Madeleine, Shyrailym wipes her face with her hand. She isn't wearing her headscarf and her dark hair falls over her shoulders.

'Laura was—' Her voice is cut off by the sound of the doorbell.

Madeleine takes a step closer, willing her to carry on. 'Laura was?'

'You have to go,' Shyrailym says abruptly, taking a step backwards.

'What were you going to say?' Madeleine takes another step forward. 'Please, Shyrailym. If you know anything about what happened—'

'You need to leave *now*.' Her demeanour transforms instantly. Moving to the counter, she takes the order of service and moves hurriedly to the shelves, where she slips it between two books. The doorbell sounds again, longer this time, whoever is pressing the button clearly impatient to be let in.

Shyrailym moves to the intercom and presses a button. 'One minute,' she says in English, and a man's voice replies in a language Madeleine recognises as Kazakh.

'Go,' she says to Madeleine, taking her finger off the speaker. Ushering her out into the hall, her expression desperate, she leaves the door ajar behind her. The lift is already there, open, and Shyrailym practically pushes her inside, before returning to her flat and pressing the open button for downstairs, as the lift doors close with Madeleine trapped inside.

Shit.

Tapping her foot, she wills the lift to move faster. She needs to know who it was who—

Ping.

The lift doors open on the ground floor, but when she steps out, she is the only person there.

Back out on the street, Madeleine looks up at the flat. Shit. Kicking the pavement, she stands there for a moment considering her next move when her attention is caught by a car parked a few vehicles along – a red Bugatti, licence plate CRYPTO1.

Her phone rings and Madeleine doesn't recognise the number. Answering distractedly, she waits an instant, and when no one speaks she repeats. 'Hello?'

'Is that Madeleine Farrow?' the man says at the end of the line. His voice is gentle but weary.

'Yes?'

'This is Jamie Tatchell, Laura's husband. Could we meet?'

* * *

Laura Tatchell's street is one of a criss-cross of residential roads that run between Green Lanes and Turnpike Lane.

A block short of the house, a series of severed ribbons tied to a lamp post and a few dropped petals on the floor are all that is left to mark the spot where the MP was mowed down on her way to work, her daughters just a few paces away as their mother crossed the road.

A black BMW with false registration plates had been found burnt-out in a field in Hertfordshire the next day. This was almost as much as they knew about the vehicle involved, and its driver. It had been stolen from a garage forecourt the night before. London has one of the highest numbers of CCTV cameras in the world, Madeleine marvels, and yet they can't trace the person responsible for mowing down a woman on her way to serve her country?

Holding her handbag more tightly against herself, she takes the final steps before turning through the small red gate that leads to number forty-two. Jamie must have seen Madeleine arrive from the window, as he opens the door before she has a chance to knock.

His opening remark confirms that he had seen her, pondering the sorry remains of the memorial along the street. 'They keep leaving flowers, and I keep having to go and cut them down before the girls see them. As if they aren't reminded enough already. They're with their grandmother this weekend.'

He holds the door open and Madeleine steps inside, noting the stack of post on the rickety dresser to the right, where an unframed photo of Laura, Jamie, Ruth and Tilly is propped against the wall. Beside it, a pot brims with keys and pens, and a ChapStick.

From the room at the end of the corridor, a radio plays low, Bob Dylan giving way to a popular DJ whose voice Madeleine vaguely recognises. 'Come through. It was good of you to come straight away.'

'Of course,' Madeleine says, following him through to the kitchen. A tabby cat meets them in the doorway, curling itself around Jamie's leg.

'Do you want tea?' His eyes are rimmed with dark circles, a beard forming where presumably he hasn't bothered to shave. They have only met once before, at a drinks event where he had looked charmingly uncomfortable amid the pomp and ceremony, Laura staying close to his side as she worked the room, clearly protecting her husband from one of the nonsense aspects of ther job – so different from his own work as a secondary school teacher. Design and technology, Madeleine recalls.

'I'm fine.' She takes a seat on one of the chairs in front of the table.

'Harriet contacted me. She said you met, that you were asking her questions.' At first, his tone sounds accusatory, but as he continues, it turns confiding, almost pleading.

225

'There are things . . .' He gathers himself, moving around to the kitchen counter and grasping the edge as though for support. 'Two months ago, we had a break-in. The house was messed up.' Madeleine looks around then, taking in the hot-potch of vases lined up along the top of the cupboards, the faded school certificates and colourful alphabet magnets spelling out random words. A Tracey Emin-style print reading *I JUST BLOODY LOVE YOU* framed on one of the walls, alongside a world map.

'Laura was . . . Shaken. Nothing was stolen but . . .' Jamie sighs, scratching his forehead where a lock of hair falls across his face. 'Laura had been distracted for a while, she was worried about something. She'd been getting threats – Harriet told me that after— It was going on long before the speech in Parliament about the Kazakhs—' He swallows. 'I guess it's not that unusual. That was the kind of MP Laura was, people took against her. She often got letters from the green ink brigade. But this was different, somehow. She seemed . . . I don't know.'

Madeleine bristles. 'Did she keep them, these threatening – what? Emails? Letters?'

'Letters, apparently. Harriet said she just threw them away.' Jamie's eyes well up but his expression remains stoic. 'She didn't say anything to me, but I could see she was scared. For weeks, long before that bloody speech. Whatever it was, she obviously didn't want to worry us. That's how she was. I can't help but wonder . . .' His face cracks, and he turns away from her. 'I just can't help but think this is about more than— What if the person who had been threatening her is the one responsible? If I'd done something . . .'

'There was nothing you could have done,' Madeleine finds herself saying. 'The person who did this, they are the one to blame. Not you.'

The one? Who is she kidding, how can she say this with such certainty? She doesn't know whether it is one person, or more, let alone why – or how to catch them. And she has no authority to find out.

She feels a shiver of unease at the way Jamie is looking at her, almost pleadingly. There is nothing she can do, apart from try to seek for some justice by bringing down people like those Laura was rallying against.

But what if they had nothing to do with this? What if this was something else entirely? As Jamie said, Laura was the kind of character who riled people, as well as moved them. What if this was connected to another of those groups?

She should never have gone directly to Harriet. It had been desperately irresponsible. Madeleine isn't a crusader or a superhero, or even a murder detective, and now she had inadvertently given a grieving young husband false hope.

'Have you mentioned all this to the team who are investigating Laura's—' she asks simply.

'Of course.'

'Then I'm sure they are exploring all possible routes,' she says, because she doesn't know what else to say.

When he looks at her, his face shines with disappointment. 'Right.' He shifts so that he is standing straight, rather than leaning against the counter.

'Did Laura ever mention a woman called Shyrailym?'

Jamie thinks and then shakes his head. 'No. Why?'

'Just someone Laura dealt with in her charity work. Look, I'm so sorry. I wish I could . . .' She shrugs. What else can she say?

When Jamie looks back at her blankly, she stands, knowing she can't give him what he wants from her. Still, she says, 'I'm going to do everything I can. OK?'

* * *

Saturday night gives way to Sunday morning. Bristling with frustration and unable to sleep, Ramona walks to Hampstead Heath and watches the sun rise from the top of Parliament Hill. By the time the joggers and dog walkers and the unbearable Pilates mums descend with their designer buggies and lightly worn disdain for their children masked by jokes about Pinot o'clock, this place will be hell. But for now, London is hers again.

Perched on the bench, safely away from the constant glare of CCTV, Ramona pulls down her hood and lets the first flickers of sunlight touch her cheeks. On the horizon, the tower blocks and office buildings dart up so that the skyline appears like the reading on a life support machine. It is still freezing, but the glass buildings in the distance glisten with the promise of a new day. Not for JJ.

Pulling her legs up under her on the bench so that she is cross-legged, Ramona takes the article from her inside pocket and unfolds it.

The Dalston News has learnt that the body of a man who was pulled from the canal on Thursday evening is a former heroin user, father and grandfather, who turned his life around. JJ Turner was a well-liked figure in Hackney who conducted charity work for the local church.

Letting her hands drop into her lap, she tips her head back and inhales the fresh morning air.

Fucking hell, JJ – what happened to you?

Lighting a cigarette, she pictures him that Wednesday morning, standing in front of her on her doorstep. Why hadn't she just talked to him, like he'd asked? She had even noticed the marks on his arms, but told herself they were nothing to worry about.

Taking another lungful of smoke, she holds it there, punishing herself for not pre-empting what had been about to happen. Only when her lungs ache does she exhale.

What had he been wanting to tell her?

CHAPTER TWENTY-THREE

On Monday, Rittler is seated at his desk when Madeleine arrives. Since her visit to Jamie Tatchell, she has found herself moving beneath a cloud.

She starts at the sight of her boss, his look one of furrowed concentration, as she enters the ground floor where his desk is positioned in the corner of the room.

Moving carefully, Madeleine closes the door behind her.

'You're here?' she says coolly, as she takes off her coat.

Rittler doesn't answer at first, and when he looks up it appears he hadn't noticed her come in. Clicking his mouse before turning his attention to his colleague, there is a pause, and then he nods courteously. 'Madeleine.'

He looks awful, his skin wan.

'What's going on? You're never in early,' Madeleine comments, and Rittler makes a face.

'Have you got a minute?'

Holding the pink takeaway coffee cup she bought from Café Concerto on the way in, she leans against the wall, waiting for him to speak. Part of her wants to raise the details that Jamie had passed on, though what would be the point? Rittler would simply ask Madeleine, as she had Jamie, whether the information had been passed on to the team investigating the case. Clearly uncomfortable at the length of the silence that extends between them, Rittler blows out his cheeks. 'The wife's lawyer is challenging the Unexplained Wealth Order. They're trying to get the jewellery back, claiming Ingrid herself is not a PEP.'

What? 'But we're not claiming that she herself is a politically exposed person—' Madeleine replies, after a beat.

'The magistrates' court dealing with the application has deemed that the husband should be a party to the proceedings, and therefore we need to serve the relevant papers on him, direct.'

'But that's not possible. We've already established that. Amir is in prison in Kazakhstan. The diplomats there had said it would be too high-risk for one of our people to deliver it personally,' Madeleine continues, taking a defiant sip of her coffee and scalding her mouth.

Wait— When had they seized the jewellery: on Friday? And now, already – by the following Monday – the magistrates' court has rejected the order?

'Absolutely – we've spoken to the FCO. The diplomats in Kazakhstan claim it's politically too risky for them to hand over the papers. As the wife claims not to be in contact with the husband, there's not much we can do.'

'What are you talking about? This is bullshit,' Madeleine says, her voice laced with anger. Whatever promises she could not make to Jamie, there was one that she could: to do everything in her power to bring down the bastards that Laura called out in that speech. Whether or not that was the reason for her death, it would be something at least.

'It is bullshit.'

Rittler shrugs. 'I know.'

Madeleine takes a moment. There is something in her boss's face that isn't right. Rittler is childish, but not this childish. This is more than a grudge about having been snubbed on a night out. What isn't he telling her?

She thinks back to Catrin's questions at Dominic's party. Obviously, Madeleine had been drunk but she hadn't just imagined the feeling that she was being mined – albeit unsuccessfully – for news about work. *You should take it easy.* Isn't that what Catrin had said? Of course she could have been debriefed by Rittler on why she is back on the home front for a while. But since when did Catrin care about Madeleine's emotional wellbeing?

'Is someone putting pressure on you, Paul?'

He looks up at her sharply, his expression turning from resignation to anger. 'Don't push your luck.'

'Rittler.' Softening, she tries a different tack. 'Look, it's me. You can tell me anything. If something—'

'What's this, a mothers' meeting and no one invited me?' At the sound of Jonny's voice, Rittler stands.

'Where are you going?' Ignoring Jonny, Madeleine watches her boss pick up his coat and head towards the doorway through which Jonny has just entered.

'Oi, Rittler. Talk to me,' she says, standing and moving ahead, attempting to block his path.

'I have an appointment. Please can you get out of my way. I'll call you when I can. In the meantime, you need to calm down.'

'Madeleine.' Jonny's voice is authoritative.

Reluctantly, she stops, studying Rittler's face before stepping aside.

'What the fuck was that? Actually don't tell me.' Jonny makes for the stairs, leaving Madeleine, still with rage.

What the fuck is going on?

* * *

When Fionn walks in, a while later, Madeleine is back at her desk. 'Did you get the bank records?' she accosts him immediately, though he doesn't seem to care that he is barely inside the office.

'Not yet,' he replies. 'I have a list of the companies they bank with. I've contacted them asking for records.'

Standing, Madeleine follows him to his desk, where a piece of paper names several well-known banks. 'How long do you reckon it will be?'

'Could be a matter of—'

Scanning the names, Madeleine turns and heads back to her desk and collects her coat and bag. 'Actually don't worry about it.'

'Where are you going?' Jonny comes down the stairs again as she heads for the door, his voice trailing after her as she slams it shut. 'What the fuck is going on?'

Madeleine calls Ramona as soon as she is out of earshot of SCID Row. 'Are you at home?'

'Yep.'

'Write down this registration number, will you? Find out who owns it. Now.'

* * *

The bank's headquarters is a stone's throw from Monument. Mid-morning on a Monday in the City of London, tourists drift towards the river, stopping to take selfies in front of the landmark commemorating the start of the Great Fire.

'I'm here to see Daphne King,' Madeleine announces as she reaches the reception desk. For a split second, she hesitates, half expecting the Facebook profile of her paramour to have been in a fake name. But the words Daphne King clearly ring true.

'Do you have an appointment?' the receptionist asks.

She ignores the question. 'Could you tell her it's Madeleine Farrow. It's urgent.'

Madeleine doesn't want to have to pull out her card and hopes the authority in her voice is sufficient to get the receptionist to pick up the phone. After a second's deliberation, discreetly surveying the expensive cut of Madeleine's suit and handbag, she does as she has been asked.

'Ms King, we have someone here who says she needs to speak to you.'

There is a brief silence while the receptionist gives Madeleine's name and awaits the response.

Hanging up, finally she smiles.

'If you wait there, Ms King will be down in a minute.'

* * *

'Well, this is a surprise.' Daphne assesses Madeleine curiously, as she passes through the retracting glass barrier into the atrium where Madeleine is seated on an inhospitably hard leather sofa.

'Is there somewhere we could talk?' Madeleine asks, standing up with an air of authority.

Daphne glances at her watch. 'I could spare fifteen minutes to grab a coffee, if you're that desperate to see me.' She smiles, cat-like. 'Otherwise we could meet after work.'

'I'd like to come upstairs, actually. Right away.'

'I'm sorry?'

Quietly, Madeleine continues. 'I work for the police. I have to ask you something, and I don't have the time to go through the formal channels.'

Pausing, she assesses the impact of her words, noting the look of horror moving across Daphne's face. Presumably she is remembering her inebriated boasting about the quality of her cocaine. Clearly, until now, she had no idea what Madeleine does for a living. So she hadn't bothered doing much more than a provisional internet search. More fool her.

'Sorry, did I not mention it?' Madeleine bowls on. 'Anyway, look, I'm not interested in your extracurricular activities, but I do need to come upstairs and ask you something.'

Indicating to the other people dotted around the waiting area, Madeleine dips her head, suggesting they might like to continue their conversation somewhere more private. 'Does that sound OK?'

Momentarily flustered, Daphne clears her throat, her whole demeanour changing as she weighs up her options, her arms crossed against her chest.

Finally, she nods. 'Follow me.'

* * *

Ramona can tell immediately that Madeleine is in a precarious mood as she watches the woman make her way towards her, on the path that runs between two sections of old gravestones in Bunhill Fields burial ground.

How she moves at such a pace in those heels is a mystery, but this Monday lunchtime on the fringes of the old City of London, Madeleine Farrow appears to be fuelled by something superhuman.

'Did you get anything on the reg plates?' Madeleine asks, once they are close enough.

'His name is Nurislam Sultanov. It looks like he and Shyrailym were engaged.'

Madeleine's eyes narrow, in a manner that is impossible to read. She pauses before responding. 'I need you to go undercover. Are you up for it?'

Is she up for it? Ramona nods without hesitation. Of course she is. Always, but now more than ever. Anything to distract from the thought of JJ, and added to that the image of Cindy's disappointed face staring back at her yesterday morning.

And then there were none.

'The wife is challenging the Unexplained Wealth Order, so she knows that we are onto her. What I want to do now is find a way to prove that Sergey, the son, is in contact with his father. If we can prove that he is visiting him in prison in Kazakhstan, then we can get him to serve the papers to Amir.'

'I thought he was persona non grata there now, because of his lobbying against legislation affecting the crypto industry?'

Madeleine makes a face. 'Maybe. He seems to have gone quiet on that front, according to what we've seen on his socials. And his business is still operating there, so perhaps a deal has been made. It seems the government is now trying to lure international investors back, so maybe he's part of that . . . Christ knows. The point is, for now he is our best way in.

'I've been through some of Sergey's bank statements,' Madeleine steams on, as they walk side by side past office workers cutting through from Shoreditch to the City, and vice versa. 'Turns out he has several bank accounts, so he's not entirely true to his beliefs in cryptocurrency, luckily for us.

'One of the regular payments is to a cleaning agency called Estate Cleaners. They use freelance contractors, zero-hours, that sort of thing.'

Because if you're a billionaire who needs the shit scraped from their toilet bowl, why pay someone sixteen pounds an hour when you could pay twelve, Ramona muses, as they pass office workers clutching salad bowls, glued to their phones.

'You want me to pose as a cleaner, and have a snoop around?'

'You've got it.' Madeleine ploughs a path for them both, people moving out of her way as if made to do so by an invisible force field. 'The jewellery seizure isn't working. The wife's lawyer – or someone influencing her lawyer – is suggesting that because she is not a so-called politically exposed person herself, we can't seize her possessions. Even if we know they were bought with the proceeds of her husband's crimes. I mean for fuck's sake, how else is a person with no job buying fifty thousand pounds' worth of jewellery? It's absolute bullshit, but I don't know right now how we get round it. And now she and her lawyer are onto us, so we have to hope we can get a grip this way. Amol and Fionn are working on the shell company that owns the building Ingrid was seen going into . . . There is a chance we will be able to seize that. In the meantime, this is the next plan.'

'And what am I looking for?'

Madeleine shrugs. 'Something that incriminates – or proof that he visits his father. I mean, we're not reinventing the wheel here: bank statements, paperwork, emails if possible . . .'

'Right.' Ramona nods. 'So, if you can't prove there are reasonable grounds to suspect that the wife's income is insufficient to pay for the jewellery – and if the SCID can't show that she is a PEP who might be susceptible to bribery or corruption – then your best shot is to prove that either the wife, or someone she is connected to – i.e. their son – is linked to criminality.'

Madeleine winks. 'You've got it.' After a pause, she adds, 'You'll be working with Jonny. There's somewhere else I need to be in the morning.'

* * *

Ramona thinks about the children of Amir and Ingrid Zhatchanov as she makes her way home, where she plans to contact Gareth and see if he has made any headway on tracking down the now vanished Time for Tuition site, given that Madeleine's IT friends seem to be making little progress.

It has only been a few days, but still: could it be so hard to trace a simple website? Ramona knows bugger all about technology but even she could tell by looking at it that this wasn't a particularly sophisticated operation. And she hadn't dared bring up the lack of progress at the al fresco meeting she has just returned from, in light of Madeleine's dangerous air.

'What the *fuck,* Ro?'

Cindy is waiting by the front gate. The sight of her friend shatters all other thoughts, Ramona understanding instantly what is about to go down. If her friend's words alone weren't enough to make this clear, then the look on her face certainly is. She has never seen Cindy angry before – but then she has never previously known her son to be put at risk.

'I'm so sorry—' Ramona concedes immediately, continuing up the path. Now that the moment of confrontation is here, she accepts that she had known it would have to come and is almost relieved.

Cindy is visibly shaking. Her slender wrists are covered in thin gold bracelets that slip up her arm as she thrusts a piece of A4 paper at Ramona. It is a black and white image of a Porsche, printed from a computer.

'Recognise this?'

Ramona swallows.

'I found it in Sonny's room. Turns out it's just like the one you and him saw last week. He looked up the model on the internet at school and printed it out, then started bragging to his friends about how his mum's mate took him out and—'

'Cind, I can explain.'

'Fuck *you*.' Cindy's voice is laced with tears. 'You were supposed to be looking after him. I trusted you. I *trusted* you. How could you?'

'It was a stupid mistake. I didn't want to let you down—'

'Didn't want to let me down?' Cindy balks. 'What, so you thought instead you would take my son on a mission to fuck over some gangsters? What's wrong with you? Are you mad? Seriously, on what planet would you think—'

'It's not like that—' Ramona bites her lip. 'I suddenly had to work that day but I didn't want to let you down. I knew if I told you where I was going you wouldn't have let me take Sonny, and I know how much you need to work.' Her voice is quiet.

'Don't you dare put this on me, Ramona. You put my son in danger.' She seems to switch gears, her rage turning to despair. 'I already have social services breathing down my neck. Do you know what that's like? If they catch wind—'

'I'm sorry, I fucked up.'

'Yeah,' Cindy replies, her eyes shining. 'You really did.'

CHAPTER TWENTY-FOUR

At 6.08 on Tuesday morning, Madeleine, perched at the counter in the kitchen, glances up from the article she is reading, and checks the time on her phone.

Bleary-eyed from yet another night of barely sleeping, she places the phone face down on the counter and steps off her stool and heads to the Nespresso machine, where she presses the button for a second double espresso.

Her stomach makes a noise and she shushes it, opening the fridge and scanning the shelves, which are empty but for the leftover takeaway from two nights ago. Removing the box and tentatively opening the lid, she sniffs its contents and makes a face, dropping the carton into the bin on her way to collect her drink.

Ramona and Jonny will soon be on their way. Gaining access to the son's house would be the money-shot. But when the chance to gain access to Sergey's offices via the cleaning company had presented itself – thanks to a regular payment listed on the bank statements she had procured from Daphne King – it had seemed rude not to give that a whirl, too.

And it had been easy enough to cancel this morning's cleaning service at AlterRon HQ, once Fionn had procured the name of the person they usually dealt with at Estate Cleaning. Madeleine had dictated the message he then sent to the agency from a cloned AlterRon account explaining that they would pay the bill as usual, but wouldn't need the manpower on this occasion.

From there, it had simply been a matter of running off some branding for the van and having a couple of T-shirts made up, before getting a small team on board. That was the easy part.

She hadn't told Rittler – surely she had no reason to – and Jonny hadn't asked.

Polishing off the dregs of her double espresso, she sighs. She really should get rid of this machine, she thinks. Much as Daphne's hypocrisy had made her wince when she criticised her for using disposable pods, she was right. Just because the world is full of devils disguised as men, it doesn't mean that plastic pollution isn't also a problem. There is space for more than one threat to civilisation, of this much Madeleine can be sure.

More to the point, it tastes like shit. The Arôme Bakery on Duke Street doesn't open until 8.30 a.m. She will pass by on her way to the office and get a proper coffee. Part of her wants to head in now. Will Fionn be there already? Probably. Madeleine has begun to wonder whether he sleeps at all.

Aside from the previous morning when she got in before him, he is almost always at his desk, no matter the time of day or night. But his time-keeping is hardly surprising – he had worked in the City before retraining as a finance lawyer and then sashaying across to the police, and old habits die hard.

Sitting up straight, she necks her final espresso and stands and heads for the shower to scrub herself clean.

* * *

The van is parked at a jaunty angle on John Adam Street. The temporary vinyl lettering along the vehicle's side panel matches the emblem on Ramona and Jonny's Estate Cleaning shirts.

At 6.15 a.m., Jonny starts the engine, and the radio, which is tuned into Magic FM, blasts through the speakers. Ramona waits for him to turn the music down, and when he doesn't she leans forward and turns the dial herself.

'Not into Boyzone?' he asks, and Ramona doesn't answer, leaning her cheek against the passenger seat window.

The journey from Embankment to Sergey Zhatchanov's office in Canary Wharf is almost a straight line along the river, the lights from the lamp posts on the bridge that connects the north of the city to the south reflecting on the surface of the river. Heading east, they drive away from the Strand. The main thoroughfare through theatreland had been largely empty when Ramona arrived half an hour earlier, apart from the homeless bundled in their sleeping bags and early morning workers setting up for the day at the chain cafés that seem to occupy at least every other shop.

Slowly, London is coming to life.

'So what about you?' Jonny asks a while later, humming along to Cyndi Lauper.

Ramona looks at him sidelong. 'What about me?'

'You've got a PI licence. So what are you doing working for us?'

'I don't work for you,' Ramona responds, looking out of the window as Jonny slows the van at the traffic lights.

'Well.' He makes a dissenting noise, pointing to their presence in the van. 'I mean, I don't want to be argumentative but—'

'This is just a short-term arrangement.'

'Right. Until you're a full-blown Philip Marlowe.' Jonny winks. 'Good name, Ramona Chang, by the way. Is it real, or a homage?'

A *homage*? He is referring to Raymond Chandler, of course. It had been embarrassing for her to realise the similarity between the name of the fictional private eye and her own assumed identity, after the fact. But it was too late to change it again.

Without answering, Ramona rolls her eyes and turns to stare once more out of the window.

'Right chatterbox, you are. There's a few bag of crisps on the back seat if you're hungry,' Jonny says. After a while, he finally accepts Ramona's silence and hums along to the radio.

* * *

Rittler is in early again when Madeleine arrives at the office, armed with a Pret pastry for herself and another for the night-hawk. In the end, she had left home at 7.30 a.m. and settled for the only place she could find open en route. The Arôme Bakery, it was not.

Madeleine says nothing as she passes his desk, heading towards the stairs.

On the first floor, she walks over to Fionn and hands him the croissant.

'What's this?'

'Food,' she replies. We humans ingest it through our mouths, she adds silently, as she takes her seat.

Her desk is just as she left it yesterday, aside from the flashing button on her phone telling her there is a voicemail. She knows before she hears Tim's voice that it will be her man in human trafficking, returning her call. She had never given him her mobile number. Even if she had done so, Tim would never have called it other than in an emergency. He is an old-fashioned gent who still believes in working hours and non-working hours, and wouldn't dream of imposing on the latter.

Madeleine, it's Tim. I got your message re the Time for Tuition bloke, happy to help if I can. Give me a call when you get in, I'll—

Madeleine hits pause at the sound of Rittler heaving up the stairs.

'I didn't expect you to be here,' Madeleine says, looking up at him as she takes a mouthful of her croissant. The implication is that if she had done, she would have got him a pastry, too. Whatever is going on between them, Madeleine isn't spiteful.

'Yeah well, I've got some stuff to catch up on,' her boss replies in a tone she doesn't recognise.

Neither of them is in the mood to continue their argument from the previous day, and Madeleine looks up at him unemotionally, noting the greyish pallor of his skin. He looks so tired.

Before she can pass comment, Rittler carries on. 'Where's Jonny?'

'He's gone to Sergey Zhatchanov's office.'

'I don't remember authorising that.' His expression is one of genuine confusion.

Madeleine considers him, her thoughts darkening. What is this, a box-ticking exercise or an effort to catch a criminal?

'I authorised it,' she says.

Rittler pauses. If he is about to chastise her, he thinks better of it. 'Right, well – anything else to report?'

Madeleine's eyes narrow. Why won't he meet her gaze? 'Not yet.'

Leaning forward and tapping the edge of her desk thoughtfully, he turns away. 'Good.'

She has barely had a chance to log into her computer when Madeleine hears the front door open and close again downstairs. Standing, she looks out of the window and sees her boss walking down the road, making a phone call.

'DS Farrow?' Fionn calls over, and Madeleine turns to him.

'Yes?'

'I have something on the shell company that owns the building that one of Ingrid Zhatchanova's cards is registered to . . . the one we followed her to in Hampstead. Two names keeping coming up: one is Nurislam Sultanov, the other is Sergey Zhatchanov.'

'You're joking?'

Fionn shakes his head, unnecessarily. Of course he isn't joking, Madeleine is pretty sure humour isn't within his programming.

'Let me see that.' For the first time since she and Bella sat side by side in the cinema on Friday, a smile hovers over Madeleine's mouth.

She leans across, taking charge of Fionn's keyboard before he can object. Nurislam Sultanov – the same man whose car she had seen parked outside Ingrid and then Shyrailym's home. 'He and Sergey are old friends turned crypto rivals, who joined forces when the market imploded. Together, they now run several legitimate companies – and several more, it would seem, less legitimate.'

'Fionn,' Madeleine says. 'You're a genius.'

* * *

The sky is beginning to lighten as they reach Canary Wharf. Carrying along towards the car park as instructed by the satnav, Jonny pulls left into an underground entrance and follows the signs to the allocated AlterRon Ltd parking space.

'Here we are,' he says, turning down the volume on *Wham!*

Thank God. Ramona isn't sure how much more of Jonny's singing she can take.

'Do we not need security passes?' she asks, reaching for the door handle.

'Fionn's sorted it.'

Her expression softening, Ramona takes the lanyard he hands her.

Stopping briefly, Jonny adds under his breath. 'Remember, I'm Albanian and you're from the Philippines, so whatever you do, don't talk.'

For the first time all day, Ramona almost smiles.

* * *

Tim was the first person that Madeleine ever worked with, one-on-one, after she moved across from the Foreign Office, not long after the organisation for which they both now work was formed. More than a decade later, as she walks through Vauxhall Pleasure Gardens with her hands stuffed deep into the pockets of her wool gingham coat, she thinks of him with a fondness that borders on nostalgia.

Older than she is, Tim is mild-mannered and slight. A gentleman, in the truest sense of the word. He had been Madeleine's senior officer when she joined. Unlike the rest of her new colleagues, most of whom had been brought across from the agency's previous incarnation as the Serious Organised Crime Agency, he was kind and welcoming and didn't give a toss that Madeleine was a posh lesbian with no background in policing.

The Black Dog is situated at the edge of the Vauxhall Pleasure Gardens, a stone's throw both from headquarters and MI6, making it a firm favourite with her lot and spooks alike. In the main, it is easy to spot the difference.

She feels the rain start as she approaches the pub.

Together, she and Tim had worked on her first stint in Vietnam before Madeleine was farmed out to the Serious Crime Investigations Department. That trip had been a baptism of fire, as they traced a network of human traffickers from a huge cannabis warehouse in Bedfordshire, six thousand miles east to Vinh city in central Vietnam.

Back in the UK, Madeleine and Tim interviewed victims embroiled in so-called debt bondage, working in warehouses and nail bars and car washes across the country. One boy they spoke to, aged twelve, had had two fingers chopped off by loan sharks after his parents died and he was unable to repay their debt. She had tried not to focus on the stump on his hand as the boy – now a teenager – explained, via an interpreter, his route to the UK after being enticed by smugglers posing as students. He had been trafficked from Hanoi airport, thirty thousand kilometres to Russia in a cargo plane. From there he had been taken by lorry to Poland, Germany, France and finally to England. Mid-winter, he was kept in the driver's cabin covered in petroleum so dogs wouldn't smell him at checkpoints, only to find himself a victim of modern slavery, once he arrived at the promised land.

Tim had brought her to the same pub where she is headed now, once they had finished the interview, and bought her a brandy.

'Madeleine Farrow.' Her former partner smiles as he looks up from his table, the same spot where he and Madeleine had sat that evening. He is drinking a pint of lime and soda. Standing, he reaches for his money clip. Madeleine loves that he still carries one.

'Coffee?' Tim asks.

Glancing at the row of spirits behind the bar, Madeleine is tempted but shakes her head. 'It's me who should be buying you a drink,' she replies, slipping off her coat and taking the seat opposite.

'That sounds worrying.'

'How's Leonora?'

All these years later, Tim still smiles at the mention of his wife, to whom he has been married more than four decades. Madeleine doubly loves him for that.

'She's doing great. Spends most of her time these days at the allotment in Barnet, growing all sorts. She would love to see you.' Settling himself back in his seat, he considers her. 'And how are you? Back for long this time?'

Madeleine makes a non-committal shrug. 'Probably not. Just taking a breather.'

Tim nods and for a moment it looks as if he might say something else, acknowledging the toll her speciality takes, but he doesn't. Why state what they both already know?

'So how can I help?' he asks, instead.

'Do you mind if this stays between us?' Madeleine leans in.

Tim reaches for his drink, and takes a sip. He is nothing if not by the book, but he is also experienced enough to know that sometimes in this job there are different books for different situations. 'As long as it's not—'

'It's nothing dubious, at least not on my side,' Madeleine says, aware of any number of ears potentially lurking at the tables around them.

'I've been looking into a website called Time for Tuition. It claims to be some sort of high-end escort agency connecting students with wealthy older men. Girls have been applying to the site and being told they need to do a practical assessment, and meet this guy in some office block and have sex with him. Then, when they get home there's an email saying they didn't pass the practical but are free to reapply any time.'

Tim makes a face. His moral compass is unwavering. For someone who spends their days investigating humanity's perversions, he is also still easily ruffled. He and Leonora never had children of their own but still he takes every case to heart, as though it was his son or daughter being wronged.

'Quite,' she continues. 'The thing is, there is no sign of any clients, or of any successful applicants. The listing at Companies House is fake. I've had a look at the office space and it's rigged with cameras. It seems to me that it's all some elaborate charade for this guy to get laid and film it at the same time.'

'You think he's selling the films?'

'Maybe.' Madeleine shrugs. 'I'm thinking we can definitely get him on a voyeurism charge, but I'm also wondering about something else.' She pauses to gather her thoughts. 'Sexual assault is going to be a hard one to make stick, but if I'm right in believing that there are in fact no clients waiting to pay for the girls' services, then would his behaviour not meet the measure for trafficking? He has arranged his victim's travel, he has deceived her, and he sexually exploited her . . .'

Madeleine looks at Tim expectantly.

Considering her words, he takes a careful sip of his soft drink. 'Well, if you can prove that there are no clients . . .' he shrugs. 'Then I reckon we're on.'

'Are you sure?' Madeleine asks. 'I'm working on proving that part. The website has been taken down, so it looks as if our man realises he has been rumbled and has gone to ground. He told my contact that she only had a couple of days left to audition. Maybe he has a job that takes him away for periods of time—'

'What if you can't find him?'

'We will.' Madeleine's tone is absolute. But it is proving trickier than she had hoped. Whatever encryption his site uses, it is more advanced than the average.

'I heard about your brother,' Tim says, with a gentle straightforwardness.

'You and the entire country. Shame everyone else seemed to know before me.'

'You weren't given a heads up?'

'Yeah, right.'

Tim hesitates. 'Look, don't shoot the messenger, but I saw Catrin earlier. She was asking after you.'

'Catrin?'

'You know, your ex-lover, now Miss Highfalutin in the MoJ?'

Christ, she really doesn't like hearing Tim say the word *lover*.

'When?'

'A couple of hours ago.' He picks up his cordial and takes a drink.

'And she was asking after *me*? What was she saying?'

'She just wanted to know if I had spoken to you.'

Momentarily speechless, Madeleine splutters. 'What? So clearly she knows that you have – but how?'

'I dunno.' Tim shrugs. As always, his very being is a demonstration of profound calm. 'You know very well that I didn't tell her.'

'What did you say?'

'I told her that I hadn't seen you, which was true. You asked me to keep this under my hat. What's going on?'

Madeleine's phone rings and she swears under her breath at the interruption. Seeing Jonny's number, she answers.

'They wouldn't let us in,' he says, over the line.

'What?' Leaning her chair back slowly, Madeleine looks up at Tim and then glances away.

'They said they didn't need any cleaners today, that we should come back next time as planned.'

'Shit.'

'Aye.'

'*Shit*.' Slamming her fist on the table, Madeleine's cheeks burn.

Tim looks up at her, several pairs of eyes stationed around the bar moving towards her.

'Are you with Ramona?'

'We're both here.'

'I'll call you back.' Hanging up, Madeleine pauses, gathering her thoughts.

Reaching across the table, she touches Tim's hand lightly and then calmly puts on her coat. 'Thanks, Tim.'

'Is everything OK?'

'Not really,' Madeleine muses.

'What's going on – can I help?'

'I'm not sure.'

'Let me know about the website—' Tim smiles and she stands, giving him a reassuring wink. 'I will. You take care, Tim.'

Considering her with a worried expression, he replies, 'You too, girl.'

* * *

Outside, rain lashes the pavements. Without an umbrella, Madeleine turns and runs towards the path that will lead her back to the tube, away from headquarters. Her chest constricts with the building pressure of an increasing number of unanswered questions.

Had she imagined Rittler's suggestion that the case wasn't worth pursuing? Had Sergey's company been tipped off about the undercover cleaners – or was it simply that having had the jewellery seized, the family now knows they are under watch and are being extra cautious as a matter of course?

Again, she thinks of Catrin. Can it be a coincidence that twenty-four hours after Madeleine calls Tim, her ex turns up again asking questions?

Obviously there is no such thing as coincidence. Everything is connected, if you delve deep enough. The question now is not *if* but how.

Stopping to lean against a wall, Madeleine feels a tightening in her lungs.

Reminding herself to breathe, she stands still in the middle of the gardens and closes her eyes, enjoying the sensation of the rain streaking down her cheeks.

A few seconds pass before Madeleine realises her phone is ringing. Taking it out of her pocket, she sees that the number is withheld.

Tentatively, she presses the accept button.

'Hello?'

'Madeleine? It's Rittler. I'm at HQ, could you come in?'

CHAPTER TWENTY-FIVE

Inside the revolving doors at headquarters, beyond the rain-slicked pavements, a yellow plastic A-frame sign reads: *Caution, slip hazard ahead.*

Madeleine catches a glimpse of herself in the reflection of the glass as she passes inside and proceeds towards the metal detector. Dripping tiny pools of rainwater onto the floor with every considered step, she pulls the lanyard from the pocket of her handbag and steps through the arch, swiping herself in through the turnstiles.

Gerald Okoduwa and Paul Rittler are deep in conversation when she enters the briefing room, stepping inside without knocking. A third figure stands with her back to them, looking out over London. The sky ahead is grey and leaden.

Her mind whirring, Madeleine peels away a lock of hair stuck to her cheek by the rain, and holds her chin a little higher.

'Madeleine,' Gerald purrs, as Catrin turns to face the room. Rittler stands uneasy between them, looking at Madeleine, and then down at the floor.

Madeleine is aware of Catrin's scrutinising gaze, taking in the sodden cashmere coat, cream suit trousers and the suede ankle boots that help give Madeleine the sense of having a firm footing, even now, when she has none. She keeps her attention focused on Rittler.

The muscle under her eye spasms as she stands there, refusing to remove her coat though it is so warm in here. Warm and damp.

'Why did you call me in?' she asks, plainly.

'Madeleine, sit down,' Gerald says. 'You know Catrin Davies, from the Ministry of Justice.'

'Yes,' Madeleine says, disconnected from her own words. She feels as if she is someone else, watching on from the other side of a sheet of glass; as though she could press her mouth up to it and scream and no one would hear.

'Madeleine, I wanted to—' Catrin begins before taking a breath and starting again. 'Paul and I have been talking and I want you to help us with something we're working on, regarding a rather sensitive case.'

Still, Madeleine doesn't look at her, keeping her eyes on Rittler, studying him for clue as to on what it is about his face that has changed. He looks thinner and heavier at once, as though any light-ness of spirit has been expelled.

'I'm already working on a case,' she says, evenly.

'Yes I know, but Paul is prepared to forfeit you for this. It is something of a diplomatic situation, and with your background—'

Blinking, Madeleine turns to Catrin, whose expression shifts so imperceptibly that only someone who has laid next to her in bed at night, memorising the grooves of her skin, would notice.

Licking her lips in the way that she does when she is unsure of herself, Catrin continues. 'We're working with Interpol on the final stages of an ongoing investigation—'

'We need our best people on this, and I've recommended you.' Rittler steps in with only the slightest glance at Catrin.

'So you're taking me off the Zhatchanov case.' She presents it as a statement rather than a question, because apparently that is what this is.

'Jonny and Fionn are all over it. Resources are over-stretched – you know how it is – and we need our best people on our most important cases. This was only ever going to be an interim thing for you.'

'An amuse bouche,' Okoduwa offers and Madeleine restrains herself from replying.

'Because you need me here,' she replies after a beat, looking over at Gerald, who gives the slightest dip of his head by way of acknowledgement.

You need me here at headquarters, where you can see me, she thinks, joining the dots.

Her gaze sharpening, Madeleine pushes her shoulders back. 'Do I have a choice?' When there is no reply, she keeps her expression blank. 'So then, fill me in.'

* * *

The following days bleed past with painful monotony, the usual muffled applause drifting up to Ramona's flat through the floorboards.

By midday on Thursday, there are two enquiries via her contact page, one from a man using the handle @ImBigTDontHateMe who believes his wife is sleeping with his friend, which Ramona instantly deletes, and a second beginning *Greetings of the Day!* from a company asking her if she wants to grow her social media following (currently zero) 'to become next big influencar [*sic*]'.

Cindy is not at the morning meeting again, and so at lunchtime Ramona takes a covert walk past Sonny's school, scanning the playground for a glimpse of him.

From a discreet distance, she finds herself watching the children running back and forth, lost in their own private games. On the far side of the playground, a girl with a series of colourful plastic beads hanging from the end of her plaits sits alone on a bench, looking at her feet as she swings her legs.

Ramona's stomach lurches.

She wishes she could walk over to the bench and sit beside her. Why doesn't one of the teachers on playground duty make the other kids ask her to play? But it's not their fault, Ramona knows that much. There are too many people and too many problems, you can't fix them all.

School is brutal. But in that sense, it is a good training ground for the real world.

Just then, another child, holding her chest with lack of breath from running so hard, jogs up to the bench and leans over to the girl, who gets up and follows her to join in the game. Ramona sighs in relief.

'Sonny!' The sound of his name being called across the playground returns Ramona to what she is doing.

Searching the playground once more, she spots him – Cindy's boy dribbling a ball through a crowd of other children. Her spirits lift as she looks more closely and sees that he is smiling. Cindy must be fine, or Sonny's face would show it. Of course she's fine, she reminds herself; it is Ramona who is the problem.

When Cindy talks about her recovery journey in meetings, her narrative is remarkably free of self-pity, even when she hints at the emotional abuse she underwent at the hands of her God-fearing parents. Her life is presented as a series of facts: she went to school locally, did well, fell in with the wrong crowd, got into prostitution way too young, and drugs followed.

She never talks about Sonny in her sharing. She never talks about how she and the boy's father, Maxy, were together since school, having grown up in the same flats where her mother and father kept themselves to themselves, other than to go to church. She never blames Sonny's dad for getting her on the game and for supplying her with a bit of this and a bit of that to soften the nerves, before taking his share of something that was never his to take.

Getting pregnant when she was just sixteen was Cindy's rock bottom – there is almost always a rock bottom – but in the end it also turned out to be her saving grace.

Sitting on a low wall a little way along from the school, Ramona takes out a cigarette. Lighting up, she enjoys the slow inhalation of smoke. Pulling out her phone, she wishes she had credit so that she could text Madeleine to see if there is any news. But she can't afford to blow her emergency stash. In any case, Ramona knows she will call once there is news to tell.

A whistle blows in the distance. Standing, Ramona glances back at the playground where the children are drifting back towards the school, and presses play on her iPod. The same tune she last listened to on her way home from Bristol plays on rotation, and she thinks of Ottilie sitting earnestly opposite her a couple of weeks earlier. The twinge of guilt she feels for not yet having found an answer to the case turns to self-pity.

What if she can't solve it? What if whatever Madeleine had told her not to pin her hopes on does in fact come to nothing?

Getting a result isn't just about appeasing Ottilie, or even about getting her the justice she craves. It is about Ramona proving to herself that she can do this. If she can't, then what will she do instead? She is approaching thirty. It's hardly old in the general cycle of life and death, but for someone with nothing to her name apart from a career that fulfils her, it is old enough to worry about the idea of starting again from scratch. She can't go back to journalism; even if she wanted to, she would have to work under a pseudonym and it's too small a world; word would get out.

Join law enforcement full-time? She shudders. It would be fundamentally at odds with who she is. It would be like asking a fox to sleep in a fish tank.

Perhaps Ramona had been naïve to believe that she could sustain herself on bits of freelance work for Madeleine, while she solved her first proper case and then waited for her PI career to take off. But if her mother had taught her anything, it's that no one is going to give you the life you want. If you want it badly enough, you have to take it – and that is what she is doing: building the world she wants for herself; it's not like she is asking for much. Enough income to cover both the electric and the rent, with enough for phone credit, would be a good start.

There is one person left who she could ask to borrow money from, if things—

Dismissing the idea no sooner than it presents itself, Ramona continues on towards Mildmay Park North.

At the sight of Madeleine on her doorstep, she slows and then speeds up again.

'Hey.' Her smile fades away as she clocks Madeleine's expression. 'What's up?'

'Can I come in?' The look Madeleine shoots her is enough to tell her that there is no use asking until they are upstairs.

'Aren't you going to take off your shoes?' Ramona asks as they step into the hall.

Madeleine looks down at her heels and then at the damp-stained carpet.

'Don't worry,' Ramona says. 'I'm joking.'

* * *

Madeleine's eyes bulge slightly, as she follows Ramona upstairs and into the flat. 'I like what you've done with the place.'

On the counter, next to a couple of cups discarded by the sink, is a clump of hair Madeleine at first mistakes for an animal, before realising it is a wig. The remnants of last night's microwave meal stand on the kitchen counter, the container having been used as an ashtray.

The resulting scene is a sort of depressing Tracey Emin installation, perked up by the wall opposite: a montage of images, each with O'Keegan's face or name staring back at her. At first Madeleine wonders if this is part of Ramona's original investigation, and then she remembers Ramona had been living somewhere else at that time. And with a little more thought, she realises these articles all relate to the story that resulted from her own exclusive exposé. A trophy wall, of sorts – except instead of medals, there was evidence of years of investigation. She can hardly blame Ramona for wanting to celebrate

255

what she had achieved, helping to bring down one of the biggest drug-dealing gangs in the world. Though she imagined Amber might have something to say about the feng-shui of it all.

The case had been excellent press for the Met, too – even though most of their information had come from Ramona's own private work.

'I wasn't expecting guests,' Ramona says now, as she moves inside the tiny flat.

There is the roach of a spliff in a glass ashtray on the table, which Ramona takes and empties. Beside it, an old copy of the *Evening Standard*; on the cover, a photo of her brother, Dominic Farrow, and the PM shaking hands. Taking her phone from her handbag and placing it on the table, Madeleine silently indicates for Ramona to do the same.

'Actually, shall we go for a walk?'

* * *

Ramona watches Madeleine with a sense of curiosity. Clearly she is relieved to be away from the flat and out of earshot of potential listeners.

Did she really worry that Ramona's home might be wired up?

'So they have pulled you off the Zhatchanov case, and now you think they might have bugged our phones and my flat, too?' Ramona asks as they walk through Clissold Park, a Bedlington Whippet chasing a Labrador across their path.

'I think it's unlikely that they've bugged your flat, but I don't actually know what is going on, so I'd rather not take any chances,' Madeleine replies, straightforwardly. 'What I do know is that I – and consequently you, as my contact – are no longer wanted on the case, and I have no idea why. I also know that my sanctimonious ex-girlfriend, who works in the civil service for the MoJ – and who is now apparently best friends with my narcissist of a brother – has something to do with it.'

'Shit,' Ramona says, and Madeleine makes a weary sigh.

'Yes, it is a bit.'

'So what are you thinking?'

She shrugs, as if it is anyone's guess. 'Something is going on, trickling down from above – most likely political. Quite possibly it has something to do with Sergey and the Tory peerage. Why else would Dominic or Catrin be interested in keeping me away? Although appointed Lords being revealed as criminals is hardly news, these days, is it? Whatever it is, someone is trying to hush it up. Maybe the sister, Shyrailym, is an asset, secretly watching her family for MI6 or the Kazakhs, or—? Christ, I just don't know.'

Madeleine shakes her head, breathing in through her nose. 'What I am sure about is that whatever is going on, someone on my team has been acting in cahoots with the high-ups at the MoJ, given that they knew I was talking to my human trafficking contact, within moments.'

'Or, to be less dramatic, someone might have been listening in on your calls, which can hardly be surprising; surely everything is internally monitored,' Ramona counters.

'True.' Madeleine nods. 'But just because calls are recorded doesn't mean all of them are being listened to all the time. Who has the resources for that? It is hard enough keeping tabs on the criminals, let alone your own staff.'

'I met him, by the way: the colleague I mentioned who might be able to help us bring a trafficking charge. He seemed hopeful.' Madeleine sees the younger woman's face light up, though until they can track him down – and the website, which Fionn claims he is still working on – they are no closer to bringing a charge.

'Do you think it could be Jonny?' Ramona asks as they follow the path towards a set of tennis courts. Madeleine feels instantly defensive. But it is true, it could be any one of them.

'No.' Madeleine is absolute. 'I suppose the most likely guess is Fionn – he's new and a shoo-in, and he is around all the bloody time – but Rittler's been pretty shady recently. Honestly, it could be anyone. Amol, Jamal . . . .' She hesitates, only slightly. 'Not Jonny.'

Madeleine turns to Ramona. 'At risk of sounding highly melodramatic, we can't trust anyone else. It's just you and me, until—'

Until when? It is a question to which she doesn't want to think of the answer.

'But we're not giving up?' Ramona says, and Madeleine smiles. 'What do you think?'

CHAPTER TWENTY-SIX

'Wow, you look . . .' Gareth begins, glancing up from his comic.

It is Tuesday morning at the shop in Hatton Garden, and through the window a blue sky is visible in a gap between the rooftops, hinting at spring just around the corner.

'Don't say anything,' Ramona snaps, cutting him short as she walks out of the loo, dressed in a Breton-striped top and pair of linen indigo dungarees that Madeleine had foisted on her after they returned to the flat from their meeting in Clissold Park.

Over the top of these, Ramona wears a navy apron with the words *Robbins & Ribbons* embroidered in the right-hand corner. On her feet is a pair of brown suede Birkenstock clogs, with just enough scuffing around the toes to seem convincingly as though they are worn day to day, but not so scuffed that they might have been taken far beyond the borders of Westminster and the Borough of Kensington and Chelsea.

'It's a good look for you,' Gareth continues, as he lines up a selection of bugs on the counter.

'Fuck you very much,' Ramona replies calmly, as she picks up the various cameras and inspects them each in turn. 'How can you not have found a trace on James Harvey yet?'

'I don't know what to tell you, the guy knows what he is doing . . .

Dare I ask where you're taking these?' Gareth says, once he has finished implanting the camera into the silk hibiscus, which Ramona slips into her bag.

'Seen Si recently?' Ramona retorts sharply, looking up at him and watching him blush as he rings numbers into his payment device.

'I'll take that as a no,' he says, pressing proceed on the transaction.

Pocketing what she came for, Ramona shrugs. 'I didn't bring my card. I'll pay next time.'

* * *

Berkeley Square is a historic public garden framed by luxury offices and Bentley and Ferrari showrooms and clubs with names like Sexy Fish. It is one of those parts of London that makes Ramona want to step off the edge of the world, safe in the knowledge that it will soon be going up in flames behind her.

Sergey Zhatchanov's house stands a stone's throw away, visible from the bench where Ramona sits and waits until the *Robbins & Ribbons* van pulls around the corner and parks up, right on schedule.

From here, she watches the woman in the apron and dungarees identical to her own, ferrying floral arrangements from the back of the van and into Sergey Zhatchanov's front door.

The sprays of white tulips, hypericum, pink waxflower and hibiscus, which Ramona knows from the company's website are R & R's signature, are the same as those Madeleine had noticed in the delivery last time she was at the house. Ramona had bought a replica from the company's bricks-and-mortar shop, on her way here from Hatton Garden. Until now, she had no way of knowing if they would be delivering the same variety today, and had been prepared to run back to the shop to change them. Thankfully, from this distance, she sees that they appear to be a match.

Six minutes and twelve bouquets after first entering the building, the flower delivery girl finally gets back into the van and leaves. From the edge of the square, where Ramona sits clutching her bouquet, she watches as she slams closed the back doors of the van, ready to head off on her next job.

At exactly the same time, Ramona stands and leaves the square, approaching Sergey Zhatchanov's home as the van turns left and disappears into the melee of central London. Without delay, she takes up the brass lion's-head knocker and bangs it firmly.

A small woman in a traditional black and white maid's outfit answers.

'I'm so sorry,' Ramona says, out of breath, before the woman can speak. 'We delivered the wrong flowers. One of the bouquets has yesterday's spray in it, it will be dead by the morning. My boss asked me to exchange it. I won't be a moment, she is just waiting around the corner. It's my first week and I am *mortified*.'

Ramona speaks with an apologetic lilt, employing her best posh North London accent, and waits a moment until the maid opens the door, reluctantly, and nods for her to come inside.

'Which bunch?' she asks sharply, and Ramona falters. She had counted twelve being brought inside for arrangement. But where to? And where was she most likely to get a line on a fruitful conversation.

'The study—' Ramona hazards a guess. Shit, what man has flowers in his study? Wishing she had plumped for the living room, she holds her breath.

But the gamble pays off.

'I'll take them.' The maid reaches for the bouquet but Ramona keeps them in her grip.

'No,' she replies firmly. 'I had strict instructions to do a quick arrangement. My boss will kill me if—'

The sound of keys on the other side of the door disturbs them and when it opens, Sergey Zhatchanov walks into the hallway. Ignoring the staff, he laughs as he talks into his phone.

Ramona's heartbeat taps a little faster. Holding her ground, she addresses the maid once more. 'Would you like to show me where to go?'

'Who's this, is she here about the party?' Sergey asks the maid, before glancing at Ramona.

'The flowers—' the maid begins to answer, but her boss turns away, no longer interested, resuming his conversation with a tell-tale sniffing sound that Ramona would recognise anywhere. Not that a coke habit is particularly surprising, given that everything about this encounter so far has been like a game of billionaire bingo.

Amusing herself, Ramona thinks of the terminology she learnt on Friday nights at the bingo, with her grandmother.

Mayfair address? *Kelly's eye.*

Phallic marble statues in the hallway? *Sweet 16 and never been kissed.*

Foreign maid? *Dancing queen.*

A thriving cocaine habit? Full house. *46 Up to tricks.*

Ramona watches almost in disbelief as Sergey turns right towards the kitchen, shutting the door behind him before continuing his conversation.

'I'm so sorry, but I better be quick. My boss—' she says now, taking charge.

Hesitating briefly as if she might turn Ramona away after all, and then thinking better of it, the maid turns and leads her up the staircase, which curves to the left as they head to the first floor.

There are three rooms. Glancing left and right, Ramona sees that one appears to be a guest bedroom. The second, its door also ajar, is a bathroom. At the end of the corridor is a sitting room with floor to ceiling books and artefacts encased behind glass cabinets, and – what else – a glass coffee table. On the far wall, above the fireplace, hangs a painting Ramona knows from her GCSE art classes is either a real Chagall, or an impressive imitation.

At the centre of the table is an oversized vase brimming with flowers.

'Is there a bathroom I can use for this? I don't want to make a mess,' Ramona says, moving towards the existing floral display, which she is relieved to see is almost identical to the one she is holding.

'This way.' The maid leads the way out into the hallway and points towards the bathroom. Keeping her back to the other woman, Ramona lifts the vase and carries it along with the new bouquet towards the bathroom. Setting them both down on a marble counter next to a marble sink, she takes a deep breath. She has never so much as arranged a vase of daffodils before.

How hard can it be? She simply has to replicate the one she has in front of her.

The camera is already installed inside the stigma of a pink silk hibiscus, realistic enough that Ramona struggles to tell it apart from the real ones as she lays the replacement bouquet on its side and unwraps the waxed brown paper.

Removing the original arrangement from the vase, she places it in the sink, aware of the maid watching her reflection in the mirror.

Willing her hands not to shake, she lifts the new bouquet into the glass bowl and arranges the stems so that the tiny microphone inside the silk hibiscus is facing her.

'This should be perfect now,' Ramona says, clearly. 'Should last at least a week.' Just then, her phone rings and Ramona notices the maid's surprise at the sight of her old Nokia.

'Hi,' Ramona answers.

'The line is good, I can hear every word,' Madeleine responds.

'Just coming, sorry. It looks perfect.' Ramona smiles, hanging up and picking up the vase, which she takes back into the sitting room and places on the table. 'Shall I take the old ones out with me?'

'No, I'll throw them away.' The maid signals towards the staircase.

'Thanks so much.' Assuming an apologetic expression, she makes her way downstairs, where Sergey Zhatchanov is standing in a room just off the hallway. 'What time does your plane get in on Saturday?' He continues his conversation, unaware of their presence. 'Don't be late, we have plenty of girls and—'

The maid coughs and Sergey looks up at the women passing through the hall. With a brief wink at Ramona, he kicks the door closed.

Turning to the maid, Ramona gives a heartfelt smile. 'You have been such a help.'

* * *

263

Madeleine watches Ramona through the wing mirror, still in uniform, as she returns to the surveillance van, parked up two streets away.

'There's a party at the house on Saturday night, with girls being brought in as escorts. I'm going to go,' Ramona announces to Madeleine, the moment she steps into the back.

Madeleine exchanges a quick look in the rear-view mirror with Jonny, seated up front in the driver's seat.

She'd had to decide whether to trust him to come in on this and not ask too many questions, or mention it to Rittler. Madeleine hasn't yet raised with him the imminent move to headquarters, on which she is due to be officially briefed the following morning, assuming she concedes – which she wasn't given much choice about – and she doubts he will find out any other way.

As far as Jonny is concerned, he is just doing his job. It is a deception of sorts, but Madeleine wasn't going to risk putting Ramona in harm's way as she herself seems intent on doing, without at least having the bare minimum manpower at hand.

True to form, Jonny is too busy singing along to the radio to eavesdrop on their conversation.

'Absolutely no way,' Madeleine replies, secretly impressed by Ramona's chutzpah.

'Why not?'

'For a number of reasons,' she responds, calmly. 'Among them, the fact that if we're dealing with a situation where sex might be involved, we'd need an undercover TPO – and even then, they would usually act as the punter, not the prostitute.'

'What's a TPO?'

'A TPO is a test purchase officer, and the fact that you don't know that is further evidence that you are not suitable for this role.'

'I wouldn't have sex with anyone, for fuck's sake . . .' Ramona huffs. 'This is ridiculous: our first chance at a proper connection with the family and you're saying no?'

'I appreciate your enthusiasm,' Madeleine continues, genuinely. 'If we knew which escort agency they were using, there would be a chance we could target that. But honestly, even then I don't think we'd ever get it signed off in time. Even if we did have time, I can't see it being authorised due to the risk to the undercover, that is, to you. There would need to be safety protocols, and in an oligarch's mansion that would be hard. Especially trying to persuade HQ to pursue an Unexplained Wealth Order. It's hardly genocide. Even if we weren't now basically working as lone agents, without the support of Rittler. It's just a no.'

Was this true – was there no one else they could trust? An image of Daphne appears in Madeleine's mind and she hesitates a moment. Was she part of this, a plant of some sort? It isn't impossible, even if Madeleine doesn't understand how or why she is involved. Madeleine had met her the night before she was pulled onto this case – by this point her superiors would already have assigned her to it. If someone high up had seen that and wanted to monitor the situation . . .

A nasty thought occurs. Daphne had been alone in her flat, hadn't she? If she was a spy . . . No. Madeleine stops herself there. She is being paranoid. Daphne works in a bank, Madeleine had visited her at work unannounced.

She had been genuinely shocked to discover that Madeleine was police. Hadn't she? Yes, the other side of her brain replies: and a day or two later, Madeleine was being pulled off a case concerning one of the biggest financial criminals in the world, whose son happens to be a valued Conservative donor. Still, Gerald Okoduwa had said it himself, the wider issue of London being used by rich foreigners as a personal launderette service is far more embarrassing than a donor who turns out to be corrupt. Besides, Amir Zhatchanov's arrest is hardly a secret, nor is the fact that he has a son. The story is already out there.

She sighs audibly.

No, this has to be about something else. Perhaps Sergey is more involved than they officially knew. Being the son of a criminal and a party donor is one thing; but if he is up to no good himself . . .

* * *

The meeting has already started by the time Ramona arrives.

The linen *Robbins & Ribbons* apron is stuffed inside her bag, but she hasn't had time to change out of the striped top and tasteful dungarees, and she feels like a fraud as she approaches the crypt.

Stopping at the door, she gathers herself. From here, she can hear Pharrell's 'Happy' playing through the speakers and can't help but wonder if this might be a misguided choice of song for an unofficial wake. Still, it's the kind of thing JJ would probably have approved of. He was both horribly sentimental and had terrible taste in music.

Unlike their usual meetings, the room is bursting with those who have turned out to send him off. Apparently, word has got around.

For a moment, Ramona considers changing tack and walking home. If she's honest, she imagines herself heading to the nearest pub, but she can't do that to JJ. Of all the ways to send him off, getting trashed is probably not the most respectful. The fact that she can think so clearly, and override any lingering urge to get messed up, is a sign of how far she has come, in part thanks to her sponsor.

Taking out a cigarette, she waits outside, unable to bring herself to go in.

She hates these things. Her relationship with the person they are here to memorialise is – *was* – a personal one; he would understand her not wanting to come to a special meeting to honour his passing. Or rather, he would understand her not feeling the need to show up simply as a mark of respect.

Ramona doesn't need to demonstrate her affection for the man whose body is right now in the mortuary on Dalston Lane, being—

Taking another drag, she pushes the thought down and nervously taps her foot.

But it would feel wrong not to be here, she would never forgive herself.

And besides, there's someone else she needs to see.

* * *

Cindy is on the far side of the room, deep in conversation with an older woman whom Ramona vaguely recognises.

Seeing Ramona approach, Cindy starts – presumably thrown off guard by the clothes – and then fixes her attention more pointedly on the person she is talking to, shifting herself around a little so that Ramona is out of her line of sight.

Slowing down, Ramona bristles as she feels a hand on her arm.

'I wasn't sure you'd make it,' Vicky says, looking at her from under perfect flicks of neon-green eyeliner.

Vicky is well-meaning enough and apart from the pointed looks she gives Ramona whenever she asks if anyone wants to share at the end of a session, she isn't pushy. Nonetheless, Ramona always feels ambushed whenever the group leader tries to talk to her directly. Perhaps it is because Ramona has the feeling that she has drunk too much of the therapy Kool-Aid.

Though in fairness, Vicky isn't the only one: JJ was nothing if not evangelical about recovery, but he never came across as judgemental or self-righteous or unnecessarily probing. Whenever Ramona had opened up to him it was always a result of him leaving her enough space to offer up parts of herself, rather than feeling like she was being backed into a corner.

He understood that, in some ways, Ramona is like a rat: when made to feel trapped she is likely to lash out.

'Well, I'm here,' Ramona replies simply, in answer to Vicky's point, trying not to sound too passive-aggressive. The way Vicky is studying her face now, Ramona can't help but feel that the other woman is trying to read her, and she hates it.

'When was the last time you saw him?' Vicky asks next, the question taking her off guard.

'Erm, Wednesday morning. Why?'

Vicky shakes her head. 'No reason. I saw him on Crossway, that same day. I was just leaving the meeting and I was going to ask if he was alright because it was weird that he hadn't been there. It looked like he and some guy were having some kind of scuff.'

'A fight – JJ?' Ramona leans in. 'Who with?'

'There were two of them. I didn't get a proper look. They left and by the time I got to JJ, he was shaken. He asked me if I'd seen you.'

Ramona narrows her eyes. 'What time was this?'

Vicky thinks. 'Half nine, ten, maybe?'

'Yeah, he came to me right after—' Spotting Cindy turning away from the person she had been speaking to, Ramona hesitates. 'Listen, Vicky, I need to have a quick chat with Cindy . . . Did you see JJ again after that?'

'No. That was it.' She shakes her head, tears forming in her eyes. Ramona feels bad for leaving her crying, but there's nothing she can do about it, so she pats Vicky on the shoulder before breaking away and following Cindy through the crowd.

Catching her up, Ramona reaches out to her friend. 'Can we talk?'

Cindy pulls away without answering.

'I'm sorry,' Ramona says, in an almost childish tone. 'I'm so sorry. Tell me what I can do to make it right.'

When Cindy starts to move away again, Ramona stops her. 'Please, I really don't have that many people in my life and I've already lost JJ and I can't lose you and Sonny, too.'

The truth comes out far more readily than she had anticipated, and she looks down, embarrassed by her own candidness.

'OK, Needy,' Cindy says. Her tone is flat but when Ramona looks at her, there is a chink in her armour.

Cindy's resolve hardens again. 'I can't trust you, Ro.'

'Yes, you can. You can trust me more than anyone. I care about you guys so much, you know that. I'm a fucking idiot and I made a really stupid mistake and I'm sorry.'

'Jesus.' Cindy shakes her head.

'Please, I'll do anything.'

For a while Cindy doesn't say anything, and then she rolls her eyes, her expression cracking just a little. 'You're a lot, you know that?'

Ramona shrugs. 'Is that a good thing?'

'No.' Cindy's face grows serious again. 'If you ever – *ever* – put Sonny in danger—'

'It won't happen.'

'I mean it, Ramona.'

'So do I.'

Cindy inhales and then she sighs. Through the muted chatter, Ramona's phone rings and a couple of faces turn to look. She hasn't worked out how to turn down the volume on the ringer and the Nokia tune is nothing if not distinctive.

Seeing Madeleine's name on the screen, Ramona's finger hovers over the button before she presses reject. She will ring her back from a payphone when she leaves, which won't be long. She isn't going to cut Cindy off just as she has forgiven her. But Cindy reads her expression.

'You should call them back.'

'Nah.' Ramona makes a face, determining to call on her way home.

'Alright, well, I need to go anyway,' Cindy says. 'Let's walk together.'

* * *

'Where's Sonny now?' Ramona asks, as they make their way towards the main road. Flooded with relief, she blinks away the threat of a tear.

Ramona isn't tall but compared to her friend, she is. At twenty-five, Cindy still looks about twelve – another rare thing she and Ramona have in common – and this makes Ramona dubious about the men who pay to have sex with her.

'At a mate's,' Cindy replies.

'I really am—'

'I don't want to talk about it again. I've said what I needed to say. And I mean it about this being your only chance. So we're good, let's just move on.'

In late afternoon, the sky is turning black as they walk arm in arm onto the street.

'Can I ask you a favour?' Ramona says.

If Cindy has an urge to be sarcastic, which she has every right to be in the circumstances, then she resists it. 'Course.'

'Can I borrow some clothes?'

* * *

Madeleine can't settle. It is nearly nine o'clock on a Saturday night, and Samantha's bar is humming.

'Can I get you anything?' the bartender asks, approaching her table, where she nurses a glass of Coke. She has no stomach for alcohol today.

'Hmm? No, I'm good.' She attempts a smile, waiting for the woman to continue on her round before standing and pulling on her coat.

Her company is not worth keeping when she is in this mood, and sadly for Madeleine, she has no way to escape it other than by making herself fall into a coma. Walking upstairs to street level, she sweeps aside the heavy red velvet curtain that leads into Soho beyond, and thinks of Ramona.

What she would give for an ounce of her spirit. Is it simply youth? She likes to think it is more than that, that Ramona will never be worn down in the way that Madeleine has been. There is no reason for Ramona to care so much about the Zhatchanov case – or for any of the other cases for which she is willing to risk as much as she does – except that she chooses to place a higher value on bringing down those she perceives to be doing wrong than she does on her own personal safety.

Madeleine had been dismissive of her yesterday, when she suggested going to the party, and she feels bad about that, but it had demonstrated just how green she is, to think she can gatecrash an oligarch's party, and what . . . force him into a drunken confession?

Admirable, maybe – but naïve as hell.

Stepping out onto the street, Madeleine takes a deep breath and turns towards home. She is barely a few paces along when she hears her name. When she turns, Shyrailym is standing on the street opposite her.

'We need to talk.'

* * *

Ramona looks like a drag queen, she tells herself, not for the first time since she left Cindy's flat. Walking through Mayfair at nearly 9.00 on a bitter evening in February, she feels eyes watching her from all around – and not in admiration.

She had said as much while she got ready at her friend's flat, Cindy lending Ramona a black minidress and platforms, carefully applying her make-up before covering her skin in something called primer and then foundation.

'No drag queen walks that badly in heels – they're not even high. What's wrong with you?' Cindy had sniped, continuing to dust Ramona's cheekbones with the same sheer sparkling powder that she then applied to her eyelids.

Actually what Ramona feels as she crosses Berkeley Square is incognito, emboldened by how unrecognisable she is dressed like this. Any one of Michael O'Keegan's men could walk right past her in the street, and she can safely say they wouldn't blink.

Cindy hadn't pushed Ramona on the question of where she was going, once Ramona gave a suitably vague answer: a honey-trap job at a party in Mayfair. But Cindy was clearly relieved when Ramona asked if she could take her phone and leave her Nokia behind, firstly so that she doesn't stand out; secondly, in case she needs a back-up recording device.

Ramona had chosen not to mention the wrap of coke in her bra, which scratches her breast as she crosses onto Sergey Zhatchanov's road. Compared to Berkeley Square, which is made up entirely of commercial properties, here on the smart terraced street where most of the houses are second homes, there is a shift in energy.

The pavement is empty. No music or obvious lighting emanates from the living room as Ramona approaches the house. Not so much as a car is parked outside.

For the umpteenth time, Ramona tugs at the hem of the black bodycon Cindy had picked out for her, with the buttonhole camera hidden inside the detachable collar she placed over the top. Lifting her head high, she stops briefly on the pavement outside the house, grappling with niggles of doubt.

What if Sergey Zhatchanov hadn't meant tonight, on his phone call? Or what if Ramona is early? She had assumed 9.00 p.m. would be a good time to arrive at a house party, but perhaps not. What if it isn't a house party at all? Or if it is, maybe every girl is already accounted for and Ramona will be immediately recognisable as a fraud—

As if by magic, the door opens. When she looks up, Ramona spots the discreet security camera trained on the porch, which will have alerted her hosts to her arrival.

If her fear was that she would not be on a formal guest list, she needn't have worried.

Stepping aside to let her in, a security guard in a slick black suit and an earpiece, with a beard so perfectly groomed it looks painted on, studies Ramona.

For a second, Ramona hesitates, and then she steps inside.

There is no going back.

'You're late,' the man says nonchalantly, closing the door behind her.

Instantly, Ramona senses something isn't right. Aside from the presence of the guard, the entrance hall is precisely how she had left it the day before: a chandelier presiding over the silent marble entrance hall, an enormous spray of flowers displayed in a glass orb at the centre. Behind, the curved staircase is entirely devoid of guests.

What the hell?

The door clicks closed behind her and Ramona tries to appear sure of herself despite the ripple of unease. It is fine, these are big houses with expensive soundproofing, everyone will be out back, in a heated seating area, or—

'Yes?'

'I'm here for the party,' Ramona says to the woman who appears suddenly behind her. She has blonde hair scraped into a high pony-tail, embellished with what Ramona has heard Cindy describe as bubble plaits. She is tall and thin and businesslike, dressed in a silk black all-in-one.

'Leave your phone there. Have you signed a form?' the woman asks briskly, pointing to a small box on the floor at the foot of a door that appears to be a closet of some sort, at the back of the hallway.

'I don't think so,' Ramona says, taking out Cindy's smartphone from the clutch her friend had also lent her, and placing it in the box.

'Sign here,' the woman says, thrusting a paper attached to a clip-board under Ramona's nose.

She knows better than to ask questions, and only glances at the details of the NDA – essentially: what happens in Vegas, stays in Vegas – before scribbling a variation of the name Marie Jones, and handing it back.

With the briefest acknowledgement, the woman opens a door leading down a dimly lit set of stairs. 'Follow me.'

* * *

Shyrailym is almost unrecognisable from the self-possessed figure in the university offices as she walks beside Madeleine.

With a heavy scarf and coat pulled around her, the daughter looks even younger than she did a week and a half ago, as she turns to face Madeleine. Her face is taut with fear as they walk under a street lamp on Golden Square. 'I meant it when I said you would leave me alone if you cared about my safety. If something happens to me—'

'You're going to have to be more clear about what you mean,' Madeleine says, the unexpectedness of this meeting causing her mind to work at half-speed. 'Who is going to hurt you?'

Stopping suddenly, Shyrailym turns to face her, taking a step forwards. 'If I help you, you have to make sure I'm safe. You have to move me somewhere else.'

Madeleine looks confused. 'You will help us bring charges against your father?'

'My father?' Shyrailym laughs. 'My father is nothing. He is a crook, yes, but he is not . . .' She looks away, gathering her breath in order to say what she is evidently holding back. 'If I help you, do you promise you'll keep me safe?'

'What are you talking about? I can't make promises unless I know—'

'The MP,' Shyrailym says, her face crumbling with relief at having said the words. 'I know who killed Laura Tatchell.'

'I'm sorry?' Madeleine says, questioning whether she has heard right.

'Nurislam,' Shyrailym continues, with a speed that suggests it is now or never, and she has forced herself to act before she can change her mind.

The name hovers for a split second in Madeleine's mind before it lands. 'Nurislam Sultanov, your fiancé?'

'My *ex*-fiancé,' Shyrailym clarifies, sharply. 'I broke up with him as soon as I realised what he had done, and why.'

Madeleine's mind snaps back into sharp focus. Aloud, she tries to work through what she is being told. Nurislam Sultanov, Sergey's business partner, is responsible for the murder of her friend?

* * *

When the door opens, another staircase – hidden until now – leads down towards the source of a throbbing bass.

'Your outfit is hanging up there,' the woman with the bubble plaits says, turning left into another room, with glazed lamps framing a large mirror.

On the walls of what Ramona sees is a dressing room, there are several silk upholstered coat hangers, each holding something indeterminate made of fishnet, and an elaborate feathered black mask. Willing herself to stay calm, Ramona reminds herself that this is an ideal situation. Ramona had wanted to catch Sergey in a compromising position, and this is it.

Just be cool, she tells herself.

Aware of the camera inside her collar, Ramona tries to think of a way to stay dressed as she is. There are no wires attached to the device: she had been sure of that. She was not going to risk being caught by one of Sergey Zhatchanov's men wearing something so obvious – not after last time. But without a camera—

'Leave your clothes and bags in one of the lockers,' the woman in the all-in-one says, her attention fixed on her charge.

'Cool. Can you give me a minute to get changed?' Ramona asks, trying to sound casual.

'You need privacy?' The woman laughs coldly, and then rolls her eyes. 'Hurry up, the party is already going.'

Under her intense gaze, Ramona pulls off her dress and lets it fall to the floor. With a step forward, she removes the hanger from the rail.

Once she has worked out how to prise herself into the fishnet underwear, she slips on the skirt, which could double up as a belt, though without the functionality of having a zipper.

Gratefully, she unhooks the mask, which is black with a pearlescent sequin detail in one corner and feathers along the top. It is unlikely that Zhatchanov will recognise her as the young woman who was in his hallway yesterday, delivering flowers, but it is a risk she would rather not have to take. Through the eyeholes in the mask, Ramona takes in the room more openly, the cameras positioned in each corner.

Can she do this? The question forms in the periphery of her mind; she doesn't allow herself to wonder exactly what 'this' entails. Of course she can. It is hardly different from any other undercover work. How far is she willing to go? This is always a question that has to be answered as she goes along. If you put limitations on yourself before you head into a job, you might as well admit defeat, then and there.

'Take that off,' the woman in the all-in-one barks as Ramona puts her bag in one of the open lockers, as instructed.

'This?' Ramona touches the collar, with the camera inside. 'But it's my signature look.'

'Now.' Her escort is growing impatient.

'Sure,' Ramona replies, removing the collar and placing this – along with the camera inside it – on the shelf, before heading towards the unknown.

* * *

Madeleine struggles to compute Shyrailym's words. 'You're saying that Nurislam Sultanov – your ex-fiancé and the man who runs a business with your brother, Sergey – had Laura Tatchell murdered because she called him and other oligarchs out in Parliament?' He wasn't on the list of people Laura had called out. Madeleine had scrutinised it, and none of the men had any direct contact to the Zhatchanov family.

Shyrailym pauses. It is evident from the way her expression flickers between hesitation and excitement that whatever she says next will be some point of no return. 'No. I'm saying he had her killed because she started sticking her nose into his businesses, and found out something she shouldn't have, and she was about to blow the whistle.'

'What did she find out?' Madeleine tries to keep her tone even.

Shyrailym closes her eyes. 'He and my brother like to party. They bring in girls for the occasion – prostitutes. One night, one of them took too many drugs, cocaine I think or who knows what, and she died.'

A sudden chill takes Madeleine off guard.

'It was an accident, they said.' Shyrailym's voice has grown small, tears fall from her eyes though her expression remains composed. 'Nurislam got rid of her body, on his private jet. Your MP, Laura Tatchell, caught wind of rumours about what was happening, and she was going to blow the whistle.'

'You knew this, but you didn't say anything?' Madeleine can't help but express the first thought that comes into her mind.

'I didn't know! I swear. It was only after – long after . . .' The young woman's face shifts into an expression of confusion. 'A British MP was there – oh yes, my fiancé and my dear brother kept good company and knew how to show their friends a good time – and there was a full-scale cover-up.'

An MP? Madeleine's thoughts move instantly to Dominic. Surely not. Her brother is reprehensible, dishonest, many things more – but covering up the murder of a young woman? Madeleine shakes her head, trying to keep a clear mind.

'So Nurislam had Laura Tatchell killed to stop her leaking information about the death and disposal of a sex worker at one of their parties?' She speaks haltingly, distilling the event to its most basic parts. The fact of it feels both unbelievable and barely even shocking, given what has come to light in recent years: not just in the news – something that happens to other people – but what Madeleine has witnessed first-hand.

Shyrailym nods, her body trembling.

'And how do you know?'

'I overheard him and my brother talking. They weren't even worried about what they had done, only that they might be caught.'

'And you never said anything?'

'It was too late by then! And I was terrified. Nurislam was my fiancé, but he was . . . You have to understand, he is very convincing. He and my brother have been friends for years, and he was fun and good-looking and he was generous. It sounds pathetic, I know, but I was flattered by his attentions.' She smiles, with a hint of sadness, and then her face turns hard. 'But he wasn't a good man, he was cruel. He started to show his true colours, gradually. He had a controlling side: making remarks about me not making enough effort, or withholding money. Then, when I started to question it, he changed again. He became kind and affectionate and I thought he was just stressed. No one is perfect.'

Listening intently, Madeleine wonders if she believes that someone as intelligent as Shyrailym had really only found out how imperfect her fiancé was so long after the fact.

As if reading Madeleine's mind, she continues. 'And then he started being violent. Not often – a slap here, a twisted wrist there – but enough for me to be genuinely fearful of him. By this point, I didn't know what to do. Nurislam was involved with my family financially, and he was my brother's best friend.'

Her expression changes again, and Madeleine sees tears glistening in Shyrailym's eyes. 'And then one day, I overheard him and my brother talking about—' She makes a gesture as though she can't even say the words 'dead prostitute' and Madeleine waits for her to continue.

'Nurislam caught me listening. He said if I ever spoke to the police, or anyone else, that I would be next. In return for my silence he gave me the money to pay for that flat, which he has had fitted with cameras so that he can keep an eye on me. But it was never about the money. You understand that? I'm trapped. If he can do that to her, he can do it to me. And now he thinks he owns me, so he comes to the flat and talks to his friends about everything he is doing as though I'm in on it. That's how I also heard him talking about Laura Tatchell. She had found out about the young woman, and told him she was collecting evidence to bring him to justice. If only she hadn't said anything . . .

'Nurislam boasted to Sergey that they didn't need to worry, that he had "silenced that MP bitch once and for all".'

Madeleine's mind spins.

'The male MP who was at the party,' she asks, tentatively. 'Do you have any idea what his name was?'

Amir's daughter shrugs. 'No.'

'But you'll go on record to the police about what you've just told me.'

She pauses and then nods. 'Please protect me.'

'I will do everything I can,' Madeleine says, and then a thought occurs. 'These parties, do they still have them?'

Shyrailym nods. 'They're having one tonight.'

* * *

Ramona's legs move uneasily on the unfamiliar heels as she heads back out into the hall. Through the slits in her mask, she notes that the proportions of the rooms underground are different from those in the main house. The ceilings feel lower, the lack of natural light making the space warren-like as she is led through sets of doors.

They are nearly at the end of a corridor when the woman in the all-in-one pauses outside a final door before pushing it open.

Taking a breath, Ramona waits. As they step inside, a swell of music erupts, a heavy bass pulsing in the darkness.

'Take a drink,' the woman instructs, pointing to a bar laid out with glasses of champagne and expensive-looking bottles of spirits. Doing as she is told, Ramona takes a glass.

Clutching the stem, so fragile that Ramona wills her hand to stop shaking, she waits for her vision to adjust to the darkness. When it does, she becomes aware of more bodies swaying in time to the music on the periphery of the room.

On the glass table at the centre of the room she registers the contents of the gold dish filled with white powder, beside it a series of tiny gold spoons.

'Don't be shy, join us.' A voice from the sofa taps the space between himself and another man, and says something in Arabic before they both laugh.

Unlike the women in the room, the men's faces are free of masks, and Ramona casts around the room for the person she is here to see. It is only a moment before she spots him, his arm around the waist of a girl with long brown hair.

'Excuse me a second.' Ramona smiles coyly and turns from the strangers on the sofa and heads towards the man she is here to see.

'Hello.' She addresses him with all the confidence she can muster, knowing she will only get one shot. 'I'm Eve.'

Sergey studies her and Ramona turns still.

Briefly, she thinks he is going to dismiss her, having already claimed his prize in the apparently younger, and more beautiful, woman beside him, but then he places a finger on her arm.

'Eve, you are very forward.' Taking her hand, he studies her as he kisses it.

'I'm Adam,' he continues with a wolfish smile, his eyes glistening as he takes a step closer towards her. 'Isn't that a coincidence? If I take you through to my garden, back here, do you promise not to bite?'

Her chest constricting, Ramona shrugs, her gaze landing on the outline of the phone she can just about make out in his trouser pocket. Without the smartphone Cindy had lent her, or the hidden lens now stuck in the changing room, she is relying on using his own phone to film him with, once she has him in a compromising position. Admittedly, Plan B is convoluted. But Plan A – come to the party, get Sergey high and drunk, and then, using her inbuilt camera, film him half-naked with herself posing as a young prostitute, taking lines – is dead in the water.

It had seemed perfect, when she dreamt it up: creating a scenario ambiguous enough – her and him, both half-naked, him taking cocaine – and then handing the photos to Madeleine to blackmail him with. After all, what would happen to his Tory peerage if photos were leaked to the press of him apparently having sex with an underage prostitute? Even if they hadn't actually had sex.

And this is precisely what she would tell him, after the fact, that she is just fifteen years old – or rather, this is what Madeleine will tell him, when she presents him with the incriminating materials. Whether or not this is true won't matter. He will have no way of knowing that she isn't underage.

Of course, Madeleine will argue at first that they can't use the photographs in court, but this was never Ramona's intention. And she could have got Madeleine on board. They both know that if Sergey threatened to go above their heads, Madeleine could simply remind him that these photos were nothing to do with her; that someone had sent her copies anonymously. If that same person also chose to leak them to the press, what could she do?

But now that Ramona is here, any remaining confidence she has in the plan falls away as Sergey takes a step towards her, running a finger down the edge of her stomach where it meets her hip.

There is a slight break in the music and then it starts again, pounding through speakers mounted in the corners of the room.

No, she won't be so easily put off. She can still get his phone, she thinks, attempting to bolster herself. Can't she? But her skin goose-pimples at Sergey's touch and she resists the urge to step back, to hit out at him.

'What's the matter?' he asks, the slightest hint of aggression in his voice as he senses her apprehension at the invitation to accompany him into a private room.

'Nothing,' she replies, trying to smile.

'You need to relax. Ease up.' He places his hand on her back. 'You haven't touched your drink.'

'I'm not—' she begins. At the flicker in his eye, Ramona silently retches. And then she smiles, lifting her glass. She pauses only for a fraction of a second before placing the edge of the glass to her lip and holding it there.

'You're right,' she says. For now, she has no choice but to play along. There is no other way through this.

And so she tips back the glass and drinks.

* * *

Madeleine dials Ramona's number for the third time. When a someone picks up, it is a voice she doesn't recognise.

'Ramona?' The woman at the end of the line answers with a question, her tone laced with concern.

Madeleine pauses. 'This is Madeleine Farrow, I work with Ramona. Who is this?'

The woman falls silent, and for a moment Madeleine worries whoever it is will hang up.

'I'm her friend. I have her phone, she's working,' she says, finally.

'Working where?'

'I'm not sure I can—'

'For Christ's sake, just tell me where she is. It's important. Ramona could be in danger.'

Her reply then is instant. 'She's at a party. In Mayfair, somewhere. She has my phone.'

'Shit.' Madeleine stomps her heel on the pavement. *Shit, shit, shit.*

* * *

Coming to, Ramona sees shapes form on the ceiling.

She is in her bedroom at her grandmother's house in Brighton; the wardrobe where her grandmother, Ai, has neatly stacked her washed and folded clothes, stands to the right of the bed. When she turns her head slightly, she sees the lava lamp her mother, Emma, bought her the year she turned ten. The shapes within the glass cylinder morph this way and that as the light flicks on and off.

When Ramona blinks, she sees it is not a light at all. It is a man holding a glass of champagne. The gold translucence of the bubbles throb as he moves closer, lifting the flute to Ramona's lips.

'You are a very naughty girl,' she hears him say, his voice too close. When she tries to lurch away from him, she can't move. A dribble of liquid rolls down her chin. Again, she attempts to move, even just an inch – to roll off the bed, or is she already on the floor?

Above her, the man takes off his shirt and places one leg over her so that she is pinned down.

'Please,' she tries to plead with him, but she can't form the words.

And then there are voices, bodies moving around too quickly for her to see them. So many people. It is so loud in here.

'Please,' she tries to call out to them. 'Please . . .'

CHAPTER TWENTY-SEVEN

After

Ramona's friend, Cindy, answers the door to the flat when Madeleine arrives bearing a carton of cigarettes, a bottle of freshly squeezed orange juice and fifty pounds of credit for her phone.

'I'm Madeleine. Can I come in?'

Madeleine notes how Cindy pauses, her hackles immediately rising. But then she stands aside to make space for the woman she clearly in part blames for her friend's condition.

It is hardly fair – Madeleine was in fact responsible for saving Ramona. From what, she doesn't like to think about too clearly. But she understands Cindy's instinct to protect her friend, and Madeleine is glad.

'How is she?'

'You can ask her yourself.' Cindy softens. 'Do you want tea?'

'I'm fine, thank you.'

The moment Madeleine spots Ramona, propped up on the sofa nursing a Jubilee memorial teacup, Madeleine doesn't know whether to laugh or cry.

'Better than grapes,' Ramona says, as she takes the offerings gratefully. The effort to smile is clearly causing her pain.

'How are you doing?' Madeleine asks, and Ramona shrugs.

'Fine.'

What else can she say, Madeleine wonders. Physically, she is unscathed.

But Madeleine had hoped that Ramona might show some remorse for the position she put herself in, along with the emergency team who swooped in to save her seconds before she would otherwise have been assaulted by Sergey Zhatchanov.

'What the fuck were you thinking?' Madeleine blurts out, before she can stop herself.

'I was thinking I wanted to get them caught – and it worked, didn't it?' Ramona responds, quick as a flash.

Madeleine opens her mouth to reply, and then grits her teeth.

However maddening this reply, Ramona is right. Thanks to her efforts, Sergey Zhatchanov has been charged with attempted assault and various other offences. Along with Nurislam Sultanov, he will also be charged with the manslaughter of the girl who died at his home, as well as conspiring to cover up her death and perverting the course of justice. As part of his plea deal Sergey has agreed to fly to Kazakhstan to serve his father with papers.

Madeleine doesn't feel in any way moved by this final victory, though. A sexual predator should be given no bargaining chips. But this is how the law works, and Madeleine knows it. It is not about morality. Besides, Sergey's brownie points won't get him far.

Is it bad that Madeleine was partially disappointed to learn that her brother had been at a conference in Davos the weekend of the party when the girl died at Sergey's party?

Yes, she knows, is the answer.

'I'm sorry,' Ramona says, unexpectedly. 'It was reckless. If it wasn't for you and Cindy, I could easily be . . .'

A single tear falls down Ramona's cheek, and Madeleine leans across to wipe it. 'I know,' she says, simply. 'But you're not. And thanks to the intel of an informant who has since been handed over to a department equipped to offer her safe haven while she testifies against Nurislam Sultanov, they are both going to go down for a long time.'

Madeleine's phone vibrates and when she reaches into her bag, she sees Fionn's number flash on the screen.

'Answer it,' Ramona says, and Madeleine pauses before doing so. 'Fionn?'

Ramona sits forward. 'What's up?'

'Madeleine,' Fionn replies, warily. 'Can we meet?'

* * *

Ramona rolls a spliff to help ease the hangover which pulses through her in tiny jabs. She had only drunk one glass of champagne, but thanks to the ketamine it had been spiked with, one was enough.

Obviously it wasn't true when she told Madeleine that she felt fine. The truth is she doesn't know how she feels. She had come close to something, but it hadn't happened. Can you be traumatised in anticipation of something that never comes to pass?

Yes, she imagines, is the simple answer. And in her case, the worst had already happened, a year earlier in the room in Somers Town. As she lay there, two nights earlier, immobile in Sergey Zhatchanov's basement, unable to defend herself against what came next, she experienced every moment of it again.

She was back there in the room with O'Keegan's men leering down at her as they pulled the wire from her shirt, reliving every kick, every punch, every—

Taking a drag, she lets the smoke out in front of her face, watching the shapes morph and change.

She had made two promises to herself after that: that she wouldn't let the experience define her or shape her, and that she wouldn't ever let it happen again. On both fronts, she has failed.

The sound of the doorbell cuts through Ramona's thoughts. She pauses, holding herself quite still, as though this makes any difference.

The curtains are open, so whoever is down there will be able to see the glow of the light from the street; there is no use pretending she isn't here.

Through the window, the moon looms over the houses on the other side of the railway line. She waits a moment and then she stands, warily, moving to the counter and taking the kitchen knife from where it lies discarded in a drawer. Holding it by her side, she moves to the door, her finger lingering over the intercom.

Cindy knows to call her phone first – who else could it be? The options are pitifully few. Inhaling deeply, she presses the button. 'Hello?'

There is a brief crackling sound and then Si's voice comes back at her. 'Hey, it's me – can I come up?'

Exhaling with an audible cry, Ramona leans forward so that her head presses against the door as she gathers herself. Si.

'Sure,' she answers, finding her voice.

Returning to the counter, she places the knife on the side and turns back to open the internal door to the flat, just as he reaches the top of the stairs.

'You look awful,' her ex-boyfriend says as he enters the room for the first time, taking in the squalor of her flat. Of all the times he had to see her new place, he had to choose the day after she was nearly killed, when it is even more of a pigsty than usual. And that admittedly was a high bar.

'Thanks,' Ramona replies, letting the door close behind him.

Before she can say anything else, Si turns abruptly and hugs her, tightly. 'Fuck's sake, I thought you were—'

Her body tenses at the familiar shape of him holding her like this, his mouth pressed against her ear, so close she can feel his breath on her skin. In spite of everything that has passed between them, she wants him to stay here, propping her up, forever.

Just as she thinks this, he lets go, stepping back and turning away again. 'Look, I need to tell you something before you hear it anywhere else . . . I was at the coroner's court the day you thought

286

you saw me following you—' He stops and composes himself before continuing. 'It was about JJ, that's why I was there. They think his death is suspicious. The police are involved and they're wondering if it might be tied to some old drug dealers he owed money to—'

'Sorry, what?' Ramona holds out a hand to silence him, allowing the confirmation of her worst fears to settle, like cement, rooting her to the spot.

'It's all unofficial for now, but there's going to be a media statement soon and I know you two were close. That's why I didn't want to bring it up, until I was sure. I didn't want . . .'

His voice drifts away and Ramona feels the floor tip; instinctively, she reaches for the wall and leans against it.

JJ, murdered?

'There is something else.' He draws breath, struggling to meet Ramona's eye. 'The reason I didn't want you to come in the night you turned up at the flat is that Holly is pregnant. It wasn't planned but it's happened.'

His voice is rushed and devoid of emotion, as if delivering a speech he has practised so many times it has lost meaning. He looks at her a moment, and then turns away.

With his back to her, Ramona watches the man she once loved – still loves? – in the reflection of the window as he raises his hand to his face and rubs his eyes with the palm of his hand. And she realises she is looking at a stranger.

A baby?

Ramona feels herself nodding. Holly and Si. Si is having a baby, without her. She tries to picture it, but her mind falls short.

'Right,' she hears herself say. 'That's . . . That's great.'

When she spots her reflection in the window beyond where she stands, she sees that she is nodding. And when Si leaves, seconds or minutes or hours later, she is still making the same movement, uncertain that she will ever stop.

CHAPTER TWENTY-EIGHT

Rittler is waiting by Madeleine's desk when she gets into the office. It is Tuesday, three nights since they busted Sergey Zhatchanov's party, and the first time she and Rittler have exchanged words since she saw him in the hastily called meeting in HQ.

Since then, she hasn't been in to the office, spending yesterday checking in on Ramona and briefing the department handling Shyrailym about the case.

As yet, no word has been offered about Madeleine's new role, but she assumes this is what Rittler is accosting her about.

'Can I talk to you?' he asks gently.

'Sure,' she says, taking a seat and waiting for him to do the same.

For once, Fionn isn't at his desk – he must have been out all day, as there was the sound of traffic when he called her earlier. With Amol and Jonny both out as well, it is just Madeleine and her boss. As she looks around the room avoiding the awkwardness of eye contact, the light catches on the tips of the leaves of an agave plant resting in the old fire grate beside Jonny's desk. Madeleine imagines spring just around the corner.

When he doesn't speak again, she fills the silence. 'I guess you've heard about our progress on the case.'

Rittler nods. 'I am actually your boss, in case you hadn't noticed. People do tell me some things.'

'Yeah,' she retorts, her tone spiky. 'Don't they just.'

She waits, expecting him to push back, but he just sits there, looking at her.

'I'm dying, Mads.'

Madeleine makes a face. Yeah, yeah, she is killing him with her underhand accusations.

'No, I really am,' he says, his voice choking up. Taking a moment to collect himself, he wipes his nose with the back of his hand and clears his throat. 'They think I have six months to a year. The boys—' At the mention of his children, Rittler breaks down.

The reality of what she is being told registers in fragments, the petals of a rose dropping off one by one until all that is left is the bare stem.

That was why he had been distracted. Rittler isn't part of a cover-up: Rittler is dying.

Moving towards him, Madeleine doesn't speak. Instead, she bends over and holds him against her waist, like a mother might.

'Hush,' she tells him. 'There, there.'

For a while, they stay like this. When the door opens and Amol steps in, Madeleine throws him a warning look.

'I've— I'll come back,' Amol blurts out and turns, closing the door behind him.

Wiping his face, Rittler sits back, trying to resume his composure. 'That's why I recommended you for the role at HQ, Mads. I want you to step up and take over once I've gone.'

'What?'

'I've spoken to Catrin, who would be a good person to vouch for you.' Rittler barrels on. 'She is keen, too. She's been asking around, and despite your best efforts to make her take against you, she can see you're the best person for the job.'

Madeleine sits there, briefly silenced. She could almost laugh.

This is why her ex-girlfriend was at Dominic's party; this is why she had been asking Tim if we had been in touch.

There is no cover-up. The case isn't being pulled – Madeleine is being taken off it in order to prove her worth at headquarters, so that she can take over the job of Detective Inspector when Rittler is gone.

Because Rittler is dying.

* * *

The Strand bustles along as usual, in that way that is hard to fathom after one has been given a shock as destabilising as the one Madeleine has just received.

Rittler is dying, but life carries on.

Fionn is waiting at Papa Luigi as arranged. Seeing him outside the office is like seeing a teacher on holiday, and Madeleine finds herself smiling in a way that ten minutes ago she would not have thought possible, given the news she has just had.

Rittler had been adamant that Madeleine mustn't tell a soul about his condition, and it is just as well, as Fionn is straight down to business.

'I found the man who runs Time for Tuition.' He lowers his voice. 'He is a policeman.'

'I'm sorry?' Again, Madeleine wonders if she has misheard.

'James Harvey is Matthew Dunston, a serving officer in the Met.'

The world stops again as she processes yet another turn in a day as unpredictable as every other: Madeleine's calls *were* being monitored, but not because of the Zhatchanov case. It was directly after she had instructed Fionn to look into James Harvey that she started to notice interference. She thinks of the website being taken down, the inability of anyone to trace it.

Had there been a cover-up, an effort from above to erase any trace of—?

The thought is eclipsed by Madeleine's phone ringing. She and Fionn both look down at the name on the screen.

Dominic Farrow.

She looks Fionn in the eye as she answers, without saying a word, simply pressing the button and waiting for him to speak.

'Madeleine, it's Dominic.' She wonders if her personal phone is bugged, too. But no, she tells herself, even Dominic knows his limits.

'I want you to come into HQ immediately, please,' he says.

'Is this a joke?'

'No, it is an order,' he replies, his voice even.

'You're not my boss, Dominic.'

'I bloody well am.' There is a pause and she pictures him, the blood vessels in his cheeks turning red as he paces his office, fury coming off him in waves.

The image soothes her, and her tone becomes calm.

'Do you really think you can stop me?' Madeleine shakes her head at the waitress who approaches and turns away again before asking for their order.

How had she got this so wrong? Not only had Madeleine misunderstood which case she was being angled away from, but she had imagined that any cover-up would be about national security or diplomacy – when in fact this is simply about her brother protecting his own, or rather protecting himself and his new role as the head of the department directly responsible for the actions of the Metropolitan Police.

'Stand down,' Dominic instructs, his voice almost a shout. Of course he knows he can't stop her, but he has been programmed his whole life to believe that he can do anything he likes, and get away with it. And the dawning realisation that he can't, compounded by the fact that it is his own sister who might be the one to pull him up, is too much.

'Goodbye, Dominic,' she says, simply.

Shaking with a powerful combination of adrenaline and satisfaction and years' worth of rage, she hangs up and dials Rittler's number without addressing Fionn, who makes no attempt to interrupt.

Rittler answers after two rings, listening intently when Madeleine tells him what she has learnt. 'Did you know about this, this Matthew Dunston—' She struggles to find the right intonation.

'Of course not,' Rittler replies. 'Until just now.'

'So.' She pauses, aware from Fionn's expression of the energy coming off her in waves. 'What do you want to do?'

She can almost hear the smile on her boss's face as he replies: 'I want you to string the bastard up.'

* * *

Si has only just left when Madeleine rings to tell her the news. An attempted cover-up by Dominic Farrow to avoid the embarrassment that the man behind Time for Tuition is a serving police officer, is exactly what Ramona had needed to catapult her out of her trance-like state.

'How did they find out in the first place?'

'Looks like Fionn's calls were being monitored – so much for Gerard Okoduwa trusting him implicitly – and someone heard about the situation and looked into it, and got there before we did, joining the dots . . .' Madeleine replies. 'Or maybe there is a wider ring of them. You know how policemen have a track record of oversharing in WhatsApp groups. What I do know is that after the horrifying stories that have emerged involving the force recently, my darling brother couldn't risk another scandal in his first weeks in office.'

'So it was Dominic all along, trying to steer you away from the investigation in order to save his own neck? Jesus.'

'With who knows whose help,' Madeleine says.

Again, she thinks of the politician Shyrailym mentioned, who was at the party where the young woman died. One day she will find out who it was, and she will make him pay.

'Thank God for Fionn,' she tells Ramona. 'Never thought I'd hear myself say those words, but whatever measures were taken to make the whole business go away, he was able – and willing – to override them.'

'So what now?'

'The arrest is being made as we speak. Voyeurism and trafficking.

Turns out Matthew Dunston lives with his wife and a daughter who is in secondary school. Can you imagine? I'm hoping they get over there before the girl's home. I'm heading to the nearest custody suite, to greet him once he arrives at the station. Jonny's driving me.'

'What about your brother?' Ramona asks.

'I suppose he'll have to resign. I'd like to say his will be a remarkably short period in office for a Cabinet member, but two weeks is quite impressive by this government's standards. Have you spoken to your girl yet?'

Ramona exhales. She isn't looking forward to relaying the news to Ottilie, in the way that she thought she would.

'It's a good result,' Madeleine says. 'You solved your first proper case.'

She is right, and yet somehow it doesn't feel like a victory.

'Perhaps you'd like to come in and watch the questioning. The nearest station to his house in Hertfordshire.'

'I have things to do here, but let me know when they bring him in.'

* * *

Ramona heads out for the first time since the party, and walks a while, filtering through her thoughts. Her mind moves to JJ, and to Si's words earlier that day. It all feels like a dream – a nightmare.

JJ killed? It doesn't make sense. And yet, what if the reason he had come to see her the day he died was because he knew he was in danger and, knowing Ramona's job, he had wanted her help? She thinks back to that afternoon, the wary expression on his face. The beanie he wore, covering his trademark red hair. Of course: he had been hiding from someone. But who? There is no way, Ramona thinks, that JJ owed someone money. He wasn't that guy. When he asked her for a cigarette, it had been the first time she had ever known JJ to ask for anything. He was a giver. He had enough Catholic guilt bred into him to believe that he could atone for his past sins by helping others.

On Kingsland Road, Ramona stands opposite the Rio cinema and pictures him, hand in hand with his granddaughter, heading in to watch a film.

JJ didn't have enemies. He had people who struggled to forgive him – including his own family – but no one who would want to hurt him.

Turning back towards her flat, Ramona tries Si's phone. She had been in too much of a state of shock earlier to quiz him properly. But she needs answers, and Si is her best port of call, even if— No, she won't think of that. Not now. Whatever is happening with Si and Holly and their—

She feels a wave of nausea as she takes out her phone. Whatever is happening in his life, she won't let her personal feelings stop her from asking Si exactly what he knows.

When he doesn't answer, Ramona starts to walk more quickly. She will head home and then go to the coroner's court herself. She is almost there, and she needs to call Ottilie, to tell her the news about James Harvey – or Matthew Dunston. That is something to be done sitting down; somewhere quiet, where she can give the conversation the concentration and respect that it deserves.

Turning onto her street, the sky is grey but daylight is holding out. It won't be dark until 5.00 p.m., if the recent pattern is anything to go by. The front gate is already open, no need for the usual kick. She closes it carefully behind her and looks up at her bedroom window, at the top of the house.

Something feels different and Ramona stops on the path, trying to work out what it is. Looking about her, nothing noticeable has changed. The bin bags are where they always are, in the plastic containers to the left of the door. A few dandelions have sprouted between the cracks in the paving stones.

She finds it unsettling at this time of year, when everything is so precarious. Once, the beginning of March meant spring was just around the corner, but these days things are less certain.

A wind blows, causing her to shiver and pull her hoodie more tightly around herself. Continuing on towards the front door, she reminds herself that what happened is in the past. What happened with O'Keegan's men has happened and she can't change it, but she is still here. Likewise, what happened with Sergey Zhatchanov is now over, and she has survived; not only that, she had helped close the case, and inadvertently helped catch a killer in the process.

Not that this feels like any kind of consolation for what she has failed to do. Though she can only move forwards, not back. There is always time to do more.

As she takes the stairs, Ramona's mind begins to settle. She will call Ottilie, and then she will go to the court in the Vestry of St Pancras and find out as much as she can about JJ's death. If the coroner or her secretary aren't there, then she will have to go and find Si. An image of Holly, with her pregnant belly bulging beneath her blouse, ambushes her and she stops, leaning against the wall for support.

From the second floor, Jeffrey's television is playing at full volume. The sound recedes only slightly as she reaches the top landing where Ramona takes out her internal key. After the events of the party, and the subsequent hangover, she is still weaker than she was and it takes even more effort than usual to open the door. If she had imagined that the taste of alcohol would propel her back into drinking, she should be relieved to learn that it hasn't. A single glass of spiked champagne had not triggered a relapse. For this she is grateful.

When the door swings open, she steps inside and closes it behind her. Her phone starts to ring and Ramona reaches into her pocket, and then she feels it, a sharp pain in the back of her head as some-thing, someone, slams against her.

* * *

'Answer your bloody phone,' Madeleine mutters into the handset as she stands behind the glass divide, watching Tim and another colleague interview Matthew Dunston.

She has had a message from Jamie Tatchell, thanking Madeleine for her part in Nurislam Sultanov's arrest on counts including suspected murder. His delivery had been quiet, almost disbelieving. She imagines there is a sense of anticlimax, almost, at such a moment. The only closure he and the girls could hope for has come to pass, and now what is left to hope for?

Accepting that Ramona isn't answering and hanging up the call, Madeleine pictures the photo of Laura and Jamie and the girls in the hallway, and allows herself to feel briefly soothed by the step towards a resolution of sorts that this will bring them, before focusing her attention back on the man in front of her. At least they can move forward, if not entirely move on.

Despite everything, there is a smirk across Dunston's face suggesting he truly believes, even now, that he will get away with what he has done. He almost did, but now that the media have been tipped off, there is no wriggling out: the same goes for her dear brother.

Judging from the manner of the lawyer at the former police officer's side, his legal representative at least knows how doomed this case is. Shame for him that he has to be part of it, but that's what you get for being a two-bit defence solicitor. Not legal aid, though, Madeleine noted. Dunston was clearly prepared to pay to fight his way out of this, and the truth is, no matter how much public outcry there is, they don't have anything on him beyond the voyeurism and trafficking charges; sexual assault and rape won't stick. Even though that, in Madeleine's mind, is what this case is.

He will likely get four years, and serve half of that with good behaviour. Her only hope is that, being a policeman, he will get special treatment from his fellow inmates.

Madeleine's attention dips in and out of focus as Tim's colleague explains to Dunston the grounds for arrest. 'Suspicion of human trafficking for sexual exploitation . . . We received a complaint from an individual who states they were deceived into sexual conduct with you through the Time for Tuition website . . . Your arrest is necessary so that evidence can be secured by way of interview and searching of properties controlled by you . . .'

Received a complaint. Properties controlled by you.

The wording is so sanitary, so banal. But that is the law, devoid of emotion. How did she end up here? Madeleine's mind moves to Rittler, and to his offer of the top job. Does she want it?

God knows what she wants. Trying Ramona's line again, she shakes away any hint of concern as the call goes to answering machine. There is nothing to worry about. Nurislam Sultanov and Sergey Zhatchanov are both in police custody, with no reason to connect the last arrival at the party with the police raid.

Slipping her phone back in her pocket, she tells herself to focus, and returns her attention to the man in front of her.

* * *

When Ramona opens her eyes, she is splayed out on the floor. The back of her head throbs and she is aware of a trail of blood on her fingertips when she pulls them away.

Above, leaning against the kitchen counter, a man in a grey tracksuit is drinking a glass of water.

'Wakey, wakey,' he says, with a laugh. Struggling to compute, Ramona looks up at him, her vision pulsing so that she can't quite make it out.

That voice, she knows it from somewhere. A distant memory that she can't quite reach, until it is there, once again, retrieved from the box she has locked it away in. And now her body seizes with the details: the clock on the wall; the white T-shirt torn around her waist; the men's laughter.

'Remember me? Oh, it has been too long, Isobel. And look, you've got this whole wall of newspaper clippings to remember us by . . . Michael will be touched.'

She sits up, too fast, at the sound of her past name.

No.

A hand moves towards her. Lunging away from it, her back hits the wall of the counter. No way out.

'Alright, alright,' the voice says. 'Calm down, you'll do yourself a mischief. There's nowhere to go so you might as well try not to make it any more tricky for yourself, yeah?'

The way he's standing, his back to the light, she can't quite make out his face.

Please.

Does she say the word out loud? There is a whooshing noise inside her head, which drowns everything else. And then, there is the man's voice again, reaching through the fug. 'I've really looked forward to this, you know that? I mean, I saw you the other day, running away from that security guard, but we didn't get to chat properly. It's been how long – a year?'

And then the voice slots into place. Daniel Knowles. The details run through her mind, just as she had typed them.

Daniel Knowles. Twenty-eight years. Born on the same estate as Michael O'Keegan. Started running drugs at twelve, by twenty-five was the brawn of the operation, certainly not the brain.

A savage. That's how she had heard Knowles described by one of the ladies she spoke to, who lived on the same floor as his mum. There was vitriol in her eyes as the woman described the hell O'Keegan and his men had inflicted on her home, and that of their other neighbours. *With their dirty money and their dirty ways. No respect for anything or anyone.*

Knowles had been one of three men there that day. He wasn't the one who— She shakes away the thought before it can fully form. But he was there, he had watched, and he had laughed.

'You're not very chatty today, Isobel. I thought you liked a chat. You always wanted to chat to me, didn't you? And the five-o. Always happy to chat to them, innit?' He jumps up to sit on the counter, his legs hanging beneath him like a kid on a swing. 'So, what's happening, where you been?'

'What do you want?' Ramona whispers.

'Me?' Knowles laughs. He has the same French crop and gold necklace he wore last time she saw him, and he pulls at the chain absentmindedly as he tips his head back and howls. 'You are a joker, Isobel. I want to fuck you up, that's what I want.'

His face grows hard now. 'Just like I fucked up your mate.'

The room grows cold, Ramona watching Daniel Knowles who studies her face in return, a slight smile forming at the side of his mouth.

He makes a clicking sound with his tongue. 'Yeah, yeah, you know what I'm talking about, innit? Ginger bruv.' He jumps off the counter, then. 'Thought he was a bad-man, that one.'

Knowles laughs again. 'But he cried when he knew what was coming. I swear to God.'

Her chest vibrates, the words sounding like they belong to someone else. 'It was you?'

'Me? Well, yeah – me and a couple of mates. I shouldn't take all the credit. It was one of them who spotted you, actually, from the top of the bus. You – the one who got Michael banged up and then fucked off – bopping down Dalston like it ain't nothing, coming out of some shop.

'My man got off the bus but by the time he gets to the shop, you're dust. So he calls me and we go and speak to the shopkeeper. Some Turkish kid. We ask him about you and when he says he doesn't know nothing we see he's lying to us, so we threaten him.' Daniel gives her a knowing wink. 'You know how it goes . . . tough love.

'But then, see, this older fellow – your ginger mate – comes in and asks what's going on. We tell him to mind his own beeswax but . . .' Daniel makes that clicking sound again with his mouth. 'Fellow won't hear it. We can tell he knows you from the way he's speaking, like "you stay away from her" and "you can talk to me, instead".'

Time slows down as Ramona listens to the words, picturing the scene. JJ leaving the fishmonger's to buy his cigarettes, and finding Michael O'Keegan's men rustling up Sami. Hearing Sami saying her name, and then stepping in.

Levering herself up with her arms, slowly, Ramona makes to stand. Her skateboard is on the other side of the room, propped up against the door.

'Do you wanna sit?' Knowles asks, jumping down and holding out a chair. 'Come, don't be shy.'

Moving away from him, Ramona backs away towards the kitchen counter, her eye catching on the knife she had left there the day before.

'Suit yourself.' With a shrug, he throws himself down onto the chair, before continuing. 'Don't get me wrong, it was quite sweet. I mean, I thought I might leave it, but the way he spoke to us . . .' Daniel shakes his head. 'No respect. The Turkish boy, on the other hand, he shat himself. He told us your name, where you live, roughly. But if he'd known your door number, he would have given it up in a heartbeat.

'Anyway, you weren't that hard to find. He told us about JJ, too, the smackhead, after he fucked off. Said you sometimes came into the shop together. I figured, from the way he defended you, you were good friends.'

'What did you do to him?'

'Me?' Knowles makes a face, like he has no idea what she is talking about. Then his mouth twists into a smile. 'OK. So, as you know, the one thing we have a lot of in our business, is heroin. So we let him leave – like I said, I wasn't going to bother with him until I clocked that he was such a good mate of yours, and it made me think. So I went round the corner and got the van, made a call, went and saw a man about a dog, and once I had all the business, we went back to the shop, and he'd gone.'

'You killed JJ to get at me?' The words seem to belong to someone else, the room around Ramona spinning so that she no longer knows whether she is sitting or standing.

'You're interrupting,' Daniel says. 'Just listen. It was lucky, actually. We looked around for a while but we couldn't see him. I was about to fuck off, but just then we saw him again. Just at the top of your road, and we got out, had a chat, and then we chucked him in the back of the van. Broad fucking daylight. You should have seen his face when he saw the needle and the bag of brown.'

Ramona sees tears splash on the floor as she pulls herself up against the counter, and wonders briefly who they belong to.

'Oh I'm sorry, you're crying,' Daniel says as Ramona winches herself up so that her back is flat against the kitchen cupboard.

'You're not going to get away with it—' she spits, a surge of energy coming from within.

'Well, that's debatable. Anyway,' he says, 'he's dead. And now . . .' Daniel takes a step towards her, pulling a blade from his bag.

In the same split second that he comes for her, Ramona pulls the kitchen knife from her sleeve and lunges, ducking and then stabbing him in the back as she propels herself past him towards the door.

She is quicker than he is, and she feels the handle under her fingers as his footsteps come up behind her.

'You fucking bitch,' he cries, and she kicks the board so that it falls in front of him as she pulls the door open.

The blade of his knife penetrates Ramona's leg as he falls, his eyes wide with horror.

Screaming in pain, she looks down and sees the blood gathering at the edges of the wound on her thigh.

At the same moment that she collapses on the floor, she hears the thump as Daniel Knowles' body hits the bottom of the stairs.

* * *

'No comment,' Matthew Dunston replies, his expression cold, in the interview room beyond the shield of glass.

When Madeleine's phone vibrates in her hand, she rushes to answer it, imagining it might be Ramona, but as she looks down, she sees the number is caller unknown. Tentatively, she answers, speaking quietly so as not to disturb the others in the room.

'Madeleine Farrow?' a man's voice says. In the background she hears chatter and the buzz of machines.

'Yes?'

'I'm a nurse at the Homerton Hospital. There has been an incident and your number was the last received call in the patient's phone. Do you know a young woman named Isobel Mason?'

* * *

'No cigarettes or phone credit this time?' Ramona asks, when Madeleine Farrow pulls open the curtain and steps inside the hospital cubicle. Through the gap in the material, Ramona spots the police-woman guarding her bed on the other side of the partition.

Madeleine's face is etched with worry. With a sense of hazy detach-ment owing to the painkillers, Ramona tries to smile, to reassure Madeleine that she is OK.

'You should see the state of the other guy,' she says dreamily. 'Are you here to arrest me?'

'No,' Madeleine says. Ramona can see from the way she pauses that she is trying to measure her words. But Ramona isn't stupid. She has killed a man.

'There are officers outside, waiting to talk to you. Once you're a little stronger. You lost a lot of blood.'

'I might lose my leg,' Ramona says, not fully understanding the words as she says them. Though she understands well enough.

Leaning back, tears well in the corners of her eyes.

'Are you in pain?' Madeleine asks.

'They gave me drugs, lots of drugs.' She tries to smile, to laugh at the absurdity of this, after everything. 'What will happen to me?'

Madeleine takes a seat in the blue chair beside the hospital bed and touches Ramona's hand, her fingers avoiding the line of the peripheral cannula feeding medicine into her bloodstream.

'It was self defence,' Madeleine says. 'Look, this isn't my area at all, but my guess would be that you will aim for a manslaughter charge with a suspended sentence.'

'But it's not a given that I won't go to prison?' Presumably Ramona knows the answer, but she needs to hear Madeleine say it.

'Nothing's certain,' Madeleine concedes. 'Just tell them the truth.'

Through the doorway, there is a commotion, and when she looks up, she sees a doctor talking to a woman, and then the police officer stepping forward, ready to intervene.

'She will want to see me. Ask her! I'm her mother for fuck's sake!'

'Mum?'

'Holy shit, darling.' Ramona watches as her mother bustles into the room, making a beeline for the bed, her glossy fringe touching Ramona's face as she leans in to hug her.

She wears no make-up or jewellery other than the thick silver ring Ramona has known her to wear all her life. Though it is still only March, she is dressed in a black vest top and a sarong over navy jeans, and flip-flops. The lines in the tanned skin around her eyes are a little deeper than the last time they saw each other. When was that?

'Why the fuck didn't you call me?' Emma says, her voice turning accusatory. Ramona recognises the edge to it – the impatience that is always replaced with something more self-possessed, more author-itative, in Emma Mason's reports from far-flung war zones.

'I didn't know where you were,' Ramona says, flatly.

'I've been in Damascus but I got back last week, didn't you get my email?'

'I'll leave you to it.' Madeleine stands, and walks to the edge of the cubicle, clearly giving them space, and Ramona wants to cry out to her to stay. But she knows she will have work to do. Madeleine had left the interview with their Time for Tuition man in order to come and see how she is, and now she knows.

Ramona is alive, and JJ is dead because of her. And now the man who killed him is dead, too.

Her attention moving from Madeleine to Emma, Ramona remembers Daniel Knowles' cold eyes staring up at her, a hint of promise in the flicker of his smile before his head hung limp, and blinks the image away.

'Mum,' she says. 'I'm tired. Can we do this another time?'

* * *

Amber is waiting at the Garden of Rest, her legs crossed over one another as Madeleine makes her way down Marylebone High Street on her journey home.

'Madeleine,' her sister-in-law calls out from the bench and waits for Madeleine to approach. Madeleine does so, tentatively, unsettled by the ambush.

Despite the grey sky, Amber wears sunglasses, presumably to obscure her face from potential recognition. Since the Time for Tuition scandal and rumours of an attempted cover-up, Dominic has been in the papers for all the wrong reasons.

Poor Amber. Madeleine almost feels sorry for her. But it is Bella she is really concerned for.

Madeleine looks around for signs of her niece, and then she sits. Despite several attempted calls and unanswered texts, she hasn't heard from her in the week since the news dropped.

'What are you doing here?'

'I came to give you a message from Bella,' Amber says, her voice low and cold.

Madeleine tilts her head inquisitively. 'She could have called me.'

'No, she couldn't. She's in hospital. She tried to kill herself, two days ago.'

'What?' Madeleine takes a step forward. 'What do you—'

'After what happened to her father, the girls at school turned on her.'

'Where is she? I need to see her—'

'No.' Amber's voice is tainted with something that Madeleine swears might be satisfaction. But that can't be. 'You will never see her again. That is the message from your niece.' She continues, enunciating each word clearly, 'She hates you. This is your fault and she wants nothing more to do with you.'

Madeleine struggles to find the words to respond.

'You know, even after all the shit you put us through with the inheritance, even with all your comings and goings over the years – your unreliability, the way you picked Bella up when it suited you and then dropped her again – we never tried to stop you having a relationship with our daughter.' Amber smiles, bitterly. 'But you've done it yourself. Bella hates you for what you've done to her father, and for what you've done to her. I can't imagine she'll ever forgive you.'

Madeleine feels the ground beneath her pull away. Her sister-in-law reaches into her handbag and pulls out the floral make-up bag Madeleine had given her niece for her birthday.

With a final triumphant flick of the head, Amber hands her the bag. 'She asked me to give you this back.'

CHAPTER TWENTY-NINE

One month later

In early April, a burst of spring sunshine has arrived and Dalston is alive with the promise of better times ahead. 'How's your leg?' Sami asks, as Ramona browses the headlines on the street outside his shop. The sentencing of the policeman behind a website that lured in young women with the promise of money, but came up with none once the girls were persuaded to have sex with him – and the episodes filmed for his private entertainment – is the lead story in most of the papers.

Ramona doesn't look up. She considers him a moment, the sheepish way he stands in front of her, his hands rammed into the pockets of his jeans. She hasn't spoken to Sami since she learnt what happened to JJ. She doesn't blame him, not really, but she will never forgive him. She could almost have forgiven him for giving up everything he knew about Ramona, without thinking to warn her. But JJ? Sami must have known there was a connection between what happened with the men in his shop and JJ's sudden death. Yet, he had looked her in the eye in the days after and said nothing.

Can she really blame him? Probably not, considering how dangerous these men are. Nevertheless, she does.

306

'Ramona?' he calls out after her as she walks away, relying on the metal crutches she leans on, more heavily than she would like to.

Cindy had offered to pick her up and walk her down there, but now that she has stopped coming to meetings, Ramona knows it would only be distracting her from her job applications. After what happened to Ramona at the Mayfair party, Cindy had been galvanised into finding a way out of sex work. Not that it has proved quite as easy as that.

Still, she has taken a waitressing job while she looks into grants for college courses. She might train to become a hairdresser, or a make-up artist. In the meantime, some days Ramona and Sonny go to meet her after school and have a hot chocolate while Cindy finishes her shift.

The meeting has already started by the time Ramona arrives. She takes the stairs down to the crypt, carefully, aware of several pairs of eyes turning to her when she steps inside. She takes a seat at the back of the room, and when she looks up, she sees the man taking to the stage is Maxy, Sonny's dad. It is his first ever meeting, he tells them. Today, I am three days clean, for the first time in fifteen years.

The room breaks into applause, and when Vicky looks up and asks if anyone else would like to share, Ramona clears her throat and stands. With Vicky's eyes on her, clearly amazed, she speaks. 'My name is Ramona Chang, and I am an addict—'

* * *

Madeleine is waiting for her outside the flat, when she returns home.

'What are you doing here?' Ramona smiles, though she is instinctively uneasy given the date.

Madeleine shrugs. 'It's your first day at court tomorrow. I wanted to see how you were . . . you didn't call.'

'I'm sorry, I've been— busy.' It is true. With all the physiotherapy and preparatory meetings with her lawyer, there hasn't been much spare time to think. And this is a good thing. Ramona doesn't want to think about what might happen, after tomorrow.

'I wanted to be there, in court, but I'm off on another assignment tomorrow so I won't make it.'

'That's OK,' Ramona says, though she feels a sting of disappointment. 'My lawyer is confident I won't have to serve a custodial sentence. Given that they've let me come home while I await trial . . . It's a good sign. Will you come in?' Ramona asks.

Madeleine shakes her head. 'I have to get things ready before I go.'

'Where are you off to?'

Madeleine taps her nose. 'That would be telling.'

'So you're not taking the job, here in London?'

'I haven't decided yet. Rittler's still—' She makes a face. 'He is doing OK. It's hard to make a decision when . . . Well.'

'How are the other guys?'

'They're good,' Madeleine replies. 'Sadie is back from medical leave next week, so full house again.'

Ramona senses a hint of disdain in Madeleine's voice and, is surprised by the pang of envy she feels that it's not her returning to SCID Row. Ramona doesn't like to look too far ahead, but staying in her own mind, in the here and now, is no easy feat.

In the periphery of her vision, she sees him, at the bottom of the stairwell once she had regained enough consciousness to pull herself to the door. The words he had called up to her. *Help me. Please.* The same words JJ would have uttered, pleading with Knowles in the seconds before he was injected with the dose of heroin that would kill him.

It is impossible to know what difference it would have made if Ramona had gone to Knowles, then; if she had called the ambulance the minute it happened, rather than waiting the ten or fifteen it took for the man at the bottom of the stairs to bleed out. She will never know. Just as JJ will never know his granddaughter as a teenager.

'Will I see you again?' Ramona asks, aware of the sudden urgency in her voice. The question is a plea for reassurance and Madeleine clearly understands.

'You know what, Ramona Chang?' Madeleine winks. 'I have a feeling that you will.'

ACKNOWLEDGEMENTS

There are so many people to thank . . . First, my razor-sharp editor Jade Chandler for believing in this series and knowing how to make it better, and the whizz team at Baskerville for working so hard to get it into readers' hands.

Huge thanks to my agent, Veronique Baxter at David Higham Associates, who had faith in the idea from the off – and to my screen agent, Emily Hayward-Whitlock at The Artists Partnership, for making things happen.

Thank you endlessly to the booksellers, librarians, critics and readers who keep me in a job. To my friends and family who keep me relatively sane – or humour me when I'm not. You know who you are.

To Sandra Fordham, Meg Clark, Luke Randolph, Penny Kirk, Ellie Porter, Parin Janmohamed, for a lifetime of support.

To my fellow writers, who take the time to read my work and say nice things, I appreciate it hugely (those who don't: you're dead to me).

Thank you to Oly Duff, Matthew Moore, Cahal Milmo and the crack-team at the *Independent* of old, who gave a chance to a wholly inexperienced reporter, way back when. To Nick Davies, Mandy Oates, Richard Hart, Alicia Kirby, and everyone else who helped.

Thank you to all the dirty bastards I've encountered along the way, for inspiring this tale.

Above all, to my husband, mum and children, for the rest. I am so lucky.

ABOUT THE AUTHOR

Charlotte Philby is a critically acclaimed author and journalist. She worked for eight years as a newspaper reporter, editor and columnist at the *Independent*, where she was shortlisted for the Cudlipp Prize for investigative reporting. She is a former contributing editor and features writer at *Marie Claire*, and has written for publications including the *Sunday Times*, *ELLE* and *Inside Time*. After living most of her life in London she is now based in Bristol with her family. *Dirty Money* is her sixth novel.